CW00872101

Spiral

by Jacqueline Levine

All of the characters in this book are fictitious, and any resemblance to actual persons, living or dead, is purely coincidental. The names, incidents, dialogue and opinions expressed are the products of the author's imagination and are not to be construed as real. The events in this book are entirely fictional and by no means should anyone attempt to live out the actions that are portrayed in the book.

For Lucky Nat, who always did it his way.
Sweet dreams, Daddy.

Part 1

DIRTERAZZI.COM
Cherie Belle and Caz Farrell
Robbing the Cradle Much?

What do you get when you mix the former Kidz Channel king everyone wants and the latest Kidz Channel princess that no one can (legally) have? Oh, only the hottest maybe-couple ever! Heartthrob Caz Farrell, 25, was spotted last night leaving Fly nightclub, with his usual Kidz Channel entourage in tow, including Dominick Furst and Amber Stiles. Mere seconds later, Cherie Belle, the sixteen-year-old siren from Kidz Channel's "Choc it Up" and Caz's co-star in the upcoming flick, This Side of Sunny, *made the same exit and fled the scene... in the same car! How the underage teen queen got into the club to begin with is still unclear. Witnesses inside the club say the two were cozying up to one another in the VIP section, well-hidden by bodyguards and friends. Some onlookers report the body language between Caz and Cherie was very telling.*

Rumors have already been swirling around the stars for a few months, and many say it would be a match made in studio heaven if the television royalty were to actually date. Of course, Caz's camp completely denies the rumors, because who would admit to dating a minor? If Caz is caught robbing the cradle, he would be labeled a pedophile for life, not to mention face serious criminal charges and spend Christmas behind bars. Since no one wants to see that, let's just pretend this didn't happen...

Chapter 1

Yesterday was the fourth anniversary of the day Dad left, but my mom didn't cry about it this year. She was too busy learning how to make latkes for tonight's Christmas-Hanukkah dinner, so the onions were the only things making her eyes tear up. Onions and the dozen roses my stepdad, Jim, brought home for her from the supermarket.

I'm torn from my thoughts by the angry pounding on the bathroom door.

"Ja-ack! Get out of the bathroom already!"

I groan. "I'm not done yet, Claudia."

I breathe deeply as my stepsister huffs and storms down the hall. When I'm sure she's gone, I resume my post-shower routine by pulling hair gel out of the drawer marked "Jack" in our bathroom's dresser. My drawer sits above the one marked "Brenton and Britney" because they're little and need the lowest drawer for their bath toys and toothbrushes. But mine comes after the drawer marked "Claudia," and hers sits below her twin's compartment, the one marked "Chloe." This is a totem pole of products and supplies that my mom carefully designed to keep all of us organized and not spread out all over her counters. If you ask me, I'd say it's just another large, invasive piece of furniture occupying space we don't have in this house. More importantly, the dresser is a giant reminder that I share a bathroom with four other people and, despite being the oldest, I'm somewhere lost in the middle.

I swirl a little gel between my palms and run it through my hair, smoothing the sides and combing my fingers through the front until it has the right height. Examining my face while I wash the remaining gel off of my hands, I scowl at how young I look. I wish I could grow a beard or something. My jaw just doesn't have that shadow yet, that look of a guy who takes a sharp, dangerous object and runs it across his face daily. I kind of want that.

Mom says I don't want a beard though, because I will seem even more like Dad. I have his dirty blond hair and his smile, and that's already more than she cares to look at every day. I think I have his eyebrows too, complete with little lines in the middle from all of the squinting I do. He used to squint at us when he was confused, and I've been confused since he left.

Claudia's back, jerking on the locked door knob with a vengeance. "JACK! God, you are such a girl! You've been in there for twenty minutes!"

I tighten the towel around my waist and sigh. A guy can't shower in peace in this house anymore. I throw open the door, meeting Claudia's hateful glower.

"Yes, Claudia?" I lean against the doorframe casually, blocking her path as she tries to push past me on both sides and fails.

She snaps, "Move! I have to shower!"

"I didn't know you could wash off ugly," I sneer.

She's not as quick as her twin with the retorts, so she releases her signature growl-scream in response. "*Moooove*—I have to get ready! They'll be here any minute!"

I move out of the doorway and let her through. "Merry Christmas!" I call backward when she slams the door closed.

"*Hanukkah*, jerk! We celebrate HAN-OO-KAH!" she yells through the door. "God!"

As I walk down the long hall to my room, I hear my mother scurrying around downstairs, followed by the clink of glasses bumping into one another in her hand as she sets the table. The warm smells of turkey and sugar cookies waft into the hall and surround me. Frank Sinatra, Mom's go-to holiday, family-is-coming-over artist, sings an indulgent ballad through the sound system of our home.

I'd trade in all the smells and sounds of Christmas for just one more holiday without the step-twins from hell.

Passing my little brother's room, I poke my head in just to check and make sure he's almost ready for dinner, which is starting in less than thirty minutes. As expected, Brenton is stretched out face-down on his bed, chin propped up in his hands as he watches some stupid video on my laptop.

Even though Jim is the new "man of the house," it's still my duty to play dad with my own siblings. I shake my head and walk over to him.

"C'mon, bud, time to get ready," I huff, swiping the computer up and snapping him out of his trance.

"Hey!" he whines, then he pouts and folds his arms. "I *was* getting ready, for your information."

My gaze moves from him to the computer screen, which is in the midst of displaying one of starlet Cherie Belle's cheesy music videos. Correction: one of her newer, cheesier music videos for a song that sounds like all of the other songs she makes for little kids like Brenton. She's one of those up and coming kid celebrities that little girls love and guys my age drool over. I don't get why Brenton's so obsessed with her, though; she's hot and all, but Brenton's ten-year-old mind can't possibly be thinking that. Or maybe he is finally noticing girls?

Rather than entertain that thought for a second more, I chuckle at him and stop the video, saying, "Are you singing this dumb song for us later or something? Putting on a little Christmas play maybe?" I turn to his closet and pull out a pair of khakis and a miniature button-down shirt that looks like it would maybe fit around one of my arms.

He squints at me as I plop the clothes down beside him. "No, Cheecho and I want to make sure we have plenty to talk to her about. Duh."

If any other person in the world had said such a thing, I probably would have inquired further with something along the lines of, "Huh?" or "What do you mean?"

But this is Brenton, and Brenton is a weird kid who has an imaginary friend named Cheecho, and he says weird stuff all of the time. For all I know, he is making a plan to have an imaginary play date with Cherie Belle and Cheecho later tonight.

So I simply shake my head at him and sigh, "Whatever, bud, just make sure you do it after you get dressed for dinner."

I turn and walk off with my computer just as he calls, "Do you have any idea who she is?"

I close my bedroom door to tune the hallway music out, but it's inescapable, blaring from the wall speakers that are littered in every hallway of our house. Jim had them installed right after he installed himself and his daughters in our home last October.

I stand back and examine my closet. Last night, Mom told me to look nice for this dinner, which means I have to wear stupid, shiny dress shoes and a shirt with a collar. I choose the same black pants and button-up shirt that I wore last month to awards night at the end of football season because the outfit is Mom-tested and girl-approved. Well, *was* approved by my now ex-girlfriend, Katrina. She picked out my clothes for the better half of a year before the twins moved in. Then she just started picking fights, and I wasn't prepared to juggle another drama queen in my life.

I check my hair one more time in the mirror and fix a few pieces that have already fallen out of place. I look down at my shirt and can't decide—undo the top button or keep them all closed? One way looks a little stiff and nerdy, and the other looks kind of dumb, showing too much of my chest like those New Jersey guidos. I try it all the way buttoned. Then I undo a button. Then I redo it.

Finally, I shake my head, wondering what happened to me and when I started giving a damn about how many buttons I button.

As I make my way down the steps, I can hear my sister Britney's antagonistic giggle and *tap-tap-tapping* of her own shiny, dress-up shoes as she evades my mom's red-nailed grasp.

"Britney, no! I said no more cookies before dinner!" Mom chides as my sister smiles devilishly, reaching for the dessert platter on the table. Mom looks harried, a dishtowel slung over her shoulder, a flour-dusted apron protecting her ornamental dress. Her eyes are harsher than normal, framed with dark eye shadow. Her hair is curled and looks nice and smooth for a change. One of Jim's daughters must have given her a makeover.

That's their way of being nice to someone on our side of the family.

The first floor of the house looks like it got a makeover, too, but that's all my mom's doing. On holidays, my mom used to go nuts with expensive decorations and the crystal ornaments that only the adults were allowed to put on the tree. She took a long vacation from playing Holly Homemaker after Dad left. First, she had to recover. Then, she had to go to work, where she met Jim. Now they're married, and she doesn't work anymore, so I'm not exactly surprised that she is reverting back to her perfect hostess ways. Mom's been reborn ever since Jim and his daughters moved in, which is great for her, I guess.

Mom scurries to sequester Britney, and she doesn't even see me when she runs past. Her frantic eyes and tight mouth tell me that, along with the decorations, good, old-fashioned Hansen holiday tension is back, too. It's a lot like the feeling you get when your parents take you to the housewares part of a department store. You're always walking with your hands clasped tightly in front of you, as if one wrong move will make all those fancy plates clash and clatter and shatter into a million pieces on the floor. Tonight's been built up by my mother as some culminating exam she has to pass to prove her worthiness as a wife and mother-figure to Jim's kids.

In truth, it should be the other way around. But in my mother's twisted, never-worthy-enough psyche, thanks to my father, she's always one wrong move away from causing this whole world she's rebuilt to crash down around her.

I think that's why there are two tables this year. She knows there will be fireworks, and she's determined to keep all of the kids in one spot far enough away that we won't be seen giving each other dirty looks or heard sniping at each other. I've been demoted to the annoyingly prescribed "kid table." I fought my mom hard on that one. I haven't had to sit at a kid table in years, partly because I haven't been a kid for years. I've been the man of the house, but I guess I've been demoted from that, too.

Really, I just don't want to have to sit with Jim's evil twin daughters all night, but I promised I would try to get along with them. It was a huge, overachieving promise; they're possibly the rudest human beings on the planet. Mom always tells me I have to be patient with them because they didn't have a mom to raise them to be ladies, but I think that's just an excuse. They're mean with a capital M, and I don't think it has anything to do with their mother dying when they were little. Mom will say anything to make me behave; she just wants to create the image of a cookie cutter family, one that gets along and says "please" and "thank you" when they pass the platters, the kind that has safe but uproarious snowball fights. In truth, if the twins are involved in anything, there won't be any pleases and thank yous, and if we have a snowball fight, it's going to get ugly.

But I promised my mother that I'd try. I promised to bite my tongue and be the bigger person. And I will, if they leave me alone.

I stop at the door to the family room and get a good look at my dungeon for the evening.

The kid table is like something you'd see in a painting. The bright red table cloth is polka dotted with the white china from Mom's first wedding. On this table, where something is destined to be broken, these old plates scream "nice enough to use for the holidays, but expendable."

My eyes travel to the middle, which is decorated with two miniature Christmas trees and a giant Menorah in between them. Jim's family is Jewish, but we're Catholic. Reason #72 this night has to go perfectly for my mom: Jim's family was apparently concerned about him bringing on board a family who practices the opposite of their beliefs. My mom is doing her best to prove her worthiness and religious tolerance all in the same night.

Sure Mom, slap a menorah in there, I muse to myself. *That makes it all better.*

Britney scampers in from the dining room. She sees me and lights up. I light up, too.

"Jackie!"

"Hey, brat!"

The distraction is exactly what my mom needs. She pounces and catches the elusive five-year-old, who thinks the chase is one big game and scream-laughs.

Mom rolls her eyes in my direction and finally notices me. "Oh, thank goodness you're finally down here. I just finished setting the kids' table." She thrusts Britney at me. "Here, take your sister before she breaks something!"

"Okay." She falls into my arms. "What're you doing, brat? Getting into trouble?"

Britney cries, "Jackie!" She climbs me like a tree and swings from my neck.

"Britney, I told you, say 'Jack.' Jackie is a girl's name." I set her squirrely body down on the ground.

"Suits you anyway."

A shiver runs down my spine. *Chloe.* She is the worst of the twins. The mere sound of her voice makes my skin crawl. If she were an animal, she'd be a nasty housecat. I see her red-orange hair flip as soon as I hear her low, menacing purr. She swishes by and casually takes a cookie off of the table, her motions taunting my sister as her eyes and smug smile goad me into battle.

It's instinctual, and I can't help it. "Shut up, Chloe."

I instantly regret it when Chloe follows Mom toward the dining room. "Eva, your son told me to shut up for no reason!" She turns and flashes me a sinister, toothy grin. It's the type of perfect grin that you hate so much because it never needed braces to be that straight. The type of grin that's about to get you in trouble.

"I was just telling him how much his shirt suits him…"

Frustration doesn't even describe what boils under my skin. Instead of sounding powerful and manly, my voice comes out like a whine. "Mom, don't listen to her, she's—" I see Britney climbing a chair to reach the cookies, and my attention is diverted. "Britney, no!" I grab her and hoist her under my arm. She squeals and twists in my grasp. The doorbell rings, and I'm sidetracked for a nanosecond. It's enough for Britney to weasel out of my hold, snatch the damn cookie off of the table, and dash upstairs. I let her go, defeated.

"Epic fail, Jack." Chloe takes a bite of her cookie and struts out of the room.

"Your face is an epic fail," I call after her. I'm pretty proud of my comeback. Mom, however, is not.

"*Jack!*" Mom appears in the doorway with her frown of disapproval. I roll my eyes and huff. I'm always caught after the fact, once I've retaliated. Mom and Jim never hear the things they say to me.

She comes to me and straightens my collar. "Jack, you promised me you'd get along with the girls tonight," she murmurs.

I want to protest that Chloe provoked me as usual, but the words fall flat on my tongue. I hate disappointing my mom. Instead, I groan, "Yeah, I know."

Mom looks around in a sudden panic. "Where's Britney?"

I hang my head. "Upstairs. She got away."

She smiles gently at me instead of scolding. "Well, at least she's not causing chaos under my feet." She stabs her pointer finger against my chest. "Be nice to the girls. You're in charge out here, so we're counting on you to set the example. Control that temper."

I sigh. "I know, I get it." In my head, I grumble, *I've had pretty good control of my anger for two years now, thank you very much.*

"Honey, why so much gel here?" She pulls at a strand of my hair, and I jerk back.

"Mom!" She knows I hate it when people touch my hair. Now I have to find the closest mirror and fix it.

"Sorry, my goodness!" She shakes her head and turns away. "His father through and through," she mutters under her breath, as if I can't hear her.

I hate when she says that. "What was that?"

"I said your Aunt Darla and your cousin Leroy just got here. Come say hello," she huffs.

I smack a hand over my eyes. "Oh, brother." I'd forgotten all about the additional cast of characters that Christmas Eve brings.

DIRTERAZZI.COM

Cherie Belle in LAX, Heading East for Christmas and New Years

Dirterazzi caught up with teen queen, Cherie Belle, in LAX yesterday afternoon, even though she was trying to hide behind her famous oversized sunglasses. Wearing Heiress boots that matched her Heiress suitcases, the sixteen-year-old looked like a walking advertisement for the designer brand as she waited in line at security with her assistant, Danika Shields. Also at her side were her adoring father, Mark, and her mother, Camille Goldman, who also happens to be a genuine MILF. Her father was more than happy to carry his cash-cow daughter's carry-ons while she texted friends and answered some of our questions. The one question she wouldn't answer: Who was on the other end of those texts she's sending?

Ahem, could it be Caz Farrell, perhaps?

Chapter 2

Leroy enters the room, the very caricature of a teenage nerd you'd see on TV. He is wearing large glasses and has a book tucked under his arm. His pants are high enough that his ankles show, and he is wearing a sweater vest *and* a tie. His book is titled, *If Your Brain Could Talk...And It Does!* He is smiling and is too happy to see me.

"Hey there, first cousin! Long time no see!" He greets me with a slap to the shoulder.

"I saw you at the wedding, Leroy. That was two months ago," I remind him patiently. I have to be patient with Leroy. Something small inside of me makes me do it, maybe a shred of sympathy for how unabashedly clueless my cousin could be to his own social awkwardness.

Plus, I need him tonight. He's my only real ally against the girls, no question about it. He's not much of an ally in this department; it's kind of like pulling in a first-year kicker when you need a senior quarterback, but he's still on the same team. It's him and me versus the Unholy Trinity—Chloe, Claudia, and Evil Britney, the girl she turns into when the twins are present.

Leroy snorts with laughter. "Well, two months can be a long time if you're a tadpole. Did you know that it takes anywhere from three days to three weeks for a tadpole to break free into water after it leaves its egg? Two months would be an eternity!"

And so it begins...Leroy will never lose his penchant for spitting out the wildest facts about anything and everything. He's got something to say about all topics, whether or not they actually make sense in the moment. Now and then he shares some pretty cool stuff, but usually it's just weird, random crap.

"Oh my God, look at this place! Eva, it's so fabulous in here!" Leroy's mom, Aunt Darla, comes floating in. She is dressed in one of her trendy, near-teenager outfits. My mom's sister is four years younger and even younger at heart, and that's putting it nicely. She's that woman who is always making references to things only kids talk about and who yawns dramatically at adult conversations. What's weirder is she couldn't be any less like her own son. He acts like he's forty, and she still thinks she's seventeen. She's divorced, too, but judging by her carefree attitude, something tells me it was her decision. Tonight she is awed and distracted by the bright lights and shiny colors of our spruced-up house.

"Jack!" She's also way too excited to see me, smiling from ear to ear as she throws her arms around me.

"Hi Aunt Darla," I reply meekly. She hugs too tight and kisses my cheek, and I can feel an inch of lip gloss left behind.

"How is my handsome nephew? You're getting so tall! You're bigger than me!" She says this every year. "So sorry about your break-up with Katrina; she was such a sweet thing. Any new girlfriends yet, or are you still on the market? How's school? What is with all the hair gel?"

I feel my face flush as she inspects me and my personal life, only pulling back when she tries to fuss with my hair. That's one thing I refuse to tolerate.

"Um, school's okay." I try to wipe off the gloss without her noticing. "Katrina's whatever." I'd tell Darla that my mean-girl stepsisters are the real reason my ex and I broke up, but she's running like a motor.

"That's so unfortunate, honey. She was lovely at the wedding; such a beautiful dress. What happened? Come, Aunt Darla wants to hear all about it!" *And she's off*! She takes my hand and walks me through the room. "Where are the twins? Did you get your senior license yet? Leroy has been practicing for his driver's test for two weeks now!" She gently rubs his shoulder. "We go out to the mall together, and he drives to the movie theatre—we saw that new Caz Farrell movie together, did you see it?"

"No, I didn't." My reply is a murmur as I peer at my hair in the closest mirror. It's fine, and so is my amount of hair gel.

Leroy rolls his eyes. "I think my mom is infatuated with Caz Farrell." When I squint at him, he mumbles, "Don't get me started."

Just as Darla is calming, the twins emerge from the kitchen, side by side, and Darla bubbles over again when she sees them.

Claudia, the only-slightly-nicer-if-you're-really-paying-attention twin, lights up and gives Darla a big hug. Claudia is Darla's number one fan. Chloe, however, is not as interested. She has a dirty look for my aunt, as usual, and looks her up and down. I've seen that look before at school, especially when I'm talking to a girl and Chloe doesn't approve. It gets under my skin then, and it really gets under my skin now.

Stay cool. Ignore her, I tell myself.

Darla sings, "Hey, girlfriend! What's happening? Look at you—is that top from Forever 21? I almost bought it the other day, but I didn't like how it made my shoulders look…"

"Oh my God, yes it is!" Claudia sings out. "You always have the best taste!"

Aunt Darla beams, idolized by someone in the room. "Just wait 'til you see your gift, girl!"

Chloe hisses, "You still shop at Forever 21? Isn't that, like, a teenager store?"

Darla, ever the optimist, shrugs good-naturedly. "You know what they say: you're only as old as you feel!"

Chloe's eyes burn with contempt. "Don't they also say act your age?"

I'm about to step in and save my innocent aunt when she simply waves the demonic cat off and fusses over Claudia some more. This makes Chloe turn scarlet with anger or embarrassment, I'm not sure which. All I know is that I don't have to do anything about it.

Suddenly, Brenton comes flailing down the stairs, his eyes alight.

"Is she here?" His head whips around in all directions, and he darts from doorway to doorway. "I thought I heard the doorbell ring. Is she here?"

I cast him the *'you're crazy'* look he deserves. "What is wrong with you?"

Brenton grabs me by the wrists. "Jack, listen to me: their cousin, the most amazing and talented actress in the history of acting, is coming to dinner. To our house. OUR house, Jack!"

I almost laugh out loud. "What cousin?"

Chloe and Claudia immediately appear, Darla-free, and scowling. "He means our cousin, Cher. You know, Cherie Belle?" Chloe replies.

I take a second to digest this news. I know exactly who that is, but I make sure my tongue doesn't come lolling out of my mouth. The heat I feel in my chest wants to rise to my cheeks. Why didn't I know anything about this?

Quite the opposite of what's happening inside, I play it cool on the outside. "The girl on that chocolate show on Kidz Network? *That* Cherie Belle?"

Brenton, exalted, falls on his knees and throws his hands to the sky. "Oh, just the sound of her name makes me crave Belgian Chocolate!"

Claudia spits, "Get up, Brenton! The last thing little miss celebrity needs is a bigger head."

I chime in for effect. "Yeah, that's not even acting, Brenton, it's just a show about chocolate." My imagination, however, pants a little at the thought of Cherie Belle walking through my home, sitting at my table...

Brenton snaps me back to reality before my imagination goes too far. "JUST a show about chocolate? Jack, it is THE show about chocolate—I mean, what a brilliant idea to have a whole show based on chocolate, only the most delectable sweet in the world!"

Leroy forgets no one was talking to him. "Is that the show 'Choc It Up?' I think I've seen it. Quite an ingenious concept; I never knew there were so many types of chocolate. Did you know that the cocoa pods symbolized life and fertility to the Mayans?"

Brenton cocks a suspicious eyebrow. "No, where did you hear that? That wasn't in any of the episodes; trust me, I have them all memorized."

Claudia is irritated but tries to feign genuine interest. "How do you know all this stuff, Leroy?"

Chloe is not as gentle. "Yeah, who has the time to memorize all this useless information?"

"Back off," I command, puffing my chest a little. I am almost a full foot taller than them. They have to listen to me, sort of fear me in that scary, big brother way, even if I kind of see their point.

Brenton defends him, too. "Yeah, there is nothing useless about chocolate facts!" Aside to Leroy, he whispers, "But how *do* you know that?"

Leroy gives his trademark impish shrug. "I read a lot, I guess." His cheeks are the color of strawberry jell-o, and I grow that much angrier. Even if they're only sophomores, the twins are still probably the prettiest girls to ever actually talk to him, and they just made him feel like a total loser.

Just then, the women of the house parade through the room with mouth-watering platters of food. In a seemingly deliberate tango performed to the tune of incessant clucking, these mavens gracefully set portions of sliced turkey, Granny's casserole, and more deliciousness around the kid table. Watching them makes me forget to be angry, forget Cherie Belle, because my stomach instantly reminds me that I've been ready to eat for over an hour.

Chloe continues her nasty assault on Leroy as the women make their way back into the kitchen.

"It's not normal for someone to memorize all that stuff," she snaps.

"Well, whatever, let's just start sitting down," I interrupt. I go to the staircase and summon my little sister. "Brat, time to eat!"

Britney comes scampering down and jumps into my arms. I set her into a chair beside me. The others begin sitting at the table one by one with a clear divide of the families. There is an empty seat beside Brenton, and Leroy attempts to sit in it.

"Hey! That's Cheecho's chair!" he complains. He's had his imaginary friend since kindergarten. My brother received the nerd gene for sure. Maybe it's because he's so much younger; it probably skips a generation or something like that. Like how Aunt Darla's so cool and Leroy's practically a savant. Well, I'm pretty cool, I think, and my brother's a complete loser.

Leroy is confused but accepts it. "Okay, I guess I'll go sit by the girls."

Chloe holds up her hand before he can sit beside her. "Uh, no way Factmonster!" They giggle together.

I roll my eyes, too busy pouring Britney's juice to reach across the table and choke them. "You girls are so stupid," is the best I can do. For now.

Brenton is flabbergasted. "Yeah, you know we need a seat for Cheecho!"

Chloe sighs. "Brenton, Cheecho doesn't exist. Let your cousin sit there."

Brenton is now at Level: Horrified. "How *dare* you!"

Claudia looks at me imploringly. "Jack, tell your super-weird little brother that his imaginary friend needs to go sit at the imaginary friend table!"

I hold my head. "Pass the turkey, please."

Leroy takes his place beside Brenton after a slight struggle. "Don't you think it would be polite to wait for Cherie?"

Chapter 3

As if on cue, we hear the doorbell chime. There is a lot of commotion at the front door. The twins instinctively roll their eyes to each other. Brenton sits up at attention. Even my stomach lurches a little bit. Mark and Camille, the twins' aunt and uncle, come fluttering through to say their hellos. They are overly tanned with blindingly white teeth and leave a cloud of obnoxious European colognes behind. They quickly retreat back into the main dining room with gusto. Finally, we hear the exaggeratedly baby-high voice of none other than Cherie Belle.

"Oh my gosh, I KNOW! Isn't it wild?" Like an angel, she enters the room, practically adorned by an aura of light. Her bouncy, blond curls help her pink, glossed smile scream innocent young teenager. Her big green eyes flash with the same "I'm perfect and I know it" sparkle that her cousins have, except better and brighter. She's the epitome of gorgeous. I shift in my chair. Do I get up? Do I welcome her to our home?

No, I chastise myself, *don't be ridiculous*. The twins notice my indecisiveness and shake their heads in disapproval. I look over at Leroy, who is already nose-deep in his book, as if none of this is happening. At least I'm not the most awkward person here.

An older girl follows Cherie into the room. She is slightly less glamorous and holds a planner in one hand and a cellphone in the other. She's not an actress who I recognize. Best friend or assistant? I can't tell. They are both dressed in matching, fluffy fur outfits.

Cherie turns and shouts over her shoulder, "Thanks Uncle Jim! Thanks Eva."

She makes sure none of the adults are looking before sticking her finger down her throat to fake a gag. Her assista-friend laughs, and they continue to walk toward the table haughtily. Cherie takes in the scene with disgust as she begins to remove gloves that reach up to her elbows. Brenton is frozen for a moment in shock and awe. Then, he rushes forward and throws himself at her feet.

"Welcome to our home!" he says, bent over like he is praying to a goddess.

"Brenton!" I hiss. "Get up!" He ignores me. If my face could get any hotter, my skin would melt.

Cherie also doesn't acknowledge me, too disgusted by my embarrassing little brother. "Seriously?" She steps over Brenton, who accepts his unworthiness while a piece of him dies. She pats his head, and he comes alive again, as if touched by an angel. As we all stare in subdued shock, the conversation with her matching apostle goes a little like this:

Cherie: "Ugh, this is so common."

Assista-friend: "So common."

Cherie: "I'm a prisoner for the next two hours."

Assista-friend: "Oh, this is totally jail."

Cherie: "Who ever heard of Westchester anyway?"

Assista-friend: "No one goes upstate except to ski or pick apples."

Cherie: "I mean, like, it's cute and quaint in that homey sort of way—"

Assista-friend: "Yeah, yeah, it's cute—"

Cherie: "—if you like that sort of thing."

Assista-friend: "—which is so not our speed."

Until this moment, I had been pretty sure this kind of stuff only happens in movies. They've proven me wrong.

Cherie, looking around with concern, stops her assista-friend in her tracks. "Danika, you don't think The

Gazer is outside, do you? These New York tabloids are ruthless, you know."

Danika replies, "I was very careful when I scoped out the place. It's clean."

"Great." She approaches the table with Danika still at her heels. "Happy Hanukkah, everyone. *Claudia. Chloe.*"

Chloe sniffs, "Why, look what the trash magazines dragged in."

Claudia will tolerate none of her cousin's insensitivity. "It's Happy *Holidays*, Cherie, not Happy Hanukkah. Notice the giant Christmas tree? We celebrate both now."

Cherie smiles daggers at her. "How nice for you." She looks at me, and my heart stops. Her eyes twinkle, and she turns on her TV smile, extending her hand dramatically toward me. "And you are...?"

There is nothing cool about how I nearly trip over myself to stand as she approaches. I'm stuttering slightly as I shake her hand. "I—I'm Jack Hansen."

Cherie studies me, her eyes moving up and down my clothes and then back to my face. She approves me with a short, high-pitched "Mmmhmm," then looks to Leroy, who is immersed in his book and has missed everything that has happened from the moment she entered. Cherie clears her throat and goes unnoticed. One of her eyebrows rises a little at his disinterest.

"I see. Curious fellow." She rolls her eyes to Danika and groans, "Well, let's get this over with, shall we?"

She sits down beside Claudia, and Danika looks at Claudia as if she should know she will have to move. I realize that the table is one seat short, and my mom will flip if she finds out she's forgotten to set a place for a guest.

But the girls are no help. Claudia growls, "Don't even think about it."

Danika looks to Chloe, who bites, "Get your own chair." The girl looks on to the next seat, which is Britney's.

Britney, always taking her cue from the older girls, shouts, "Get your own!"

"Brat, don't be rude," I scold quietly. I stand again to give my chair away, but Brenton quickly scoots his chair all the way to that end of the table to offer it to the girls. He sets it right beside Danika, who takes it with a short, "Thanks."

He practically salutes her. "Brenton Hansen, at your service. I'm Cherie's number one fan." Brenton, breathless, puts his hands on his hips and declares, "Any friend of Cherie is a friend of mine."

Chloe scoffs, "You may have to lose Cheecho with that mindset."

"Yeah, Cherie doesn't believe in imaginary friends," adds Claudia unhelpfully.

Oh no. "Okay, we should really start to eat—" I announce.

Danika looks at Brenton, bemused. "Wait, you have an imaginary friend? What are you, five years old?" He shrinks a little, his jaw hanging slack.

Britney counts on her fingers before cheerily crying out, "I'm five!"

Brenton grows quiet and turns pink. "I—I'm ten—"

My nerve endings spike, as if I smell the eruption that is about to take place. *No, no, no, don't pop Brenton's bubble, please don't do this here and now...*

But Cherie does it. "Ten? Wow, buddy, time to lose the faux friends," she snickers. Looking at the hurt on Brenton's face, I suddenly want to hide, embarrassed for him, but even more embarrassed to be related to him.

Chloe lets out her own obnoxious laugh and looks right at Danika. "Someone should take their own advice."

Cherie turns snake eyes onto her cousin and hisses, "This coming from the girl who doesn't have any friends, real or fake." Danika high-fives her.

Aunt Darla reappears, like an angel of peace, chanting, "I hope you've saved a seat for me! I just cannot sit at that boring old adult table!" She looks around in dismay. "Oh poo, not a seat left here."

She sees Cherie and brightens. Her heels make *tip-tip-tip* sounds as she scurries to her side of the table and hovers over the starlet. There is a collective groan from the rest of the table, except for me. I'm still trying to be a gentleman, but I'm apparently the only one. Even Leroy is exhausted by his mother's presence.

"Oh, Cherie! I didn't see you come in! I'm so sorry you couldn't make the wedding, I was so looking forward to meeting you."

"And you are?" Cherie looks like she's about to shake the hand of a vagabond. I'm starting to not like this girl at all; all the blond curls in the world don't make up for what she lacks in manners.

Like she does in response to Chloe's snarky remarks, my aunt plugs along, oblivious. "Darla. Aunt Darla, if you like! So glad you could make it tonight; I've heard so much about you on the news—and that new movie you're doing! Girl, you have got to tell me what it was like working with that Caz Farrell. Is what the magazines said true? Were you two dating?"

Cherie glows, clearly flattered by the implication. "Oh, not at all, Darcy."

"It's Darla, dear," my aunt reminds her.

Cherie is unfazed by her own error. "Right, whatever—Caz is a great guy, but he's really just a friend. I'm too young to be dating Caz."

Danika adds, "Yeah, she's way too young to date Caz, he's much older."

Claudia is quick to remark, "Let's be real, Cherie."

Cherie scrunches her nose in disgust. "Speculate all you like, but I am as real as they come."

"Right down to your ridiculous fur coat," Chloe says with another eye roll.

I smell the fight brewing again. "Can someone please pass the turkey?"

Chapter 4

Cherie pauses and looks at the table as if seeing it for the first time. "Turkey? Oh no, this won't work; I'm a vegan."

Danika squints at her. "But we had turkey wraps on Sunday—"

Cherie scolds her, "Yeah, and I did the interview on Channel 5 with Jules Cinque on Tuesday, stupid! Remember? When we were on commercial break, she told me to go vegan?" She looks at the rest of us as if we were supposed to be aware of this bit of information. "That's what Dr. Forrester told her to do."

The memory comes back to Danika. "Oh yeah."

Chloe sighs, "Fancy that, a vegan who wears real furs."

The connection is lost on Cherie, who gives Chloe that mean-girl look that says, *"No one here knows what you're talking about."*

Claudia asks, "So you do whatever anyone tells you to do? That's not going to get you very far."

Cherie finds her new victim and patronizes her. "Uh, no, it got me a TV show, sweetie. What has dressing like Hannah Montana done for you?" I feel almost badly for Claudia, who certainly doesn't have the wits required to develop a sufficient comeback. She gawks at her cousin and then looks down at her clothes in disbelief.

Leroy, blessed Leroy, finally interjects, but on no one's behalf. "Did you know that vegans make up about 1.3% of the population?"

Everyone looks at him for a moment of silence.

Cherie, possibly unaware of how mean she truly sounds, whispers with fascination, "It speaks."

Claudia is frustrated, but she takes it out on the wrong person. "Seriously, Leroy? Don't you have anything normal to say?"

I try to jump in again, but Chloe beats me to it and throws her napkin down dramatically. "I'm not sitting at this table of freaks." She gets up and storms upstairs.

Aunt Darla is mortified. "Chloe! Oh, my!"

"Good! We don't want to sit with you either!" Cherie stands abruptly, and Danika follows as she storms away from the table to the dining room. I hear the sounds from the adult room promptly cease.

"Angel, what's wrong?" Cherie's father, Mark, calls as he rushes to her side.

"I'm leaving, Daddy!" she sniffs. "I'll have Fernando come back for you."

"But, Cherie darling, you promised—" he tries to say, but she won't have any of his coaxing and shakes her head.

"No, I promised you I would try, but they're impossible. I just can't take another minute! Chloe and Claudia are being rude as always, and then there's a kid saying weird stuff…"

As she whines on, I lower my head and shake it with a sigh. Everything she is complaining about is sort of true, and she's not exactly exaggerating, which is the saddest part. I hear her patient father trying to soothe and calm her, but she bulldozes through him and the front door.

"See, Leroy? I told you that people don't like to hear all those facts!" Aunt Darla scolds. She chases after her. "Wait! Cherie!"

Brenton glares at Claudia. "Look at what you did! You chased her away!"

I clear my throat and give a low warning, "Brenton, let it go." I've got to try to keep some order around here.

I may not have power over what the girls do, but I can prevent my little brother from continuing the fight.

My tone falls on deaf ears as Claudia scoffs, "She was totally mean to you, Brenton! Why do you even care?" I kind of have to agree with her there, but my brother doesn't care.

"Brenton." My eyes dart to him to stay quiet.

Brenton, however, is indignant. "That doesn't matter! You're just jealous of her!" I kind of agree with him, too. I'm feeling helpless, a mere spectator to this catastrophic game of nasty ping pong.

But I try anyway. "Stop—"

Claudia throws her napkin at him and shouts, "Go play with your imaginary friend!" It misses him and whizzes right past my nose.

"Hey!" I cry out as I watch it slap against Leroy's face.

Brenton gets up, punching the table with both fists. "I will! At least I'm not a Miley Cyrus wannabe!" He throws a bread roll that almost clocks Britney in the head.

"Cut it out!" I bellow, leaning in front of my little sister and blocking the roll.

"She started it!"

"No, you did!"

I jump up and yell, "I said cut it out!"

And that's when they, the suspicious adults who are suddenly attuned to the commotion, fill the doorway of the family room. That moment, which should end up on the cutting room floor, is all they see. They're all there: Jim, Mom, Grandma, Jim's mother and father, and Cherie's parents. The adults see me, and only me, on my feet and red with anger, yelling, as the table clears in a heartbeat. Brenton stampedes up to his room. Britney whimpers beside me. Claudia lets out a scream-growl and storms away in the opposite direction.

I only care about my little sister right now. "I'm sorry, Brat," I murmur softly, sitting down to comfort her.

But she pulls away. "I'm not eating with these freaks!" She scampers off before anyone can catch her. I am left alone at the table with Leroy.

"Claud, what's going on?" Jim calls after her.

"I'm not hungry!" Claudia cries out. A door slams. The adults, minus Darla, look at me as if I'm somehow responsible for what has happened. Cherie's parents, Mark and Camille, shake their heads at me. Leroy is reading again as if none of this has happened in front of him. He might as well be putting a finger to his nose and shouting, "*Not it!*"

My mom is afraid to say my name. Or too angry to say it. "J—boys, what happened here?"

I feel a thousand times worse than she does, but there's no way to convince her it wasn't my fault.

"They were all just… just… being mean, Mom," I sort of whine. I didn't know what to say without going through every detail. Jim looks at me sternly and shakes his head. I have to hold back the glower I want to give him. He doesn't know how cruel and inhuman his daughters are, he only knows about my violent past, so I'm immediately the problem.

Still, I can't shake the guilt that somehow I am actually responsible for this debacle. One look at my mom's disappointed frown tells me that I'm accurate in my assessment.

My mom and Jim march up the stairs, and the other adults return to the main dining room in muted mumbles, leaving me alone with Leroy.

"Well, that's one way to clear a table," Leroy nervously jokes as the room clears. "I guess that means more food for us."

I do everything I can to control my anger, concentrating it all into my tightening hand until I crunch my empty soda can. Leroy keeps his eyes forward, and I can tell he's afraid he'll be next.

I mutter, "Those girls ruin everything. I can't take them anymore! Look at me—I'm so angry, I'm sweating like a pig!"

Leroy closes his book slowly. "Many teenage boys suffer from night sweats."

I turn in my chair to look at him, and he flinches. I clench my jaw, hating that my whole family still perceives me as some kind of loose cannon. "Relax, I'm not going to hit you, Leroy. Can you just not do the fact thing right now?"

Leroy relaxes a little and shrugs. "Well, I could say what I really think."

I cock an eyebrow. "Oh, yeah? What's that?"

He serves himself food as he speaks. "That you're sweating because you were nervous around Cherie."

"Are you kidding? I wanted to strangle her!" I guffaw.

Leroy laughs at me. "Could've fooled me. It's okay; she is a pretty girl." He passes the tray of turkey meat. "I think you've been asking for this."

I take the platter, but I set it to the side. "Hold on a sec—you were reading. You don't even know what just took place here."

He smirks at me and shakes his head. "I notice a lot more than you think, Jack."

I feel my cheeks grow hot, and I force myself to take a deep breath. "Well, you noticed wrong."

Leroy and I spend the next twenty minutes in silence. He eats and reads. I eat a little here and there; I'm only human. There was no way I'd sit at that table for all that time without touching any of the amazing food I'd been lusting after all day.

A soundtrack of clinking glasses and forks scraping plays in the other room, accompanied by belly laughter and cheer. How do adults manage to go a whole night without arguing over anything? Well, these adults at least. Mom never had that kind of luck with my dad.

Still, Mom and Dad got to choose to live together. Dad got to choose when he'd had enough of living together. Dad didn't just get up from the table when he needed a way out; he left the house. No one lumped Mom and Dad and their relatives into one home and said, *"Here, deal with it."*

"Wanna go for a drive?" I ask, suddenly claustrophobic and anxious for fresh air. I love my car. It's my space, the one place where I have total control, and no one else gets to share it unless I ask them to jump in. Right now, I just want to get in and drive.

Leroy seems game, and we are about to leave the table when Aunt Darla, Mom and Jim come down the stairs with the rest of the brood, marching each of my siblings back to the kid table with resignation.

"Where do you think you're going?" my mom asks me, perturbed.

I look back at Leroy. "We were going for a drive. We finished eating."

She shakes her head. "Oh, no, mister, this holiday dinner is happening. Sit down. Besides, it's snowing, and the roads are bad."

I sit down with a heavy sigh, looking at the disgruntled faces around me. No one looks happy to be at this table. I think of how hard my mom worked to make this dinner for them, and I feel like none of them deserves to be here.

Not even me.

"Where's Cherie?" Brenton asks.

"She went back to her hotel," Aunt Darla says softly, patting his shoulder when his face drops. "Her driver will come back for Aunt Camille and Uncle Mark later."

The table is full of scowls and folded arms and upturned noses.

"Look guys, I know not everybody gets along," Jim begins, and I watch his eyes rest on me. *What did I do?* "But if you can just try—at least for tonight, for our sake—we really would appreciate it. Look, it's snowing outside, how many times is there a true white Christmas? And look at this table—we can't let all this good food go to waste! Besides, you may actually have a good time tonight if we just forgive each other for our differences for a few hours. Whaddya say?"

The twins shrug. Brenton pouts and sighs dramatically, and Britney holds up her half-eaten cookie to me.

"No, thanks." Jim shoots me a look, and I have to recover quickly. "I was talking to Britney. She tried to give me a cookie." *But also no to your whole* "we can be a cookie-cutter family, too" *speech*, I grumble inside my head.

"I know you kids will make the best of it," Mom says at last, putting her hand over Jim's. "As for Cherie, well, we will just have to talk about how to treat guests at another time. As a *family*." She lets those last syllables hang in the air for a moment.

Jim's father, Elliot, comes to the door and announces it's time to light the menorah. Claudia and Chloe rise dutifully from their chairs and walk to the dining room.

Brenton turns to Leroy, oblivious. "So what else do you know about chocolate, Leroy?" Leroy and Brenton begin to talk chocolate, and I have to nudge them while simultaneously taking Britney's hand.

"C'mon guys," I say half-heartedly. "We have to do this, too."

I lead all three of them toward the adult table, where the others are crowded around a half-lit menorah. It may be Christmas Eve, but it is also the fifth night of Hanukkah. As we stand in the room and listen to the prayers being sung by only six adults in the room, I realize that this, too, is a visual metaphor for my life. A hodgepodge of people, all clustered together, the adults trying to harmonize in a sacred song, the kids refusing to participate, and I'm supposed to set the example when I don't know the words.

Chapter 5

There's a certain feeling everyone wakes up with on Christmas morning, and it's never dread. Usually, you tingle with anticipation, as if the gift you were hoping for will be sitting at the foot of your tree, or, as you get older, outside in the garage. For some people, it's the serenity of quiet, because lush snow is falling and the house is still, and no one else is up yet. For me, it's usually the grumble of my stomach because Christmas morning means tons of food, both fresh and leftover, and Mom's amazing hot chocolate.

But I wake up to the sounds of muffled sobs, not my growling insides. I look down, and Britney is curled in her usual spot between my chest and my arm. Maybe she was talking in her sleep...

I hear the heavy, near hysterical whimpering again, and this time it's farther away. I look at the clock; 3:30 a.m. Did Brenton finally discover that Santa doesn't exist? Did one the twins tell him just to be mean?

Oh, someone please shoot me.

I look down at Britney again; she's still asleep. I don't want to wake her. I pull my arm out from under her head with well-practiced, ninja-like skill. Britney doesn't stir, so I slide carefully out from beneath the sheets and fumble in the dark to find my t-shirt.

Footsteps pad softly past my door, and the crying sounds like it's coming from downstairs now. There are voices, too. I soundlessly turn the knob of my door. I look back at Britney and feel bad leaving her. I know if she wakes up in the dark of my room, alone, she'll freak out, but waking her is much more deterring.

In the hall, I pull the shirt on and listen intently. The voices are muffled, interrupted by sobs and cries that are muffled, too. It sounds like a lot of voices. They're coming from the family room. I find my way down the steps, each one becoming clearer as the light from downstairs pours through the railing. I know Aunt Darla and Leroy were staying in the guest room in the basement. Could everybody be awake right now?

I pause at the bottom step and find that yes, everyone is up, and there are police officers in the house, dressed in black uniforms, looking somber. Everyone turns to look at me, and I take a step forward.

"Mom?"

"Oh! Jack, honey!" my mom bursts, her face red and swollen, but she's trying to hide it. "I'm sorry if we woke you!" She hurries to me and hugs me so tight I can barely breathe. I haven't seen her look like this in a long time, and my guard goes up immediately.

My eyes find Jim. "What's happening?" I demand, wide awake and anxious.

For the first time since I've known him, Jim looks like an old, broken man. His hair looks more white than gray, as does his skin, and the tears he must have already shed are no match for what he starts to release when he says, "There's been an accident…"

I shrink into myself a little as I watch Jim crumple, and I grab my mother's arms gently, looking to her for some sort of answer.

"Mom, please…" I can only think of my brother. My pulse builds in speed and force.

"It's, um, Mark and Camille, sweetie," she says finally, dabbing at her eyes with the sleeve of her shirt. It takes me a moment to place faces with the names, but when I do, I'm floored.

"Cherie's parents? What happened?" I repeat.

"They—there was ice on the road, and, I don't know. They say the car skidded, and slipped, and it went over the guard rail." She has that look on her face, the look that says she blames herself. *For what?* I wonder. *She feels guilty for having Christmas Eve dinner on Christmas Eve? It's not her fault it snowed!*

"Are they okay?" I ask hesitantly, although I know by everyone's reaction that this is a stupid question.

A police officer steps forward. "Son, I'm sorry to say your aunt and uncle were killed in the crash. I'm very sorry for your loss." I'm stunned into silence and stare at the cop, slack-jawed. *Killed.* He definitely said killed. Those two people that were here tonight, singing songs and laughing, they're gone. Dead.

No, *killed.*

The cop pats me on the shoulder, and I know I don't deserve the sympathy. *Aunt and uncle?* I met them once, at the wedding, for about six minutes.

I didn't even speak to them tonight, didn't even know their daughter was a famous actress, and Cherie was such a tornado of mean that I made a special effort not to spend more time with them than I'd had to. Now I'll never have a chance to see them again. No one will, not even their daughter.

Suddenly, that thought arrests my mind. "Where's Cherie?"

Mom coos at me, "She's in the other room, honey. The officers brought her here; she's too young to stay alone. Maybe you can talk to her? I'm sure she's very upset and might want some company."

I nod stiffly and follow my mom as she points toward the living room. I don't see Cherie at first, as if she blends with the expensive furniture that no one is supposed to sit on. Not only is she perched on one of my mom's fine satin sofas, but she's holding a glass of water. Food and beverages are supposed to be another no-no in this room. Clearly, tragedy knows no rules.

"Um, hi Cherie," I call softly.

She looks up at me, stone-faced, her green eyes slicing through me. Her features are so small and delicate, like a China doll. Her cheeks are ashen and her eyes are a little glassy, as if there is a giant waterfall of tears on the brink of gushing through them. Despite all of this, she still manages to look glittery like Hollywood with her trendy clothes and her sparkly makeup. She's dressed markedly different from the Cherie I saw at dinner, not as prim and proper but more... risqué. Had she been out somewhere when this happened?

"Hey." She mouths the word more than she says it.

"I'm..." *I'm really stupid,* I think as I struggle to find the right words to say. "I heard what happened. I'm really sorry."

And just like that, her face crinkles, her dam breaks, and she's in tears. Full-on, face-in-hands, body-quaking, sobbing. I stumble over myself and my words.

"Oh, uh, okay—I—I'm sorry," I sputter and make my way to her side. *What did I say? She was fine a moment ago!* I look around; I don't have a tissue or a napkin or anything I can give her.

She doesn't need it. She swivels and buries her face into my chest. At first, I'm frozen and incapable of thought. Cherie Belle is practically in my lap, hysterical and latching onto me like I matter. My stomach twists. What do I do? Am I allowed to touch her? My inner-gentleman, the one who's used to handling crisis situations, is oddly slow to respond. I make a careful hoop around her small body with one arm.

"How?" she whimpers. "How could this happen?"

You must mean: how could this happen in a world as perfect as yours? I'm shocked at my own rude thought. I shake it from my head.

"One minute, I'm talking to this guy, and the next I'm being escorted in a police car back here!"

I should be ashamed of the twinge of jealousy I feel as my mind runs away with another mean reaction. *What guy? Where is he now? Why am I stuck picking up the pieces of this night and not him? Where's that girl she brought to dinner with her—isn't this her job?*

I look around. "Where's, um…"

"I can't even find Danika," she murmurs into my shoulder. My shirt is now wet with her tears, but I don't care. They're celebrity tears, which are probably like Holy Water or something. "I've texted and called—stupid idiot! What am I paying her for if she can't even be with me at a time like this?"

My thoughts exactly. "Oh, so she is your assistant," I conclude.

"How can I go on without them?" Cherie cries into me. "Oh, Daddy!"

I hesitate, digging into my mental rolodex of things people used to say to my mom when she'd cry like this in our mandatory post-Dad family therapy sessions. "You'll find the strength." The reasoning fits, so I go with it. "You're a strong, brave person, and you have a lot going for you. A lot of people love you. You'll be okay."

"No! No, I won't!" she hiccups, pulling away from me to reclaim her breath. "Oh, God… why? Why did this happen?"

I shake my head, spilling more memorized lines. "No one knows why God lets these things happen, but we can't let them break us. We just have to keep going."

She quiets.

I'm good at this, I think proudly. *All those months of therapy were good for something.*

Wrong. All wrong. She looks at me like I have four heads. "How could you act like this is no big deal?"

I'm a sputtering, fuel-less engine again. "I—I didn't mean—it's just—"

She's angry with me. If she could grow spikes and a tail, she would. "I just lost not one but *both* of my parents, and you tell me to move on?!" Holy God is she mad.

"I'm sorry; I didn't know what to say. I've never..." I stop and think. I've never had someone close to me die except my grandparents, and that was years ago. Well, then Dad left, so maybe that's kind of like losing someone.

I turn that thought off like a light switch. "I've never lost someone before," I tell her. "Maybe I should get Chloe or Claudia... their mom died, you know."

She's looking at me funny again, and I realize she probably already knew that. Her eyes narrow into slits. "You just made all that up?"

I shrug sheepishly. "Kind of. I'm sorry."

She sniffs and drags her sleeve beneath her nose. "You'd make a pretty good actor." She looks longingly at the window.

Thank you, a different topic, no more crying! I nod slowly. "Yeah, but I've got a perfect face for radio."

She turns, and a ghost of a smile plays on her lips at my joke. My insides are pretzeling as I ponder how to keep her on this path and not the crying one. I'm great with jokes, not good with crying.

"Don't be silly; you are definitely pretty enough."

Pretty? "Pretty?" I ask, almost offended, although I'm not really sure if I should be offended. I would prefer "hot," "handsome," or "heartthrob." Pretty is a word reserved for girls. But Cherie Belle just called me pretty, so that's probably a good thing.

"Yeah, like little boy pretty. Trust me, they like that at my studio; I could set you up with an audition." Her chest falls suddenly and she slumps. "Oh my God, I can't go back to work like this! This is going to be all over the news—I'm going to have to give all sorts of interviews..."

I watch her collapse into the couch, silent tears running down her cheeks again. People think of the weirdest things when they're devastated.

"Do you have to go back to work?" I ask meekly. "Maybe you could just take a break and stay home."

She looks at me. "Stay home with *who*, Jack?"

She remembered my name. Even says it like we've been friends for years. I'm a little shocked, but I don't let on to her. I try to think about her question instead. There is the glaringly gray area of who her guardians are now.

"Your grandparents?"

Cherie rolls her eyes and takes a sip of water. "I can't live with them; they're in an assisted living community."

"Well, if your mom and dad had a will, then..."

Waterworks again, and this time I can only blame myself. The conversation of wills, legalities, her life being in the hands of others; these were all things she had not yet thought of and normal kids shouldn't know about. My dad's exit from our family opened a whole world of things to me that only adults have to know. Cherie's not there, yet. She's not there yet, but she will be soon because her parents are dead.

At sixteen. On Christmas Eve—even if she is Jewish.

I hear wailing upstairs. *Britney*! I curse to myself and jump to my feet.

"What's that?" Cherie practically spits.

My mother calls out, "Jack? Jack, is that your sister?"

I look from Cherie to the stairs and start to inch my way toward them. "I, um, I have to get my little sister. I'm not there, and if she wakes up and I'm not there—you see, she sleeps with me, at night. Like, not in a weird way but, like, she climbs into bed with me—" It is sounding worse the more I babble.

"Go. Just… go," Cherie insists, closing her eyes as if the sound of Britney's crying is nails on a chalkboard to her ears.

I race up the steps and burst through the door, probably scaring Britney even more. Her face is warped with anguish, but she still holds her arms out for me to pick her up.

"I'm sorry, Brat," I mumble into her hair, holding her close. "I'm here." She still cries for a little in my arms, but the screaming has stopped.

Now the whole house is awake. I hear Brenton race down the stairs, shouting, "Santa!" Claudia and Chloe are brushing their teeth in the bathroom next door.

Oh, no, I think. *Now they'll start crying, too.*

I close my eyes. Part of me wants to return to Cherie and sit with her. I don't know if the terrible twins will be nice, or if Brenton will pester her about her show.

I look down at Britney, who twists a lock of her hair between her fingers and stares vacantly, listening to the sounds of the house. She's my obligation right now. Cherie has plenty of people to worry about her tonight.

Maybe Danika will finally see her text messages and come running, I think, slinking to my door and closing it softly. Then I carry my little sister back to bed and lay down with her tucked inside of my arm. She nuzzles me and sucks her thumb, a habit Mom's trying to break. I let her be for tonight. I've officially had my fill of teary-eyed females for one evening.

DIRTERAZZI.COM
TRAGEDY STRIKES CHERIE BELLE: BOTH PARENTS KILLED IN CHRISTMAS CRASH

It was a blue Christmas indeed for sixteen-year-old Cherie Belle as she lost not one but both *parents in a terrible car accident this morning. Mark and Camille Goldman were braving some unexpected New York snow on their way back to the hotel from a relative's home in the suburbs when the driver, Fernando Suez, lost control. After hitting an oncoming car head on, the limo spun and crashed into the highway's guard rails with such force that the vehicle flipped over the sides and made an almost 18-foot drop to the ground below. All three passengers, Mark, Camille, and the driver, were instantly killed.*

Fortunately, Cherie Belle was not in the car at the time, and she is currently staying with an uncle in Westchester County, New York. Unfortunately, she wakes up today an orphan, and the only list she will be on this Christmas is CPS—Child Protective Services.

Dan Friedman, VP of Kidz Channel, gave this statement this morning when he heard the news: "The Kidz Channel community is deeply saddened and shocked by this awful tragedy, and we are keeping Cherie and the Goldmans in our thoughts and prayers." Dirterazzi also extends its deepest sympathies to Cherie and her family during this time. Reps for Cherie have yet to return any of our calls, but we will keep you updated as we learn more.

Chapter 6

With Christmas abandoned and nothing worth getting up for, I stay in bed even after Britney leaves me. I stare at my cellphone as it charges on my nightstand, secretly hoping one of my friends will call and give me a reason to leave the house. They're all busy with family stuff, though. I know I could be busy too, but not with the open-presents-and-have-breakfast kind of family stuff. I do my duty and shovel the driveway and the walk, but I watch movies and sports highlights on my laptop and altogether campout in my room afterward.

My mom finally demands my presence for dinner at six o'clock. Cherie doesn't join us for the meal, opting to instead stay hidden in the basement/makeshift guest room of our house. While the adults sniffle and force smiles at the table, the kids use manners to pass the plates of food around. It feels like I'm caught in a strange dimension where the twins care and our parents aren't forcing conversation. We don't open our presents, which are still sitting under the Christmas tree/Hanukkah bush, sad and lonely. We all help to clear the table, and Claudia loads the dishwasher. Chloe carefully puts the leftover food into plastic containers. Brenton brings plates of food down to Cherie and Danika, ever the grateful servant.

My mom almost cries just from how nice and civil we are to one another. The twins hug her. Britney hugs Jim when he starts to cry. I take out the garbage, lower my head, and retreat back to my room.

Mom comes by with a soft knock on my door later. "Can I come in?"

I get up from bed and unlock it, swinging the door open. I don't make eye contact but go right back to my bed. I pause my fifth movie of the day and avoid her gaze, waiting for her to speak. I don't want to see her eyes rimmed with red, her nose pink and swollen. It bothers me to see my mom sad; it brings me back to a time I don't want to remember.

"How are you doing?" she asks, sitting on the foot of my bed.

I check my empty email inbox for the twelfth time. "I'm fine. How's everyone else?"

She shrugs and sighs. "As good as can be expected, I guess." She tugs on the leg of my sweatpants then sighs when I won't look up at her. "Hey."

"What?" I don't mean to groan it, but I do.

"I know why you keep hiding in here, Jack, but it's not going to make it go away," she says.

"I'm not hiding," I reply. "I just don't feel like being around a bunch of people crying all day."

"Jack, don't be insensitive," she chastises. "I didn't raise you to be that way." That's the dreaded Mom argument that she always uses on me—as if I'm making her fail some test by not being perfect. I roll my eyes.

"I'm not being insensitive. I just don't have anything to say."

"You don't have to say anything, Jack, you just have to be there for them. We have a lot of people here who are very deeply hurt by this tragedy. I know you can shut everything out, but—"

"Mom, I'm not shutting it out, I don't feel like being out there right now. I don't even know any of these people!"

Mom purses her lips at me because she knows the truth. She knows I've seen enough crying and hurt to try to avoid it at every turn. She cocks her head and murmurs, "Treat them like family, Jack. That's who they are. It's not Brenton and Britney who need you to step up this time."

I'm annoyed with her for bringing *that* up. We don't talk about *that*.

I'll do anything to stop this conversation from going forward. I close my laptop and cast an icy glare at her. "Fine. Where's Cherie?"

She waves a hand toward my window. "She's with her publicist and her manager, I think. They're helping her prepare statements for the press."

Mom pauses before adding, "But Jim's sitting downstairs by himself. Why don't you ask him to watch a game with you?"

Because he doesn't watch sports, he watches the History Channel, I mutter in my head. But I can offer, especially if he is alone, and especially if Cherie is already occupied. I nod and grunt as I roll off the bed.

DIRTERAZZI.COM

WHAT WILL HAPPEN TO LITTLE ORPHAN CHERIE?

While Kidz Channel star Cherie Belle, 16, prepares to bury her parents after a terrible car accident claimed both their lives early yesterday morning, her handlers are scrambling to find out just what lies ahead for the teen queen. Sources very close to the family tell us that Cherie's parents had a will and designated her uncle, James Goldman, as their executor and Cherie's guardian years ago. Goldman, however, has twin teenage daughters (super-hot 15-year-old daughters, apparently) and recently remarried to Eva Hansen, a woman with three children of her own. All of them reside in Pleasantville, New York, a suburban area of the state in which Cherie is none too keen on settling. Though Mark and Camille had a trust prearranged for Cherie, adding another child to James Goldman's house may be too much. Carl Shwartz, Cherie's longtime manager, is pushing for Cherie's grandparents to step in as her temporary guardians and move to California with her so that she can continue her career. With movie deals, a new album, and ad campaigns on the horizon, Cherie's entire brand hangs in the balance until a decision is made. Things would be so much less complicated if Cherie were 18 years old!

Somewhere in LA, Caz Farrell is thinking, "Now you know how I feel…"

Chapter 7

Just as Cherie had imagined, the word of this catastrophe is all over the news, and Mom tells us to leave the TV off so our houseguest doesn't have to listen to any of it. I genuinely feel bad for Cherie. She is bratty and self-centered and all, but she doesn't deserve this kind of attention at a time when she just wants to disappear. I know exactly how she feels.

The Jewish religion insists on quick burials, so it's 48 hours before we find ourselves standing in the cemetery, dressed in suits and dresses. Everyone is ankle-deep in fresh New York snow, watching the two caskets descend into plots that Jim's parents had purchased for themselves many years ago. Today, they're using those plots to bury a child and his wife who hadn't bought their own plots because they hadn't planned to die the way old people do. The thought makes my insides curl.

Cherie had been right about the paparazzi, too, who are suddenly everywhere, snapping photos, following our cars and the hearse. Her limo leaves the funeral home first, and ours follows.

"Don't say anything to the reporters," Mom warns all of us as we pile into the limo. "Let Cherie's publicist handle the questions."

You would think people would be respectful and give a family space at a time like this. I've never seen such chaos over one person before. It doesn't help that some of her celebrity friends show up, too. Danika made sure to call her agent, her manager, and her every last co-star. It's like Hollywood threw up in my neighborhood. Naturally, I don't have a chance to feel star struck. Instead of meeting starlets and rubbing elbows with guys

I've seen on TV, I'm officially in charge of rounding up the youngsters and making sure we are all ready in time and no one is bleeding or dirty.

The service is sad and crowded with a motley crew of Hollywood C-listers and average suburban New Yorkers. Cherie, donned in black from head to toe, has the aura of a tragic victim more so than any regular girl. With big, face-swallowing sunglasses, a large black hat and a black fur wrap, she looks like the wealthy widow from a cheesy movie. She stands stoically beside the caskets, dabbing occasionally beneath her sunglasses with a small handkerchief. Her grandparents clutch tightly to her and can barely stand as the rabbi reads the burial prayers. But Cherie doesn't waver; she doesn't even flinch when she is given the shovel to throw dirt onto each of the caskets. Like a dainty china doll, she deposits a tiny smattering of earth upon each casket. Then she stands off to the side as the rest of us do the same. Mom is behind her every step of the way, waiting to be needed, but she is more of a mess than Cherie has ever been in the last few days.

Megastar Caz Farrell is here, much to my dismay. The women all ogle and obsess over him as he does his part and tosses dirt onto the caskets. Aunt Darla makes it a point to introduce herself, and he is generous enough to give her an autograph discreetly. He makes his way to Cherie as the relatives and friends begin to disperse. Cherie greets him with a warm smile and sparkly eyes and a kiss on the cheek; I am close enough to smell the confidence on him, and it is nauseating. I can't see what the big deal is, but I do notice that he is definitely *my* definition of a pretty boy.

"Thanks for coming, Caz," she says softly.

He smiles the perfect, white smile of a modest hero. "Of course. I'm so sorry, Cherie. I'm praying for you. If you need anything, please don't hesitate to call me."

He's good, I think bitterly. I hadn't thought to say anything like that.

Well, whatever. Isn't he 25 years old or something— and an actor? He's supposed to know what to say and what look to give.

She eats it up and grins a little brighter. "That means a lot. Thank you."

"Will you still be joining me for the New Year's special?" he asks.

She nods emphatically. "Yes. I should be fine by then. Just have to get some things straightened out."

He grins again. "Well, I look forward to seeing you then. If you're back in the Hills this week, text me; we'll get lunch." I resist shaking my head, thinking over and over how a 20-something-year-old taking a 16-year-old to lunch has to be against the law somehow. He nods briefly at me and smiles, but I can only glare at him when I tip my head in response.

With that, Caz is off, headed for his own limo, accompanied by glamorous and extravagantly dressed celebrifriends and assistafriends, and they're all swarmed by photographers as they reach the cars. When I look back at Cherie, she is listening half-heartedly to the rabbi. He tries to give her words of encouragement before she departs. She's all polite smiles and head nods.

Jim lays a hand on my shoulder and murmurs, "Can you keep an eye on Cherie while I get everyone to the limo?"

I nod and stay by her side, hands shoved deep into my pockets, watching as Jim shields his parents from the same photographers. He helps his old, shattered mother into the limo with a gentleness I've never seen him use, even with Mom. Then he returns to help my mother through the snow, holding out his arm for her like a gentleman from the 1800s. The twins and Leroy follow, and Aunt Darla carries Britney and holds Brenton's hand. It feels like a scene straight out of a drama Caz would probably star in.

A stout older man and an Aunt Darla-type woman approach us. "Hiya, sweetheart." The man hugs Cherie, then holds out his hand to me, and I shake it, staring at his bulbous nose.

"Carl Schwartz. I'm Cherie's manager. This is Betsy Calves, her publicist. And you are?"

"Jack Hansen," I reply, hoping my handshake is firm enough for Hollywood bigwigs. I don't add a title; I don't think I have a title. Cherie's step-cousin? That just sounds weird.

Her manager looks me over before turning his beady eyes back to Cherie. "Coming, sweetheart?" he asks, and he points a fat thumb toward their Rolls Royce limo.

She smiles and shakes her head. "It's okay. Maybe you can take Danika with you?" She turns to Danika on her left side, who looks disappointed to be dismissed. "I'm going to ride with my uncle and grandparents this time, and their limo's pretty crowded."

I'm surprised by this revelation, and I'm almost tempted to ask, "*Why*?" It seems so unnatural that she'd want to continue to mix with us commoners.

Betsy, a pretty, middle-aged woman, gives her a big hug. "Okay, baby. We'll be in touch with you soon, okay? Don't worry about the press; I'll take care of it. Just keep your phone off. Don't even look at Dirterazzi.com—just keep clear of the Internet completely. I'll update your blog in a few hours with a thank you to the fans or something."

Cherie nods gratefully. "Thanks, Betsy." She looks up at me. "We should probably be going, right Jack?" I nod quickly, realizing she needs me to get her out of the conversation.

"Yeah, they're waiting," I say stiffly.

As we turn to leave the cemetery, I take a cue from Jim and give my arm to Cherie, helping her brave the ocean of snow that covers the cemetery grounds.

"Thanks," she whispers tightly, resting one hand in the crook of my arm and the other on the top of her drifting hat. She plods along in giant heeled boots that bring her head to just above my shoulder, and I wonder inwardly if she couldn't have chosen a more unfortunate shoe for this event. She tries very hard not to stumble or struggle as we walk, and I immediately realize why when I hear the distant sound of cameras snapping away. I look up to see photographers intently capturing her every step through the cemetery, cursing at each other to get out of a shot.

They'd love nothing more than for her to fall right now, wouldn't they? They'd love a shot of this overdressed little girl, this Hollywood princess with the not-so-fairytale life, falling in public. I scowl at them and make sure Cherie, in her high heels, with her fancy black dress and big hat and big fur wrap, makes a graceful exit into the waiting limo. I scowl at the photographers again before sliding into the empty seat next to her.

As the car pulls away and we are encased in silence, Cherie makes a sound like she is releasing the longest breath ever held by a person. Her head drops and her sunglasses slide down her nose, revealing eyes tightly scrunched in agony. Her mouth twists into a silent scream, and she doubles over onto herself. She's disintegrating, the prim and proper façade gone, and now I realize why she wanted to be with us. No one else gets to see what's behind the elaborate outfit, the passive line her lips make. No one else gets to see the stuff that happens once the door of the lavish limousine hides all of us from their prying eyes.

I've only seen one other person this hurt before, and I shudder from the memory of my mother lying on our kitchen floor, my father's farewell note clutched in her hand.

Looking out at the sea of red, worn faces in our limo, each set of eyes welling with fresh new tears at the sight of Cherie's breakdown, I realize I'm the last person who should be sitting beside her. While the picture moves everyone else to sobs, I feel like I've been punched in the gut, and I don't know what to do.

"Oh, sweetheart," Mom murmurs. She moves from her seat and trades places with me, throwing her arms around Cherie's shoulders and crying with her. She is finally needed.

Britney crawls into my lap, which is the distraction I need.

DIRTERAZZI.COM

WHO IS CHERIE'S MYSTERY MAN?

At the snowy funeral for Cherie Belle's parents today, tears and celebrities were to be as expected as the cold New York temperatures. What was not expected, however, was the heat between the mourning Belle and a mystery friend who stood stoically at her side. Onlookers noticed a tall, handsome youth doting on Cherie and assisting her in and out of the cemetery throughout the day. Those in attendance at the funeral identified the young man as Jack Hansen, James Goldman's stepson, and the oldest child in Goldman's Brady Bunch-ish family.

We don't know what role Jack is playing in Cherie's life right now, but we hope it's a reoccurring one. He just might give some competition to Cherie's rumored beau, Caz Farrell, who also happened to be in attendance, though only briefly. Jack is around Cherie's age, which is already an improvement from Caz, and he has that young, brooding James Dean look that makes the ladies here in our office say "Mmmhmm." (Their words, we swear. We were more interested in Hansen's smokin' hot stepsisters (click here for pics!)). One thing is certain: if Cherie does end up imprisoned in suburban New York until her 18th birthday, at least she's in good-looking company.

Chapter 8

Jewish people do something called Shiva when a person dies. They gather at a house to visit with the family members of the deceased and drink coffee. At one point in the night there are some prayers said and some songs sung. It's a lot like a wake, except it goes on for days and the overpowering smell of flowers is replaced by an overwhelming cloud of freshly-brewed coffee. Fortunately, there's a lot of food. There's a lot of talking, too. During the very first hour, I overhear family members debating Cherie's future, both as an actress and as a person.

"Terrible, just terrible—a girl that young?" their great-aunt Elyse whispers to a distant cousin over the top of her lipstick-stained Styrofoam cup. "Eh, no good. I imagine she'll wind up on the path of some addict and get arrested, or worse." She nods her head and gives a raised-eyebrow, *"that's-a-fact"* look. I load a small plate with cookies and pretend I can't hear her, but the comment sits inside of my gut and ferments, making me anxious. I try to imagine Cherie doing anything that would mess up her hair, let alone her reputation, and it's laughable to me.

But still, I wonder, *Could that really happen? Or are those ladies just being old and catty?*

My phone buzzes with a new text message in my pocket. I check it quickly, and it's my friend, Josh.

I open the message, grateful for the distraction. Maybe he's throwing a party I can escape to. Then, my stomach drops. "Did I just c u on TV?"

TV? I'm on TV? I want to turn one on, but then I stop. Cherie's sitting right next to the one in the living room. Mom's rule echoes loudly in my head. I rush upstairs to my laptop, closing the door to my room soundlessly. When I do a quick online search of Cherie Belle, the first few links are to news reports about the funeral. Sure enough, Channel 5 has posted video coverage of all of us standing in the cemetery. I see myself, which is weird, because I'm watching myself react in a moment that I still remember clearly. I note with a small amount of pride that I'm taller than Caz Farrell, and I'm a little bigger, too.

A knock on my door yanks me from my daze. "One second!"

"Your mom is looking for you," Claudia calls from the other side.

My pulse pounds. "Tell her I'll be right there." I close my laptop before my mom can catch me completely breaking one of her only rules about this whole mess and head back downstairs.

I take out my phone and am about to reply "Yes" to Josh, but I stop, my thumb hovering over the send button. I look up and see Cherie, who sits stoically beside an old woman and nods with a somber frown as the lady rattles on about what great people her parents were.

Looking back at my phone, guilt gnaws at me. I promised my mom I wouldn't talk about this with anyone, and I don't want to tell anyone what is happening anyway. I don't want the questions that will follow, and I don't want the phone calls harassing me for information. Even more, I don't want to be just another person putting her private life on display.

Instead of hitting send, I hold the power button down until the phone turns off.

I dodge Cherie for the rest of the night, which is hard to do now that she's staying in our basement for the week. I know I'm supposed to be supportive and helpful, so I work overtime to do little chores around the house and keep Britney and Brenton occupied, which keeps me from crossing Cherie's path too often.

As one day passes into the next, however, she begins to surface more. I run into her the next evening after Shiva when I go scrounging for leftovers. She's in the kitchen, sitting in silence with Danika at our dining table.

I feel compelled to ask, "How are you? Do you need anything?"

Danika gives me the stink eye, as if to say, *"Back off, kissing up to her is* my *job."* I try to pretend she's not the world's biggest bitch.

Cherie whispers, "No, thank you, Jack," and a sad smile follows. I like when she says my name, and I'd give anything to take the hurt out of her voice when she says it.

On Wednesday morning, Mom comes in my room and closes the door like she's about to tell me a secret.

"Jack, honey?"

I don't open my eyes, but I turn over when she sits down and shakes me gently.

"What, Mom?" I look at the clock. 8:00 a.m. This clock had better be three hours slow.

"Honey, wake up a second; I need a favor from you," she says. Whenever she starts off like that, I know it's not just a favor. When Mom wants something simple, she just tells me to do it. *"I need a favor from you"* is code for a whole day of babysitting or a list of chores.

I still refuse to open my eyes. "What?"

"We have to take Danika to the airport and meet Jim's parents at the lawyer's office."

I groan. I already know where this is going.

Mom rattles on. "Chloe and Claudia are going to the mall with some friends, and I'm sending Brenton to Raine

Johnson's house for a sleepover. I don't want him to have to sit through another Shiva—"

"Mom, what's the favor?" I just want her to stop talking; she's giving me a headache.

She hesitates. "Well, I need you to keep an eye on Britney, and I was hoping you'd help me with Cherie."

I lift my head. "Cherie?"

Mom leans in to confide, "She's not eating. I'm a little worried. Danika said something about her being a vegan, so I don't know. Maybe we don't have anything here for her to eat. Would you take her to the store for some groceries?" She sees my eyes roll back into my head, and she hurries to say, "I'll leave some cash for you to get a few things you like, too."

I'm about to protest, but then I think better of it. I weigh the con of being alone with a teary-eyed Cherie with the pro of a chance to eat frozen foods and not get a lecture about preservatives. Mom's good. She knows my weak spots.

Maybe Cherie won't be so bad. We'll be out in public. She'll be too proud to cry or anything. She might be nasty to someone, but that's okay, as long as it's not me. I can deal a little better with Mean Cherie than Sad Cherie.

"Okay," I concede. She tousles my hair, and I jerk my head away. She laughs and bends to give me a kiss. Her strong, going-to-something-important perfume envelopes me.

"Thank you, sweetie. I knew I could count on you," she whispers. "I told her you'd be ready in an hour, so try to get up soon, okay?"

"What?!"

But she's out of the room and the door is closing behind her, and I have no choice other than to get out of bed.

I should have known that gathering Britney and setting up her car seat would be easier than rounding up Miss Belle, who is thirty minutes late for our supermarket appointment. I use the first ten minutes to really clean up the inside of my car, kind of spruce it up a little extra for the occasion. Then I have to play a spelling game with Britney for the next twenty minutes to avoid honking the horn.

"Spell... snow."

"S. N. O."

"W. Snow has a w at the end. It's a tricky word." I sigh and throw my head back against the headrest. "Spell tree."

Give Cherie time. Don't be a jerk, I remind myself. I try to remember that she's not one of the twins, and that she has the potential at any time to run into people wanting to take her picture. She wants to look good. Hell, even I made sure to put jeans on instead of my sweatpants today.

When she finally does emerge from the house, I can sort of see why my mom's worried. Her cheekbones are a little more prominent, her skin is paler, and the bones of her hands and wrists stick out. The rest of her is covered by heavy, layered sweaters, a scarf, and big sunglasses. Her legs look like the heels she's wearing: long and impossibly skinny. She sways a little when stepping down off of the porch, and she has to grab the banister for support, as if walking makes her dizzy. This girl definitely needs to eat.

I get out and shuffle to the passenger side to open her door for her, a gentleman's move that always earned me bonus points with girls in the past. Cherie, so used to being chauffeured, merely murmurs a thank you and slides into the front seat as if my chivalry is no big deal.

"Cherie!" Britney cries out. I think she loves her as much as Brenton does, but for different reasons. Cherie is a princess in Britney's mind; one with pretty makeup and fancy clothes that she might let Britney play dress-up in.

And she's a star on TV. That never hurts.

"Hey sweetie pie," Cherie coos, turning in her seat. "What a pretty braid! Who did your hair?"

"Chloe." Britney grins and bats her eyelashes. I try not to groan audibly.

Cherie turns and puts her seat belt on, saying, "Your sister has the most gorgeous eyes. Who has blue eyes in your family?"

I stiffen and busy myself with pulling out of the driveway. I hate having to talk about my father. "Our dad."

She nods. "Oh, yeah. I keep forgetting about him. Where does he live?"

I almost have to clear my throat to answer. "I don't know."

From the corner of my eye, I can see her nose scrunch as if she doesn't understand this. I can tell she is going to ask more questions, so I change gears instead.

"Got a list of food you want to buy?"

She waves her hand dismissively. "Oh, no, I didn't make a list. I really don't want anything; this is very nice of Eva and all, but I just don't have the stomach to eat anything right now."

"You'll have to eat eventually," I say, and I hate myself immediately for it when her face falls. I may as well have said, *"You'll have to get over their deaths eventually."* We silently agree to drop each other's uncomfortable conversations.

"This car is nice," she says, but she says it in a way that should have the phrase, "for a high school kid," attached to the end.

Still, the compliment makes me beam on the inside. There's nothing I'm more proud of than my car, not even my football trophies. I spent a lot of time lifeguarding last summer to earn this car, and it means a lot that she would pay it a compliment.

"Thanks. Do you have a car back in California?"

She nods. "I have a couple, but they're in my parents' names. Probably have to give them back now. Whatever; it doesn't matter anyway. I haven't gotten a license yet. Haven't had the time to take the test."

This is abhorrent to me. How does someone not have the time to take the most important test of their life? "So why do you have cars?"

She shrugs, and the answer is implied, hanging heavily in the air over my head. *She's rich and famous, dummy! She probably owns monkeys that she doesn't need, too.*

"Here it is," I announce, pulling into the parking lot of our local shopping plaza. I look in my rearview mirror at a car that is *thisclose* to hitting my bumper. "What the hell? Why is this guy on my—"

Cherie takes one glance back and mutters, "Dirterazzi," as if she's bored by the word. "I guess they finally found your house. I thought I saw them following you when we pulled out of your road."

"Jesus," I murmur, turning around to see not one, but two beat-up sedans pulling into spaces near me.

"It'll be fine," she sighs as I put the car in park. "You take care of Britney while I give them a quick statement."

I marvel at her boldness as she throws open the car door and steps out elegantly. The photographers are out of their cars faster than spitballs from a straw, and they have no hesitation in approaching. I do what I can to pretend they're not five feet away, snapping with their cameras, while I reach into the backseat and unbuckle Britney.

In the background, I hear Cherie spinning the same comments Betsy and her other handlers have prepared and rehearsed with her. "...deeply saddened by... respect my privacy at this time... so fortunate for the support of..."

Britney is quiet as she watches this spectacle and twists a blond curl around her finger while she waits beside me. I hold her hand a little tighter, but it may be for my own comfort rather than hers. My stomach is doing little flips and flops just in anticipation of those cameras turning on me.

Cherie walks over to us, her camera-ready smile fading, and Britney reaches out to her with her free hand. Cherie extends her own out and sways from the suddenness of her own movements. Her heel catches in a crack in the ground, and she cries out. Her body begins to fly backward as she tries to right herself.

Immediately, my football reflexes snap to attention. Before she falls over, I catch her in midair against my forearm and grab her wrist, like I've dipped her after a dance. Britney bursts into a fit of giggles.

"Oh, God!" Cherie grasps at the sleeves of my jacket for dear life. Her wide, surprised eyes trap mine and hold them hostage.

I stare at her, entranced. "Are you okay?" I whisper.

She's breathless. "I think so." I am frozen in the moment, so close to her I can see the flecks of gold shimmer in her lip gloss. I suddenly can't look anywhere but her mouth. My mind is racing faster than my pulse. I hear the click of a camera, and it jerks me out of my stupor.

"Smooth, Jack! Great shot."

"Good catch, man! Hey, Cherie, you should keep him around!"

"Yeah, you two look good together."

Suddenly, the cameramen are on top of us, snapping frantically, and Cherie is scurrying to find her footing. I tuck Britney out of the camera's view and cast them a dirty look. My cheeks burn.

I want to tell them to get lost, but my tongue is numb. All I can do is tilt my head toward the supermarket. Cherie follows obediently, one hand still gripping the sleeve of my jacket while we walk. Britney leaves my side like I'm yesterday's news and takes her new idol's free hand.

I send the girls inside and grab a shopping cart, stealing a glance over my shoulder as the photographers compare their stills of us. I can't help but wonder what Cherie and I look like together.

Supermarket shopping without a list is hard, but following someone as slow and distractible as Cherie is nearly impossible. I have a clear goal: frozen pizza and chips, and I find my stuff in less than three minutes. But Cherie parades up and down each aisle, wondering where things are, texting, examining the firmness of fruit, reading nutrition labels. It's torture.

To add salt to the wound, we end up with four items by the time we get on line. I set a box of expensive granola bars, apples, Doritos and pizza on the conveyor belt. When Britney begs for a bag of Skittles, I don't think twice and add two bags of the candy to our sad bounty.

I don't want this to be my fault, so I ask one last time, "Are you sure this is all you want? Is there any other fruit you want to buy? You looked at a lot of fruit."

"I'm good," Cherie says quietly. She seems distracted again, but this time she's staring past the cashier to the massive windows. The cashier gives her a double-take, and then she looks around to see if any of her co-workers realize they are in the presence of greatness. Cherie doesn't notice the woman's sudden interest in her and stares forward, her eyes glazed.

Cherie had faded in and out the entire time we shopped, so I don't pay attention to her. I don't follow her gaze, and instead I proceed to pay the cashier. Britney asks to carry the grocery bag, and I fiddle with her coat to make sure it's zipped. We're immersed in our own worlds, our normal routines. I wish that for just a second I had noticed the growing media storm outside.

Because when we emerge from the supermarket, we are swarmed by humans with cameras for heads. There are all types—fans holding up cellphones, professional photographers, and news reporters with video cameras and microphones that they immediately thrust in her face.

"Cherie! Cherie, how are you?"

"We love you, Cherie!"

"We're praying for you, Cherie!"

"Stop wearing furs! Do you know how many defenseless animals are killed for your stupid fur coats?"

"Cherie, will you still be hosting the New Year's Ball with Caz?"

My head is spinning. We take a step left, and they step in our path. We swerve right, and there they are again, blocking our path. I look down at Cherie, who keeps her sunglasses down to hide her eyes. I can tell by her stiff, unsmiling mouth that she is unnerved. Her head hangs low, her shoulders curve inward, and she tucks her arms against her body. She is shrinking inside of herself.

But they don't seem to notice. Or care.

"Cherie, are you going back to work on *Choc it Up*?"

"Cherie, is it true you were drinking at a nightclub the evening your parents died?"

"Cherie, is Jack your new boyfriend?"

Britney cries out, "Jackie!" before I have a chance to digest that last question. I look down and see she is engulfed by the photographers.

I've tried to keep my cool up until now, but these people have crossed a line. Frustrated, I command, "Move!" They part immediately. I lean down and hoist my sister up in one arm. I reach out with my free hand and grab Cherie's. Gritting my teeth, I lower my head and plow through the crowd like we're one yard short of a first down, and I have been given the ball. Surprisingly, they get out of my way.

But it doesn't stop the questions.

"Jack—Jack, are you and Cherie dating?"

"Cherie, how does it feel to be an orphan? Can you give us a statement?"

The barking continues to swirl and swim around my head as we walk hastily forward. I do my best to tune them out and protect the girls. They both look like they're about to cry, and I'm not sure who needs more shielding. I quickly deposit Cherie into the front seat.

"Buckle Britney in when I put her in the car seat," I command, and she nods. I swing around to my side and drop Britney, who has started to cry from all of the commotion, into the back. It's the first time I have ever set her down in the car without checking that she was safely buckled, but I trust Cherie to take care of it. I jump inside, start the engine, and throw the stick shift into reverse.

The cameras are everywhere. I honk my horn and gesture for them to move. I can get in trouble if I hit someone, and I would definitely lose my license. Frustrated, I shout, "Get out of the way!" I'm almost ready to hit someone anyway. They seem to sense I've reached my limit of patience and start to back away from my bumpers.

"Thank you! Geez! How the hell did all those people know we were there?" I mutter, more to myself than to Cherie. "Only two guys were outside when we first got there!"

"Those two guys tell two guys, and pretty soon you have a gaggle of them at your door," she replies.

I'm baffled. "Tell me that this is not every day of your life."

She shakes her head. "It wasn't this bad before." That is a little sobering. I can barely believe that this attention is all due to her family tragedy.

Vans and cameras follow us back to the house. I'm lucky to be able to pull into the garage since Jim and Mom are still out. As the door folds down to hide us from their prying eyes, I turn off the engine and stare forward.

Cherie notices my trembling fingers, my wide, *what-the-hell-just-happened?* eyes. "I'm sorry," she whispers. I see her eyes shine with looming tears.

I look over to her and shake my head. "It's not your fault. I've just never seen something like that before." I try to let the adrenaline melt away.

Her eyes gloss over, like tears are making their way out of hiding. I don't want her to be upset. I'll do anything to keep her from crying.

"Let's go inside. Britney wants you to put makeup on her."

"Yay!" Britney squeals from the back, and Cherie shakes her head.

But she's smiling.

DIRTERAZZI.COM

CHERIE BELLE RETIRING FROM ACTING?

Rumors are circulating around pop TV star, Cherie Belle, again! This time, sources close to Cherie say she is considering stepping away from acting and Hollywood for good. It seems the starlet needs more than just a little healing time after the deaths of both her parents in December. "She just wants to be a kid, you know?" says our source, who asked to remain anonymous, about Cherie's top secret plans. "She's been acting for over five years, and now she wants a break so she can focus on herself and her healing."

Carl Schwartz, Cherie's manager, insists this is hogwash and claims his client is merely taking a few weeks off after promoting her movie, This Side of Sunny, *to clear her head. We're pretty sure Carl, who was spotted recently enjoying a lavish dinner with Cherie and other members of her entourage at the swanky Manhattan restaurant, Curve, would have the 411 on Cherie's true plans.*

Chapter 9

"I just don't get it; why does she sleep with him every night?"

I wake up, but I don't open my eyes. I fell asleep on the couch after eating my pizza, and now I can't be sure what's going on around me. I feel Britney curled up on top of my chest, and she doesn't stir. The conversation is behind me, spoken in hushed whispers.

I can definitely make out Claudia's voice. "Oh, I know, it's so weird," she moans.

Someone replies, "I think it's cute actually. But why does she do that? Is she just super-attached to him?"

It's Cherie. My heartbeat stills.

Claudia's quiet for a moment. She lowers her voice even more, but I can make out most of what she's saying. "They're... all messed up. Dad said... their dad left... she went on sleeping pills... couldn't hear Britney crying at night. Jack had to take care of her."

Rage ignites in my chest. I could kill Claudia right now. How dare she tell Cherie that? Even worse, how could Jim tell his daughters all of that? I want to jump up and scream at her, but I stay put, waiting to hear what else the little weasel has to say about my family's secrets.

"So she just neglected them?"

Claudia's quick to say, "No, it's not like that. She was just really, really depressed, and she needed the meds to sleep at night."

"Does she still take them?"

"I don't think so."

"So Jack had to take care of Britney? What about Brenton?"

Claudia snickers. "He made an imaginary friend, remember? They're the total textbook example of dysfunctional products of divorce."

Leave my brother alone. Leave all of us alone.

Cherie says, "I don't know; Jack seems pretty normal to me." Her words come just in time to keep the steam that is building inside of me from whistling out of my ears.

Claudia continues on her mean marathon. "He's not. He's a super narcissist; always hogging the mirror and fixing his hair and stuff. *Loves* his hair."

"He doesn't strike me as that at all. I've met lots of conceited guys before, ones with way less to be conceited about than him."

"Well, trust me, he is the most screwed up of all three. Chloe says he has to keep the outside looking perfect because the inside is so effed up. He would never sit and just talk like we are now. He's always locked up in his room like a hermit, and God help you if you invade his space."

Cherie seems to laugh at this. "That's just 'cause he's closed off."

"Closed off?" I'm glad Claudia's asking because I don't know what that means, either. I strain my ear muscles and try not to breathe to hear what she says.

"He probably has a hard time with trust, and that's why he doesn't open up to anyone," she says. "I'll bet if you try to talk to him about his dad—"

"Oh, no, don't do that," Claudia says quickly. *Good girl*, I think, feeling the steam rising into my ears again.

"What? Why not?"

Claudia's voice goes real low again, and this time it's harder to make out what she's saying. "He does not... his... That's one... things our Dad... promise not to do...

got a serious temper... in school... therapist... he runs..."
There's a long pause.

"Really?" Cherie whispers, sounding shocked.

"Yes," Claudia hisses. "He doesn't talk about it. Like I said, textbook example."

Cherie seems unconvinced. "I don't know; I bet I could get him to open up."

Nope. No way.

Claudia scoffs. "Your funeral." They're quiet for a moment as she realizes her poor choice of words. *What a dummy.* "Sorry, I didn't mean it like that."

Cherie lowers her voice. "It's okay." But she drops the conversation and clams up completely. I lay as still as I can, listening as they sit in deafening silence. There is some pounding on the steps and someone swishes by. Based on the heavy cupcake-smelling perfume that follows, I am positive it's Chloe.

"Hey," she says as she enters the kitchen.

"Hi," Claudia replies. Cherie says nothing.

"What time are people going to start coming over for Shiva?" Chloe asks. I hear the refrigerator door open behind me.

Claudia sighs and continues to be insensitive. "Six. It's always six."

"Right." She pulls out a chair and sits down. "What're you guys up to?"

"Nothing. I was just telling her about..." I don't hear her say my name, but I can only imagine she's pointing in my direction when Chloe groans, "Oh."

Finally, Cherie excuses herself from the table, murmuring, "I'm gonna go lay down," and she retreats downstairs.

Chloe whispers, "What's her problem?"

"Who knows?" Then Claudia snickers, "I think she likes him."

"Ugh, serious?"

Wait—what?!

"Yeah," her twin laughs. "She was saying how he's such a nice guy and all. Idiot."

Chloe dismisses her. "Grief makes you say lots of crazy things, trust me. Plus there's not much else to look at in this town."

I don't have a chance to be offended; their words echo in my mind and almost make me start to believe them. *Cherie likes me? Is that really possible?*

Claudia "Mmm-hmm"s her. "You see the article on Dirterazzi.com?"

Chloe is the one to "Mmm-hmm" this time.

"Do you think it's true?"

Chloe guffaws. "No, but it would be hilarious if it was. That's a train wreck waiting to happen."

What is? I'm irritated they're speaking in code. Even more, they're openly defying my mom's orders of not going on gossip sites.

Claudia snickers then sighs again. "We'd better wake them up and clean the living room before Eva gets home. You know how she gets when people are coming over."

"Yep, nothing can be out of place," Chloe chortles.

"I'll get Britney," Claudia mutters. Suddenly, she pushes her chair backward on the floor noisily and approaches the couch. I can feel her bear down on the top cushions as she leans over the side.

"Britney, wake up," Claudia sings softly, and I feel my sister's weight lift off of my chest. "We have to get you ready, sunshine."

I hear Britney whimper and whine a little, her sounds growing softer and distant as Claudia carries her toward the stairs.

"WAKE UP!" Chloe shouts in my ear. I'm startled but expected it. She squeals with laughter and races toward the staircase after her sister, who cackles maniacally with her.

I open my eyes and stare at the ceiling, my brain so on fire that I'm numb.

***

"Cherie?" Mom calls, poking her head around the living room wall into the kitchen and looking right at me, blessedly interrupting an all-too-long conversation I've been having with Jim's second cousin about choosing the right college.

"Jack, honey, do you think you could find Cherie? Rabbi wants to do the Kaddish." I nod, knowing exactly what she means even though the words she's saying still sound so foreign to me. I shrug and smile half-heartedly at my captor as he relinquishes his hold on me so I can fulfill my duty.

"After Kaddish, I'll tell you about my time at BU," he says with a wink, like I should be impressed. I shake my head and withhold the groan I want to release as I walk away. If one more person tries to talk me out of going south for college, I'm going to hit something.

I search the basement first, since Cherie has been notoriously retreating downstairs this week when she wants to escape others. The basement is empty except for a few shopping bags of new clothes and the remnants of wrappers for some toiletries my mom picked up at Target a few days ago. In the corner sits an open, oversized suitcase with clothes splaying out over its sides haphazardly. By the looks of her suitcase, I'm not sure why she needs all the new clothes, but then again she may not have packed the amount of black dresses and shoes and tights and sweaters and scarves she has been actually wearing this week.

I climb the stairs, taking them two at a time, and search the crowded first floor for her again. It's then that I realize Britney is also gone. I take a chance and head up to the bedrooms, stalking through the hallway straight for Britney's room, which is tidy but empty. My chest tightens a little.

"Brat?" I call out, checking my mom's room, then Brenton's. Heat rises, and my nerve endings spike. What if she went outside? What if those paparazzi vultures got to her?

Suddenly, I hear Britney giggling. The sound comes from my room, and I sigh with relief, throwing open the door with force.

Cherie and Britney are in the midst of a complicated form of patty cake, sitting cross-legged across from each other on my bed like they're in their pajamas at a sleepover and not in fancy black mourning dresses at a Shiva.

"Hey!" Cherie gasps in surprise, clutching at her chest as if her heart stopped.

Befuddled, I stare at them and say, "My mom's looking for you; time for the knish or something."

They exchange glances at each other and explode with laughter. Apparently there is a joke I'm not in on.

"Silly, it's Kaddish, not knish," my little sister corrects me, and Cherie giggles some more. I guess Britney converted to Judaism overnight or something.

I shrug and my cheeks burn a little. "Yeah, whatever, it's time for it."

Cherie purses her lips and slides off of the bed with that look that says she's exhausted being on call all of the time. I guess this must be what it feels like for her to be in movies and on TV, constantly trying to be a kid in between getting called to stand in a certain spot or say some line with the right expression on her face or the perfect emotion in her voice.

Right now the only emotion I see in her is sadness, which is punctuated by my sister's pout.

"Can we play when you're done?" Britney asks. I know she can be a pest, so I try to step in.

"Cherie has to be downstairs with everyone else, Brat," I say softly.

But instead, Cherie shakes her head at me and smiles at Britney. "No, I can come back, if you promise to wait right here for me."

Britney beams, and I do a little, but only on the inside. I won't let on to it, but I like that she'd give this kind of attention to my little sister. Maybe Cherie's not such a spoiled brat.

"Okay, I'll be right back," she says over her shoulder. I follow her out of the room like a shadow. She slows until we are in step, side by side with each other.

"Sorry that I was in your room," she says, looking up at me. "I hope it's okay."

I shake my head. "It's fine." I don't know why, but I didn't care at all. I realize now that I should have; Cherie Belle was in my room. On my bed. Just hanging out. It seemed harmless enough, but what if she wasn't playing with Britney the whole time? What if she looked through my things? What if she went in my nightstand? My cheeks still haven't stopped burning, and now they're getting hotter.

"I saw all of your football trophies," she adds with a small, teasing smile. "What position do you play? Quarterback? Kicker?"

I look over at her in disbelief. "You know football?"

She bites her lower lip and glances down in shame. "No, I don't; just those words. And touchdown."

It's my turn to laugh at her. "Oh. Well, I play tight end, which is an offensive position." She scrunches her nose. "Uh—I come out when we are on offense. That means my team has the ball. I can catch and run with the ball, or I can block people during the play."

"Oh. Well, you must be very good. You have a lot of trophies," she remarks as we descend the stairs.

I hope she isn't looking at me as I shrug again and say, "Nah, they give those out to everybody every year. It's just like good sportsmanship and stuff."

She is looking up at me. "I saw one that said captain on it."

My jaw clenches. "JV. Just for a month or two. But I was on varsity this fall, so maybe I'll be captain next year."

"Why just a month or two?" she asks. I don't know why she's so curious about this. I feel like I'm being interviewed, but I'm not sure for what.

I'm slow to respond, especially as we enter the crowded living room together. But Cherie turns her eyes to me as if I'm the only person in the world and she's totally invested in whatever I'm saying. It puts me under a sort of spell, and I feel obligated to answer.

So I tell her the abridged version. "They made me captain of the JV team last year, mid-season. I didn't start freshman year with all of the other guys, so the coach didn't know what to expect from me."

"I guess he liked what he saw then." I nod dumbly, my eyes transfixed on her pouting, shimmery lips. "Did you just start to play football last year?"

What does any of this have to do with anything? I think to myself. "No, I used to play a lot as a kid. I just wasn't able to play for a little while, so I started late in high school."

Her head cocks to the side. "Why?"

I shrug, and the response is automatic. "I couldn't. I had to take care of Britney and Brenton." *Aha!* As the words leave my tongue, I finally realize why she's pressing me so much about my football history. Her conversation with Claudia comes burrowing through my thoughts and breaks me from the trance. As if I really could believe that this girl had any sincere interest in my football woes!

I gesture to the rabbi, who is still chewing my mother's ear off. "I think they need you now."

A hint of a smirk plays on her lips, as if she senses she has been caught red-handed but still feels victorious in her mission. She nods at me and floats over to my mother's side. I turn and march back up the stairs to tell Britney she's going to take this patty cake game down to the basement from now on.

DIRTERAZZI.COM

AND CHERIE'S GUARDIANS ARE...

James and Eva Goldman, you've just won an all-expenses paid trip to Hollywood! Your only obligation? Raise America's sweetheart and keep her from spiraling out of control like every other child star who has faced some sort of serious, life-altering tragedy and turned to drugs and alcohol and bad influences to feel better!

What's that you say? You're not excited? Yeah, we aren't either. Good luck, Goldmans; you're going to need it.

Chapter 10

After Shiva, Mom pokes her head into my room. "Sweetheart?" she calls, smiling sweetly. "May I come in and use your laptop? Jim left his at the office, and he's using mine to get caught up on some work."

"Yeah," I grunt, turning off my latest movie and handing the laptop to her.

"Thank you so much." She sits down at my desk and begins to type and click away. I lie down and stare at the ceiling for a few seconds before growing bored. I pick up my phone, realizing I haven't spoken to anyone outside of this house in almost four days. When I flip through my missed calls and messages, I see I've neglected about a dozen messages from my friends, Frank and Josh. I have four texts from guys on my football team and a few from numbers I don't recognize.

What the hell? I wonder as I sift through them. The most recent text is from Josh, asking if that was me he saw on the news again last night and why haven't I called him back yet. The question blares at me in big, shouting capital letters. I peer up at my mom, who obliviously clicks and types at my desk. I text him back quickly and tell him to grab Frank and meet me in the food court of the mall tomorrow.

Another set of texts are from my ex-girlfriend, Katrina, who also asks what is going on and if the "rumors" are true. I'm not sure what this means. As I start to type, "What ru talking about?" my mom begins small talk in my direction.

"Did you have a nice time with Cherie today?" she asks in a faint, hopeful voice.

"Not really," I mutter. "Some photographers followed us. They almost trampled Britney."

On my phone, Katrina replies, "U and Cherie Belle?"

I stare at the screen, stunned. I type, "What rumors?"

My mom sighs. "Yes, I see they found the house finally. They are brazen, aren't they? I'm sure you took care of her. You always do." She clicks the mouse pad. "Ooh, a coupon for Kohl's! Didn't you say you needed socks?"

Katrina's scathing text replies, "Like u don't know."

My eyes nearly roll back into my head. I text back, "I don't. What is it?"

"What the hell is going on then?" Katrina persists. I can feel jealousy radiating from her, and I don't understand why or where it's coming from.

"I don't know what ur talking about," I type back. No response.

My mom calls, "Jack? Did you hear me?"

"Yes, socks," I say quickly. I sit up and roughly throw my phone into my night stand's drawer.

Mom turns and looks at me with a raised eyebrow. "Something wrong?"

"Nothing," I mutter. "There are some kinds of rumors going around about me and Cherie in the news, and Katrina's mad at me."

She squints at me as if she finds that hard to believe. Her lips purse to the side, and she tilts her head. "I know all of this media attention is hard, honey. Jim and I are trying to figure out the laws and find out what rights to privacy we have. It's all very confusing. For now, we can't really stop them, so just remember not to answer their questions."

"Yeah," I grumble. I twist onto my side and close my eyes to turn off all of the conversations around me.

Finally, Mom stands and pats my legs gently. "Thanks, honey. You can go back to your movie."

"Pass me the laptop?" I ask, too lazy to get up. She rolls her eyes and laughs, handing me the computer before leaving.

In true Mom fashion, every tab is still open. I start to close each tab, one by one. A bunch of Mom-sites flash before me: Kohl's New Year's sale items, Couponclipper.com, a Shoprite weekly flyer. Her email is still open. As I bring the cursor to the little red "x" at the top, the first email catches my eye.

Jim's email address glares at me, and my interest is piqued the minute I read the subject line.

Cherie.

I blink. I squint at the screen and swallow. What about Cherie?

Should I read it? I want to read it.

I shouldn't read it. I shake my head to myself, and I almost want to slam the laptop closed and walk away before I do something I shouldn't. Almost.

But I can't stop myself. Hesitantly, I click on the email's subject and open the message.

From: Goldman, Jim
(jgoldman@goldmanopticals.com)
To: Eva Goldman
Subject: Cherie
Did you see this? Should we talk to them?
www.dirterazzi.com/articles/cherie-belle-new-love-affair-A-Romantic-Comedy/
Sent from my iPhone

Love affair? With who? Who's *them*? I read and reread the link over and over to myself. Twinges of curiosity are overshadowed by flames of jealousy that resonate through my limbs. I want to look. The mere title of the article makes me furious. Now I know I shouldn't go any further. I don't want to know who she's dating.

So even Jim's reading the gossip sites? What is wrong with everyone?

My hands are sweating. My heart beats rapidly inside my chest. I don't know why this is getting me this upset, but it is, and I get even angrier that I am so angry about Cherie's stupid love affair and Jim's gossip site prying.

I am also mad that my thirst for the details of that article is begging to be quenched. My curious side begs, *If everyone is going ahead and reading about her and forwarding it around, why can't I*?

No, I can't do that, I tell myself.

I don't want to know who she is dating. I didn't want to know that she is dating someone at all.

I pace between my window and my front door, trying to calm down, trying to count to ten, but none of it is working. I have to go for a run. I have to clear my head. I pull up the blinds of my window and scan the dark street for photographers. There are a few waiting in their cars beside our sidewalks, so I decide to go out of the back door.

After pulling on my sneakers and my sweatshirt, I pound down the stairs and into the kitchen. Cherie is sitting at the table, painting bright pink polish on Britney's fingernails, and the image of them sitting together, Cherie doting on her so lovingly, does something to melt my insides as I step closer. They both look up when I enter the room.

"Jackie, look!" Britney is glowing, holding up a set of perfectly painted nails that match Cherie's.

"Nice," I nearly grunt, trying to show approval with a small smile. Oblivious, Britney returns her attention to the table.

"Hey," Cherie says cheerily. I smile tightly. She is wearing an over-sized sweater that swallows her whole upper body and tiny shorts that do very little to cover her legs, which are long and thin. Her hair is held in one long ponytail that drapes over her shoulder. Her green eyes look so big on her drawn, hollowed face, but she's still as pretty as pretty can get. I don't know if it's because she is a celebrity or if I'm just that attracted to her, but she gives me those butterflies like movies and books always talk about. It's really annoying, and I hate it.

"Hi." I head straight for the refrigerator and pull out a water bottle, trying not to stare at her.

"Where are you headed?" she asks with pep.

"For a run," I say quickly. I feel bad speaking so brusquely to her, but I feel like a thousand curses will fly out of my mouth right now if I open it too much.

She glances at the clock and then back at me. "It's almost 8 o'clock at night."

I shrug, growing irritated. "So?"

Cherie squints at me. "Is everything okay?"

I hate being such an easy read. "Yeah, fine. Just want to work out, that's all."

"You just seem... I don't know, angry or something." Her face falls. "I hope I wasn't prying too much before, you know." She thinks I'm mad at her, I'll bet. I'm not, but maybe I sort of am. I shouldn't be though, and I'm definitely not angry with her for the reason she thinks.

"No, it's fine. I'm not mad, I promise," I lie quickly. Britney's eyes dart between us, and she impatiently slides her hand closer to Cherie on the table.

Ignoring Britney for a moment, Cherie says softly, "Okay. Well, be careful." I hear something in her voice; disappointment maybe? I'm not sure.

I turn for the door. When my fingers touch the knob, she calls out, "Hey, Jack?"

I pause and look back at her. "Yeah?" She whispers something to Britney, and my little sister bounds out of the room enthusiastically. Cherie watches after her for a moment, smiling, then turns her attention to me.

"Sorry, I didn't want her to hear this, but... I'm driving down to New York City this weekend," she says. "I have this New Year's thing to do with Caz to promote our movie. After that, I'll probably go back home."

"Oh, really?" *She's leaving*? That was... quick. It feels almost too sudden, and my heart sinks a little more. "Well, I'm sure I'll see you around, right?"

A hint of a smile plays on her lips. "I guess. I just wanted to say thanks. You know, for everything this week."

"I didn't do anything special." My insides scream at her, *I shouldn't have had to do anything. Your boyfriend should have had to deal with all of this. Who is he? Caz? Is that the guy?*

She laughs a little. "You did, though. You... you made me feel really safe today. And you were so kind all week." She gets up from her chair and crosses the room toward me. I can feel every hair on my body stand up as she swings her arms up and folds them around my neck. "Thanks for being there for me."

I slip an arm loosely behind her and give her a quick hug in return, but she doesn't let go. Cherie holds on tightly, like it's a goodbye-forever hug, and her body lingers dangerously close to mine. Her vanilla and flowers scent intoxicates me and clouds my senses. My insides go nuts, and a million bursts of electricity sting my skin. I pray she can't feel my pulse pounding.

Finally, she leans back and gives me a quick peck on the cheek. It's the friendly kind of kiss girls give people all of the time, but it sends shockwaves up and down my spine. I close my eyes for a second and try to get a hold of myself.

"I hope you'll come out to visit me in California soon," she says, stepping backward and releasing me. "Maybe next month. Don't you guys get a week off in February or something?"

I look down and nod. "Yeah, I think so. That would be fun."

Her stare burns through mine. I've forgotten what I was supposed to do and why I'm even down here. I remain in place like an idiot, trapped by her eyes again. There's something in them that I can't quite read; it's something she wants to say, and I'm desperate to know what it is.

Before I can ask her, she says, "Sorry, I didn't want to keep you from your workout."

"Oh, yeah. See ya later."

I want to ask what she's thinking. I want to know why she's looking at me like that. I push it to the back of my mind and get out of the house before I can admit that she tossed my anger right out the window.

DIRTERAZZI.COM

CHERIE BELLE LOVE AFFAIR: REAL LIFE ROMANTIC COMEDY

Celebrities really are just like the rest of us: they trip, they fall, and they are caught in midair by a handsome prince charming that can't tear his eyes off of... um... yeah, keep dreaming folks. That kind of stuff only happens to princesses, and celebutante Cherie Belle!

Cherie Belle stepped out yesterday for the first time since the funeral for her parents, who were killed in an automobile accident on Christmas Eve. Escorted by her new family member/possible love interest/arm candy, Jack Hansen, Cherie made her way to a local grocery store in upstate New York. Following our last report about Cherie's dwindling waist size, we're not really sure she's going to eat the food she was buying, but that's another story.

Our reporter on the scene claims the moment between Hansen and Belle, pictured above, was the kind of stuff romantic comedies are made of, as Cherie, who was sporting her signature high heels, suddenly tripped and soared toward the ground. In a blur, Hansen, the 6'2" tight end (ahem, get your mind out of the gutter, ladies, it's a position he plays for his high school football team) thrust his arm out and caught the teetering Belle just in time. Then, they stared into each other's eyes, forgetting everything and everyone existed, even Hansen's five-year-old sister. All these love-struck kids needed was a little Maroon 5 ballad playing in the background and some rain to make it a magical movie moment.

Cherie's reps are keeping mum about Hansen's relationship to their client, insisting he's just a nice kid who is trying to help Belle for the short time she is in his hometown, and they want to emphasize the word short.

No decision has been made yet about whether or not Cherie's grandparents will be her permanent guardians, but Cherie isn't letting an uncertain future keep her from fulfilling her duties as a star of the upcoming flick, This Side of Sunny. *Cherie will be on the first flight back to Hollywood after she and Caz Farrell perform in Times Square for the Kidz Channel's New Year's Special. According to Carl Schwartz, Cherie will promptly begin touring and giving interviews to promote the movie.*

From the looks of this picture, however, Jack Hansen isn't letting Cherie out of his sight too easily. Even though she plans to perform with Caz Farrell on New Year's Eve, one question still remains: Who will Cherie kiss when the ball drops?

Chapter 11

The front lawn is a minefield of cameras and reporters on Saturday morning. They are waiting for a sign of Cherie, their perfectly tragic teenage victim, to have to leave our house. For some reason, I'm good enough, and they pounce the moment they see me.

Reporters emerge from vans, shouting questions at me. It's hard to get to my car unscathed by a flurry of strangers. I don't want my picture taken anymore, so I keep my hood up and my sunglasses on. I don't stop to listen to the questions or tell them to go to hell, which is what I really want to do. This time, I don't have Britney around to protect, or Cherie to make a path for. This time, I could just give them a piece of my mind. But Mom said not to talk to anyone, and I promised her that I wouldn't. I jump into my car and head for the mall.

As soon as I am within feet of Josh and Frank, Josh thrusts a magazine into my chest.

"Seriously?" Josh says. I look down and unfold the magazine. In the upper right hand corner of the cover page, there's a picture of Cherie walking through the cemetery, adorned with the line: "Cherie Buries Her Parents With New Beau By Her Side."

In the picture, I walk beside her, her arm tightly curled around mine.

I gawk at the magazine and then at my friends. "Where did you get this?"

"In the deli. Is this for real?" Josh demands, his eyes wide.

"What's 'beau' mean?" I ask, flipping through the magazine pages until I find the article, "Love for Orphan Cherie?" It's three pages long, and one page is devoted entirely to a shot of us in the Shoprite parking lot. Cherie is in my arms, staring longingly into my eyes, and I look ready to kiss her. I remember the moment vividly, and they've captured it to look romantic, not anxiety-ridden as I recall. Another page is littered with pictures of us at the cemetery, coming out of our house, driving in my car. I'm so taken aback by the photos that I can't even read the article. In some pictures, I look extremely attentive and attached to Cherie. It's as if they've crafted the images to make it look like we're dating.

"It means boyfriend, you idiot. When were you going to tell us?" Frank chastises me. "This is insane!"

"It's not what it looks like." I glance around the food court, suddenly self-conscious. *I'm on the front page of a magazine? I'm described as Cherie Belle's boyfriend?* "Jesus Christ…"

I'm Cherie's supposed new love affair, and it's a total lie. I can't deny the relief that washes over me, and I feel foolish for having been so angry about her fictional love affair last night. I toss the magazine back into Josh's arms.

Frank scoffs beside me, "Why didn't you call us? I texted you all week—you coulda just answered!"

Josh elbows him. "Dude, I'd rather hang out with Cherie Belle, too." I roll my eyes.

Frank groans, "Get over it! She's, like, fourteen!"

"She's sixteen," I correct him. "She'll be seventeen this summer."

He cocks an eyebrow at me. "Wait—is it true? Are you dating her?"

"No!" I nearly shout. "Not even close. She's my stepdad's niece."

"Well, you better tell Katrina that 'cause she's real upset. She's been crying all week to my girlfriend—"

"So that's why she texted me last night," I grunt, realizing now why she sounded so angry. I rub my forehead. "Guys, I've done nothing all vacation but deal with this crap—can we talk about anything else please?"

"No way!" Josh cries. "You've been hanging out with celebrities all week, and you're not gonna share one detail? It's Cherie Belle!" Josh nudges me. "Is she hotter in person? Dude, have you seen her naked?"

I shove him away, and it's harder than I meant to. He almost falls, but Frank catches him.

"Ow, man, take it easy," he complains, rubbing his arm. "You'd better get used to answering questions— inquiring minds wanna know!"

"Get over it, Josh! He said it's not like that," Frank groans. He seems relieved that the rumors aren't true.

"Thank you!" I exclaim, walking away from them and toward a table. "You guys wouldn't believe what a circus my house is right now."

Frank gives me a reassuring pat on the shoulder. "Sorry dude, that sucks. If you want to stay at my house, it's no problem. My mom loves you; she'd probably let you live with us if your mom would allow you out of her sight for two seconds."

I groan in response as I sit down. "I wish."

"So what's going to happen now?" Josh presses, sliding into the seat across from me.

"Not sure," I say with a shrug. He gives me a doubtful look. "She's going to go back to California after New Year's."

"Really?"

"Yeah," I reply, taking in their doubtful looks. "Why? What?"

They look at each other and then at me. Frank scoffs, "Dude, I wouldn't be surprised if she has to stay with your family. I mean, your stepdad is her freakin' uncle, right? Is he her only uncle?"

I nod. Their point is coming to me, but slowly. "I'm sure he's not the only person in her life."

"Well, is there any other family who could take her in?"

I shrug. "Her grandparents. She'll probably live with them. Maybe they'll move out there with her."

Frank smirks. "What are they, like 80? Not happening. You're looking at another roommate, buddy," he says matter-of-factly.

The possibility frightens me. "That's—nah, it can't happen. We can't have another person in that house. Besides, the twins hate her. It would never work."

Josh laughs and slides the magazine across the table. "Well, the entire world thinks a loser like you is dating Cherie Belle because of this stupid picture, so anything can happen, right?"

I gulp quietly. They have no clue how bad it would be for me if they're right. The thought of another girl in that house... a diva that brings media chaos... even if it is Cherie...

I will beg Frank's mom to take me in if that's what Jim has planned.

DIRTERAZZI.COM

YOU DON'T KNOW JACK: JUST WHO IS JACK HANSEN?

Jack Hansen, Cherie's rumored love interest, has turned a lot of heads the past few days. You've seen him brooding beside her at the funeral and catching her in grocery store parking lots, but Dirterazzi asks the question: What do we really know about this kid? The mysterious teenager with the serious eyes and dashing good looks has Cherie Belle fans asking if he is really deserving of Cherie's sudden attentions, or if he is just taking advantage of being in the right place at the, ahem, right-ish? time. We here at Dirterazzi have the same question, so we did a little investigating of our own!

Jack, 17, was born and raised in the swanky suburbs of Westchester County, New York, just about an hour from Manhattan (That means he's got some money, y'all!). At Thomas Jefferson High School, where he is a junior, Jack plays football and gets mostly A's in courses like AP U.S. History and Pre-Calculus. Friends say he has applied to some Big East schools in the hopes of achieving a football scholarship. Teachers at Belleville praise his exceptional manners in and out of class, and a few have called on him to tutor struggling peers. Sounds like your all-American boy, right?

Well, not exactly. Classmates tell us there's a darker side to Jack, due in part to his biological father leaving the family when Jack was just 13. Jack's childhood friend, Josh Parker, tells us, "It really messed him up for a while. He was so angry, and he used to get into a lot of fights with kids." Others label Jack as a womanizing misogynist, who even broke up with his most recent girlfriend because she wouldn't have sex with him. Teammates use the words "standoffish" and "cold" to describe him.

So is this the right guy for Kidz Channel princess, Cherie Belle? We can't be sure yet, but something tells us Cherie is latching onto a kid who is just as broken as she is. Only time will tell if this is a match made in heaven or in haste... stay tuned!

Chapter 12

I close the front door behind me at around 12:15 that night, and I'm hoping I won't get caught by Mom or Jim. My normal curfew is midnight on weekends, but sometimes stuff happens, and I get side-tracked. Or I'm avoiding my house at all costs and don't really want to go back, like tonight.

As I turn to race up to my room, I find both of them approaching, faces plastered with huge smiles. If it wasn't for the smiles, I would be fumbling to come up with an excuse.

"Hi, honey," my mom coos. Her arms are folded, though, and I know that means she's nervous.

"What?" I ask, immediately sensing a fresh bomb about to be dropped.

When she hangs back, Jim moves forward. "Sit down, Jack. We want to talk to you about something."

No, I think to myself. *No, no, no. Nothing good ever starts with that line.*

Like a man walking on death row, I follow him to the dining room. We sit across from each other, and I think I could melt ice with the way my eyes burn into his.

I want to say, *"Don't say it, Jim. Don't say what I think you're going to say."* But I don't. Instead, I just try to convey it with my glare.

He clears his throat. "Well, bud, as you know, a lot has happened in the last few days," Jim begins, resting his elbows on the table. "We, uh, we went to meet with my brother's lawyer, and we discussed the terms of my brother's will and custody for Cherie."

"What does that mean?"

My mom's tone is gentle, like a kindergarten teacher explaining to her students how to add. "It means that Mark and Camille wanted Jim to take Cherie should something happen to them, which, well..." Her voice trails off for a moment.

"I know what custody means." I'm growing more and more impatient as I wait for them to hit me with it. I can't bring myself to ask, *Cherie's moving in, isn't she?*

"Well," Jim chimes in, "Cherie is now my responsibility, so she's kind of like a daughter to me."

I toss my glare back and forth between them. "Yeah, I got that."

"She wants to step away from acting, which I think is really good for her right now. She could probably use some time to herself." He glances at my mother. "But she wants to be in her home, too, because it's her home, and it's close to her studio for when she decides to go back to work. The social worker we spoke to thinks the consistency would be good for her, and I can understand that as well."

I nearly sigh with relief. "Okay, so she's moving back home, then?"

Jim nods. "Yes, she is." He pauses, and I hate that. It means something else is coming.

"We've talked it over and, since it's been deeded to us as Cherie's trustees, we think it will be good for all of us to move with Cherie to her home in Hollywood next month."

DIRTERAZZI.COM

CHERIE BELLE: CAZ FARRELL COMMENTS ON HER RUMORED LOVE AFFAIR

We caught up with Caz Farrell today in the Grove and just had to ask if he believed the rumors surrounding Jack Hansen and Cherie Belle.

With a shit-eating grin, the Hollywood heartthrob told us, "That wasn't the impression I got from Jack or Cherie at all, and I was at the funeral. I'm sure Cherie is just concentrating on healing right now, and we should all try to give her the privacy she deserves during this very difficult time."

You know what they say: Denial *is a river in Egypt...*

Chapter 13

I stand up from the table. "That's it; I'm going to live with Frank."

My announcement comes as more of a shock to my mom than it does to Jim. I almost expect her to ask, "*How could you do that to me*?" I swallow hard, my stomach twisting in knots until I'm ready to vomit. But I have had enough. I have to stand my ground.

"Jack—"

But I've thrown up my hands already and move from the table, not giving them an ounce of time to talk their version of sense into me. I'm practically foaming at the mouth. "I can't do it. It's not fair, and I've already put up with all of this." I gesture around the house wildly, but they know what I mean. "Now you want me to pick up and move to California—in the middle of my junior year?"

Mom tries to be patient with me. "Jack, sweetie, I know it's hard, and I know we are asking a lot of you. Trust me, I do." She looks at Jim as if this was not her favorite plan either. "But we all have to think about a much bigger purpose here."

"That's fine, Mom, I get it, but I'm not moving across the country just because tragedy struck someone else's family."

My mom pulls back as if I've spit at her. "Jack, they were *our* family. I know you don't know her well, but Cherie's your family, now, too, and she's all alone in the world. She's—she's an orphan, Jack."

She looks me dead in the eye. It's a cold, hollow stare. "Jack, think of Britney."

"This isn't about Britney," I grumble, but I know what she's getting at. Her words take an imaginary knife and slice me open. Now she's staring at my wounds, and I can't close them up fast enough.

"Just think of what you would want someone to do if this happened to her. Wouldn't you drop everything and help her and do what's best for her?"

"I did that once, Mom. Remember?" She blinks back tears, but I don't feel bad; she started it.

In a trembling voice, Mom adds, "Jack, we all had to stick together then, and we all have to stick together now, too."

"No, this is different. This is way different. How can you expect me to give up my life and move to a different state and be even more miserable?" I huff. "You keep changing things. You keep adding to a house that's already full. God, you're gonna end up like a cat lady—only with kids!"

She sighs and a tear falls down her face. I hate myself for making her cry, and she twists the mental knife deeper. "Maybe you're right, but I can't turn a child away, not like this, Jack. I'm sorry. She needs us right now, and New York is not the place for her. They have a beautiful estate out in Hollywood that we can all live in very comfortably. You'll still have your own room, and the weather's always nice—"

"Mom, I get it. Go! *You* do that—*you* go live in California with all those kids, and you have a happy life. I want to stay here, in New York. I can just live with Frank, or Aunt Darla."

Her tears fall faster now. "You know that's not an option, Jack. Besides, I couldn't go a day without you—and what about Britney? She'd be heartbroken. You can't be so far from us!"

"Then don't go," I insist, putting my foot down. I look at Jim, and I can feel the frost of his icy glare. He's mad at me now, but I don't care. Man to man, this is what it comes down to: who will she choose? I feel like some soap opera organ music should be playing in the background, with some announcer exclaiming, *"What will Eva do? Will she stay for the son who's always stood by her, or will she follow the man who came around and put a band aid over a missing limb?"*

And I have my answer when she looks at him, passing the baton in this awful relay. It's his turn to speak.

"Jack, I know this hasn't been an easy transition for you," he begins.

"That's an understatement." Mom's nostrils flare at my snarky tone.

Jim takes in a deep breath. "I know it must be hard to live in a full house."

"How would you know? You're never around!" I snap. It's true; Jim has so little experience with the day-to-day routines in this home. It's like he dropped his daughters off at a permanent day care. I wasn't surprised that Christmas Eve was the first night he discovered Britney sleeps in my room. He didn't even know she was afraid of the dark.

My tone should have gotten me in trouble, but he continues patiently. "Here's the situation, Jack: a very long time ago, before she was famous, before she was rich, Cherie's parents left me and my late wife as her guardians, and I vowed to take care of her and raise her as my own in the event of some catastrophic incident. Here we are, 16 years later, and I unfortunately have a duty to fulfill.

"Now, I understand how this looks like it could be as simple as staying here in New York, but I'm also aware of the size of this family, the size of this already shrinking house, the lack of privacy a celebrity like Cherie would have in a small town like ours, all of this."

"She is going to be famous anywhere, Jim," I say with authority. "And that, by the way, is not good for the rest of us to have to live with forever. It's dangerous; the reporters almost stampeded over Britney the other day. There are pictures of all of us everywhere."

"I know. I've seen them, and I'm not happy about it," he says. I feel like he means to say more, like he's not happy that they're labeling me as her boyfriend. I feel my face flush a little.

"But that's not all, Jack," he adds, his voice lowering. "Your mother and I have been talking for some time about starting fresh in a new place. As you know, the housing market is awful, and we couldn't sell this house if we tried. I never dreamed one day we would have a space to go to freely, no questions asked."

So many thoughts swirl in my head at once, and I have to step back. The only words that I think are appropriate to say out loud come tumbling out of my mouth.

"This is wrong. This is so wrong."

"Jack," my mother says in her warning voice.

"So, let me get this straight," I continue, my hands piecing the puzzle together in the air. "You've wanted to—were planning—to move, but you didn't tell me. Now, you're looking to use Cherie's situation—the death of your brother and his wife!—to make your dreams come true? What kind of people are you?"

"Jack!" My mother is horrified at my accusation, but I stare at her, unwavering.

Jim is red-faced. "Call it what you will, but I am taking lemons and making damned lemonade, and you will not make me feel badly about it!" Jim's in my face now, but I'm taller, which I'm sure intimidates him.

He snarls, "What we do for the betterment of this family shouldn't matter to you anyway. You're applying for colleges all over the east coast, aren't you? When you're playing football in Florida, is it going to matter where your mother lives?" His chest rises and falls with fury. I am reminded that he lost his brother a few days ago and that he isn't entirely responsible for what he says or, worse, what he does.

"That's not for another two years," I say, hating that his argument kind of makes sense.

"Well, this is a decision we need to make now, for her, and for everyone else," he says stiffly. "You can go wherever you want when you're ready, but right now you have to come with us while we support Cherie."

I growl, "She's your responsibility, not mine. You won't make this my problem, too." I force myself to take another step back.

"*Jack!*" my mom cries.

As I storm away from the table, I catch sight of Cherie and the twins standing in the doorway of the basement, spying on our conversation. Cherie's mouth is set in a hard, angry line, but her eyes are glistening with tears ready to fall. It socks me in the gut and I wince inwardly. She whirls around and flees back down the stairs. Chloe's sinister eyes glower at me from the dark corners of the stairwell before she follows her cousin, and Claudia just frowns. I'm not sure if she's disappointed in me or feels sorry for me, but it makes me feel worse.

Shit.

I lay in bed replaying the conversation and standoff in my mind. Jim obviously wants to cash in on his brother's death, but at what expense to the rest of us? She could live anywhere, like Manhattan, or somewhere swanky in Westchester with... someone. Her grandparents. Aunt Darla seems to love her. Someone else.

Lots of people would adopt her, so that's an option.

No it's not. Who am I kidding?

I think of California, with its surfer dudes and all those rich people that we don't really belong with. If we move to Hollywood Hills, I'll have to go to a Hollywood school. I don't want to be surrounded by rich, snobby daughters of movie producers and guys who think they're so cool because their parents party with Kanye West or something.

Nope. Can't do it. I'll move in with Frank. I'll live with anyone else.

I pause and sit up, remembering my father's email address. That could be my ticket out of here! I'll send my dad an email and beg him to take me in; who cares if he abandoned us? Who cares if he never called or offered help when times were really bad? *All is forgiven, Dad!* I'll do anything but move to California with this circus.

I flip my laptop open and go to my email inbox. I type his address into a new message and move my cursor to the empty body.

Hi,

That's as far as I get. I stop and lean back, staring at the screen, my fingers trembling over the keys. What does someone write after all this time? I try again.

You owe me, and it's time to pay up.

I quickly delete it and shake my head. There's no way he'd invite me to live with him after I leave that kind of message, even if it is what I'm thinking. I clear my throat and start to type again.

What are you up to? I hope things are good. Things aren't so good here.

Terrible. What a dumb idea. I slam my laptop closed and fall back onto my bed, my head pounding with frustration. I am not in a good frame of mind to write this now.

I hear the creak of my door and look up. Britney's pushing through the small slit between the molding and the door, and she closes it silently behind her. She is carrying her blue Care Bear. It was my Care Bear, but I gave it to her when she was born. She scurries to the foot of my bed and clumsily climbs aboard, crawling toward me on all fours. I pretend to be asleep, which I usually am during this routine.

She burrows inside of my arm and rests her head against my shoulder, sighing softly. I smell the Johnson's Baby Wash in her hair and the bubblegum toothpaste my mother's convinced her to use. She always smells like candy and clean and home.

I open my eyes and stare at the ceiling. I hear my mother's voice. *"What about Britney? She'd be heartbroken."*

I'm lying to myself if I think I can abandon Brenton and Britney the way Dad abandoned us all.

DIRTERAZZI.COM

JACK HANSEN AND CHERIE BELLE REPORTEDLY NOT SPEAKING AFTER MAJOR FALLOUT

Seems like Hansen's fifteen minutes of fame is about to be up because he and Cherie Belle are no longer speaking to one another. A source close to Cherie says the lovebirds exchanged heated words after Hansen learned his family was moving to California to support Cherie's career, which is said to be stronger than ever in the aftermath of her parents' deaths, despite previous reports of Cherie's possible exit from acting. The Goldman family's plan to move to her Hollywood Hills pad next month solidifies what Carl Schwartz told us last week: Cherie is not quitting acting.

The move is not sitting well with Hansen, however, who is in the middle of his junior year and doesn't want to leave the east coast. As we told you last week, he has big plans to attend college down south in two years, and his current football coach is known to facilitate some seriously sweet scholarship deals for his star players. Apparently, Jack has forgotten that Cherie is a super-rich megastar celebrity who could pay for him and all of his siblings to attend college wherever they want. Or maybe Jack just doesn't want Cherie within driving distance of Caz Farrell. Either way, it appears the spark we witnessed in the parking lot a few days back has already fizzled between these two crazy kids. Teenage love can be so fickle…

Chapter 14

Cherie is alone at the kitchen table, typing on her laptop, when I come downstairs. It's noon, and the house feels practically empty. Is it Saturday? Sunday? I've lost track. I think it's New Year's Eve. I always lose track during the Christmas Break. All I do know is that I don't have to be in school, or my mother would have had me up much earlier.

She looks up at me with contempt, and I'm immediately reminded of my argument with Jim the night before.

"Hi," I say, trying to smile at her.

Her eyes quickly drop to her screen, and she ignores me. I walk around the table and reach into the refrigerator for some orange juice. Her cellphone rings, and she promptly answers it. Her voice is all sunshine and flowers.

"Hello? Oh, hi, Chris. Yes. Yes, I am. Thank you, that's kind of you. I'll be okay. 1:30? Of course! Okay. Yes, I'll be ready. Thanks, Chris, see you soon." She hangs up on Chris and types out a text message.

My mind spins briefly. *Who is Chris? What's happening at 1:30?* Suddenly, it comes together. "Are you still doing that New Year's Eve thing?"

She ignores me again, keeping her back to me, and resumes typing on her laptop. When I look down at her screen, I see she is posting something on her blog. The font is too small to read.

I swallow hard and consider ignoring her back, but some gut instinct urges me to apologize. "Look, I, um—"

"Save it, jerkoff," she huffs, and she slams her screen down, swipes the computer up into her arms, and heads for the basement.

I'm stunned and don't know how to respond to that. "Excuse me?"

She spins around and glares at me. "I heard everything you said last night. You're a real asshole, Jack."

I smooth the back of my hair and feel my cheeks burn with shame. "Yeah, about that—I'm really sorry—"

"No, you're not." She spits the words at me like fire, and I'm growing defensive. I try to remember she needs extra patience. "We're not family. We're not even friends. Why would you care what happens to me?"

"Cherie, I really didn't mean it—I was just mad," I try to say, but she waves me off.

"I said save it, Jack. I don't need your apologies, or your fake sympathy. I am not anyone's *problem*!" She scoffs, "You don't really think I want any of this, do you? I don't want your stupid family moving into *my* home and getting in *my* space!"

It's becoming harder to have patience now. "Please don't talk about them like that."

"Just shut up, Jack," she hisses, and I actually find myself complying. She's practically shouting as she steps forward, her teeth flashing and her eyes wild. "Don't talk to me—ever! Don't pretend to care, don't act like you understand what I'm going through, and just don't speak to me! Is that clear?"

I nod, and she turns toward the basement. She stops in the doorway and looks back with hatred. "We have one month stuck in this house together before we move. You stay out of my way, and I'll stay out of yours." With that, she disappears and slams the door behind her.

That night, at a New Year's Eve party at Frank's house, I'm immediately surrounded by the kids from school who haven't seen me since the start of break. Their attention is overwhelming, and I have to dodge a myriad of questions about Cherie and the chaos at home. I'd never been a really popular kid before, but now it feels like everyone is trying to be my best friend. Of course they all only want to talk about the one person I wish to discuss least in the world.

"What's Cherie like?"

"Are you really dating her? That's just a rumor, right? Frank said it was a rumor."

"Is she pretty in person?"

"Sorry about your aunt and uncle. It's so nice of you to be there for Cherie—you're such a good boyfriend."

"Why didn't you tell anyone you were dating Cherie Belle? That is so cool!"

One meddlesome kid asks, "Is that why you broke up with Katrina?"

Automatically, I look up and find Katrina just feet away, glowering at that question. Pouting and huffing, she walks past me and the nosy guy, making sure to roughly slam her shoulder into my arm.

"Katrina—" I try to call out, but she ignores me and storms out of the room.

It's almost 11 before I find a chance to pull my real friends aside and tell them that I have to move. Frank shakes his head, Josh's eyebrows raise, but neither of them seems terribly surprised.

"When?" Frank asks.

"February," I say quietly. "Over break."

Frank's jaw drops. "But that's in, like, a month! That's—it's too soon!"

Josh nods and harrumphs, "Better make the best of the time we have I guess." He hands me his half-empty beer.

Frank is less easily comforted. He grumbles, "There's got to be another way. It's junior year. There's just gotta." I'm too clouded over with misery to tell him not to say anything to anyone. Shaking his head, he walks away and over to his girlfriend, who looks from him to me as he relays the news. Then she's off, going directly to a group of girls with the information. Pretty soon, the whole junior class knows about it, and kids are coming over to pry further.

I curse under my breath, swallow the beer in my hand, and prepare for another round of questions.

On TV, Cherie sings a duet of "Baby, It's Cold Outside," with Caz Farrell in Times Square before the ball drops. I drink more beer and cheap champagne than I should. When the ball drops, Frank sheds a drunken tear as he hugs me, Josh razzes me about how in love Cherie and Caz look, and Katrina asks me to go upstairs with her. I look at the TV, watching Cherie exchange hugs and kisses with her celebrifriends. She and Caz hug extra-long. Without a second thought, I take a swig of my beer and follow Katrina to the guest bedroom.

DIRTERAZZI.COM

CHERIE BELLE COZIES UP TO CAZ FARRELL AT NEW YEAR'S PARTY, GETS WASTED! JACK HANSEN NO WHERE IN SIGHT

It was a wild night for Cherie Belle as she proved to the world she will go on, despite facing the ultimate tragedy this week. First, she and Caz sang and danced a near perfect duet of "Baby, It's Cold Outside," a romantically charged number full of that breathy, sex-kitten voice for which Cherie is famous. The heat between the Kidz Channel alum and his costar did not go unnoticed, and neither did their escapades afterward. Cherie followed Caz and his entourage to New York hotspot, Pulse, for a post-party to remember, or forget, based on reports of Cherie's level of sobriety (or lack thereof). It is being reported that Cherie drank an intense amount of champagne for a little girl, and her ever-shrinking frame did not handle the overdose of alcohol well. She spent the night stumbling and slurring, and eventually passed out, needing to be carried out by a friend. Caz, who is not known for his chivalrous ways, stayed at the club and partied the night away with his buddies. Whatta guy!

Another thing that did not go unnoticed: the absence of Jack Hansen, Cherie's parking lot prince, who is no longer speaking to her. Something tells us that if Jack Hansen had been there, he would have been the one to carry Cherie out of the club... or drag her out by her hair, caveman-style, depending on whose version of Jack Hansen we believe. All we do know is that Cherie is going to wake up with a serious headache—and we don't mean the one Kidz Channel is going to give her when they scold her for underage drinking. Stay tuned!

Chapter 15

The month that follows is a whirlwind of chaos as my mother files and registers and calls and books and altogether drives all of us crazy to pick ourselves up and make this haphazard move across the country. Sometimes I feel like she is possessed by some woman who actually believes this move is a great idea and that everything is going to be just fine, which has become her mantra.

When I remind her how all of my SAT scores and my college applications have our current address listed, she informs me that she can call the admissions offices and take care of the change in the morning.

"The acceptance letters will find their way to us, honey. Everything will be just fine," she nearly sings.

As I ask her for more boxes for my things, she says, "Of course, dear, I'll go to the post office tomorrow to get some. Not to worry, everything will be just fine."

One day, I catch her obsessively cleaning out the bottom shelf of one of the kitchen cabinets, wiping what seems like the same spot over and over, muttering curses to herself. I offer to help her and she jumps in fright, as if I snuck up on her. Throwing off her rubber, yellow gloves, she shies from my hands, which are reaching out to steady her. Before I can wonder if she's finally on the verge of cracking, she breaks into tears and runs to her room, slamming the door and hysterically whimpering, "I'm fine! Everything is going to be fine!"

That's just my mom. The twins begin to have goodbye ceremonies with different friend groups every night the week before we leave. It starts with the cheerleading squad, who come over with a pizza and cans of frosting and pretzels and lots of tissues. It starts out as a night I wouldn't mind hanging around, until the tissues come out. The next night, a few girls from their hometown come by with shoe boxes of ticket stubs and postcards and pictures. The next night, a mix of freshman and sophomore girls from my school fill my living room and play a DVD slideshow of pictures from the past couple of months that's set to a mix of Kesha and Lady Gaga songs.

I'd be jealous of all the attention they're getting if it wasn't so nauseating and disingenuous. The twins started coming to school with me when they moved here in October. These girls that keep coming over have known them for precisely four and a half months and can't possibly be the true friends forever they claim to be. Katrina used to say some of those girls latched onto the twins in an effort to get closer to me, and I never believed her before this week. Now those same girls are throwing themselves at me like they have nothing to lose, and a few of them are actually pretty cute. I marvel at all of the opportunities I ignorantly missed out on these past couple of months.

The one all-girl party I do attend is, of course, Britney's. When her kindergarten friends hold a party to bid her farewell, there I am, holding her coat, watching her throw herself around the bouncy castle with all of the other five-year-olds. I'm an anomaly to the moms and dads, who don't quite understand why I'm there and not my mother. I have to explain that my mom is chaperoning the twins' ski party out in Orange County and that my stepdad is taking Brenton to a laser tag party with his friends. They nod knowingly but are still perplexed. That's when I turn my attention back to my little sister and the parents continue to stare, wondering, whispering. I'm used to it, and they should be by now, but they're not, so I breathe deeply and try to be patient.

Cherie, however, is the only one who isn't drawing attention to us anymore. She generally flies in and out of the state for different premieres and interviews, so she is barely around, and the gaggle of gossipers are even more scarce. When she is present, she keeps to herself in the basement or is chauffeured to some red carpet event by Danika. I vaguely remember hearing that she has a movie to promote or something. Every now and again I secretly hope we will be forced to sit together and talk, and maybe I'll have the chance to apologize. The longer we go without speaking or seeing each other, though, the less I have to say and the more I begin to forget about her.

The evening before we leave for California, I'm sitting in the middle of my barren room, which has been stripped of all of its furniture and posters. Another moving truck will come in the morning to pick up the rest of our boxes. My childhood home has never looked sadder.

I examine the map Jim's printed for me, which details our route for travel to California. I've never been on a road trip like this before, especially not as a driver. It's a little intimidating, but the alternative was leaving my car in the hands of strangers on some train ride and joining the RV of Hell. Even Brenton begged to ride with me instead of with the collection of misfits riding together in the RV Jim has decided to rent and captain. My mom almost caved when Brenton threw himself at her feet, but then he got the flu and threw up at her feet a few days later. Now she wants to watch him every minute of the trip and reneged on her original promise, only allowing him to stay in the one hotel room we are renting for Britney and me.

Naturally, Princess Cherie is flying out to LAX in the morning. She would never ride in a rented RV like a commoner. Her handlers actually flew in to New York last night just to make the trip back out with her tomorrow. Betsy picked her up earlier for a "dinner meeting," but I never heard of a dinner meeting requiring a limo and an entourage of hair and makeup people. Either way, she's out of the house for the night, and I won't have to see her.

There's a knock on my door, and I call out, "Come in." The door pushes open, and Claudia comes inside.

"Ready for tomorrow?" she asks, pointing to the map. In Brenton's place, Mom gave me Claudia as a co-pilot. Not my first choice, but at least it's not Chloe.

"Yeah, looks easy enough," I say. "Did you need something?"

She smiles and sits down next to me. She fiddles with a corner of my sleeping bag. "Are you nervous?"

"It's just a couple of highways," I say with a shrug, trying to sound confident. She is putting her life in my hands for a few days, after all.

She laughs. "No, I mean about moving. To Hollywood. Isn't it crazy?"

I nod. "Yeah, I guess a little." I'm confused; Claudia never tries to talk to me, let alone have heart to hearts.

"We've been out there to visit a bunch of times. It's nice and all, but I don't really know if I want to live there. They're all probably rich and snobby at school."

"School will be weird, I guess," I say.

"Yeah," she sighs. "It sucks; we feel like we just got settled here in your school, you know? We made so many friends already."

I tilt my head and raise my eyebrow at her. "I'm sure you guys will be fine; you'll make lots of friends again, especially with Cherie around."

"Oh, she's not going to school," she tells me, then rolls her eyes.

"Why not?" I probe, intrigued and a little annoyed. "Princess doesn't like school?"

Claudia shakes her head, and we share a smirk. "Well, she was always tutored on the set and stuff, so I don't think she's gone in a really long time anyway. But she's taking time off from everything—school, acting, you name it."

My stomach drops, and I instantly remember how fragile she seemed at the grocery store that day. "That makes sense I guess," I grumble, turning back to my map to avoid Claudia's gaze. "How's she doing?"

Claudia laughs again. "Why don't you ask her yourself? She's staying downstairs tonight."

"In case you haven't noticed, we don't talk much," I say with a forced grin, "and I prefer it that way."

My stepsister groans. "No you don't, come on. I think you like her."

I scoff, "Yeah, right, okay."

She waves me off dismissively. "It's not like you're the only one; every guy loves her. You don't have to pretend."

I hope my cheeks aren't as red as they feel as I train my eyes on the map. "Yeah, but they don't know how nasty she is. Mean girls are ugly girls."

"Yeah, right! Look me in the eye and tell me she's ugly," she chides, poking at the paper in my grasp until I look at her.

"Stop!" I push her hand away. "You're going to rip it."

"See? You can't even answer me," she snickers.

I can feel myself turning violet, but I force myself to look at her. "I told you: no! She's not hot, and I don't want anything to do with her."

She blinks rapidly. "You're gonna live together for a long time. I mean, what, are you not gonna talk to each other for the rest of your lives?"

I play it nonchalant. "That's the plan."

"You don't mean that, Jack," she says. Again, she gives me that disappointed frown, and I'm growing tired of her questions and prying.

"Look, don't worry about either of us. We've co-existed in this house for the last month just fine," I say.

"That's just because she's never around," Claudia laughs. "She's always flying out to LA for premieres or something. What are you going to do when we're in her house and she's around all the time?"

"She said if I stayed out of her way, she'd stay out of mine, so that's good enough for me."

"Fine," she says, giving up. She looks around my room and sighs. "What time are we leaving tomorrow?"

I make a face. "Six." She makes the same face and rolls her eyes again. I watch her curiously as she gets up to leave.

"Hey."

Claudia stops in the doorway and looks down. "Yeah?"

"Why do you care so much anyway?" I ask.

Her face falls, and she shrugs. "I—I think she needs someone to talk to."

"Why?"

Claudia looks around and puts a finger to her lips. She closes the door a little. "I don't think she's okay."

"What do you mean?" I press, suddenly absorbed.

"I hear her crying at night sometimes. She holds it in all day around all of us, but when she's alone, she has these meltdowns." Her voice is a whisper now. "Dirterazzi says all this crazy stuff about bad things she's doing and clubs she's going to."

"You're not supposed to be reading that stuff," I remind her, but the information she's spilling to me makes me want to look the stories up for myself.

She cocks her head and folds her arms. "It's kind of impossible to ignore, Jack. And the things they say—if they're true, she's in trouble. I think she needs someone to talk to her about her parents. Someone who can relate to her, like you."

I look down at the map as anger stirs inside of my gut. "My dad didn't die, Claudia." My voice is edged with bitterness.

"That's not what I mean," she says quickly, but I hold up a hand to stop her.

"I gotta go," I say quickly. She looks at the clock, surprised, as I stand up and avoid her gaze. "I gotta go to Frank's house and say goodbye."

"Okay," she murmurs. "Have fun." And she leaves in a whirl of frustration.

***

"Surprise!"

I'm jolted by the chorus of shouting coming from Frank's living room. There are a slew of my friends from school inside, raising red plastic cups and blowing on noisemakers leftover from New Year's.

"What is this?" I laugh. Frank and Josh grin like idiots. Frank slaps his hand on my back, and Josh gives me a cup full of cold beer.

"It's your going away party, man!" he cries. "We couldn't let you leave without a proper sendoff!"

"You serious?" I look around the room in awe. Frank's mother, Donna, comes up and gives me a tight hug.

"Ma!" Frank whines.

"I know, I know, I'm not s'posed to be here," she mutters in her thick Brooklyn accent. "I gotta say goodbye to my second son ova here!" She squishes my face between her hands and gives me a big kiss on both cheeks.

Taking my hands in hers, she says through teary eyes, "Now you listen, Jack: you visit often! You come right here and stay with us; don't you go stay in no hotel. You're family!"

"Thanks, Ma," I reply, feeling a little sick inside. This woman has been like a second mother to me for a long time now; she was the first person to take notice that I needed help a few years ago, back when I had gotten really bad. Now I have to leave her behind, too, and that kills me. If I had ever before felt like I didn't want to move to California, it was nothing compared to how I feel now.

"Ma, c'mon." Frank nudges her away from me. I want to tell him to leave her alone, but she gives me one last kiss, wipes a tear from her eye, and turns.

"I know, I know, I'm gone, alright?! Have your party; enjoy. Bye, sweetheart."

"Thanks, Ma," Frank and I call out simultaneously. We laugh at our joint response, but the feeling is suddenly bittersweet. I look away from him quickly and make my way around the room to say hello to our other friends.

"C'mon, man, let's have a drink!" Frank says finally, pulling me away from the crowd and urging me to raise my cup.

I gesture to my watch. "I can't stay long, you know. I just came to say goodbye. I'm driving all day tomorrow."

Frank squints at me and mutters, "They get you forever; we can have at least one night."

His words hit me like a punch to my gut. Josh is quick to neutralize the feeling.

"Eh, leave 'im alone, man," Josh grunts. "He's probably gotta rest up for all the road head Cherie's gonna give 'im!"

I glare at Josh and shake my head. "You're an idiot."

He snickers and taps his cup against mine. "Happy travels!"

Frank and I shake our heads, but I lift my drink anyway.

***

The air is frigid as I open my door and step out onto my curb. My breath floats in small puffs over my head. I lock my car door and step quietly onto the walk. I pause and lean against the trunk, staring at the house. I just want one last small moment of peace with my childhood home before leaving it forever. The house looks just like I remember it did when we first moved in over 13 years ago, though somewhat worn and faded in parts. Despite how hard I try to will the memories away, I can still picture those first few years we spent here.

When we first moved in, I was the only kid, and it seemed as though that was how it would stay. Just the three of us: me, Mom and Dad, in this little, green-shingled home with the white shutters and the white birch trees. The backyard was my kingdom, and my dad built a tree house as my castle. He'd call me 'sport' and would teach me how to throw a football and tousled my hair when I made a good pass. I ruled on high for three years. Then Brenton came along, a little bit of an accident, and he wasn't interested in bugs and dirt and sports like me and Dad. We didn't understand him, so we kept doing our thing together in the backyard, hoping he'd come and join us one day. Mom insisted that she couldn't be alone in a house full of boys, so Britney came next, much to Dad's chagrin. Mom wanted everything to be perfect for her little girl. She had her name picked out, and she was buying dresses and pink blankets. Dad had to build a new addition on one side of the house just to accommodate the little girl who would need her own room and privacy. Then, she came home, and she was anything but Daddy's little girl.

I remember how my sister would cry every night that first month she was home. Dad couldn't even pick her up. She'd cry and scream all night, and my mom couldn't figure out why, let alone stop her.

Sometimes I think Britney was the straw that broke my dad's back.

My moment of darkness is immediately brightened by the glare of headlights. The screeching wheels of an oncoming car that almost missed the turn onto my road shatters through my thoughts. I have a hard time seeing, but the queasiness in my stomach tells me it's Cherie and her hangers-on in their fancy limo.

I watch the car roll to a dramatic stop at the tip of the driveway. The blistering February cold forces me to shove my hands deep into my coat pockets and shrug my shoulders up to my ears. No matter how glacial my skin feels, I can't tear my eyes away from the windshield. I smell trouble.

The driver hops out and runs around to the doors at the limo's rear. A lot of cackling laughter and smoke billow out of the backseat, and the driver reaches in like he has to drag something out. I get a creeping feeling that the something he's trying to pull out is Cherie.

Sure enough, as the driver backs up, I see one tiny, impossibly long heel poke out and wobble as it touches the ground. I step onto the lawn, hoping to make it inside before I'm spotted, watching the scene from the corner of my eye. A stout man emerges from the other back door and runs around to Cherie and the driver, as if he has to help in some way. I recognize her new helper from the funeral; it's Cherie's manager—Carson? Carter? I don't remember his name. Fortunately, he doesn't seem to notice I'm there, so I spy some more, undetected.

Cherie flops out of the car, practically unconscious. Her eyes are closed, her makeup smeared down her cheeks like she's been crying, and she looks like she's little more than a marionette as they try to manipulate her body forward. She's the very definition of a hot mess.

"C'mon, Cher, we're home! Just a few more steps and you can go to sleep, okay?" Mr. Manager says in an ugly, gruff old man voice.

It's almost comical as he urges her forward, her arm draped behind his neck. She laughs a little and says, "Carl, you're not very good at this." Her impossibly short dress rides up a little and threatens to show too much.

"Yeah, well, you're not very good at handling a few drinks, little lady," he scolds. That's when I've heard enough and turn away, hoping I'm an inconspicuous shadow.

"Oh, hey Jack!" *Crap*. "Jack, right? Hey there, gimme a hand, would ya?"

I press my lips together and turn around. Carl and the driver help Cherie stumble toward me, and she practically collapses. Instinctively, I reach out and catch her.

"Good reflexes, kid! C'mon, sweetheart. Up, up… there we go!" He rights her, but he leaves her in my grip. The driver hurries back to the warmth of his car.

"Jack!" she shouts out as if we're best friends. She slaps her hands against my chest and gasps, "Jack, I had the best night!" She smells like smoke and liquor, and she's beautifully wrecked. The tiniest of voices invades my psyche, echoing the words of one of her pessimistic aunts in the days following her parents' deaths.

"She'll probably end up on the path of some addict or get arrested or worse..."

I'm so confused that I can barely make a sentence. "What—why...?" I look down at her, and then I glare up at Carl, speechless.

"Thanks, bud, can you get her inside? I don't wanna wake your parents," he says breathlessly. He then has the nerve to roll his eyes and shake his head, as if this is not his problem. I want to shout at him, but my mother instilled stupid manners in me, and I hesitate.

Cherie backs away from me, pulling down the hem of her dress, and slurs, "I can do it myself, Caaarl!" She opens her eyes to look at me and then squints like I disgust her. "I don't need *your* help with ANYTHING."

What the hell? Now she's pissed at me again?

I don't have a chance to snap back; instead I'm jumping forward to catch her before she tips backward onto the icy sidewalk. She almost takes me down, too, but I drag her onto the snow.

"Ah!" she cries. The slush surrounds her feet, slipping into the sides of her shoes. "It's cold! Help!"

"Shh! You're gonna wake everyone up!" I hiss. "Carl, wait!"

But he's already gone, climbing back into his smoky limo and shouting at the driver something about stopping at the Regency. The car door slams closed behind him.

"Jack, move!"

"Okay, okay, be quiet!" I guide her out of the snow and back onto the walk, toward a drier patch. She is clumsy and noisy, the worst combination. Every step she takes is a wobble or a slip, and she screeches then giggles each time.

"You have got to get better shoes," I mutter as she tips toward the front porch, her stilettos making scraping sounds along the sidewalk. She is dragging her feet, and the heels get stuck on almost every crack or bump in the walk. Inevitably, she trips, and it's a two-hand job just to keep her moving up the walkway to the front door. I try to be careful about where I put my hands, afraid to touch her or grab her in a way that's going to get me labeled as a molester.

"Jaaaack," she groans, slumping against me as I try to dig my keys out of my pocket. "I still don't like you," she grumbles. I'm tempted to step aside so that she can fall.

"Yeah, well, you're not my favorite person right now either," I huff.

"Jerk." I grimace, but I don't need to move for her to fall; suddenly, she's sliding down the length of my leg to the welcome mat.

"Cherie? Cherie!" I whisper as she hits the ground.

"I just wanna sit here for a minute," she mumbles incoherently.

"Huh? Cherie, you can't sit there. Cherie?" I nudge her with my foot, then reach down and grab her arm. She jerks it out of my hold and lets her head droop forward heavily. "Cherie, it's cold on the ground. Get up." I feel like I'm dealing with Britney.

"Leemee alone, Jack," she whines. "I'm just gonna sit here a lil' while."

"Cherie, it's cold. You gotta come inside," I say in my gentlest tone. I'm getting frustrated though, and I'm cold, too. I'm standing out here on the porch like an idiot trying to talk sense into someone who openly hates me. What is wrong with me?

"Cherie?" She doesn't respond. "Cherie, did you pass out? Cherie?"

She gives me the slightest shake of her head and the back of her head bops up as she takes a deep breath. "I'll come in inna minute."

I curse under my breath. What the hell am I going to do now? I drag my keys out from my pocket and unlock the door, nudging it open with my foot. Then, I squat down and sweep one arm under her knees and the other behind her back.

"Hold on," I murmur futilely, and I lift her dead weight with all the strength I have. She is limp in my arms, but she's surprisingly easy to carry, and I catch myself feeling almost thankful that she's been wasting away for the last few weeks.

I sidestep into the house, fitting her neatly through the doorway. I push the door closed behind us and step lightly through the house, navigating down the hall in the dark. I look to the couch, knowing I could just drop her there and let her face the consequences in the morning. Jim should find her like this and know what she really does with her Hollywood entourage. My conscience nags me to not be so cruel, and I begin maneuvering around the breakfast table in the kitchen as I make my way to her quarters in the basement. She looks like a corpse, stone-faced with her head tipped back.

I flick the light switch upward, and a yellow glow floods the basement. The stairs prove to be trickier as I can't really tell if my foot is on each step before moving down. It's a narrow area, too, and she just barely fits between the bannister and the adjacent wall. Her body begins to feel heavy. I panic that I'm going to miss a step and go crashing down to the floor or smash her head against the wall. I want to congratulate myself when I get on solid ground again, but then there are all of the boxes to contend with, strewn and stacked about the room like pieces in a game of chess. Her bed is barely visible in the distance, but it's still there, well made and in one piece. Why was mine all packed up and ready to go two days ago?

'Cause she's a damn princess. Isn't that why you're carrying her around, stupid? I grumble in my head. I careen around the boxes, her weight getting heavier as my arms grow tired. By the time I'm at her bedside, my shoulders are burning. I'm desperate to release her. I set her down as carefully as my tired muscles will allow and double over, trying to catch my breath. I stretch and twist my arms to relieve them of the ache.

Cherie is motionless, and I can only tell she is breathing by the slight rise and fall of her chest. She looks peaceful. She almost looks nice. I unfold a blanket from the end of the bed and drape it over her.

I find myself wishing I'd had the chance to get closer to her. Memories of the first few days she spent with us sweep through my mind, and I picture her, sad and fragile, gripping my arm, burying her face in my chest, relying on me. She would always hold her emotions together in a vise-like grip for the public, and then she'd crumble whenever we were alone. I hated to hear her cry, but I sort of miss her needing me like that. I miss her trusting me.

I turn her onto her side in case she gets sick in her sleep, and she curls her fingers around mine, grasping my hand. Electricity zips through my arm. When I try to pull away, she stirs, and her eyebrows come together.

"Stay," she moans into the pillow.

"Cherie, I gotta go upstairs," I say softly. I shake my hand a little bit to loosen her grip, but she is holding on tighter than I'm fighting to get free. "Cherie?"

"Stay with me, just a little," she slurs. I wonder if she even knows who I am or where she is.

"Cherie, I can't stay, I gotta go to my room. C'mon, you'll be okay. You just gotta sleep it off." She shakes her head quickly once, then again, and tightens her hand around one of my fingers. She plants her face beside my knuckles.

"Shh, please just stay," she whispers, her lips brushing against my fingers as she speaks. Her warm breath caresses my skin. I get a chill that rocks from my hand to my spine and down to my groin.

Checkmate. I close my eyes and obediently lower to my knees beside the bed.

I can wait a few minutes until she's really asleep. It's the least I can do.

PART 2

DIRTERAZZI.COM

UNDERAGE CHERIE BELLE SPOTTED IN HOLLYWOOD NIGHTCLUBS

Just when you thought you couldn't get enough of Cherie Belle, she has done all of us the honor of spreading herself around town. In what one could only describe as the biggest "I told you so" moment in Dirterazzi history, Cherie has taken to the nightclub circuit to drink, er, dance her worries away with her favorite Kidz Channel buddies.

There is no shortage of eye candy when a herd of Kidz Channel alum walk into a room, but Cherie steals the show with her voracious appetite for shots—um, we mean short dresses—and pole dancing—we mean partying. The underage star is taking Hollywood nightlife by storm as she flaunts her way into the clubs, gives onlookers a show, and then stumbles into someone's care at the end of the night. No one knows if her guardians are completely aware of her hijinks, but someone ought to tell them before Cherie gets in serious trouble with the law.

Just kidding! This is Hollywood! Carry on, Princess Cherie.

Chapter 16

Brenton and I reach the new house first, and I let him tap in the code that opens the massive wrought iron gate. He was permitted to ride the last leg of the trip with me because Mom was convinced he felt better. I don't know if I'm completely convinced, though, since he spent half the ride sniffling and sneezing and sleeping, but I preferred anything to riding with Claudia and her annoying boy band music.

I get out of the car and look up at the big, beautiful beige home that towers over me and stare in wonder.

"C'mon, Jack!" he yells impatiently.

"Okay, okay. Relax." I unpack the trunk, and he races forward with my set of keys to unlock the door.

When we step into the house, he whistles low and looks up at the high ceiling of the main foyer. There are two winding staircases leading to two different wings of the house on opposite sides of the entrance. We step forward hesitantly on the marble tile, like it will break under our feet.

"I take it you approve of your new home?" I laugh, but even I can't ignore how overwhelming the mere size of our new residence is, let alone the intricacies of the carved columns and expensive furnishings. In the past month, Jim flew back and forth to get the house ready for us, and each time he returned home, he would gush about something new. Still, I had never expected it to be this massive or beautiful.

Brenton echoes my own thoughts. "This isn't a house, Jack. It's a palace!" Of course he's thrilled to pieces. He's a ten-year-old who lives with his favorite celebrity of all time and gets to call this mansion his home. There's even a giant in-ground pool in the backyard. What's not to love?

Behind us, I hear the RV rumble into the driveway, and a chorus of screams, commands, and giggles erupt from the brood inside. Chloe, Claudia, and Britney pound past us in a flurry of pink and white, the scent of suntan lotion and vanilla wafting behind them.

"Oh. My. God!" Claudia gasps.

"I call biggest room!" Chloe shouts.

"Oh, no you don't!" Brenton growls, chasing after them as they race upstairs. I save my breath and let him go; he'll figure out eventually that Jim came out a few weeks ago to designate and prepare rooms for all of us.

Speaking of which...

"So, where do I go?" I ask softly, remembering the three suitcases in my hands. I don't meet my mother's gaze.

She forces a smile. "Don't you want to take a look around?" she says.

"There's a big pool in the back," Jim adds, emptying his arms of the baggage that the girls left behind.

"I saw. I'm good." I take in as much of the main rooms of the house as I can from this spot. There is a giant kitchen and a huge island in its center. The living room has high ceilings, too, and windows that stretch from the top to the bottom of one wall. I can't see it completely from where I'm standing, but that room has a stone fireplace and a giant TV mounted over it. I instantly picture spending football season planted in that room, unless my mom will finally let me have my own TV in my room.

"So, upstairs?" I add hopefully, "Basement...?"

My mom has *that* look; it's a smile she's trying to hold in but really can't because she's too excited. "Well, Jack, when Jim came out here for some interviews in

January, he took a good look at the house and planned it out for the family. We both thought a lot about what you said when we first mentioned we were moving, and you're right, you've had to deal with a lot of change really fast."

"I can remember being your age, buddy," Jim says, clapping a hand on my shoulder as he walks past me. "There are a lot of young people in this house, but you're the oldest, and the oldest boy. There's about 7 years separating you and Brenton. Heck, you're practically a man. We have a little less than two years before you're off to college."

I'm getting nervous. Are they kicking me out? Do they have boarding school plans for me?

"We know you need your own space," Mom continues. I watch Jim walk toward the kitchen.

"Follow me, Jack. We have a surprise for you." I'm moving in slow motion. I think I know what they're getting at, but I'm trying not to get my hopes up.

"We know you're a good kid, Jack, and we really feel like we can trust you," Jim is saying as he leads me to a set of doors in the kitchen. The doors are all glass. They lead to the pool, which truly is immense. I look around the backyard as Jim urges me outside.

"Man this place is fancy," I murmur to no one in particular. It even has a pool house.

Wait...

"What's that?"

Jim's smile grows large and bright. "That, Jack, is a casita. It's kind of a like an apartment, or a guest house. And we set it aside just for you." He winks at me.

I'm in shock. "Huh?"

Mom is beaming, too. She takes my hand and pulls me toward the casita. "This will be your new room. It's a space you can really call all your own. You have a bathroom, a small living area, and Jim spared no expense making sure you have all of the, uh, amenities, so to speak, that you would want."

He rattles them off like a car salesman. "Sixty-inch TV, wireless sound system, leather sectional—the works," Jim adds triumphantly. He takes a key from his pocket, unlocks the door, and sweeps his hand forward as if to encourage a king to cross a threshold. My eyes can barely take in all of the completely awesome things I see at once. I know he wants desperately to earn my favor and has been unsuccessful for the past year, but I think this move definitely catapulted him from 2 to a 7 on my rating scale.

The casita is huge—the bathroom is the size of my old bedroom. I have a giant tub *and* a shower. The TV takes up a generous portion of one wall, and he managed to hook up two of my video game consoles already. Around the room, I see small, in-wall speakers. The room is light blue, and there are windows everywhere. There's even a wet bar, which Jim humorously stocked with sodas and Gatorades. It's not simply a guest house. It's an elaborate, five-star hotel suite.

"This is mine?" I can barely squeak out. Jim and Mom nod. I want to hug them. I want to strip off my clothes, hoot like a tribal warrior and do a back flip into the pool. I resolve myself to stand stoically still and simply nod, but I can't hold back the grin that's spreading across my face.

Jim places the key into my palm. "Now, of course you know this comes with rules. No guests after eleven, and no one in here we don't know about, period. Keep it clean; the usual. When you're out here, you're *in here* and not *out there*." He points over the stone walls that guard the property. "Same curfew rules as home: come back by midnight on weekends, ten on school nights."

"Absolutely," I murmur, unable to take my eyes off of the amazing space. Suddenly, my heart drops. "Wait—what about Britney?"

My mom looks down. "Well, Jack, Jim and I have been thinking about that, too. We think it's time we have her stay in her own bed. We'll need your help with that one. She's not to come out here or leave her room at night anymore. You need your privacy, and you need your sleep, and she needs hers."

"But how are you going to stop her?" I ask, looking at the pool, my newfound enemy. "I don't even hear her when she comes in sometimes. What if...?"

Jim, ever the tech-geek, says, "We're putting motion detectors in her room, which will wake us up if she gets out of bed. She won't get to the stairs without one of us getting to her first."

This new twist both excites and unsettles me. I don't know if I'm ready for Britney to grow up. I kind of liked being her hero, her security blanket, even if she did occasionally get in my way.

Outside, I can see the twins, Brenton, and Britney making their way out to the pool as a noisy, wild unit. My mom shouts at them that they need to unpack before going swimming. Someone yells back, "Cannonball!"

I look around at my new sanctuary and clutch the key tightly in my hand. This could work out.

***

I've forgotten about Cherie completely until she materializes in my doorway while I am unpacking. I turn and nearly jump in surprise. She is wearing a little yellow sun dress and oversized sunglasses that swallow most of her petite face.

"Oh hey," I say with a grunt as I unfold my legs and stand up. The truck with our furniture has not arrived yet, so I spent the past three hours on the floor sorting through the clothes in my luggage and putting them into the new dresser at the front of my room. The floor is still a bit of a mess, so I have to climb over boxes and piles to get closer to her.

I grab the sound system's remote and fumble with it, trying to find the right buttons to turn down the music. Cherie is still standing in the same spot, motionless, and staring at me. I can tell by the hard line her mouth makes that she is unhappy.

"I was just unpacking a little; do you need something?" I ask quickly, trying to fill the silence. I shift uncomfortably. I don't like to be stared at.

"This should have been my room," she says icily. I'm caught off guard and don't know what to say. She steps forward over some of my mess and tips her glasses down on the bridge of her nose to meet my wide eyes. Her stare is emerald green and mean.

"Huh?" I manage to utter. Even angry, she's pretty; like makes-me-forget-what-I-should-say pretty.

"Take your stuff, and—" she takes a manicured, slender finger and pokes my sternum with the tip of a hot pink nail "—go."

"Ow!" It actually hurts, and I wince, stepping backward.

This makes her smirk. "What a baby. You need to be upstairs with the rest of the Jungle Gym Nation, not me."

I feel my eyebrows knit together. "What is your problem?"

"YOU ARE!" She's practically barking at me. "Uncle Jim gave you the only corner of solitude in this whole damn house—*my house*!—to appease you. No one took into consideration how I would feel having to live with a bunch of strangers around me!"

"Yeah, take a number," I mutter, folding my arms across my chest.

Her mouth twists in confusion. "What's that supposed to mean?"

"I'm not here by choice either, Cherie," I remind her.

She rolls her eyes. "Not my problem," she snorts, echoing my harsh comments over one month ago.

I hold my head high defiantly. "Whatever. I'm staying in this room, and you can figure out how to deal with it until I go away to college."

I turn around to resume my unpacking. She shoves me hard from behind, and I stumble forward. I catch myself on the corner of the dresser before I fall.

"Hey!" I spin around, but she's yelling at me before I have a chance to say more.

I'm dumbfounded, backed into a corner of my own room as she continues jabbing her finger into my chest. She's half my size but twice as scary. "Don't turn your back on me when I'm talking to you! Who do you think you are?"

I hold my hands out against her shoulders to keep distance between my chest and her pokey finger. "You need to relax—this is ridiculous!"

"Don't touch me!" she hisses, slapping at my hands. "You threw your temper tantrum back in New York and got *your* way, so now I'm gonna throw *mine*!"

I feel like I am trapped in Crazytown. "*Got my way*? What're you talking about?"

"This!" she shouts, gesturing to the room. "Take your stupid stuff and go upstairs to my old room. You can even have the stupid TV. Just get out! I deserve this space! This is my house!"

"No way," I guffaw. "In case you forgot, I didn't want to move into *your house* to begin with. You can throw as many tantrums as you want, but I'm not giving up this room." I flinch again when her hands ball into fists at her sides.

"Well, I'm not living in that animal house with your loony family!"

Now I'm offended. She's lumping my mom, sister and brother in with her crazy cousins and uncle. My own hands ball at my sides instinctively.

"Watch it."

Her eyes are cruel, but her words are worse. "No, you watch it, Jack. If I were you, I'd cede this place to me now, because otherwise you're going to wish you never stepped foot in it."

I don't even know what to say. I'm actually a little threatened, and very confused. Am I not being fair by keeping this room for myself? Am I supposed to do this for her since she's been through a lot? I'd heard that grief makes people do and say crazy things, but this is sheer insanity!

"You don't know what you're saying," I conclude finally, and I return her stony expression with an equally hard stare. Looking into her eyes this way makes my blood boil for a dozen different reasons, but the most prominent is how much I can't ignore how hot she looks when her eyes squint and the red flush of anger fills her cheeks.

Finally, she takes a step back. "Okay then, Jack Hansen. It was nice knowing you." As she begins to turn away from me, I see the glimmer of a vengeful smile on her lips, and I know I'm in for it big time.

***

Mom calls us to dinner at six o'clock, sharp. She's prepared pasta for dinner, and we each grab a plate and get on line. It's just my mom's same old cooking, but it looks like a catered event in this elaborate kitchen on someone else's fancy dishes. There's a platter of pasta, a big bowl of salad, breadsticks, and brownies. I feel like I'm in the cafeteria, only I can reach over everyone's heads and take what I want without having to wait. This causes some complaints and elbowing, but nothing will stop me from getting back to my mini-castle. I eat as I serve myself, starving from the move and all of the unpacking I've completed.

Cherie hovers over a plate of salad at the end of the kitchen's island, but she doesn't seem to be eating. She pushes lettuce back and forth. A cherry tomato rolls along the end edge of her plate. She glowers at us, visibly disgusted by our typical dinner routine. I realize this is the first time she's joining us for dinner and never observed the chaos that goes into feeding seven people.

Trust me, Cherie, we'd all like to be only children, I think bitterly, cramming more ziti into my mouth before I swallow the first bit.

"It's good tonight, Mom," I say. I reach over Brenton's head and snag a Coke from a collection of unopened soda cans.

"Gee, that's nice to say," Chloe replies sarcastically from behind me. "And please don't talk with your mouth full; it's gross."

I turn and chew in her face while saying, "Sorry if I offended you, Chloe."

"Jack, stop," Claudia groans.

"I'm gonna eat in my room anyway," I call out over the din, quickly heading for the door.

Mom looks up at this, and she's all scowls. "Jack..." she says in *that* tone, the one that warns me to make a better choice.

"The Knicks are tied!" I tell her indignantly, and that one reason alone should absolve me from the mandatory family dinner. But I know I have to make a better case. "Besides, I got a lot of unpacking done—I'm in the zone!"

Jim looks up from his plate of food and cocks an eyebrow at me. He's never been one for basketball, so I know he doesn't get my need to see the game, but he can appreciate my play at my mom's weak spot: accomplished chores. I see a hint of humor in his forced stern gaze. I shrug, wink, and continue to push the sliding glass door open.

"I'll come back when it's over, promise!" Before either of them can argue, I rush back to my sanctuary. Before I can close the casita's door, I hear Cherie's shrill voice complain:

"Well, if he doesn't have to stay—"

DIRTERAZZI.COM

MISERY LOVES COMPANY: CHERIE BELLE MOVES BACK TO LA PAD WITH NEW GUARDIANS AND JACK HANSEN...DID SOMEONE SAY AWKWARD?!

It's official: the moving trucks rolled into Cherie Belle's driveway this afternoon, as did the Goldman family and, you guessed it... Jack Hansen! Hansen was the first to arrive to the swanky 10-bedroom mansion Cherie's parents purchased back in 2009. Cherie was out for the day with some friends as her new family unloaded their things in her home. Sources close to the situation tell us tensions are high, especially now that Jack and Cherie will be around each other more often.

"They're still not speaking to one another," our anonymous source tells us. "She has bigger things to worry about, and he's not worth her time."

Maybe so, but he's worth someone's time: 216,042 someones to be exact, which is the number of members belonging to the newborn site, WeLoveJackHansen.com. Veronica Page, the site's owner, tells us, "We earn almost ten new members a day. The people love him; in fact, a lot of the members think Jack can do better than Cherie. They feel she's too shallow for him." The site has a complete bio on Jack, as well as pictures gleaned from the numerous internet reports about him and Cherie over the past two months. When asked why she started the site, 29-year=old Veronica says, "I'm a sucker for the underdog, and he's a total underdog. He's gotta compete for a celebrity like Cherie with a guy like Caz Farrell— that's tough! They're young, they clearly like each other, but the odds are stacked against Jack, so I thought he needed a cheering section." Veronica likes the idea of a Belle-Hansen relationship. "I, personally, am rooting for Jack and Cherie to be together. I think Jack is just what

Cherie needs right now; he's a good kid and a normal boy who could help her have a normal life. It's the situation that's tearing them apart, and it's just sad; they're a tragic couple who aren't supposed to be in love, like a real life Romeo and Juliet."

It isn't clear if our Romeo is aware of the site or his popularity with the ladies yet, but one thing is certain: his Juliet is not one of the site's members. Stay tuned...

Chapter 17

It almost feels like a giant fist plunged through my chest and clamped down on my lungs. My voice coughs from my throat, the air frozen in my esophagus as I stare forward, horrified.

"No—"

I had only wanted to retrieve my iPod. I was committed to staying in my room and avoiding any further run-ins with any of the girls, particularly Cherie. It was never my intention to get into a fight tonight.

Instead, I gawk at my egg-yolk covered car and feel my veins throbbing with an impending murder spree.

"Are you kidding me?!" I finally shout. My car—my beautiful car—soiled with the grossest, slimiest substance in the world. The sight alone makes me wretch, not to mention the smell.

I can only think of three possible, logical culprits: Claudia, Chloe, and my newest nemesis, Cherie.

"Which one of you did it?" I bellow, storming through the front door of the house. My strides eat the ground beneath my feet as I soar toward the stairs.

"Jack?" Mom calls from the kitchen. "What's wrong, honey?"

I'm so angry that my voice rumbles through the house like thunder. "My car! They egged my car; there's yolk all over the hood—whoever did it is *dead*!"

Mom's nose scrunches. "What? I'm not following, dear."

"Go look!" I command, pointing to the front door. "Someone trashed my whole car with eggs! It's one of the girls—or all of them. You've got to do something, now! Or I will."

Jim appears in the foyer, his hands resting on his waist, looking me over like I've gone nuts. "What happened?"

I grind my answer out between my teeth, "Your niece happened. My car's covered in eggs!"

Neither of them seems to believe me. "Let me see," Jim says, and he follows me out to the driveway. He pauses in mid-step when he sees my beautiful, black coupe polka dotted with white egg shells and dripping with slimy yellow yolk.

His first question doesn't surprise me. "How do you know this was Cherie?"

"Really?" I ask, folding my arms over my chest and pitying his uselessness as a father and as an intelligent adult. "If it wasn't her, it was your daughters."

"Well, I know you're convinced it's one of the girls, Jack, but I wouldn't be surprised if it's just some crazy fan of Cherie's or some of those paparazzi folk."

Paparazzi folk. I'm reasoning with someone who calls them "paparazzi folk." I hang my head and rub my eyes with my hand to avoid grabbing the man and shaking sense into him.

"I guess we can check the video surveillance cameras," he says suddenly, and I look up.

"Huh?"

"The property has a pretty good security system of cameras. I haven't really tinkered much with them yet, but we can do it together if it will help us get to the bottom of this," he says with a smirk. I want to punch the smirk off of his face.

But I'm willing to do anything to catch one of those rats in the act. After her threats this afternoon, I can't think of a guiltier party than Cherie.

"Fine. Let's go," I reply.

Jim leads me to his study, which used to be his brother's study, based on the nameplate on the desk. One wall is covered with full, oak book shelves that span from the floor to the ceiling. The other walls are garnished with family photos, awards and trophies belonging to Cherie, and her parents' college degrees.

"Let's see here." Jim turns a giant computer monitor on an angle and double clicks on a small icon in the bottom left corner of the screen. I lean down and peer over his shoulder.

The screen instantly divides into 8 squares, each displaying a corner of the massive property. I can see the heads of some neighbors walking past the front gate, the entire pool area in the back, the garage, the driveway, and two gardened portions on the sides of the house. I marvel at this little piece of technology and exchange awed glances with Jim.

"Pretty cool, huh?" he says. I nod, and I watch him nimbly type and click his way into the main controls of the videos. He manipulates the square showing the driveway and makes it rewind, but he goes back to two days ago.

"Too far," he mutters, adjusting the playback over and over as he skips forward and back in time. I'm growing impatient, already past the fascination with the cameras and refocused on the witch hunt for my car's vandal.

"Well, this is just a few hours ago," he murmurs. My eyes flicker around the screen, hopeful for a glimpse of something. Wouldn't it be my luck that my car is just beyond the periphery of the camera's point of view? I can see my front bumper and that's it.

"Ugh. Of course," I groan.

"Hold on, let's watch and see if anyone walks by," he suggests. He speeds up the video, and I watch intently, hoping for a glimpse of something viable. The only thing we see is a dark shadow that flickers past the screen like a ghost in a horror movie.

"What the—come on!"

"Look," Jim sighs, defeated. "It's not that I don't believe you, okay? I will talk to them about this, but you and I both know they're going to deny it. I can't punish them for something I can't prove, especially when there are a lot of sick people out there who would do this out of anger or jealousy toward you."

I stare at him. "Huh? Me? Like who?"

He cocks an eyebrow at me. "Well, people who don't like Cherie would do this, but it's more likely people who do like her and are mad at you because they think you're her boyfriend."

My chest tightens instantly. "How do you know about that?" I demand, feeling the back of my neck burn.

Jim shrugs. "I see the news and the magazines in the stores, Jack. It's impossible to ignore. I just ask that you keep things like that in mind before you blame the girls for crazy things like this. I know they like to tease you, but I don't think they'd go as far as to throw eggs at your car."

"You don't know Cherie that well," I mutter under my breath, still unwilling to believe that some nutty stalker is so obsessed with Cherie that he or she would take it out on *my* innocent car.

His mouth twists to the side. "I know this whole thing has been rough on you, kiddo. It can't be fun to have your name in the papers and stuff, and then things like this happen and you don't know who is to blame. The other day, I found a stuffed animal covered in red paint in the mailbox with some death threat attached to it, addressed to Cherie."

"What? That's nuts!" I shake my head at the gruesome picture in my mind. "Did you call the cops?"

"Of course, but it's not the first time I've received something like that unfortunately," he sighs. "And the cops, they'll investigate and find some sicko who hates that she wears fur. So, you see, it's possible the girls didn't do this. Just try to take it all in stride, okay? It was probably some nutcase with a crush on her. How they got the eggs over the gate, I'm not sure... but I'll look into that in the morning..."

He squints up at my doubting frown. "Can we squash it for now at least?"

I purse my lips and nod. "Yeah."

He claps a hand on my shoulder as he stands and says, "C'mon, I'll help you clean the car off."

Chapter 18

I can't pretend it doesn't give me just the slightest bit of satisfaction that it's raining today and the twins can't go to Venice Beach, a venture they desperately wanted and begged Jim to do. It took their father and me two hours to clean the eggs off of my car, eggs I'm still convinced those girls are responsible for. Last night, as I was picking shells off the middle of its roof, I realized I was conveniently parked below Chloe's bedroom window. If my car was a dartboard, my roof was practically her bullseye.

So this morning, when I glanced out my window and was met by gray skies and fog, I actually laughed out loud. It wasn't the type of Karma I really wanted them to encounter, but it was good enough for now. Unfortunately, I had no one to share the perfect moment with.

That's when I realized I had slept alone for the first time in years. Britney wasn't there to jump on me or force me to cater to her whims or whimper that she needed me to follow her to the bathroom because she was scared. Mom wasn't coming in to remove her from my bed and get her ready for breakfast or school. She and Jim actually kept their promise and made Britney stay inside.

Oddly, I was kind of bummed.

When I first settled in to go to sleep, I tossed and turned for a good hour. I checked the door, opened it and closed it, just to make sure Britney wasn't wandering around the pool in the dark. I put the TV back on and watched highlights from the Knicks game on ESPN for a little. It must have been almost two o'clock in the morning before I finally fell asleep.

The silence in the room is deafening. There are no arguments or shrieks of discontent outside my door. My mother's big band music and Jim's NPR blah-blahing radio can't be heard for miles. Brenton isn't asking me to play with him.

I could get used to this. I immediately put the TV on and hang out in bed, because what else is there to do on a crappy day during winter recess? It isn't like I have to be at school yet.

School. Just the thought of the word gives me a chill. Mom and I are going in extra early next Monday to get me registered for my classes. I'm consumed by the realization that I don't know this building, I don't know these teachers, and I certainly don't have any friends there. I will be on my own, except for the twins, who are definitely going to drop me like a bad habit the second some tool says hello to them.

I turn over and reach for my cellphone to flip through pictures. The first few pictures are from my going away party. I linger over one of Josh and Frank performing a keg stand, smiling at the memory. I forward it to them along with the message, "Thanks a lot for the party."

When they don't respond immediately, I'm sort of confused. Usually, I'm the one who is slow to text responses. I send them a few pictures of my new room and tell them about all the cool things Jim put in it. No response. I wait and wait, watching for their replies, but then I remember that California is three hours behind New York time. School also started for them this week. Mom planned our trip out perfectly so I wouldn't have to miss a day of classes in either state. *Thanks, Mom.*

The thought of my mom gets my stomach growling, which encourages me out of bed. I brush my teeth and, for the first time in a long time, take my time in the bathroom. When I am finally ready to leave the casita, I find a folded note on the floor just beneath my door. I scan it quickly.

Jack—Went shopping. Be back by 3. Please finish unpacking.

"Sure thing," I mutter to myself. I look out at the house. Does that mean the girls went with them? Is it possible I can explore the castle freely? I decide to take my chances and cross from the patio to the kitchen door. When I slide the door open, I poke my head inside and listen. Nothing.

"There is a god," I whisper. I close the door behind me and immediately raid the fridge. I glower at a near empty carton of eggs. Below them, there are a few pieces of string cheese and some apples, so I grab one of each for my journey and begin to explore.

I wander around the quiet house, strolling through the long halls and staring up at the high ceilings. Along the walls, Mark and Camille have placed a gallery of expensive-looking paintings and family portraits. Often, they are pictures of Cherie. Sometimes they are stills of her in her TV show, and sometimes they are regular kid pictures made to look fancy on large canvases. Despite how much I don't like her right now, I can't ignore how gorgeous she is when she smiles. I haven't seen her smile since the night she came home wasted with Carl, which seems like years ago now.

She never even thanked me for taking care of her drunk ass that night, I think bitterly. She passed out on me after demanding I stay, and I never had the gumption to get up and leave. I must have sat on the basement floor for hours, fading in and out of consciousness, listening to her breathe, my arm stretched out so that she could hold my one finger inside of her fist. I'm a sucker and an idiot. I was hoping I'd earn myself a one-way ticket back into her good graces that night, but no such luck. I went upstairs before she even woke up, and then somehow she was ushered out and onto a plane before I could see her. I don't even know if she is aware that I helped her. If she is, she still hates me enough that nothing I did for her even mattered.

Cherie will hold my words against me forever, and now this casita business has really cemented her distaste for me. Cherie hates me so much that I don't think there is any way we can get back to being friends again.

Shaking my head, I continue down the hallway to the elaborate staircase. I make my way up to the second floor, which is huge. The rooms are all pretty far apart from each other, and now I have no idea what Cherie is complaining about. This is more than twice the size of our home back in New York.

She has no idea what it means to not have privacy! I think bitterly.

I walk through each room, marveling at the size of each one and how every bedroom gets its own bathroom. One room is hunter green and full of Brenton's toys. The bed is well-made, complete with a brand new comforter dotted with rockets and moons. A poster of the planets hangs just above his bed, and a giant telescope faces a broad window.

"Looks like we all got an upgrade," I murmur, examining the telescope closely. It's hefty and expensive, and perfect for nerdy Brenton. I'll bet he could rattle off the model number and everything. I lean down and peer into the eyepiece. I'm not sure what I'm looking at, but I know it's something in space. I wonder if it's only a matter of time before Brenton starts using this to spy on girls in neighboring houses.

Brenton must have gone nuts when he saw this gift. I step back and shake my head, realizing we may have all received bribe gifts that would take the sting away from being uprooted.

Next to Brenton's room is a pink, frilly room designed with Britney in mind, I'm sure. I'm positive when I see the ridiculously big dollhouse in the corner. It looks custom made to match this house, as if Cherie passed down her own dollhouse to my sister.

That's all I need, I think bitterly. *A mini-Cherie.*

My old Care Bear is sitting merrily atop the watermelon-colored bed and snuggled against more pillows than any one child should need. On her white dresser is something that looks like a walkie talkie. I can only conclude that this baby monitor contraption must be Jim and Mom's big plan to keep Britney trapped in her pink prison.

"Good luck with that," I scoff, turning the monitor over in my hand.

Much farther down the hall are two rooms, side by side, covered in clothes and half-hung posters and smelling familiar of sugary perfumes and flowery body lotions. I shudder and keep moving, not even curious enough to look inside of the twins' rooms to see what lavish presents Jim and Mom gave to them. Much to my delight, I find Jim and Mom are taking up residence in the bedroom across the hall from the twins. Jim must be prepared to keep a close eye on his menacing daughters. I can't help but laugh.

There is one set of double doors at the end of this hallway, and they are closed. I'm intrigued. I try the left knob and find it unlocked. Quietly, I push the door open and peer inside.

The room is immense, with plush carpeting the color of sand and a huge fireplace surrounded by big, beige armchairs. It smells of wealth; a heavy cologne of potpourri and leather hangs in the air and envelopes me. There are large vases of silk flowers that look real, not like the cheap stuff my mom used to decorate our old house in. The bed is gigantic, bigger than anything I've ever seen, with an intricately carved wooden headboard. The comforter looks like it's made of gold silk. I turn to check out the bathroom, but quickly stop in my tracks.

A large, framed wedding portrait of Mark and Camille punches me in the ribs and quickly turns this room of opulence into a ghastly mausoleum.

Staring at their smiling, loving faces as they get lost in each other's eyes, I retreat backward and into the hallway. I close the door quickly behind me with a click that resounds through the empty, expansive house.

I turn on my heel to head back toward the stairs and lock in place, my bones nearly jumping out of my skin. I almost cry out from the shock. Cherie has appeared soundlessly on the other end of the hallway, posed in a no-nonsense stance with her hands balled into fists at her sides.

There she is, standing in the doorway of the farthest room, staring at me. No, glaring at me. It's like coming face to face with a ghost that's always been haunting you but you never saw before. And now it wants to kill you.

"H-Hi," I stammer, trying to calm my nerves. She doesn't reply, her big eyes boring into mine, looking through me, hating me. I try to pretend I wasn't just snooping around her dead parents' bedroom. I want to tell her I got lost, that I would never have gone in that room if I had known, but all that comes out is, "Is, uh, is anyone else home?"

She shakes her head ever so slightly.

I step forward. "Do you know when they'll be back?"

"Get out," she growls.

I feel my eyes widen. I'll never be as obedient in my life as I am in this moment. I lower my head like a scolded child and hurry down the steps and out of the house, back to the safety of my casita.

Chapter 19

When I open my eyes the next day, the first thing I can think is, *What hit me?*

There's a gentle knock at my door. I look up and find the alarm clock. It's nearly noon. My body is achy and hot and my eyelids will barely lift. I'm hung over without the awesome drunken memories of a wild party to go with it. Maybe it's from helping Jim unpack all those suitcases the other day.

Or maybe Cherie poisoned the dinner plate my mom left in the fridge for me last night. After how Cherie looked at me yesterday, I wouldn't put anything past her. I had been so nervous about running into her again that I didn't even go inside when Mom called me in for dinner. Instead, I snuck in once everyone was asleep to eat out of the fridge like a scavenger.

I crawl out of bed to the sing-song sound of my mother's voice.

"Jack? Jack, honey, are you up yet?" I stumble to the door and pull it open. The bright sunlight makes me squeeze my eyes shut. Heat from outside hits me like a warm blanket, washing over my limbs and suffocating me. Now I feel worse.

Yep, definitely poisoned. Cherie's trying to kill me.

"What?" I say when I'm finally able to peer out at her from behind my scrunched lids.

She looks harried but forces a smile for me. "Oh, good, you're up! I have to go inside and make lunch. Please come outside and watch Britney and Brenton in the pool?"

I look over her shoulder and spy two very capable teenage twins already frolicking with Brenton in the pool. Princess Cherie is sunbathing just feet from Britney.

"Seriously?" I'm about to slam the door closed on her. She holds her hand against it and turns her imploring Mom-gaze at me. For once, I'm too beat up to care. If she had a way to extract the jackhammer that's chipping away inside of my head, maybe I'd be willing to help.

"You know the girls aren't going to pay attention, Jack," she whispers conspiratorially.

"They're *in* the pool, Mom," I reply.

"Please, Jack, you have your CPR certification and, Britney, well, you know…" Her voice trails off and leaves me defenseless. Mom's biggest fear about moving here has been the easily accessible in-ground pool. To her, that's just a living nightmare, especially after Britney's near drowning episode last summer at a birthday party for Brenton. I shudder to think what would have happened if I hadn't been there. Britney easily flies under the radar around the girls, and they wouldn't notice if she decided to join their game.

"Gimme a minute," I mutter. I retreat into my room to brush my teeth and tame my hair. I grab my sunglasses and meet my mom at the door of the casita.

"Thank you, sweetheart," she coos, and she disappears into the house through the sliding doors.

I scan the property briefly. I feel dizzy and weak and want to lie down, but not near Cherie, who is smack in the middle of the small collection of cushioned pool chairs. There's a patch of grass near the edge of the pool, and I drag myself toward it.

Brenton calls me to come into the water. "Maybe later," I reply half-heartedly. He squeals with delight as Claudia lifts him and throws him into the deep end.

I drop onto my stomach in the grass and prop my chin onto my arms. The sun feels extra hot on my skin. Maybe California's sunlight is stronger than New York's. My neck and shoulders still ache, and my eyelids are just so heavy. I watch the twins and Brenton playing and splashing in the shallow end. Across from me, on the other side, Cherie looks asleep in her chair, a pair of shades covering her eyes and her head tilted back toward the sky. She is wearing what is possibly the slightest pink bikini that a girl could wear. I force myself to look away.

Britney is quietly playing in her sandbox to my right. Chloe and Claudia have their backs to her as they toss Brenton around in the water. I know it's not a good idea, but I close my eyes. *It's just for a moment*, I tell myself as I slip somewhere between awake and asleep, a dreamlike state that erases all of my aching.

In my dream, I am drifting on a cloud, gazing down at a vast ocean below. Water swishes gently in the ocean. The sun is soft and soothing, and somewhere distant I hear the light laughter of children playing. I float along without a care.

A dull weight bears down on my back, pushing my cloud down closer to the water. I look back, but there's only a shadow, nothing else. The weight grows heavier and heavier, spreading down the length of my torso to my legs and up along the tops of my shoulders. It's pushing me down, down, down. The water is close now, and I can almost touch it. I can't move, or even breathe. I'm trapped beneath the weight of this shadow. I can't even see the sun anymore. The water begins to lap gently at my legs, and it is frigid. I shift but still can't really move.

"Jack," I hear a voice whisper into my ear. I'm panicking now, and my body is on fire with adrenaline. My heart beat quickens. I can't feel my hands or my arms, only the terrible weight and the water on my legs. It feels like icy fingernails scraping against my skin. It's driving me insane.

"Wake up, Jack!"

My eyes snap open. It takes me a second, but I quickly realize I am engaged in a full-on assault. Cherie is straddling my back and leans over, meeting my eye. The girls are back there, too, on top of my legs, soaking wet and giggling maniacally. Brenton stares at me from the pool, half-horrified and half-humored.

"He's awake!" Cherie announces.

"Hold on!" Claudia shouts.

"Get off," I insist, trying to unseat them. I push my upper body up, and I'm sure I can throw them off if I can just get partially up. I overestimate myself, and Cherie promptly digs her nails under my armpits, causing me to jerk my arms back and fall down. There is a chorus of laughter and shrieks. Individually, they are waifish little girls. Combined, they exact over three hundred pounds of body weight on top of me. I don't know what they mean to do, but dread creeps into my chest.

"Get off," I grumble at them.

Cherie's lips are beside my ear. "Now's your chance, Jack."

"Get off of me—I mean it," I growl. I'm hoping my voice sounds as threatening as I need it to be.

"I'll let you go, if you cooperate."

I'm fuming. I wriggle beneath them but can't get free. I refuse to wave a white flag, and I won't call my mom for help, either. I won't give them the satisfaction.

"I'm not giving up the room, so forget it," I bravely say.

"Oh, really?" she taunts.

A buzzing sound circles my head. I try to turn to see what she's doing. The buzzing comes closer, sounding vaguely familiar. "What is that?"

"I know how much you love your hair," Cherie teases. "I'll let you keep it if you move out of the casita."

My stomach squeezes. "Cherie, cut it out; this isn't funny!" I reply through clenched teeth. I'm sweating now, both from panic and from the stress of trying to pull out of their hold. I reach back and swipe at the empty air over my head.

"Careful," Chloe warns. "One wrong move, and you could lose a finger."

"C'mon, Jack," Cherie whispers. The shaver comes close to my ear, and I can almost feel it vibrating against my flesh. My skin crawls. "It's just a room. Is it really worth going bald right before school starts?"

"Don't do it, Cherie," I warn. Anxiety builds when she doesn't answer, and I squirm beneath them wildly.

She suddenly runs the shaver along the back of my neck. I freeze, grinding my teeth and scrunching my eyes, locked in fear, and she relishes every second of it.

"Stop!"

Her voice is menacing. "Give up yet?"

"No!" I insist, though I am frantic to say yes and give in. The twins are enthused by my outburst, and they squeeze their legs around mine even tighter.

I can't let them do this to me. If I have to risk getting cut by that shaver, I will. In a move of desperation, I drag myself forward with all of my strength and twist beneath the twins. They scream and try to hold on to my legs. I squirm away and turn around, unseating Cherie, who rolls off of me and onto the grass.

She curses and scrambles to escape. I grab her by the ankle before she can get far. She kicks back, but it doesn't faze me; she must have forgotten that I have grown up with a little brother *and* a little sister. I pounce, sweeping her underneath my body and deftly gathering her skinny wrists together into one my hands.

The twins know better than to stick around, and they run into the house in a fit of screams and laughter. Cherie is trapped and must fend for herself against me.

"Get off of me!" she spits. The shaver buzzes noisily just a few feet away, and I pick it up to turn it off. Her eyes grow wide and wildly dart between my face and my hand. "Don't you dare!"

Her terror incites me to draw the moment out a little more. I wave the shaver closer.

"So, what was that you were saying about going bald?" I taunt. She strains and writhes against my grip. I lean forward and press her wrists down to the ground above her head.

My face is now almost inches from hers, and I pause, forgetting what I was doing because her mouth is so close to mine. Cherie stops moving and stares defiantly at me like she knows I've gone stupid again just from looking at her. A deep chill passes through me. Her eyes darken and her lips seem to almost pout, as if she's daring me to kiss her.

She says, "What are you waiting for? Scared?"

"I'm not scared," I murmur, entranced, all rational thought held prisoner somewhere in the back of my mind.

But my heart does stop when I hear my mother's harsh tone coming from the kitchen. "Jonathan Hansen the Third!" I look up to find my mother's furious eyes resting on me, and I snap out of my daze.

"Off. Right now," she commands.

My jaw goes slack. "But Mom, *she* attacked *me*! She was trying to cut off my hair!"

"Let her go!"

I release Cherie and get to my feet. She clambers to hers and looks at her wrists as if I had sawed her hands off. "They're *red*!" she cries. Her hand flies forward and slaps me hard across the face.

"You asshole!"

I step backward, stunned. My cheek is ablaze. I reach up and can almost feel the outline of her handprint on my burning skin.

"Hey!" my mom yells. "Cherie, that is not okay! Apologize right now!"

"No way! He deserves it! We were just fooling around with him!"

"Well, it's not okay to hit someone like that!" Mom insists. I can't see her face. I'm blinded by a thick red haze of hatred for Cherie. I turn and storm into the casita—MY ROOM—and slam the door shut.

In the bathroom, I look at my face. There's a big handprint along my jawline. I can even see white lines where her fingers bend. Finally, I check the back of my neck, and I realize she had run the shaver just below my hairline. Relief is replaced with more fury. Words are forming at the back of my throat that I don't want to unleash. My body is aching even more, and now my face hurts, too. I'm going to kill those girls. I hate them so much.

No, I hate Cherie. She is a terrible, cruel human being, and she should never have been allowed into the world. She needs to be locked up, institutionalized, and not released until her fiftieth birthday, or something really old.

I'm boiling. I need to cool down, and fast. I mop my sweaty forehead with the back of my hand and check the thermostat on the wall. It reads 64 degrees, but it feels like 80. I lower it to 60 and collapse onto my bed. I hear my mother outside arguing still with Cherie, but I can't make out their words. I'd listen if I could stop the words that are echoing in my ears.

"What are you waiting for?"

Did she see it in my face? Could she have possibly known in that briefest moment that I couldn't ignore my proximity to her mouth? Did she feel it, too, or was she just trying to taunt me?

I never before experienced anything more intense than that single second of my life, and now I can't stop myself from imagining what that scenario would have been like if we hadn't been trying to kill each other. If we had actually wanted to be physically entwined.

If she had wanted more.

Forget it, I scold myself. I try to shake myself of the thought.

Don't even think about it. Stop thinking about her. You can't think about her like that.

Shit.

Chapter 20

A few hours later, I'm woken up by a soft knock at my door. The room is darker, but I can still see daylight peeking through the blinds. I'm frozen to the bone, shivering, and I wrap my arms around my body. I glance at the time, but the quick turn of my head makes me dizzy.

A knock again. "Jack, honey?" It's Mom.

"I'm not hungry," I call out. Surprisingly, I'm not. I maneuver the comforter around my bare skin and shake beneath it, teeth chattering. I fumble for a pair of sweatpants and a sweatshirt and pull them on hastily. Then, I climb out of bed and stumble to the thermostat. I raise it to 80 degrees and retreat back to my bed.

"Jack, I'd really like you to come inside and talk to Cherie, please."

No way, I think to myself. "I just need some space, Mom, okay?" I actually couldn't sit across from her and hold my head up right now if I tried. *Why am I so exhausted?*

My mom hesitates, but I can tell she's still at the door. She knows "space" is a hard word for her to argue with, especially when I say it. "Okay, I understand, but I really think it's important that you two talk before the end of the night."

"Why, is she catching a train back to hell?" I smirk, but my mother sighs heavily.

"Jack…"

"I'll find her later. Just not now, okay?" My head pounds a little more.

"Promise?"

"Yes, I promise!" *Now leave me alone!*

I want to go back to sleep, and I do. As I bury inside of my blankets and close my eyes, my teeth click against each other.

***

BANG BANG BANG!

I wake up in a pool of sweat, and it is nighttime. I groggily look toward the door. The knob twists back and forth violently, but it is locked.

I look at the clock. It is near midnight. Someone pounds at my door again and the knob jiggles. Could it be Britney? Suddenly, I sit upright in alarm.

What if she snuck out? "Hold on!" I burrow my way out from under my sweat-soaked blankets and throw off my damp sweatshirt. I nearly lunge at the door.

But when I open it, there's no one on the other side. Could I have been hallucinating?

"Hello?" I call, poking my head out and looking around. "Britney?"

I hear rustling in the grass. A close palm tree shakes slightly. My pulse quickens as I realize it might not be Britney who's out here. I suddenly think of all the possible crazies and stalkers who could be in our back yard and take a step back toward my door.

"Hello? Who's there?" A girly giggle follows, and I release the breath I had been holding for the last fifty seconds of my life. I move toward the tree.

"Britney, you're not supposed—oof!" Something hard slams against my back. For a second, the air is knocked out of me and, before I can stop myself, I'm flying face-first into the pool.

It happens so fast that I don't have a chance to keep from inhaling water. I'm engulfed, body and lungs, by the warm, chlorine-treated liquid. It stings my eyes and chokes me as I fight to get to the surface.

I hear their cackling laughter as soon as I come up and take my first drink of air.

"Oh my God, did you see his face?" says one.

"Priceless! Did you get it, Claudia?"

"The video's too dark, but whatever! It was perfect in real life!"

I'm gagging, barely able to find the pool floor with my feet. "You girls—are so—dead!" I gasp between coughs, clearing my vision and looking up. They cackle harder. Claudia, Chloe, and Cherie are standing just out of reach along the sides of the pool, pointing at me and throwing their heads back with manic laughter. I dive toward them, and that sends them into a tornado of shrieks as they run away, still laughing. My wet sweatpants weigh me down like a set of twenty-pound dumbbells on my legs, and getting out of the pool takes every ounce of strength I have left. I know I won't be able to chase them down before they reach the house. I collapse onto the cool stone along the pool's perimeter and pant for air.

I notice Mom's bedroom light is suddenly on and can't help but groan. The girls quietly slip into the house and vanish. My mother races into the kitchen and turns that light on, too. She is quick to throw the doors open, her eyes frantically searching the pool.

"Brenton? Britney?!" Her voice is urgent. She fears the worst, just like I had.

"It's fine, Mom, it's just me." I get to my feet slowly.

She steps closer. "Jack, what are you doing in the pool at this hour?" she nearly scolds. Behind her, the girls are back, making faces at me from the kitchen windows. They promptly disappear as Jim appears in the kitchen. "You're soaking wet! What were you thinking?" She pulls a towel from a wicker ottoman and rushes to me, tsk-tsking.

"The girls pushed me in," I tell her, grateful for the dark that hides my shame. Ganged up on and outsmarted by a gaggle of girls twice in one day. How humiliating and frustrating this whole week has been. Cherie has kept true to her promise, and I regret ever challenging her on something as stupid as a room. It's just not worth another two years of this.

Mom wraps the towel around my upper body and rubs her hands over my arms. "What? Oh, honey, I'm sorry. Those girls! I'll make Jim talk to them."

I nod but covertly roll my eyes. I know they're both powerless against the sneak attacks of Cherie and her minions.

My mother smiles at me as if realizing it's been a while since she's really looked at me. "My handsome boy, just look at you." She leans in like she has a secret and whispers, "Maybe they tease you because they like you."

I'm disgusted and pull away. "Ugh, please don't start."

"Oh c'mon now, honey, no sense pretending it's not possible. They're not related to you by blood, and you're all at that age..." She pushes my wet hair off of my forehead.

"Okay, okay, I've heard enough," I sigh, turning from her.

"Hey, what is this?" she asks, pulling me back and letting her hand linger. She feels my forehead then my cheek with the back of the same hand. "My goodness, Jack; you're burning up! Are you sick?"

That would explain a lot of things. I suddenly allow my posture to fall into a slump and hang my head. The minute Mom diagnoses me with a fever I'm through playing tough and resilient. I fold into her arms when she pulls me close.

"We have to get you some Tylenol, and, oh, you're so warm! We just may have to fill your tub with ice!"

I draw the line there. "I'm fine, Mom, it's probably just Brenton's stupid flu."

"You need medicine and some TLC," she whispers, standing on her tip toes and kissing my temple. "My poor baby; I've been neglecting you, haven't I?"

I don't answer. I don't need to. She knows I would never say that out loud, but it's been a long time since she's been this aware of me.

"Come on, we have to dry you off—Jack, it's a furnace in here!" she exclaims as she steps into my room.

"I was cold before," I mumble pathetically.

"Oh, this will not do," she replies, and she flips on a light switch. She rummages through my drawers for new pajama pants and a sweatshirt, and she marches me back outside.

"You're sleeping in one of the guest rooms tonight," she tells me.

I plant my feet, indignantly protesting, "No—Mom, no! I can't do it—please don't make me stay in the same house with them. They're evil, Mom!" Fear is pouring out of me now, and I worry I may actually cry. God, I hate being sick. It turns you into such a pile of mush.

"They'll leave you alone, trust me. I will see to it. I simply cannot let you stay in here—you're practically incubating more germs in this place. I have to disinfect the whole room and clean your sheets!" She urges me toward the house despite my hesitation. "Let's go, we have to get you out of these wet clothes."

I groan audibly and follow her to the house, my head hung low. I'm now forced to go into the house anyway. Point: Cherie.

Chapter 21

The girls do leave me alone for the night, and I don't hear from anyone but my mother throughout the next day. She mentions taking me to an urgent care facility each time she enters the room because my fever won't go down. She checks my temperature once an hour and feeds me pills once every four hours. She brings tea and a cool washcloth that she runs over my head and neck. I can't begin to describe how much I've missed her shedding all of this attention on me. If I didn't feel like I was on death's doorstep, falling in and out of consciousness every other hour, I'd actually be able to enjoy this.

It isn't until nighttime that I finally hear from Cherie, who taps on the open door to the guest room and wakes me. I glance up and see her standing there with a tray in her arms, her hair falling in angelic ringlets around her shoulders and her lips shiny with gold gloss. I don't want to see her like this, while I'm all weak and pathetic and she's...

Well, gorgeous and perfect.

I lower my eyes. "What do you want?" I mutter gruffly.

"Your mom asked me to bring this in. It's chicken soup," she says, setting the tray down on the nightstand.

"I'm not hungry," I lie. "I'll eat it later."

She doesn't leave, so I glance upward. Her mouth droops to one side as she studies me. "You're pretty sick, huh? Aunt Eva says you've had a fever all day. She says you haven't eaten anything."

"What do you care?" I grumble, pulling the bed sheets up to my chin. "It's probably from some hex you put on me."

A laughing smile replaces her pitying frown, and she nods. "I must say, I'm pretty good at hexes."

I roll my eyes and turn away from her, burying my face under the sheets. "Just leave me alone, please."

I feel her weight on the bed behind me, and my heart thumps. *What does she want? Why can't she just go away?* I pray she won't be cruel enough to mess with me now; I wouldn't have the strength to fight her off.

"C'mon, Jack," she urges. "I'm trying to call a truce." Her fingers gently slide through the back of my hair.

Usually, I hate when people touch my hair. Cherie causes a different feeling, however. First, chills rocket through my spine, then warmth spreads down my neck. I shake her off quickly.

"Don't."

Her chest falls with a heavy sigh. "Okay, okay. Sorry I touched your precious hair."

I sit up and glare at her. "Why are you here?"

"I told you, I'm trying to call a truce," she murmurs. "It got really ugly yesterday."

"*Yesterday*? It's been ugly since January. I know you and the twins egged my car the other day," I reply, and I cross my arms over my chest. I'm trying to stay mad at her, but it's not working. Frowning at someone who looks like her is hard to do because really all I want to do is make her smile, and I blame the flu for this flaw in my logic right now.

She doesn't confirm or deny my accusation. "I've never hit anyone before," she pouts. "I lost control. That's not me, and I'm really sorry."

I still don't believe her. "Did my mom send you in here?" I demand. "'Cause I don't need some fake apology from you."

She looks genuinely hurt, and I feel like a jerk. "No one forced me to come in here, Jack. I'm trying to make it right, okay? I got, you know, scared when you held me down, and I just—I freaked out." She clams up suddenly, shaking her head like she's trying to get rid of water in her ears. Or a bad image in her mind. Something; like maybe she knows I was *thisclose* to kissing her.

I feel compelled to say, "I wouldn't have done anything."

She nods and breathes deeply. "Yeah, I know." She changes the subject quickly. "Want a little soup?"

I'm rocked to the core right now. What am I missing? What freaked her out? I may have punched a lot of people in the past, but I never hit a girl before, so what would make her think I'd hit her?

I follow her thumb as it gestures to the tray. I nod dumbly and reach for the bowl, but she takes it into her hands and says, "Here, I'll do it."

Now she wants to feed me soup? What the hell is happening? My inner machismo has to put a stop to this.

"I can do it," I try to argue, but she already has the spoon up and ready. She brings it to my lips, but I turn my mouth away. "You're not feeding me."

"I don't mind," she insists, setting the spoon back down. She winks and teases, "You'll be much neater if you're being fed." I'm too suspicious to laugh at her joke with her, and I feel my cheeks burn.

I hold up my hand when she brings the spoonful forward again. "Wait a sec. Why are you being so nice to me all of a sudden?"

Her smile fades a little. "I feel bad that you're sick."

"Why do you care though? You hate me."

"I don't hate you, Jack," she replies, looking hurt again.

I cock an eyebrow at her. Suddenly semantics matter? "Okay, you strongly dislike me."

She shrugs. "No matter how I've treated you, you've been there for me when I've been… out of it." Her head hangs a little. Finally, she peers at me from under her long, black lashes. "Consider this my way of making up for that last night in New York."

I gulp. "Oh. I didn't think you remembered."

She nods. "I remember everything." The air stills between us, and she drops her eyes again. "And you were really nice the first couple of days after my parents died. I kind of liked having you around, you know, before you said that stuff to Uncle Jim."

Meeting my gaze again, I see a thousand nights of tears in her eyes, and I feel really, really badly.

"I'm sorry, you know, for what I said that night."

"It hurt a lot," she concedes quietly. "I already felt so alone, and then you, the only person I actually felt safe with, even you didn't want me."

ME? Oh, now it's like she's kicking me in the stomach over and over. "I'm sorry." I don't know what else to say. "And I didn't mean to hurt your wrists yesterday."

She smiles sadly. "I'm fine. Deserved it, I guess." Now I feel even worse. She stirs the bowl of soup and sets it down, lays the spoon beside it, then looks at the clock.

"Well, I've gotta go get ready," she says. I want to ask why and where she's going. I don't know why I even care, but I do. I don't really want her to leave.

I nod. "Thanks for bringing the soup in. I'll, uh, have it later."

Her lips purse together, and she slowly walks away. She pauses at the door and turns back to me.

"I'll, um, I'll see you later, Jack," she says. "Feel better."

I smile a silent thank you and try to look away. When she finally disappears, I release the breath I had been holding for the last thirty seconds. Her sad expression and sadder words haunt me as I slump down and stare at the wall.

I think my fever finally breaks that night because I have some delirious, trippy dream filled with all of sorts of colors and sounds. Cherie is in my dream, too, lying next to me and stroking my hair, and I actually let her, which is how I know it can't possibly be real. She is bathed in this white aura of light, looking like an angel. I try to talk, but it comes out in garbled, nonsensical sounds. She giggles and tells me I'm cute. She even kisses my cheek.

When I wake up in the morning, I'm ache-free and alert. My skin is cool and every trace of my fever is gone.

Except for the delirious dream part, because my pillow smells like Cherie.

Chapter 22

It's clear that Cherie must have taken some sort of kindness pills last night because they have worn off when I finally walk out of the house and toward the pool. Danika is sun-tanning by her side, furiously typing away on her phone. She looks up at me and smirks as I pass.

"Hey, Danika," I force myself to say. "Long time no see."

"Hello, Jack," she replies icily.

"Hi, Cherie."

Cherie barely looks in my direction, even when I sit down in the other chair beside her. She keeps her face pointed to the sky, her sunglasses set over her eyes so I can't even tell if she's awake.

"Nice out today," I say quietly, kicking my feet up and laying in the chair next to her, trying to be casual. *We're friends now, aren't we?*

She turns her head the slightest bit, looks in my general direction, then turns back to the sky. "Yeah, nice."

And we're back! "Yep." Why do I sound so meek? I clear my throat and work up the nerve to ask, "Hey, did you come into the guest room at all last night? Like, really late?"

She glances over at me and tips her sunglasses down, examining me like I've gone crazy. "No."

"Oh. Yeah, I didn't think so." I feel myself turning pink. Of course she wouldn't have; that was just some dumb fantasy my brain conjured in my delirium. "Listen, I don't know if I said it before, but—um—thanks for bringing the soup by last night and stuff."

She doesn't respond. She instead looks kind of annoyed that I'm there. She turns to Danika and says, "Did you hear from Caz yet?"

I'm not sure why, but his name sparks a twinge—*just a twinge!*—of envy. I try not to look over when Danika answers that she has indeed spoken to Caz.

"He said we should meet him and Dominick at Blue Moon at 4."

"Fabulous," Cherie sings with a grin.

I let this news stew in my brain for a few quiet moments, and then I get up to walk to my room. *So she's meeting up with Caz Farrell today. Just great.*

I hear Brenton behind me asking Cherie if she wants to play with him, and she flatly denies him.

"Nope," she replies.

Brenton, brokenhearted, murmurs, "Okay." Now I'm really bitter. She knows he adores her; can't she take the time to play with him for five minutes?

She says to Danika, "What time should we leave?"

Brenton floats toward me as I near the casita. "Jack, wanna play Marco Polo?"

I shake my head. "Not now, buddy, maybe later, I'm still kind of sick." It's not even an outright lie; my whole interaction with Cherie has made my stomach churn and my skin reach a new, feverish temperature.

Brenton sighs and floats away, muttering, "And they all wonder why I have an imaginary friend..."

"Sorry, bud," I sigh, and I watch him paddle back to the middle of the pool. My eyes find Cherie again, and she is sitting up in her chair, rubbing lotion down her legs and then across her waist. Danika catches me looking and throws up her hands.

"God, would you stop staring at us?! It's gross!" Her words make me cringe, and they ignite flames inside of me.

The words come flying out before I can stop them. "Don't flatter yourselves." I disappear inside my room before our exchange can get any uglier. Cherie's shouting something else and laughing with Danika, but I slam the door to tune her out.

My mind is spinning with fury, wondering where I went wrong and what I did now to make her mad. What could have happened between the moment she left the room last night to the moment I woke up to bring us back to square one?

Danika. Of course, it all makes sense. She can't be nice to me in front of other people because that would go against everything she's been doing for the last month. She doesn't want anyone to know she was actually kind to me last night and that her nastiness toward me is all just for show.

Or maybe I was the one she's lying to; yes, that's it. I should have gone with my instincts; my mother definitely sent her in to apologize. She didn't really mean it—she was just messing with me yet again. Messing with me so she could lure me into a moment like just now where I look like a pathetic puppy desperate for her attention, giving her the chance to kick me.

My blood is even hotter now, and I'm absently pulling on my gym shorts and a fresh t-shirt. Cherie and her bitch sidekick know no limits. I yank on my sneakers. I've got to run. I've got to burn all this anger off somehow. I throw open my door and see my mother emerging from the house.

"I was wondering where you were!" my mom sings out, carrying Britney onto the patio. "We just went up to check on you—wait, where are you going?"

Britney holds out her arms for me as I slide past. "Jackie!"

"Not now, I'm going for a run," I mumble gruffly, even though neither of them deserves my tone.

"But Jack—you just got over a fever! School starts in two days!"

"I'm fine, Mom!" I keep walking to the front of the house, my strides swallowing the ground. As I head through the front door, I hear Cherie's voice plaguing me from the patio.

"I don't know; he just got mad all of a sudden. He's pretty moody, Eva."

Once outside the gate, I break into a run, my feet hitting the pavement in hard, rapid steps. I follow the sidewalk to the end of the street and keep going, running blindly, my fury leading me down this road and up that hill until I am lost and have come upon a part of town that actually has buildings and alleyways. I can't stop to think about where I am or if it's a neighborhood where I could be in danger. I'm swimming in muddled, bitter thoughts about the humiliation Cherie's exacted upon me within the past seventy-two hours.

She was so nice last night, so... perfect. She apologized—she called a truce! Had I really for even a minute thought any of that was real? *She's a professional actress, stupid!* She was putting on a show—my mom probably gave her a good tongue-lashing for slapping me, and Cherie thought she'd make nice to get out of trouble. That's all. She doesn't care about me one bit. She doesn't like me.

And I have to stop liking her. It isn't healthy. It isn't going to go anywhere.

But with her fiery eyes and her gorgeous smile and how nice I know she could be sometimes, it's becoming impossible to avoid thinking about her almost every minute of every day.

My anger bubbles to the top when I stumble over a fallen garbage can that's rolled into the middle of the alley. I crash onto my knees and palms, and I'm a mess of scrapes and blood almost immediately. I curse and pick myself up, turning on the dirty, metal can with full venom. I throw my foot against it and send it colliding against the wall of a building.

A voice rips me out of my blind fury. "Whoa, my dude! Take it easy; it's just a garbage can." A kid approaches me, his hands out as if he could be next. I'm too angry to be embarrassed. He looks like he might be about my age, maybe a little older. He's black and short and lean, and he's watching me with laughing brown eyes.

"Sorry." I'm breathing hard, staring at the garbage can as he rights it.

He smiles with genuine friendliness, and his eyes are alight with humor. "That's girl problems, right there. What's her name?" I drop my gaze to the ground. How did he know that?

I don't even want to say her name out loud because the first syllable alone may force my foot to fly forward into the trash can again. I also don't want him, if he doesn't already recognize me, to recognize her name and put two and two together. It's a terrible thing when you can't be honest with anyone.

"Trouble," I grimace.

The kid laughs heartily and holds out his fist toward me. "I heard that! That was my ex-girlfriend's first, middle, and last name."

I bump his fist with my own, and we share a grin.

"What's your name, dawg?"

"Jack Hansen." I wait for it. I wait for him to say, *"Hold on, that Jack Hansen? Cherie Belle's Jack Hansen?"* He doesn't, and I'm relieved, even a little embarrassed that I actually assumed some random person would recognize my name.

"I'm Mica Williams, nice to meet you."

"Same. Where you from?" I ask, noting the accent I hear in his voice. It sounds like home.

"Originally? New York. The Bronx. You?"

I smile. "New York. Westchester."

"Aight, aight, I heard of it. Upstate, right?" he chuckles. "So whatchu doin' here, besides beatin' up innocent garbage cans? You on vacation?"

"We just moved here. I live on Palm Court." I'm not even sure how far away that is from here, and for the first time I realize I'm really lost.

His eyebrows raise. "Word? Them some big houses. You got that Westchester money, huh dawg?"

I shrug. "Not exactly. Kind of just landed in our laps." I feel dirty admitting to it.

"Ah, gotcha. Wish I had that kind of luck." He gestures to the garbage can. "So, this whatchu do for fun, Jack Hansen?"

"No, I'm just a little on edge is all."

"There's a gym not far off. You look like a big dude; why don't you lift some weights or somethin'? Work that aggression out," he advises.

I shake my head. "Not what I needed today."

The light bulb seems to go off. "Oh, you got that burn like you wanna hit some *bodies*! I gotchu dawg, I gotchu. Yo, you spar?"

"Spar?"

"Like in boxing, you know? Tyson-Mayweather-style." He bounces back and forth, his fists up to his temples. He throws some air jabs. I marvel at how he moves; it's graceful, like he knows what he's doing.

"No, never tried that," I admit. I suddenly wish I could punch like him.

"Aw, you gotta try it. There's a trainer off Route 1. He's got a gym. I go every day." I'm immediately interested. While I know the last thing I need is to awaken my violent side, I always wanted to learn how to actually box. It's probably better to take boxing lessons from Mica than to violently explode on friends like I shamefully used to do years ago.

He sees the enthusiasm in my expression. "I could teach you, ya know?" He grins. "I'm not too bad, if I don't mind me sayin'. Yo, if you down, meet me there tomorrow. It's called Rocco's. We'll get you on the bag, see what it do."

"What time?"

"Anytime. I'm off from school right now, so I spend most of my morning there."

Curious, I ask, "What school do you go to?"

"Worthington High School. It's not too far from here."

This is good news. Very good news. "That's where I start on Monday!"

He laughs at my excitement. "Word? That's cool, man. Thought you'd be in some private school or some shit like that."

"Yeah, not quite," I reply quietly. "So what time should I meet you at the gym?"

He shrugs. "It's Winter Break, Jack Hansen. Meet me when you get over there."

I watch him replace his earbuds and trot off. My chest swells a little. I just made my first Californian friend, and he's from New York. What are the odds?

Once I come off of my high, I realize I have no idea where I am, and where I am doesn't look good.

"Hey, Mica—wait up!" I call out. He turns and removes one of his earpieces. I jog toward him. "How do I get home?"

He smirks and shakes his head, waving me to follow him.

Chapter 23

The next morning, I make it my business to wake up at 8 and look up directions to Rocco's gym. I'd like to run to it and really prove I'm still somewhat of an athlete, but it probably isn't the best idea after how lost I got in the not-so-nice neighborhoods yesterday.

I'll be dead before I get there, I think to myself as I search the refrigerator for something to eat.

The front door opens, and Cherie walks in with Britney at her side. My sister sees me and runs over, arms outstretched and a smile just as wide.

"Jackie!"

"Hey, Brat, where were you?" I ask, catching her against my leg and patting her head. I raise my suspicious eyes to Cherie. Her hair is pulled up into a tight ponytail, and she's wearing a loose shirt that hangs off of one shoulder. My mind pulls up the word "sexy," and I immediately dismiss it. I've got to stop that kind of thinking.

She leans over the other end of the island and shrugs. "We just went for a walk around the neighborhood," she says with a bright grin like everything between us is fine and dandy. "Uncle Jim's at work and your mom is meeting with the principal at Britney and Brenton's school."

"A walk?" My mind begins conjuring images of stuffed bears covered in red paint littering the sidewalks and crazy stalkers in black ski masks hiding in the bushes while paparazzi snap pictures of my little sister and Cherie, who walk by, blissfully unaware. "Alone?"

Her eyes narrow. "Yes, alone. We were getting some girl time in." Tons of replies are forming on the back of my tongue, but I can't seem to get any of them out at the moment. My mind races with all of the things that could have happened to either of them while they were out.

"What are you up to?" Cherie asks finally, noticing I haven't spoken. Britney looks up expectantly, as if she's hoping I will offer to be part of whatever it is she and her new best friend are up to next.

"Going to the gym," I reply stiffly, trying to shake horrific images from my head. Britney frowns and gives up on me, moving to Cherie's side.

"Don't you usually work out at night?" Cherie's voice is soft and almost genuinely interested in what I have to say.

I don't have a desire to be kind back and harrumph, "I didn't realize you were keeping tabs."

"I'm not; *don't flatter yourself*," she bites back, sarcasm suddenly dripping from every word. Britney senses the tension between us and wisely chooses to disappear upstairs.

Cherie is oblivious and continues her mean assault. "Something about seeing you awake before noon makes me feel like I'm in an alternate universe."

I shake my head. "Whatever. I gotta go." As I gather my water bottle and banana, I look up at her again and point toward the stairs. "And don't go out alone with my little sister anymore. I don't want her surrounded by those paparazzi morons or those nutcases who obsess over you."

"No one was there, it was just us—" she begins to argue.

I hold up my hand to stop her. "I don't care; just don't do it."

"Why are you being such a jerk?" she demands.

I shake my head and say, "Just stay away from my little sister."

Cherie glares at me, folds her arms and juts out one hip, challenging me with her pose as she says, "I'll do whatever I want; you don't make the rules."

My blood begins to really churn into a froth. I stalk forward and stand within feet of her. She steps back, intimidated, and that's exactly what I want her to feel.

"When it comes to Britney, I do make the rules. Keep away from her."

"Or you'll do what?" she needles smugly.

I glare down at her and warn in a low growl, "You haven't seen me really angry yet, Cherie."

"You don't scare me, Jack." She swallows hard but tries to maintain the confidence in her words. I keep my gaze locked with hers for what feels like a full minute before I finally have to tear myself away. I walk past her and head through the front door.

I'm glad I'm driving to the gym now because I can't wait to punch something. Hard.

***

"Hey, my dude!" Mica shouts from the water cooler in the center of the gym. The machines match the hard, cement floor: mostly gray and black. I am out of my league in age and size, big time. If it weren't for Mica, I would have turned and run back to the parking lot.

But Mica is all smiles as he comes over and pulls me into a bro-hug like we've been friends for years. "You came, huh?" I'm confused why this impresses him so much.

I don't have time to ask because he's already off and running with a very clear agenda.

"C'mon, let's show you 'round, introduce you to some regulars," he says, and walks ahead of me with a cool, confident sway to his stride. I'm calmed and intimidated all at once. I follow him through the gym like a lost puppy, trying not to stare too long at the burly men violently dancing in the center ring, swinging at each other with graceful venom.

I'm only half-listening as Mica rattles on about the different guys working out through the free weight area. They eye me with suspicion, neglecting to wipe beads of sweat from their brows and upper lips. Occasionally, one will nod or give a half-smile, half-grunt. I return the gesture, mindful of my distance from Mica.

"So, whattya wanna do first, Hansen?" I jerk to attention, and Mica is waiting for me to take an interest in any particular area of the gym.

"Uh, boxing, I guess?"

He almost laughs at me. "Still got that aggression to get out?" He pats me on the shoulder and gently nudges me toward a closet.

He reaches inside and pulls out a black jump rope, handing it to me with a sly grin. "Let's get you warmed up."

***

An hour later, I'm annihilated, lying flat on my back on the gym floor, as the throbbing of my muscles dominates my senses. Mica leans over me, laughing.

"My dude, you alive?"

I close my eyes and croak, "Yeah."

"One more set. C'mon, you got this!"

I look over at the jump rope, officially the new bane of my existence, and swallow hard. "I don't know; I think I might puke." Mica put me through a bootcamp far more exhausting than any football practice I had ever been to. Push-ups, squats, jump rope sets—those really did me in—basically, a constant circuit of cardio and strength training designed to kill me. He didn't just watch me and coach me through them. He actually did every exercise alongside me.

And still Mica laughs, dragging me up onto my feet. He thrusts the jump rope into my hand. "One more. Let's go!"

After my final set of jumping rope, he leaves me to catch my breath and rummages through the closet once again.

He hands me bandages for my hands, saying, "Here, wrap yo' fists up—gotta support yo' wrists." When I've wrapped them tightly, he pushes two heavy gloves on my hands and makes sure they fit well.

I follow Mica back through the gym, and instead of leading me to the ring in its center, he introduces me to a giant punching bag.

"This here is the bag," he says, gripping its sides like a girl he's about to slow dance with. He sees my eyes flicker between that and the ring and almost laughs out loud. "My man, you can't be thinkin' Imma put you in the ring just yet! You gotta crawl before you can walk, son!"

I'm not sure I understand what he means, but I'm pretty sure he is telling me I'm not ready to spar with someone in the ring. "So, what, you just want me to punch the bag?"

"Yeah, just the bag," he replies, his eyes twinkling with humor. "Imma teach you a few moves and stuff before we get to hittin' people." He leans in and winks, "It's not as easy as it looks."

Mica directs me to hold my hands higher, then not that high, then twist them a little straighter. Then I have to change the position of my right foot. Frustration starts to climb into my chest after his third direction to do something different with my stance. I wipe sweat off of my forehead with the back of my forearm.

"Let's try some punches," he says, sensing my impatience.

Mica makes me connect my fist to the bag in a slow-motion jab, then a slower-motion right hook, then a gentle uppercut. I have to do these over and over, mimicking every move he does. Finally, he tells me to hit the bag without direction. Unsure of myself, I give the bag a few thuds with my gloves.

"What in the hell is that?" he scolds. "C'mon, Hansen, hit the bag! Show me whatchu got!"

I grind my teeth together and release all of my frustration into one huge right hook, my go-to punch from my more violent days. Mica jumps back as my fist connects, and the bag rocks from the force. I surprise myself with the hit, too. It's been a long time since I've thrown a real punch; maybe it's the fact that I'm older, or maybe because I'm bigger, but I don't remember ever having that kind of power before.

"Whoa! My man!" Mica laughs, his jaw a little slack. I steal a look around and see a few eyes on us. "Alright then. Alright. Now let's do it again; but this time, we gotta watch yo' form."

Chapter 24

"Dress nice. Honeys they're like ballers; can't look like no chump if you wanna get in with the females."

Mica's words echo in my head as I look at the clothes in my closet, rubbing the aching muscles of my arms. Mica gave me the run-down of the whole high school, from the teachers to the students to the best place to sit at lunch. Now I just have to make a good first impression. If this were home, and if I were going back to the same old school with the same old people, I wouldn't care what I wore. Tomorrow feels like the first day of the rest of my life for some reason, and I can't help but deliberate over my limited choices.

I hear voices outside my room, and I move closer to the window, listening intently. There's giggling and hushed whispers. Peering through the blinds, I see Danika, the twins, and Cherie sneaking around the perimeter of the pool in their bathing suits. My guard goes up immediately, and I'm prepared to face another attack. I look at the clock, which reads 11:50. Is this seriously the only thing they can be doing the night before school starts?

Oh yeah, Cherie doesn't have to start school yet. She hasn't ever attended high school and won't have to until next year, so she has all the time in the world to play around. I stare at the door, waiting for them to knock, expecting round three of Operation: Terrorize Jack.

But then I hear a distinctly male voice. More than one. I look through my blinds again, and I realize the girls have been joined by a trio of guys in swim trunks with towels draped over their shoulders. They all sneak into the hot tub at the pool's far end, holding bottles in their hands that I can only assume are booze. I'm surprised the twins would participate in a potential hangover on the night before their first day at a new school. My instinct is to open the door and put an immediate end to their little party, but I withdraw from the window instead.

"Not my problem," I mutter to myself, shaking my head.

I pause, conflicted. *But if something bad happened…*

I shake my head again. *Not my problem and not my business.*

I try to tune out the hushed laughter and horseplay that resonates right outside my room, concentrating hard on the closet in front of me. My mind, however, keeps wandering to the party in the hot tub, and I catch myself wondering who the guys are and what they're all doing in there. Bigger question: Why don't Jim and Mom hear any of this?

My cellphone is sitting on my dresser, begging to be put to good use. I could call Mom or Jim and just tip them off. That would bode well for me; the girls would get in trouble and no one would have to know I did it.

It feels cowardly, though. A small part of me wants to be big and bad and walk out there to chase the guys away. I might be bigger than those guys. I'm bigger than Caz Farrell. I throw a solid punch.

But then I'm reminded by a larger, sorer part of me that wants to avoid additional pain that there are four girls out there who don't like me, and that they are accompanied by three guys who probably like them. My odds don't look good in that equation, especially when I consider the things those three girls have been capable of doing to me this week without any extra help.

Nope, I'm not getting mixed up in any of this.

***

A loud pounding on my door jolts me out of a deep sleep at two o'clock in the morning. I sit up and look around in a haze, wondering if maybe I was just dreaming. But then the knocks come again, and I know it has to be the girls outside my door, up to no good. I pull my pillow over my head and try to ignore it.

I hear Cherie's voice calling, "Jack, open up!"

There's no way I'm falling for that. For all I know, she could have her minions, including those guys, waiting to ambush me. I lay as still as I can in bed, hoping she will give up and just go away.

"Ja-ack!" she whines. "Wake up! I want to talk to you!"

I hear a familiar, inebriated slur in her voice, and I know Drunk Cherie is waiting on the other side of that door. "No, go to sleep!" I finally shout back.

"Jack, come *onnnn*!" she whines again. I groan. I get out of bed, shuffle toward the door, and lean against it.

"What do you want?" I ask quietly.

She wiggles the knob. "Unlock the door please? I want to talk."

I scoff, "No way. I'm not falling for that." I can picture those three dudes standing behind her, waiting for me to be dumb enough to unlock the door so they can pounce on me and do her bidding.

"Jack, I promise I'm not going to do anything. I'm by myself. Please just open up?" She's genuinely begging, and I want to believe her.

Resisting the temptation to let her in, I reply, "It's two in the morning and some of us have to go to school tomorrow, Cherie. I know that's a foreign concept to you."

"Har har, Jack," she grumbles. "C'mon, it'll only take a second. Don't be such a baby." She's not going to let up, but I am not going to be jerked around tonight either.

I sigh and look around my dark room, catching sight of my baseball bat in a far corner. I retrieve it and unlock the door slowly.

"Yay!" When she opens the door and sees me standing with the bat in my hand, she erupts with giggles. "What are you doing?"

"Where are your little boyfriends?" I demand, peering behind her. The smell of vodka and chlorine oozes from the top of her head and wafts into my room. She looks dry, but her hair is stringy, and she's wrapped in a towel that's cinched across her chest. Two thin strings are tied loosely behind her neck, and I have to stop myself from immediately picturing what she's wearing under that towel.

She giggles again and pokes my side. "Ooh, someone was watching us! Jealous, Mr. Hansen?"

"Stop." I jerk back and push her hand away, thankful it's dark enough that she can't see me blush. "I'm not jealous," I grunt. "I just don't want some guys lurking in the bushes, waiting to beat me up in your honor."

She laughs loudly then. "Oh, darn, I didn't even think of that!" She notes my scowl and purses her lips. "I'm *kidding*, Jack. And they're not my boyfriends. They're just some friends, and they're gone, okay?" She gestures grandly out to the pool for emphasis.

I nod and relax, realizing she really is alone. I step back to allow her inside and set the bat aside.

She sweeps her hand along the side of the door and finds the wall switch, flicking it up and bathing us in harsh yellow light. I have to scrunch my eyes closed against it and quickly turn it off.

"Too bright." I fold my arms across my chest. "Just tell me what you want, Cherie."

She wanders into the room, her eyes rolling, ignoring me. This close, I can smell the alcohol on her stronger

than before. "They sure did change this place for you."
She stumbles over something, maybe her own feet, and I
reach out and catch her before she falls. Her towel slips
off of her body and pools at her feet. She squeals and
twists inside of my arms, her fingernails clawing into my
flesh while she finds her footing. Feeling the soft, bare
skin of her back against my stomach makes me dizzy.

"You're drunk," I grumble, promptly stepping back
and releasing her. She laughs again.

"Maybe just a little." Her fingers squeeze together,
and she squints one eye like a pirate.

"Cherie, I have school tomorrow," I remind her
again, and she waves me off, making her way to my bed. I
should be used to seeing her in a barely-there bikini by
now, but I can't stop myself from staring at the perfect
lines of her body. She plants herself on top of the
mattress and looks at me with doe eyes.

"Can you close the door?"

Jim's voice resonates in my ears. *No guests after*
eleven. No one in here we don't know about. But does
Cherie count?

"Jack?"

I'm uneasy, but I do it. It doesn't help that she pats
the mattress beside her, insinuating I should sit down. I
comply with even more hesitation, making sure there is
plenty of space between us. She turns to face me and
curls her legs beneath her body.

"What did you want to talk about?" I ask as patiently
as I can. My adrenaline is pumping, and I'm kind of
nervous about being alone in a room with her when she's
drunk. The last time this happened, I spent the night
trapped in her grasp.

She shrugs. "Nothing. I just don't want to go back
upstairs."

My shoulders drop. "Are you kidding me?"

She is hard to see, her face only slightly visible in the dark, but I can feel her eyes boring into mine. "No."

"Cherie, come on!" I am beyond annoyed now, and I won't do anything to mask it. "This thing about the room has got to stop—"

"I know, it's not that," she mumbles, fumbling with her inebriated speech. "I'm sorry. I just—I can't go back up there right now. I can't be down the hall from…"

Her words fade away, and I am too irritated to put it together. "From?" I'm waiting for her to say my sister, or her cousins. Instead, she takes in a deep breath and spews out the reason in one long exhale.

"From where they used to sleep!" She's a puddle of tears and sobs suddenly, and the anger dissolves from my body. I stare at her, paralyzed by the crying and immediately feeling like the biggest jerk in the world as it all starts to make sense.

Cherie doesn't covet this room because she wants to avoid my family; she wants to avoid the room of her deceased parents that sits just across from her own.

"I—I'm sorry," I murmur weakly. I don't know what else to say, so I reach out and pat her shoulder awkwardly. She's hysterical, holding her stomach and whimpering things like, "Oh God!" and "It hurts so much!" I want to call for my mom because I'm not equipped to handle this outburst.

Without warning, she crawls into my lap the way Britney would, and she buries her face into my neck. I wonder why this is always happening to me, why she cracks and breaks down with me when we are alone but acts like a cold-blooded monster whenever there are other people around. I can't keep up with her mood swings.

"Maybe you should talk to my mom," I say.

"No, I don't want to. Promise you won't say anything to her, Jack," she whimpers.

"But, Cherie—"

"Please, Jack?" I fall silent. "I don't want them to worry."

My logical conscience starts to scold me. *This is a big deal. I shouldn't be the only person to be privy to this information, and I'm certainly not the right person to help her through it. She needs adults. She might need professional help.*

We sit like that for a long time as she sobs and sniffles and cries, and I beat myself up for not knowing what to say and focusing more on how much of her skin is pressed to mine. My body begins to convince my mind that this is nothing terrible.

Maybe she wants to be my friend now, I think hopefully. *I can do this; I can be there for her. I have been before.*

Then I remind myself that she is drunk, and it is my duty as a gentleman and a human to just be quiet and supportive when she falls apart like this. Soon enough, she will work it all out of her system and go back to hating me and smacking me with her words or her hand.

I feel her grow heavier against me. "Cherie?" She's calm and still, and I think it's possible she's passed out. "Cherie, you should get to bed."

Her lips move against the skin of my neck while she mumbles, "Can I just stay here?" I get a chill, and the sensation spreads through my whole body.

Bad idea. I try to urge her off of my lap and onto her feet. "Cherie, that's not a good idea—"

"Please, Jack? I'm just so tired," she says, and she snuggles against my chest. I grind my teeth against giving in, which would be an easy thing to do when my whole body is determined to say yes.

"Cherie—"

Her hand stumbles up to my mouth and covers it. "It's okay." Her fingertips brush my lips, and I tremble in a dangerous place. "Just for tonight."

Every neuron in my brain is telling me this is going to get me in trouble, either with Jim and Mom or with her. I have to say no. But then Cherie twists out of my lap and collapses against my pillow.

Cherie is almost naked. In my bed. My brain fries, and I look away quickly.

"Fine, but just for tonight, okay?" I say to the floor. She mumbles something incoherent in response, and curls up beneath my comforter. I look around the room, spy the couch, and know I should go to sleep there instead of next to her.

But she's pulling on my elbow, urging me to lie down next to her. "Come here, Jack," she insists.

"I'm going to stay on the couch," I tell her, urgently pulling away.

"No, please stay here?" she pleads. Stupidly, I listen. As I lie back, she clutches my arm and presses her face to my shoulder. Her cheek is still damp with tears. She murmurs, "I don't want to be alone," and slips out of consciousness.

I stare up at my ceiling, my thoughts spinning wildly and my heartbeat fast. For all the things I hate about her, I'll never be able to ignore how unbelievably gorgeous she is.

But I can't let the physical attraction I have for her dominate my rational thought.

This is dumb. This is such a dumb chance I'm taking.

And she's a mess. I know I have to tell someone, but then she will get in trouble for drinking, and she will really have a reason to hate me. I don't want her to hate me anymore.

I pull the sheet of the bed around her to cover her and keep her warm. And I tuck it in the small space between our bodies to keep our skin from touching, because I don't think I can physically handle it much longer.

One night, I convince myself. *This is just for one night, and this will never happen again.*

But when I wake up the next morning to my agonizing alarm clock, I look over and see that she is gone. I don't know when she left or how she made it out of the room without waking me. For some reason, I'm disappointed in myself for missing her exit. I'm irritated that I fell asleep at all. Most of all, I kind of miss her.

Correction: *Worst* of all, I *do* miss her.

DIRTERAZZI.COM

BOOTY *CALLED IT*! CHERIE'S LATE NIGHT TRYSTS WITH JACK HANSEN?

Hold onto your seats, folks. Dirterazzi may just be about to make "I told you so" history...

We don't want to toot our own horn yet, but an anonymous source is claiming that Jack just became Cherie's midnight booty call. It appears living in close quarters has finally broken down the Berlin Wall of Silence between Cherie Belle and former love interest, Jack Hansen. A source very close to the family tells us that Cherie and Jack secretly spent the night together last night after she spent a wild night out with friends. Cherie was drunk, according to the source, and determined to see Jack. The big question, of course, is whether Jack is Cherie's first or if he's merely receiving Caz's sloppy seconds. Stay tuned!

Chapter 25

It's easy to be the new student in September, when everyone is just getting back from the summer. New cliques are forming because so-and-so suddenly got hot, or they earned credibility with a sports team, or their parents bought them an awesome new car. You can completely change your position in the high school hierarchy, like plotting a winning Jenga move. It's a fresh start for anyone who puts their piece in the right place.

But February? You're just glaringly, embarrassingly new when someone plops you into a pre-calculus class in February. First, it takes me twenty minutes to find the door to my class, which is not inside of a hallway; it's out in a courtyard because this is California, and everything in California has to be different from New York. And the door looks like every other door in the courtyard. Then, class is stopped when I enter, and I'm introduced to my class as Jonathan Hansen, because that's my real name, and I have to politely say, "I go by Jack," before the whole class starts yelling out "John!" or, worse, "Johnny!" So now I'm late, flustered and holding up class to repeat my name to a group of kids who couldn't care less about my name because they're not going to talk to me anyway.

"Ah, well, welcome Jack," the pony-tailed teacher says with a warm smile as he shakes my hand. "Just one second." He shuffles inside of a cabinet and pulls out a thick textbook for me. There's a low hum of whispers among the waiting kids, and I try not to meet any of their gazes.

The teacher, oblivious, hands me the book and a syllabus. "This is your book. We're on page 352 right now. You can find a seat."

The smile is warm but the words leave me cold, sending me into a blind search. The class stays silent as they wait for me to find my seat. I feel twenty pairs of eyes on me and wish the teacher would keep teaching and let me do my thing without an audience. I finally find an empty seat in the back, and of course it's too small for me, but I have no choice but to sit and try to stretch out my body without invading someone else's space. The desk makes a deafening noise as I scrape it backward to give my legs room and not put my feet anywhere near the expensive-looking bag that belongs to the girl in front of me. She swivels her head to look at me and then my feet, as if she's thinking, *"He'd better not be stepping on my bag!"*

But that's not what she's thinking. Instead, she whispers, "Are you *the* Jack Hansen? Like, *Cherie Belle's* Jack?"

I stare at her dumbly. That just happened. And it's only first period.

The recognition and the questions follow me as I go from classroom to classroom. There are at least five people, mostly girls, who recognize me from some magazine or entertainment news show. My Business Economics teacher actually makes a joke about a gossip blog she's read about Cherie and me. I do the same thing I'm supposed to do when any other person asks me something: Press my lips together, smile tightly, and say, "Just rumors."

But each time they ask, I feel her skin on mine, and her warm body curled around my arm. Sometimes you wish rumors were true.

Mica promised to meet me during fifth period in "the courtyard." Lucky me, there's three of them, and it's a whole text conversation just to figure out which one he meant. It's the only period we have together, and we both have a study hall. I finally find him in Courtyard Two, outside of the science rooms, and I shake off a few girls who are following me with more questions about Cherie.

"But do you guys really live together?" one short brunette asks.

"I, uh, I gotta go," I stammer pitiably. "Nice talking to you." I make a beeline for my friend, who's all smiles.

"Jack Hansen, my man!" he laughs, thankfully clueless. "I see you made a few friends of the female persuasion already."

I'm so fortunate he has no idea who I have been made out to be in the press, and I pray he never finds out. "Yep, looks like it."

"You okay? How's Worthington High treating you? You look like you been thrown outta a bus!"

I chuckle shyly and immediately reach up to check my hair. It feels fine, still in place. "Just disoriented, that's all. How's your day so far?"

He waves it off. "Just had chemistry. Ain't nuthin. It's my best class! What'd you have?"

"English with Mr. Cannon. Seems easy enough; nice guy."

Mica snickers. "That's my worst class. He wants to me write all poetic, and then he tells me my grammar's bad. I say, 'tell that to Jay-Z'!"

I laugh with him. He has a way of relaxing me with his jokes, and I'm grateful.

"Let's go walk around; I'll take you on a tour," he says, then adds a wink and a nudge of his elbow. "Maybe we'll talk to those new twin biddies along the way."

I start to nod, even though I'm not totally sure what a biddy is. Then I notice he is pointing at the twins, who are aptly surrounded by a gaggle of overdressed guys. I was used to the attention they attracted at our old school, but this new place, with these snake-eyed guys, makes me feel like I should step in and check on them. Conflicting emotions instantly surge through me.

Mica reads my expression like a book. "What? You know them or sumthin'?"

I purse my lips and nod. "Remember how I told you I live with an annoying stepfamily?"

He grins. "No way, man! You kiddin' me? Them twins live witchu?"

I cringe from the higher octave in his voice. "Yeah, they're my stepsisters." He laughs full on.

"Hook a brotha up!" he says, clapping a hand on my shoulder. When he sees I'm not laughing, he adds, "I'm kiddin' man."

"No, you're not."

"No, I'm not. They some fine a—"

He's cut short by Chloe, who is shouting my name from across the courtyard. She sashays over to me while her admirers look on with a mix of curiosity and humor. I know what they're thinking, and it gets my blood coursing.

I force myself to look down at her. "What?"

"I just wanted you to know we're going to hang out after school with some friends, so you don't need to drive us home," she says with a noticeably disapproving look in Mica's direction. I'm not sure if it's his baggy shirt or his skin color that she disapproves of more, but her awfulness as a person makes me even angrier than her news.

"Oh, yeah? I doubt Jim wants you going home with Miami Vice over there," I shoot back, tilting my chin in the direction of her arrogant entourage. "Better bring that pepper spray your dad gave you."

She huffs heavily at me. "Don't be a jerk, Jack."

Mica cuts in with his jovial grin and an outstretched hand. "Hello, I'm Mica Williams. I'm Jack's friend. Nice to meet you, uh…?" It's the clearest, most eloquent sentence I've heard him speak since I've met him.

Unfortunately, he might have been the same old Mica for all my stepsister cares. She stares at both of us like we have cooties or something. "Chloe," I say when she doesn't move to speak or shake his hand. Finally, she remembers a fraction of her manners and forces herself to shake his hand.

"Hi. So nice to meet you." Her saccharine smile makes me grind my teeth. "I'm so glad Jack has been able to find someone willing to hang out with him."

"Well, I'm sure he feels the same for you," he says with all of the pleasantries of a British gentleman. I snicker when her stupid smile transforms into a blazing glare.

She locks her eyes on his but says to me through gritted teeth, "I'll see you at home, Jack." With that, she flips her hair, turns and storms back to her new boyfriends and Claudia.

"I am really sorry about her," I say quickly.

"Eh, I'm used to snobs like her. This school's full of 'em."

"But what you said was awesome—did you see her face?"

Mica bumps my fist and encourages me to keep walking, chuckling, "Guess I see why you hate bein' home, playa. Can't believe there's two a dem!" I grin to myself; he's right back to the Mica I know.

"Three," I correct him. "There's another one just like them, but she's at home." I suddenly feel badly lumping Cherie in with those two.

"Triplets?!"

"No, just their cousin."

Maybe it's the way I smile at the thought of her, or maybe it's how I speak of her, but Mica picks it up. He reads me again, and I want to kick myself. "Ah, is that Miss Trouble?"

I try to shake my head, but I'm forced to add a disclaimer when he laughs at me. "It's not like that, really. She's their cousin; that would be weird."

"Ooh, that's double trouble right there!" he smirks.

"She's actually the reason we moved out here."

"Word?"

I nod. "Yeah, her parents were killed in a car accident this Christmas."

He winces. "Damn, that's rough. I'm sorry, man. But, uh, why she livin' witchu?"

"Something about the will; her parents left her in my stepdad's custody." The concept must sound nuts as it comes out of my mouth because Mica gawks at me.

"Say what?" His voice rises in pitch again. "That's some craziness right there! What 'bout your pops—couldn't you just stay with him?"

My guts twist into a pretzel. I swallow hard, looking for anything to say but the truth. I shake my head, coming up empty. "It's, um, it's complicated."

He respects my silence. "A'ight. Why's this cousin at home and not here?"

Boy, is he nosy. If I keep going, he's going to put it all together. "It's a long story."

"We got time," he prods. "If it's not too personal or nuthin.'"

I take the out. "I don't know if she'd like me talking about it." I feel terrible dismissing him, but he shrugs and grins.

"It's cool, I respect that." He sighs, "Well, I wish you luck, Jack Hansen. Sounds like you gots a lotta chaos at home."

I grimace and nod. "You have no idea."

"Since you've been, uh, relieved of yo' drivin' duties to Miss Congeniality, how bout we go to the gym after school and work it all out of yo' system. You in?"

I roll my eyes and laugh, rubbing my sore shoulder. "Yeah, I'm in."

***

It's nearly 6:30 at night when I finally pull into the driveway. I'm drenched in sweat and my hair is matted against my head, but I'm starving and can't decide if I should shower first or eat. The thought of sitting next to Cherie looking like this makes me decide to shower first, and I walk around the outside of the house instead of through it to get to the casita.

As I pass the windows of the dining room, though, I notice there are three empty seats at the dinner table. My mom looks downtrodden as she cuts something on Britney's plate, and Jim is busy peering out into the living room to catch part of the news. Brenton is building a pyramid with some ears of corn on a platter.

Where are the girls?

I open the door, and my mom jumps to attention.

My mother looks harried yet relieved. "Oh, Jack! I'm so glad you're here, I was worried. I just put dinner on the table—have you heard from the twins at all?"

I look around and ask, "Where is everyone?"

"Jackie!" Britney sings, and she pushes her face upward, her lips scrunching together. I bend for her to kiss my cheek and hug her.

"Hey, Brat. Miss me?" She nods emphatically.

"Jack, did you hear from the girls?" Mom repeats impatiently.

I shake my head. "Chloe and Claudia went home with some friends they met today." I can tell this doesn't sit well with her or Jim, who instantly joins the conversation.

"What friends? I told you guys under no circumstances to go in cars with other people!" he nearly scolds. I squint at him.

"Don't look at me; I didn't break the rules," I say. He rolls his eyes. "I told them it was a bad idea."

I look around and listen for Cherie stomping around or blasting her whiney indie music. "What about Cherie?"

My mom hangs her head and avoids eye contact with all of us. "I, uh, I don't know. She said she was going to lunch with that boy Caz and Danika, but that was this afternoon. I haven't heard from her since."

I grunt in response and shake my head. "She shouldn't be going anywhere with Caz, Mom. He's not a boy. He's old." I try not to let on how jealous I suddenly feel.

Jim cocks a concerned eyebrow. "Yeah? How old is old?"

I shrug, trying to be casual. "25 maybe?" His jaw clenches. I grab a roll from the basket on the table and take a bite, adding, "I'd get on that if I were you, *Psuedo-Dad*." He growls something incoherent, and I smile smugly.

"I'm sure it's nothing," Mom reassures him while shaking her head at me. "They're probably doing some interviews for that movie they're in together. Speaking of which, the premier for the movie is next Monday, and we are all going, so I need to get your suit dry-cleaned. Please make sure you give it to me before you go to sleep tonight."

"Whatever," I groan, pretending I don't care about her or her premier. But as I walk out to my room, I feel everything but indifferent. Sickness creeps through my stomach as I think of her out with Caz, as I realize I have to attend a movie premier where everyone thinks I might be her boyfriend, and as I keep this huge secret that she slept in my bed last night. The thoughts swirl and crash into one another in my brain, conjuring fury and frustration that manifest into a pitch of the bread roll over the top of the casita.

DIRTERAZZI.COM

DRUGS, BOOZE, AND SEX: IS CHERIE BELLE A TRAINWRECK IN MOTION?

Another night, another bender. Cherie Belle is growing her party girl reputation by the hour, and it's starting to make a few people more than concerned. After snapping a picture of Belle smoking what appears to be a marijuana joint last night, Dirterazzi did some investigating and found out that the teen queen has been adding drugs to her growing list of things she'll do for a good time, along with body shots, cigarette smoking, and dancing like a stripper for anyone who will watch. Some say she's just having some fun, but it looks like a cry for help to us. We've seen this behavior before in other disturbed actors and actresses who crumble under the growing pressures of fame, and the end result is often tragic. Hopefully, the Goldmans will realize she's in trouble and step up to their duty as her guardians. If not, here's a photo gallery of the <u>ugliest moments in celebrity train wreck history</u>, which can only be described as little windows into Cherie Belle's future if no one steps in to stop her.

Chapter 26

It's past midnight, and Cherie's in my room again. I forgot to lock my door, and this time she just slips inside, quietly closing it behind her. I hear her turn the lock.

I lift my head from my pillow wearily and see her shadow inching closer to my bed. "Cherie?"

"Oh!" she gasps with a start. "I didn't know you were up."

"Well, now I am," I grumble, shifting onto my back. "What are you doing?"

"I just came to hang out," she replies. Now she's close, and I can smell the aura of vodka around her once more.

"You've been drinking again," I mutter, feeling the mattress dip beneath her weight as she crawls in beside me. I'm foggy with sleep and dumb enough to slide over to make room for her when she nudges me. She smells of smoke and weed, too. "Where were you tonight?"

"At a party," she sighs. I wonder where the party was and if Caz was there. I don't want to sound jealous, so I don't ask. I picture her making out with Caz, and my skin grows hot.

As if she senses my envy anyway, she adds, "It was a lame house party."

I don't feel any better. "Cherie, you can't keep coming in here. It's—it's weird." But I'm defenseless when she burrows inside of my arm and rests her head on my chest.

"It's fine, Jack," she slurs. "Just for tonight, okay?"

"You said that last night," I sigh. I can tell this is going to be like dealing with Britney all over again, except she's not my baby sister. She's a beautiful, famous girl my own age who thinks it's no big deal to sleep with a guy. A guy she's not dating. A guy she sometimes hates.

"I like it here, with you," she murmurs. "You get me."

Now I know this is high-talk, or drunk-talk. "I get you, huh?"

"Shh," she shushes me, and I feel her arm drape across my stomach, pulling me tightly against her. I'm torn between forcing her to leave and just closing my eyes because it feels kind of good to have her there. I didn't like being alone every night anyway, so I can tolerate this I guess, right?

The fear of getting caught looms over me. How embarrassing it would be if anyone found out about this. The twins would scream, "*Gross!*" and make fun of us for the rest of our lives. Jim would be mad at me, and my mom would probably be upset that I have a girl sleeping in my bed.

But, I try to convince myself, *maybe she'd be proud of me for being nice to Cherie.* I can't be sure. I don't know if I care right now anyway. I promise myself that I'll talk to Mom tomorrow and get Cherie the help she needs.

When morning comes, though, she's gone again, and I think better of telling Mom anything. I'm sure that it was the last time, and I'm pretty confident Cherie is just going through a weird phase. Even if it happens again, it won't last forever.

I go about my day, going to school, and dodging the questions from my classmates about her. I join Mica afterward at the gym. I try to forget all about Cherie until it's time to go to sleep. Just as I'm about to lock my door, I pause, as if my hand doesn't want to do what my brain is telling it to do. I don't lock the door, just in case. Sure enough, when I wake up hours later, she is snuggling up beside me, telling me it's not a big deal.

And it happens Wednesday night, too. I pretend to be asleep, and she comes in as quiet as a mouse. She tiptoes to my bedside, calls out my name, and then climbs in beside me when I don't answer. I knew before I went to sleep that I should lock my door and stop her from coming in, but I couldn't bring myself to do it. It's become part of my nighttime routine: push-ups, crunches, brush my teeth, wash my face, stare at the door debating whether or not to lock it. I begin to wonder if there's something wrong with me for practically inviting her in every night.

By Thursday morning, I'm positive I'll get in trouble if I tell Mom. I've let Cherie sleep with me for a few nights, and my mother will definitely ask why I didn't tell someone sooner. She'll scold me for not caring enough to stop Cherie from drinking or hurting herself. I won't know what to say to that because deep down, Cherie getting hurt is becoming my newest fear. I know it can't be healthy for this girl to be getting drunk all the time, and I am beginning to worry that something will happen before she gets home to me. Each night I find myself staying awake later and later, holding my breath, waiting until she comes through that door before I can breathe easy again. Dread plagues me, even during the day when I'm at school. I constantly wonder if she's okay and who she's with.

Tonight, she doesn't tiptoe inside. Instead, she runs in and jumps on the bed, high on life.

"Jack!"

I'm wide awake but still startled. "What are you doing?"

She giggles maniacally and sits on top of me. "Oh my God, I had the best night! It was so fun!"

"Great, I'm glad," I mutter. I shift her off of me and turn onto my side. "Did Caz show you a good time?"

"Very funny, Jack," she laughs, pulling on my shoulder until I'm on my back. "It was a girls' night, for your information. We went to Fly, and—"

"Cherie, I need to go to sleep, and you need to go to your room," I say firmly. But a huge weight floats off of my chest when I hear that Caz wasn't with her for once.

"Can't I stay here, with you?"

Her voice is small and pouty and makes me angry. She is so proud of herself for being able to manipulate people with that voice, but I refuse to be just some other tool she has wrapped around her finger.

"No, you can't keep staying here. You're keeping me up every night. I can barely stay awake at school."

She giggles. "Oh stop, you're always passed out when I come in. Aren't you?"

Dammit! I turn on my side again to hide my reddening face. "Yeah, but that doesn't matter, you're keeping me up right now. Go to bed. In YOUR room."

She's relentless tonight. "Why do you keep pushing me away, Jack?"

The question hits me like a brick. I look over my shoulder and see that she is genuinely hurt. Her expression is a punch to my gut, but I try to stay strong. "Because this just isn't… *right*."

"It's not wrong, either, Jack," she fires back. "What are we doing besides keeping each other company?"

I grunt, "I don't need company, Cherie. I'm fine. You're the one who keeps coming in here."

"And you let me in, don't you?"

I fumble for an answer. She's on to me. "You come in. I don't let you in," I bite back.

"Oh really? You could lock that door if you wanted to, but you don't."

"Because I don't know where you'd be if you didn't come in here, and that worries me," I admit finally.

"Well, then why haven't you told on me?" I don't have an answer for that, and she pounces. "You must want me to be here because you'd find a way to keep me out like you do to everyone else," she says firmly.

I sit up and turn to her. "What's that supposed to mean?"

"It means you try to pretend you don't need anybody, but actually you do," she says. "You like having me around because I was abandoned by my parents, and you know what that feels like."

I stiffen immediately. There's nothing more I hate than someone psychoanalyzing me. The heat of shame turns quickly into an angry fire. She has no idea why I actually like having her around, and it has nothing to do with being abandoned by my father.

Does it?

That's it. I've had it with this girl! Now she's making me question my own psychological stability. She's the only person on this earth other than my father who makes me question myself.

"You've been talking to Claudia too much." I hear the hardness in my voice, and so does she.

Her mouth twists to the side. "Yes, she told me a little bit. But it's nothing I couldn't figure out on my own, Jack."

"Cherie, enough. Our situations are totally different," I reply. I stand up and walk to the bedroom door. "I'm not talking about this right now."

"Why?"

"Because I don't want to. It's nearly three in the morning, and I have school in a few hours. Just go upstairs!" I open the door and moonlight pours in like an interrogation lamp. I turn away from it bitterly.

She slides off of the bed and walks toward me, and I'm blazing again, but it's for all the wrong reasons. I scan her tiny black dress, which only hits the tops of her thighs and plunges low on her chest. A long, glittery necklace draws my eye to her cleavage. She looks amazing, even with her hair frazzled and her makeup slightly smudged. She doesn't look pretty and perfect, like that teen princess I first met on Christmas Eve who was all pink lip gloss and bouncing yellow curls and innocence. She's hot and ragged, the dangerous kind, when a girl looks a little bit like you were the reason she got that disheveled. Suddenly, my mind is conjuring all sorts of alternate endings to this night, and I'm desperate to block the desire to take her back to my bed.

She stops and stares at me. "Do you hate me still?" Her sad tone snaps me out of my daze, but her wide, black rimmed eyes keep me imprisoned. "I thought we were past all that."

I swallow hard, trying to find my voice. "I don't hate you," I say softly.

"Then what is it?"

I can't answer. I can't tell her I feel like a yo-yo, wound up tightly until she feels like playing with me, and then thrown back and forth at the flick of her hand. Mean, nice, friendly, evil, perfect, wild. I'm subjected to whoever Cherie feels like being on a given day. I certainly can't tell her how badly I want her. I can't let her know that she makes my blood boil and my heart pound and my skin tingle all at the same time. Cherie, who has been trying to break me for the last week, is causing at least one part of me to crack without even knowing it.

"Oh, Jack," she sighs, pushing her lower lip out. "Are you still mad that I took your sister for a walk?"

I feel air catch in my throat and try not to stare at her mouth. "No, that's not it," I reply.

"Then what is it?" she presses.

I have to look away. "I'm just tired, Cherie, okay?" I sigh to the floor. "I go to school all day and then the gym and then you have me up all night—I'm tired and need sleep." I don't even believe my complaints, and they're mostly true.

"Oh, the gym, huh? That's where these abs are coming from," she teases, playfully running her fingers over the muscles of my bare stomach. It sends a red alert straight to my groin and sparks a rash of goosebumps across my skin.

I push her hand away quickly. "Don't." My voice sounds choked and tortured, and she tilts her head like a dog, picking up on it. I didn't want her to know that she affects me that much.

"Gosh, I was just paying you a compliment, you big grouch!"

"Cherie, can you be serious for one minute? I mean it."

She sighs and looks me dead in the eye. "If you really want me to leave, I will. But I really want to stay. I promise I won't bring up your abs again."

I swallow a chuckle and shake my head. I can't put my foot down with her. I know I should tell her to go. I know that letting her stay means a lot of things are going unsaid. She may not feel the same way about me as I feel about her, but spending all these nights together is digging me into a deep hole, that's for sure.

I rub my eyes. "If we get caught, we could get in trouble."

"Get in trouble for what?" she laughs, heading back to the bed. "It's not like we're doing anything bad out here."

Yet, I think, watching her crawl into the bed, in her tight, short dress. *We're not doing anything bad yet*. I feel a thousand pounds settle back onto my chest as I slide into bed next to her.

She curls up around me, and I lie flat beside her, staring at the ceiling, trying to calm my racing heart.

I try to convince myself that she's right; I'm not doing anything wrong—*we* are not doing anything wrong. My imagination, however, has a whole playbook of wrong decisions I desperately want to make. But I can't; I keep telling myself she's like Britney, only older. And not my sister.

And ridiculously hot.

A tiny part of me hopes that someone does find out and puts a stop to this before I reach a point where I can't stop myself.

DIRTERAZZI.COM

CHERIE BELLE OUT FOR ASSISTANT'S 25th BIRTHDAY PARTY: NO BOYS ALLOWED!

In the first night all week, Cherie Belle was seen out without Caz Farrell or any other Kidz Channel boys as she celebrated the twenty-fifth birthday of her assistant, Danika Shields. The girls, all twelve of them, started the night out at the uber-swanky Sake restaurant for some sushi and a birthday cake shaped like a puppy. How cute! Then, Danika brought her posse, including Belle and other ladies of Kidz Channel fame, to their favorite hotspot, Club Fly. The no-boys-allowed rule was upheld even on the dance floor, where the ladies shimmied and shook together and kept it relatively clean for once. Belle was spotted drinking throughout the evening, but she left the club on her own two feet, another first for the week. Maybe things are turning around for the starlet...

Chapter 27

"Hansen!"

I'm startled out of my slumber and jump to attention. I'm in the middle of the cafeteria, and Mica is staring down at me with genuine concern.

"You okay, my man?" he asks, sitting across from me.

I rub my eyes and nod weakly. "Yeah, just tired."

"You look it. Am I workin' you too hard at the gym?" he laughs, nudging my shoulder with a light jab.

I shake my head. "Maybe." I'm exhausted, staring at my sandwich, thinking it is too much work to lift it and chew it.

"You look beat. What's up?" he presses, stealing the french fries off of my tray. "Studying for a test or somethin'?"

I harrumph. "Something like that."

"Well, I was gonna ask you if you wanna meet up in West Hollywood tomorrow night, but seein' how you need a nap and all..."

"Very funny," I grumble. I try to think what day it is, and I realize it's Friday. "What time?"

He grins wide at me. "'Bout ten. My friend, D'shawn, gots some honeys meetin' up wit' us, too. Betta dress nice."

I squint at him. He says that to me a lot, and he's starting give me a complex, like I don't dress well or something. "What's that supposed to mean?"

He laughs at my defensiveness. "Means we goin' to a club, and we gotta look the part, you dig?"

"What club?"

Mica winks. "It's called Fly. It's hoppin'." I cock my head because the name sounds familiar. Then I remember hearing Cherie babble one night about being there before coming home to me. Now I'm intrigued.

"How will we get in?"

"We got the hookup, kid," he says reassuringly. "D'Shawn knows the door guy. It's his cousin." He chuckles deeply at my doubtful frown. "Don't worry, I got you, son!" He tousles my hair like I'm a kid, and I smack his hand away. He struts off, calling over his shoulder, "We gon' play with the big boys tomorrow night!"

***

"Can you keep a secret?"

I peer down at Cherie, trying to make out her features in the small light from my window. I can't tell if she's joking, but I hope that she is.

"Haven't I kind of been doing that already?"

"I'm serious!" she giggles. Her smile makes me smile. Behind her mess of wild blond curls, the digital clock reads 3:30.

"What?"

"Swear not to tell." Her hand absently pets my shoulder, giving me a tame version of chills.

I sigh. "I swear not to tell."

She giggles again. "Okay, so, I tried E tonight."

My heart misses about three beats. "What?"

"E. You know, Ecstasy?"

"Cherie, I know what E is," I huff. "I mean *what* were you *thinking*?"

"My friends were doing it, and they offered it to me. I figured why not?" Her grin grows big. "Oh my God, it was so fun."

"It's so stupid, that's what it is."

She rolls her eyes and closes them. "Come on, you're not seriously going to lecture me right now, are you?"

I prop myself up onto my elbow. "It's not a lecture, it's a reality check. That's dangerous stuff, and you shouldn't be doing it."

"Don't act like you've never done drugs before." She narrows her eyes when I shake my head. It seems gleefully shocking to her. "Serious? You've seriously never done any drugs before?"

"Nope. We get drug tested for football season. I'm not going to jeopardize my chance at a scholarship for some stupid curiosity." I feel like an old man as I add, "And you shouldn't either. You could get in big trouble for that; people are always watching what you do and talking about you. You'll get arrested or addicted or worse."

She smiles playfully and rubs my shoulder. "Aw, do you care what happens to me?"

I blush a little but admit, "Yes, I do. You know that already. I wonder all the time if you're going to make it home or not. The drinking is bad enough, but drugs are a whole other story."

"Sweetie, save me the D.A.R.E. talk, okay?" she says, squeezing my chin in her hand. "It was just this once, and I'm totally fine. See?"

"Yeah, good for you, but you're lucky nothing bad happened. A kid at my old school did E once, and it messed him up big time," I tell her.

"That only happens when you don't drink water or take too much. Only dumb people overdose, Jack," she says flipping her hair over her shoulder and across the pillow. "My friends know what they're doing."

"You do know that the term 'intelligent celebrities' is an oxymoron, right?"

She laughs at this and turns to face me. "You hate that I'm famous, don't you?"

"No, I hate your famous friends and your stupid entourage who bring you home drunk and feed you drugs."

"They don't feed them to me, Jack," she corrects me, offended. "They ask if I want to try them, and I say whether I do or I don't. I only try drugs with someone if I trust them."

"Oh really? Celebrities are trustworthy drug specialists?" I scoff. I can't believe she's this dumb sometimes. "I love it. What does Caz say, 'trust me because I can play a doctor on TV?'"

"Oh, I wasn't with Caz this time; I was with Carl and Betsy," she says, as if that's supposed to make it any better. "And don't pick on Caz. He's a not a bad guy."

I grunt, "Yeah, he's a real Prince Charming."

"Oh, my! Someone sounds jealous of Caz," she sings.

"Did I say that?" I look away, my cheeks stinging from her truth.

"You don't have to; all guys hate him! Look me in the eye and tell me you're not," she laughs. When I won't look at her, she straddles my stomach. I turn my face, but she pulls it back and makes me meet her eye. "Are you jealous of Caz?"

"I'm not," I say defiantly. "I think it's stupid that you are dating a guy who's so old."

"I'm not dating him," she replies with a smug smile. "We are just friends."

I jerk my face from her hand. "Sure you are."

She drops her jaw and gawks at me. "You *are* jealous!"

"No, I'm not. Get off of me please," I push gently at her knees, but she won't budge, tightening her grip around my sides. Her hands rest on top of my chest, sending warmth through my skin.

Her face is serious all of a sudden. "Jack, you don't really think he and I are dating, do you?"

"Does it matter what I think?"

Cherie's eyebrows knit together as if she isn't sure. "But why do you think that?"

"It's all over the news, Cherie," I say stiffly, turning my eyes away again. It's hard to look up at her when she's on top of me like this. It makes my mind swirl with a thousand different scenarios I'd rather have happening right now than a conversation about Caz.

"Aunt Eva told you not to pay attention to that stuff, remember?" she says. She looks disappointed in me.

"I don't. People at school ask me about you," I mutter in my own defense. She dismounts and plants herself beside me, her legs folding underneath her body.

"Really?" This news sounds more exhilarating to her. "Kids ask you about me? What do they say?"

"Did you think you weren't relevant anymore or something?" I joke, shaking my head. "They ask if you guys are dating, they ask if we're dating—"

"They ask about you and me?" Now she looks nervous. "What do you say?"

I shrug and explain, "That it's a rumor the magazines made up, and you just live with my family."

"Oh." Is that satisfaction I see or disappointment? I can't tell, and before I can ask, she says, "Good. Keep saying that."

It's my turn to be offended. "It's the truth; you're not my girlfriend."

"Well, I'm not Caz's girlfriend, either."

"Then why do you hang out with him so much?" I pry, knowing I'm asking more than I should, and possibly asking for more information than I want to know.

She shrugs. "The producers of *Sunny* think it will be good for the movie if we are seen together a lot, so we get together sometimes. Keeps people guessing."

The celebrity world perplexes me more every day. "The producers for your movie make you stage a relationship? To make people *think* you're dating? Why can't you tell everyone it's not true?"

"I do, Jack," she says. "I tell them we are just friends. No one believes me because it's more fun to believe the rumor. Isn't it more scandalous to think a sixteen-year-old girl would have some twenty-something-year-old heartthrob wrapped around her finger?"

She adds with a wink, "It's even more scandalous if they can make a love triangle out of it by throwing you in there and saying we are dating, too. Clearly, that's not true, right?"

Her explanation makes sense, and it even burns a little. I'm still unconvinced about Caz, though. She's a pro at lying, and I feel almost like I'm the newest victim of her believe-me smile. "Do you like Caz?"

She shrugs. "Not particularly. He's a little shallow. He has jerky friends, and he gets nasty when he's around them."

I laugh out loud. "He sounds perfect for you."

Cherie gawks. "How dare you!" She digs her fingers into my side to tickle me, but I'm quick to grab her hands and hold them hostage. She squeals and squirms to free herself, but I twist my upper body and pin her arms beneath me.

"Watch it. My mom's not here to save you this time," I warn.

"You wouldn't do anything to me," she taunts, struggling to free herself.

"Not true."

She lifts her chin and says breathlessly, "Then do something." I smell booze and smoke and trouble.

Once more, her lips are too close to mine; my heart stills as if it's afraid to beat, and I can't inhale or exhale. I've never been locked in that awkward moment between play and intimacy with her before, and it scares me how easily I could seize the opportunity to make a move. That dark look flashes through her eyes again, and I'm dangerously close to doing something that could get me slapped again. Or maybe she wants me to, I can't tell with her right now. Is she tempting me on purpose? Is it the ecstasy talking? Does she have any idea what she is doing to my brain?

I release her hands and fall back onto the bed. "Nah, it wouldn't be a fair fight."

She's quiet, watching me with those big, green eyes. I swallow hard and look over at the clock, or anywhere that isn't her face or her body.

"Jesus, it's late," I mutter.

"Yeah," she whispers.

I don't want to tell her to leave, but I don't think I can stay next to her for another minute. "Are you staying here?"

Please say no.

"Just for an hour or so. I try to get in the house before your mom wakes up." She pauses and blinks at me. "Can I?"

I should say no. I should say no right now.

Say no, stupid!

"If you want."

She smiles and presses her hands together beneath her cheek instead of curling around my arm or snuggling against me like usual. It's like she knows my whole body is on fire and she'll get burned. I turn my face to the ceiling and close my eyes.

"Jack?"

I feel her staring at me and risk looking over. "What?"

"Are you coming to my premier on Monday?" she asks.

"To the movie?" I shrug. "I think so, yeah. I have to, right?"

She scrunches her nose, insulted. "No, you don't *have* to do anything."

"I'm kidding. Of course I want to go."

She smiles and says, "Good. I'd like to have you there."

I try not to grin on the outside as much as I am grinning on the inside. I watch her watching me for a second, her eyes twinkling. I don't know if she ever closes those eyes because I have to turn my whole body away from her.

DIRTERAZZI.COM

CHERIE BELLE: WITNESS CLAIMS SHE TOOK ECSTASY

Well, we had high hopes, folks, but Cherie's hopes were just to be high it seems. A member in Cherie's entourage claims the starlet experimented with ecstasy last night. Our source reports, "They were all doing it, and she wanted to try it, so they gave her some. They only gave her a little, and it worked its way out of her system pretty fast." It is unclear who "they" are, especially since it seems Cherie was out with her handlers, Carl Schwartz and Betsy Calves, along with a few This Side of Sunny *costars, such as Caz Farrell. It is possible Schwartz and Calves were unaware of her little experiment, but it seems unlikely due to their proximity to her. Dirterazzi just wants to know: Is no one watching out for this little girl?*

Chapter 28

"Dude, that's crazy." Frank's voice echoes through the bathroom as I finish styling my hair. I wipe my hands on my towel and carry my cellphone back into my bedroom.

"I know, right?" I reply, setting the phone down on the top of my nightstand as I get dressed. "Sick room, huh?"

He laughs, "You're the luckiest shit I know." He sighs and is quiet for a moment before asking, "What about Cherie? What's happening with her?"

I pause and look down at the phone. It's only been about a week since I last heard from Frank, but it feels like a year's worth of drama has taken place. It's too much to tell, and I don't know how much I really want to tell him anyway. What if he tells someone else, like big-mouthed Josh? I can't take that kind of a risk.

I finally say, "Nothing's happening. I never see her around." I hate lying to my best friend. I've been lying to everyone else about her, so it feels natural all the other times, just not with Frank. Lying to Frank makes the secrecy I have to maintain about Cherie awful for reasons I can't define.

"There was a thing on the news about her partying in clubs and stuff," he continues. "They say she's a train wreck waiting to happen."

Sickness pools in my stomach and I nod absently, knowing full well that those stories are mostly true. They've got to be. "Really? What else do they say?"

"Eh, that she's with that tool, Caz Farrell, all the time, and that she drinks. Don't you ever pay attention to the internet, man?" My jealousy burns the back of my eyes. "They got all these pictures and videos of her hanging out with some trashy sluts, getting drunk and whatever. My girl showed me one picture of her hanging all over some fat old guy, and she looked bombed."

Carl, I'm sure. Carl and Betsy, her trusted keepers, are the biggest parts of Cherie's problem. Carl and Betsy and Danika... a motley crew of bad influences that Cherie needs to lose, fast.

"Hey, you know, it's not my problem." Lie number two. It is definitely becoming my problem.

My phone beeps. I won't deny that my heart flutters a little when I see Cherie's number pop up on my phone.

"Hey, can you hold on a second? I have another call," I tell him, and I immediately switch to her call before he can reply. "Hello?"

"Hey! What are you doing today?" she sings on the other end.

I feel ridiculous for smiling at the sound of her voice. "Nothing. Just got back from the gym. You?"

"Well, your family is going to the beach today, and I was thinking of hanging back here at the house. Were you going with them?"

I want to laugh at her and shout, "*No way*!" Instead I just say, "Nah, I don't think so."

"Good!" she cries. "Come outside to the pool!"

I hold my head a second and try to steady my thoughts. Cherie wants to hang out with me? Sober? In broad daylight? This has got to be breaking a ground of some sort, right?

"Uh, yeah, sure. Hold on," I stutter, walking toward the door.

"Well, not yet," she says. "They haven't left. Give it, like, half an hour. Okay?"

I stare at the phone. So I can hang out with her, but I can't hang out with her in front of anyone? Not even our family?

"Jack, are you there?"

"Yeah, okay," I reply stiffly. "I gotta go; I have a friend on the other line." I hang up on her quickly.

"Frank?" There's no answer. "Frank?"

He's already hung up.

***

"Hey!" Cherie sings when I finally step outside, forty-five minutes later, just to be sure. "Look, I made you lunch!"

She stands over the patio table in a yellow bikini top and a skirt-looking thing wrapped around her hips. My eyes dart from the curved lines of her bikini top to the eclectic spread of food to which she gestures. From celery and hummus to something that looks like grilled tofu, the table is a vegan's heaven.

"Nice," I force myself to say. "I didn't realize you cook."

She beams shyly as she arranges a plate of food for me. "I love to cook. It's how I got started with *Choc it Up*, actually. My mom and I used to take all these cooking classes together, and I would hold cooking parties with my friends as playdates. One of my friends' dads happened to be a casting agent, and he thought I'd make the perfect host for their show."

She hands me my plate, adding, "The rest is history."

I think of her taking mother-daughter classes with her mom and feel a little cold inside. It reminds me of my dad for some reason, and I begin to visualize how we used to play football in the backyard of my old house.

"Cool," is all I can say in response as I pretend to be invested in eating. Her food is actually not so bad, and I start to take bigger bites. Pleased with my contentment, she rattles on some more about how she got started with the Kidz Channel and all the fascinating places around the world she got to visit to investigate chocolate.

"...but I think it's time I step away from it for a little while," she concludes after a good ten minute monologue about the acting business.

"Think you'll ever act again?" I ask finally.

It takes her a moment, but she eventually nods and looks up at the sky wistfully. "I'd like to think that they wanted me to, so maybe one day."

"You don't have to just do what they wanted you to do. You wouldn't be dishonoring them or anything," I say.

She lowers her gaze to me and squints. "Where do you want to go to college?"

I cock my head. "Huh?" That question came out of nowhere.

"Where are you planning to go to school?" she presses.

I shrug, my ever-ready answers flying off my tongue before I even think about them. "South Carolina, University of Miami, if I'm lucky."

"Why those schools?" she presses.

I'm so perplexed by her sudden topic shift. "Good football schools."

She nods pensively. "Who taught you to play football?"

I stare at her, feeling instantly exposed as I prevent the word "dad" from escaping my mouth. I sit back in my chair at the table and watch a smile slowly spread across her face. She has a really funny way of telling me to follow my own advice.

"Touché," I murmur.

***

"Truth or dare."

I look up and see Cherie bobbing around me inside of Brenton's blue inner tube, her smile twinkling with mischief. The sun makes her tanned, wet skin glisten and her blond hair glow like a halo. Her sunglasses cover her eyes, and I can't tell if she is luring me into a trap or truly still a little girl at heart.

I shake my head and lean back in my floating chair. "No way. I'm not playing truth or dare with you."

"Come on, Jack, don't be such a lame-o," she pushes. "Please?"

"What are you, twelve?" I reply.

"Truth or dare, Jack! Come on!"

"Fine. Truth." I don't trust her enough to say dare, but I brace myself for what will probably be a question that is too personal.

"Oooh, truth, huh?" she says with a giggle. "Okay. Hmm. Let me think..."

"You wanted to play this stupid game but you don't know what to ask?" I scold playfully. "Disgraceful."

"Well, I was expecting you to say dare, so now I have to think about a question."

"Well, we all know thinking is hard for you. This may take a while," I joke.

"Shut up!" she laughs through her dramatic gasp and splashes me. "Okay, hold on, I got it. Truth: How many girlfriends have you had?"

I don't know why I'm embarrassed to say it, but heat creeps across my face when I reply, "Three." Maybe that's not enough. Maybe she'll think I'm a loser to have not had more than three girlfriends.

"What were their names?" she asks quickly, but I wag my finger at her.

"Nope, you only get to ask one question at a time," I tease. Besides, it's my turn to ask a question, and now of course I have to know how many boyfriends she's had. "Truth or dare?"

She senses that I want to ask the same question, and she avoids giving me the satisfaction like the plague. "Dare," she whispers through a wince, as if I'm about to say something really awful, like tell her to run around the pool naked. Not that it's a bad idea or anything.

I squint at her and at this game she's playing with me; not the truth or dare one, the one where she's asking questions she wouldn't want to answer herself. I'll make her regret it.

"I dare you to call Danika and tell her she's fired. Right now. And you have to hang up immediately."

Cherie's jaw drops. "No, I can't!"

"You have to; it's the rules."

"Jack—no! She'll believe me!"

I harrumph, "Good, you don't need that bitch around anyway."

Now she is horrified. "Don't call her that, Jack!"

"What? She is." I can't even believe I would have to defend the word. Cherie tilts her head and gives me a look only my mom would give me: the *"don't be a jerk"* look. I roll my eyes and look away.

"This game is no fun," I mutter.

"Well, if you're going to pout about it like a baby," she sighs and swims to the edge of the pool. I watch her pick up her phone.

"You're doing it?!" I feel my eyes nearly bug out of my head. Cherie shakes her head at me, and it's her turn to roll her eyes while she puts the phone to her ear.

I can barely hold back the laughter as she says in her flawless actress voice, "Danika? Hi, what're you doing? Oh, that's nice. I know, right? So, um, listen: we have to talk. I—I just don't think this is working out anymore. Yeah, I'm sorry; I have to let you go. Don't take it personally or anything, okay? Okay? I gotta go, but I'll call you and we'll do lunch laters. Okay? Don't cry, please? It's not you, it's me. Okay? Love ya!"

She hangs up and turns a frown toward me that says, *"See? I'll do your dares, but I won't like it, and you're gonna pay."*

But I'm too busy celebrating the prank to be worried about the retribution. I pump a fist in the air victoriously and cry out, "Yes!"

"You're a Neanderthal," she grumbles, texting rapidly, probably a quick apology or something. "Your turn: truth or dare?"

I know better than to ask for a dare after making her do that. "Truth."

"Truth? Okay, truth: Did you and Katrina break up because she wouldn't have sex with you?"

The question spins my head. "Whoa, what?" It got really personal all of a sudden.

She sets her devil's eyes on me and smiles sadistically. "Did you break up with Katrina because she was a prude?"

I suddenly can't see straight, so I sit up and take off my sunglasses. "Katrina? How do you even know about Katrina?" I ask, rubbing the shock out of my eyes.

She shrugs and her mouth twists with a coy smirk. "I know things."

The twins. That sounds like a Chloe and Claudia rumor if I ever heard one. My face burns a little more now, and I'm not sure if it's from sunburn or how exposed I feel. It doesn't matter that her idea of me is completely inaccurate, I don't like the mere fact that she knows the name of someone I dated weeks before I even met her. What else have those girls told her about me— and why are they even having these kinds of conversations about me?

"Stupid twins," I mutter absently.

"So it's true?" she demands, squinting at me as if the thought is vile and inhuman. "Did you really break up with a girl over that?"

"No, of course not!" I groan. "Sex had nothing to do with it. Chloe was really nasty to her whenever she would come around. Katrina started to get paranoid that Chloe liked me and was trying to break us up. I just couldn't take the drama anymore. She didn't trust me, and then one night she accused me of cheating on her with Chloe because I didn't answer her phone call."

I lie back down. "So we broke up."

Cherie floats closer. "Did you?"

"Did I what?"

"Cheat on her with Chloe, duh!"

I cast her a dirty look. She knows something, but I don't know how much. "Chloe's my stepsister."

"So?"

"So there's no way I'd do something like that," I say firmly.

Cherie's eyes glisten with mischief when she knows more than she's letting on, and right now her eyes are shining. "But Chloe would."

I roll my eyes. "You sound just like Katrina."

She's too smart to be discouraged from pressing. "Well, you're not denying it."

I sigh, focusing on the cup holder of my floating chair and running my finger along its rim. "It was a stupid mistake. She'd had a few drinks at the rehearsal dinner, and we were all just hanging out, and she tried to kiss me. I stopped her right away."

Cherie nods like she knows this already. But who would tell her? "And your girlfriend found out?"

"Well, yeah, because my friends are stupid and can't keep their mouths shut," I mutter bitterly. "It became the running joke, and my friend, Josh, let it slip in front of Katrina."

"Why did you tell your friends at all? That seems kind of mean," she chastises, and I shake my head in shame.

"I know, that was dumb, but I was freaked out. I didn't know what to do—this girl just tried to make out with me, and she was 24 hours away from being my stepsister. They were moving into my house!" I look down and sigh. "I shouldn't have said anything and shoulda just pretended it didn't happen."

"Chloe must have been mortified when you turned her down," Cherie says, but her evil grin tells me she doesn't feel so bad for Chloe.

I nod. "Of course she was, and she's been a bitch to me ever since. Her and her little minion, Claudia. They made up all sorts of rumors about me at school, including that sex one, I guess."

She pauses and mulls my words over in her mind. Finally, she asks, "And what about Katrina? Did you guys ever… you know?"

"That's none of your business," I say as I put my sunglasses back on, doing anything to avoid looking directly at her. "Your turn: truth or dare?"

"No—wait a minute! Did you and Katrina have sex?"

My ears are ringing with her questions and her prying. I want to run from them. I know I should bail on this game before the questions can get any deeper. I'm too proud to tap out that easy; I want her to walk away first.

Instead, I guide the floating chair around in a circle and call over my shoulder, "I already answered way more than one question. Now it's your turn. Which will it be?"

Cherie grunts, "Ugh! We are so coming back to this Katrina stuff when it's your turn!"

"Why do you care so much?" I ask, glancing back.

She shrugs. "Because you are clearly dodging the question! Whatever, you're going to have to tell me eventually. I choose truth."

"Okay, fine. Truth: have you had sex with anyone?" Once it's out there, I can't take the question back, but I wish I could because only an asshole asks a girl a question like that. I feel like I'm no better than Josh, and I wonder what possessed me to pry into her privacy like that.

Of course, the little kid in me cries, *She started it!* But I know that's not how it works, and that girls aren't supposed to kiss and tell, even though guys are allowed to talk about that stuff. I can already feel irritation rising inside at the thought of her having sex with some other guy, and the status of her virginity is probably one of those truths best left unsaid.

This whole time, as my mind spits scolding words at my impulsive jerk side, Cherie is silent. I look back, dreading her answer but hoping she answers all the same. Cherie watches the water rippling around us, and for the first time since I've known her, she looks too shy to speak. Her blushing cheeks and her reserved eyes dart between me and the water.

My inner-gentleman finally steps up to the plate. "Never mind, you don't have to answer that."

She looks relieved, and says, "Well, are you going to ask something else?"

I think and think, wondering, *What's a nice, softball question I can lob at her to make up for my asinine question?* "Did you have any pets growing up?"

She cocks her head at me and sighs with frustration. "Seriously?"

"What? I want to know," I reply, watching her shake her head at me.

"If that's the kind of question you're going to come up with, then I'd rather answer the other one," she pouts.

I groan and rub my eyes. I can't win with her; when I'm a jerk, she won't answer. If I'm nice and ask an easy question, she still won't answer.

Finally, I say, "Okay, fine. Truth: Why aren't you getting any counseling about your parents' deaths?"

Cherie is quiet for a moment, looking at me as though I'd stabbed her in the heart by bringing up this topic. I feel badly, sort of. She floats a few inches away from me before stopping and coming back. She refuses to run away from my questions, either.

Her voice sounds almost robotic as she, sweet-faced, replies, "I have a lot of help and support right now. I have the good fortune of being surrounded by a loving family, faithful friends, and devoted fans who give me all of the strength I need to face this tragedy head-on."

I guffaw, "Oh my God, that is the most manufactured response I've ever heard! Can't you be real with me for five seconds?"

She tilts her head. "That's my truth, Jack."

"No, it's not," I reply, refusing to soften my tone, even as her jaw tightens. "That's what they make you say. Your truth is you drink and party and try to pretend none of that stuff happened last month. Your truth is denial."

"The words they give me have to be my truth, Jack. If I don't believe it, I can't sell it, and my job is to sell, not become some social services case." Her mouth sets in a hard line. Now she's angry. "Your turn. Truth or dare?"

A chill shoots through me. I know where this is going just by her expression. To protect myself, I say, "Dare."

"Dare?" She takes off her sunglasses, revealing her piercing, vengeful eyes. "Okay. I dare you to tell me about the day your father left."

I freeze, my eyes locked with hers. Breath catches in my chest and sits there, useless. My tongue becomes dead weight in my mouth. I need a witty come back, or a sly joke, anything. But my brain just shuts down like a jewelry store getting robbed, complete with steel doors and ringing alarms.

Game over.

I look away and shake my head. "That's stupid—that's not even a dare."

"Sure it is," she shoots back. "A dare is something uncomfortable that you make someone do because otherwise they would never do it."

"Well, I'm still not doing that," I insist, rolling off of the floating chair and into the water. As I head to the pool's edge, I hear her swimming after me.

"Stop running away, Jack!" she calls. I pause at the wall and feel her glide up beside me. "You asked for a dare, and I gave you one, so now you have to do it or you'll lose."

I shake my head and start to lift myself out of the water. Suddenly, I pause, wondering if she means I'll lose something other than this dumb game, something bigger. Like her.

I think about it for too long, and she grows impatient. "Jack?"

"I lose then." I push down on the side of the pool.

"Why?" she presses, grasping at my arm and pulling me back into the water. "Why won't you talk to me about him?"

I turn and glare at her. "You won't talk to me, either! You just gave me your publicist's bullshit answer when I asked for the truth. Excuse me if I don't have a prepared statement to hide behind."

"Okay, fair enough," she says slowly. She looks down at the water and after a few moments she says,

"Therapy's for weak people who can't handle the hard times in their lives." I swallow hard, thinking of the therapy I had to take part in after Dad left, knowing full well that if I hadn't had someone to talk to, I would still be getting my frustrations out by beating the hell out of anyone who crossed me.

She continues, "I don't need some doctor telling me how to get over their deaths; I just need to be strong and move on."

"Yeah, except you're not moving on, Cherie." I move closer and say, "Therapy can be a good thing. You can let your guard down; you don't have to be strong all the time."

She pins me with an angry stare. "You know, you should really practice what you preach."

I shrink back from her. "I had to be strong for other people. I didn't have a choice."

"What makes you think I have a choice? The whole world is watching me and waiting for me to crack!" I have to agree with her; maybe she does have to pretend everything's okay just so the rest of the world doesn't see her fractures.

"And what about now—do you still have to be strong for others?" she pushes.

I glare at her. "I don't know, you tell me. You're the one who comes to my room every night—what would you call that?"

I thought my words would incite her, hopefully make her too angry to continue, or too embarrassed. I thought it would derail this whole conversation.

Instead, she shakes her head and wags a finger at me. "Don't even go there. I mean this wall you put up when anyone tries to bring up your dad. You're still trying to act all tough like it doesn't bother you, but it clearly does."

"I found a way to cope with it, Cherie," I lie. I'm as good at lying as she is when it comes to this subject. "It's not like it haunts me every day; I just don't like to talk about it."

She shrugs. "Well, I'm finding ways to cope that don't involve some prick prying into my psyche while the photographers follow me in and out of his office!"

"No, instead they follow you in and out of bars and clubs! You think drinking and partying are better coping methods?" I shoot back.

She shakes her head. "You make me sound like I'm an alcoholic, Jack."

"You kind of are," I say. "Even my friends at home have heard about how you drink and stuff every night. The paparazzi are following everything you do anyway, and they're recording it and gossiping about it. What they're saying isn't good—would you rather they say you're getting help from a therapist or developing a drinking problem at sixteen?"

She rolls her eyes. "I don't have a problem, Jack, and I know what I'm doing, okay? I'm just having a little fun, and I think I deserve it after what's happened to me. Please don't nag me. Can you just be my friend?"

"Friends worry about what happens to one another, Cherie," I reply.

She meets my gaze and retorts, "And friends talk to each other about stuff that bothers them, Jack. You can't claim to be my friend and to care about me if you won't open up to me about your own problem."

My shoulders grow cold at her biting honesty. "It's not a problem. My dad leaving us isn't anything but the past. I shouldn't have to talk about that to be your friend."

"Why can't you, though?" she murmurs, floating toward me. I feel the familiar pulse of anger rising into my chest and spreading through my body. Cherie raises her hand and rests it lightly on mine, and I stare at the contrasting sizes and skin tones as she begins to weave her fingers through my own. A million bolts of electricity fly through my skin into my bones and up my arm, dulling the anger. The last time she was sober and held my hand, I was dragging her through a parking lot to save her from prying eyes. Now I feel like I'm the one getting dragged, only she's dragging me back in time against my will.

In a voice that rises barely above a breath, with her eyes burning a hole through my skull, she begs, "Please let me in, Jack."

The touch of her hand, the urging in her voice—all of it comes together like a tsunami rising and washing over my stoic barricade. She's got me, and she probably knows it. She has to know I'd do anything for her if she'd be brave enough to force this conversation.

"I don't want to." It's a last, weak effort to keep my secrets locked up, but I know and even she knows that they're right there, at the brim, ready to flood.

"Why, Jack?" she presses.

I swallow the lump that's forming in my throat. "Because." I feel my anger stirring; anger at her for forcing me to talk about something so hurtful, and anger at my father for making it hurt in the first place.

But I suddenly realize that no one is forcing me to do anything. Cherie just has some uncanny ability to pull me in and make me stay, even as she crawls under my skin and gets me madder than I've ever been. She gets away with things I never allow other people to do, from touching my hair to digging for the truth about my dad. I would have run from this pool had anyone else been asking these questions, but here I still am, just trying to get her to drop it, but not even really trying that hard anymore.

I guess I don't want her to drop it that badly. Maybe I want to tell Cherie. Maybe I'm ready to tell her what I won't tell anyone else.

I train my eyes on the water and stiffly reply, "I woke up one day, and he was gone. I found my mom on the kitchen floor, holding the letter he left her."

My words must paint an intense picture for her because she curls her fingers around my palm tightly. "What did the letter say?" she asks, hanging on my every word.

It feels like nails scraping down the walls of my stomach as I relive that awful moment. "That he met someone. That she shouldn't try to call or write or find him because he didn't love her anymore." I close my eyes, seeing vividly his blue script on the yellow legal pad paper that I found crumbled inside of Mom's tight fist that morning. I'd revisited this memory tons of times, mostly in nightmares, but always by myself. I hear my own voice coming out in wavering sounds, as if a ghost has taken over my body and is passing a message to the living.

I continue babbling. "That she could have everything—the car, the house, the savings, us. Just to please let him go and live his new life."

"Oh my God," she whispers. "That's terrible."

I shake my head and avoid Cherie's eyes. "I had to get my mom to her bedroom before Brenton woke up so he wouldn't see what a mess she was, and I got him ready for school. Britney was crying and hungry. She was still a baby. I didn't know what to do or how to feed her, but I had to figure it out because my mom couldn't come out of her room."

"How old were you?"

I take in a deep breath. "Thirteen."

"That must have been so hard for you to see," she says softly. "How long did it last?"

I can't even force myself to look at Cherie. I fix my eyes on the wall of the pool and say, "About a day and a half. The next day was Christmas Eve, so Aunt Darla was coming over for dinner. She realized what was happening and got things under control. She had just gone through a divorce herself, so she knew what to do, and she got my mom some professional help. Mom eventually went on anti-depression meds so she could sleep at night and forget about it, and she basically became a vegetable for two years. I was on my own, taking care of Britney and Brenton, while Aunt Darla tried to help Mom figure everything out with a lawyer."

"Did your dad ever reach out to you or try to explain his side to you?" she asks. It hurts just to shake my head in response.

"I'm sorry, Jack." Cherie is unmoving in the water beside me, just holding my hand and staring at our fingers, entranced. "I guess you felt pretty alone, huh?" she murmurs.

"Not at the time, no. I was just mad. Mad at him, mad at the world."

She tilts her head. "Mad or hurt?"

"Both, I guess," I reply. My voice lowers as I force out the words I've never said aloud to anyone. "I mean, how could someone tell you they love you and then just pick up and leave? Makes you wonder if they ever meant it at all."

Cherie whispers, "I'm sure he loves you, Jack."

"Yeah, well, I guess we'll never really know, huh?" I say, keeping my eyes trained to the wall of the pool.

She doesn't say anything in reply for a few moments, then, "So how did you adjust to life without him?"

I shrug and tell her the truth. "I had to quit football for a little while just to be able to help take care of Brenton and Britney. Our town was small, and everyone knew about how he left her. I stopped talking to my friends. At school, I got into fights and stuff with kids who gossiped about it."

"Fights?"

I nod, gritting my teeth. It's all out there now. No turning back. Maybe it's better that she knows. "Yeah. Lots of them. I got suspended. I had 'anger issues.' I probably still do, I just handle it differently."

She finally has a reason to let go of my hand, but she doesn't. Instead, she holds it tighter and asks, "Did you ever hurt someone? Like, bad?"

I swallow hard. *Here goes.* "Once, when I was really out of control, I turned on my friend, Frank. He was the only person still trying to talk to me. I turned on him because he'd finally had enough of my moody shit and told me to get over it. His mom came out to stop me from doing worse."

I close my eyes against the memory. Cherie urges me to continue. "Then what happened?"

The words are hard to force out. "I turned on her, too."

"You hit her?" she gasps.

I lower my head in shame. "Almost. I stopped myself just in time, but I was about to."

I can hear her gulp. "What happened then?"

I shrugged. "I turned and ran as fast as I could for as long as I could until I just wasn't mad anymore, and that's what I've done ever since."

"So that's why you always go for a run when you're angry," she concludes.

I nod. "Yes. I never want to feel that out of control again, and running is the only thing that mellows me out."

She sighs, "Well, having a drink now and then with my friends is the only thing that mellows me out. It takes the edge off of all of this. Can you understand that?"

I glare at her in disbelief. "Do you hear yourself? You know that's like a line the alcoholic character on TV shows says right before they get too drunk or arrested, right?"

"Jack, nothing's going—"

"No," I interrupt, finally looking at her again. "Don't tell me nothing's going to happen because something will. What you're doing is practically textbook—*young celebrity experiences tragedy and goes from American sweetheart to party animal to overdosing addict!*"

She huffs, and it's her turn to roll her eyes.

"You don't see it, do you?" I demand.

She shakes her head with sass. "Nope. Won't happen. This isn't TV, Jack. I'm smarter than that."

"Oh, really? You're smarter, huh?" I sigh, "Well, I see where you're headed, even if you don't. Even if nothing bad happens, you'll still be known as some sloppy drunk, or end up high and useless all the time like my mom was."

"She snapped out of it eventually, right? I will find my way, just like she found hers," she replies evenly.

"But at what cost?"

Cherie shrugs. "Whatever it is, I can afford it."

I growl, "Not money, Cherie. I mean at what cost to your reputation, to your life, and to me and everyone else who cares about you?"

Her lower lip juts out, and she coos, "Aw, Jack, do you really care that much about me?"

"Yeah, I do." How could she not know that by now? I quickly add, "A lot of people do." I don't know why it's so hard to admit how I feel about her out loud.

"Oh, a lot of people, huh?" I hear the sarcasm in her voice, as if she's aware I'm hiding my feelings and is resigned to play along. "Well, I'll be fine. Promise. Maybe I'll just go for a run later."

I shake my head. "You're impossible, you know that?"

The hint of a playful smile softens her face. "Maybe. You can be a pretty tough nut to crack, too."

Frustration and fear tornado inside of me at once. I could tell her right here, right now, how much she is really starting to mean to me. I could just lay my whole heart out there and hope it means enough to make her stop being so careless with her life. I risk her stomping all over my feelings, but I also risk never knowing whether or not she gives a damn about me.

"Truth or dare?"

Cherie swallows hard and blinks rapidly.

I take another deep breath and say, "Well? Truth or dare?"

She is silent for a moment, as if she never expected me to continue her dumb game. "Um, truth, I guess."

I nod. "If I asked you to, if I told you it mattered to me, would you go and get real help with a therapist? Would you stop drinking and all that other dumb shit?"

"That's really more of a request—"

"Maybe; you just have to answer honestly," I say, finally raising my gaze to hers. She quiets and presses her lips together. I add, "You can say yes or no, but it has to be the truth. Would you stop all this and get help—for me?"

She thinks about the question carefully and silently. My skin is chilled and my knees sort of quake. It's as though the world has stopped spinning on its axis as I cross my fingers and hold my breath and wait for an answer, hoping she will say yes, hoping she cares about me just a fraction of how much I care about her.

At last, she shakes her head and murmurs, "No."

My world explodes. I can't look her in the eye, I can't breathe, I can't think. I have no real meaning in her life; she's just using me to make it through the night, so she doesn't have to feel so alone. She didn't even want our family to know we are hanging out together today. I can't believe I thought for a millisecond that I mattered to her as anything more than a fill in for when she's lonely.

Crushed and defeated, I don't even have the strength to pull myself out of the water. I sigh and slowly slink around her to the stairs of the pool.

"Where are you going?" she asks as I curl a towel around my waist and walk toward the casita.

I point over my shoulder to the house. "They'll probably be home soon—wouldn't want to ruin our little secret here."

"Oh." She smiles sadly, knowing I'm lying, probably knowing she just punched me in the gut, too. "Well, thanks, Jack."

"For what?"

She shrugs. "For letting me in." She says it as if she knows I won't ever let her in again. I even want to tell her that it's never going to happen again, physically or other. She is spiraling out of control, and I don't want to be sucked in any further than I already am.

But I just nod and close the door gently, wishing I had never left myself so open in the first place.

Chapter 29

"That's right, that's right!" Mica shouts, greeting me in a parking garage off of Hollywood Boulevard with a quick embrace and a laugh. He appears annoyingly impressed with my clothes. "You look like a pimp, Hansen!"

"Thanks, I think," I reply, looking down at my shirt and pants. Mica's accompanied by an entourage of big dudes and tall girls, and I feel underdressed despite his approval. I count eight others, maybe two or three years older than us. There are about five girls, all wearing glittery dresses and high heels. They are trying much too hard to look older than they are, and a few of them are successful.

One girl is a modelesque brunette, with long, tan limbs and eyes rimmed with thick, black lashes. Her hair is long and dark, cascading down her bare back in waves. Her full, rosy lips smile at me shyly when she catches me staring.

I look away immediately and step closer to Mica.

"Who are all these girls?"

"Some friends of D'Shawn's cousin. They in college," he says with a wink. "Can't be bringin' too many playas to the party, if y'know what I'm sayin'."

Mica introduces me to D'shawn and his friends, and I feel my cheeks growing red when he begins to tell them about how we met.

"My man here's got crazy girl problems, yo," Mica laughs. "Lives with a bunch of nasty stepsisters at home. You should see 'im in the ring, swingin' all wild like a rabid animal!" His friends laugh, and I grit my teeth, stealing a glance at the beautiful mystery girl with the hopes that she isn't listening.

But she is, and she purses her lips in playful sympathy. I immediately find myself comparing her to Cherie, like how her smile has that same brightness but her eyes are smaller. She's seems taller, but Cherie is always wearing those ridiculously high heels, so it's hard to tell.

Mica follows my gaze and summons her closer with a flick of his wrist. "Carly, meet Jack Hansen," he says with a broad smile. I cringe hearing my name out loud, thinking this just might be the moment Mica finds out who I am. But when the girl seems not to recognize my name, I relax a little.

He murmurs loud enough for her to hear, "Jack, this is Carly. She got an ass that'll make you forget all about Miss Trouble, and she likes younger men." My jaw drops and my cheeks burn at the embarrassing things he says.

I try to smile politely and shake her hand. "Hi."

She says, "Hello," in a sultry voice and rolls a dirty look in Mica's direction. She does not want to be presented like an escort he's providing for me.

"I apologize for him," I say quickly, shoving my hands deep into my pockets.

She giggles and says, "It's okay. I've hung out with Mica a few times. He's got no filter."

"That's for sure."

Mica urges all of us to start walking toward the club, and I fall into step beside Carly, feeling out of place both in this group and among the other people on the boulevard.

"You look familiar," she says, squinting at me.

Here it comes, I think nervously.

"Have you come out with Mica before?"

I nearly sigh with relief. "No, we just met last week," I say, directing my gaze to the concrete at my feet and staying mum about Cherie. If she can't place me, I won't help her. "I just moved here from New York."

"New York?" she asks. I nod. "Why did you move out here?"

I smile tightly. "It's a long story. What about you? Are you originally from California?"

"No, Las Vegas, actually," she says, laughing when my eyes widen.

"Vegas? That's so cool." She nods and flashes me a shy smile. "Why'd you come here?"

"I was discovered by an agent, and he convinced my parents to move us out here," she replies with the touch of modesty that Cherie definitely lacks.

"So you're a model?"

My guess is flattering but wrong, so she laughs. "No, but thank you. I'm a singer," she tells me. "I'm working with a producer right now."

Before I have a chance to feel embarrassed or ask what the hell she's doing hanging out with us, our group stops at the front of a crowded club. There is a line of people waiting behind a long stretch of red velvet rope. D'shawn walks right up to the doorman, and they exchange a quick hug and some friendly words. Soon, the rope is pulled aside, and our group is ushered inside.

Mica is at my side, practically bouncing with excitement. He hears a song he likes playing through the club and is already dancing, moving his feet deftly and grinning from ear to ear.

"He's crazy!" Carly shouts over the music, her eyes reflecting the colored lights of the club as she watches him. I can only nod in agreement, my words lost because I'm watching her, captivated by her smile.

As we follow D'shawn through the club, the scent of incense mixes with sweat and smoke and devastates my sense of smell. It smells like Cherie, and I suddenly feel bad about my attraction to Carly.

It doesn't last long.

"Stay close, hun," Carly calls over the music. She grabs my hand and weaves in and out of the crowd. A buzz shoots through my veins from my fingertips to my gut. She glances over her shoulder, just to ensure I'm still at her heels. I force a blank stare, like having her hold my hand didn't set off a thousand alarms inside.

Bodies dance around us, bumping and sometimes slamming into me as we walk through, linked tightly. It is easy to get unhooked from someone in a crowd like this, so I make sure to keep up and not get distracted.

Until I see *her*.

Unexpectedly, Cherie is before me, dancing—no, writhing—like a stripper on a table in the club's VIP section. There are people cheering her on, and a few have the wherewithal to catch the moment on their phones' cameras. She is dancing with another girl, who stops her and turns her around. The girl tugs on her hair so that her head snaps back, and she quickly pours a shot into Cherie's open mouth. The crowd goes berserk.

As much as I feel like pretending I have no idea who she is, I can't help the horror and jealousy and urge to protect her that simultaneously explode in my chest. I'm drawn closer and closer like a magnet until I am on the perimeter of the crowd she's attracted. I stop and stare up at her, debating whether I should drag her down from the pedestal by her hair or punch the guy who's trying to get his camera under her tiny dress first.

Suddenly she sees me, double takes, and then waves emphatically. "Jack!"

She uses the people beneath her like stepping stones and finds her way to the floor amid a chorus of boos and protests. She loses her footing and almost crashes, and I quickly thrust my arms out to catch her. I get a wave of déjà vu because I've been in this situation a few times now.

"Jack!" she shrieks excitedly, wrapping her arms around my neck in what is probably the most extreme show of affection she's ever displayed in public since I've known her. She stumbles again, but this time I already have her in my grasp. She giggles maniacally as I help her stand upright.

"Jack, what're you doing here?"

In my swirl of astonishment and anger, I forget why I am even at the club. "What are YOU doing?" I demand. "You're wasted!"

"I'm fine, Jack," she replies with a wave of her hand. "Come! I want you to meet my friends—"

"Wait, Cherie. You're drunk. People are taking your picture," I tell her, holding up my hand to block someone who is recording us with their phone.

"Who cares?"

"You should! This is going to be all over the news—you'll get in trouble!"

She laughs at me and pets my cheek adoringly. "Oh, Jack, you're so sheltered. I won't get in trouble for any of this—the club might, though!"

"I mean with Jim and Mom," I say, squinting from the flash of a different person's camera. I finally recognize that I've been holding her close to me this whole time, and now I'm in every picture that's been taken for the last thirty seconds. The headline *"Cherie's New Beau Sneaks into Nightclub with Her"* flashes through my mind, and I shudder. *Great, now I'll be in trouble, too, and it's not even the truth.*

I release her and take a step back, glaring at the photographers. Two girls come bounding up by her side.

"Hi, I'm Amber," one says, and I recognize her as Amber Stiles, another beautiful star from Cherie's network. The other girl looks familiar, too, and is also pretty hot, so my mind starts running through all of the Kidz Channel starlets to come up with her name. It takes me a minute to recognize this scantily dressed vixen is Danika, who looks more like the real Danika's evil, whorish twin.

Danika watches my jaw drop and smirks. I immediately remember the dare I made Cherie pull on her earlier, and I can tell by the look on her face that she is now in on the joke and doesn't find it funny.

"Oh, hey there," I say, forcing a smile.

"Hi," she says too cheerily. "Have a nice afternoon?"

It almost hurts to look her in the eye. "Yes, it was fun. I—I'm sorry about the, um—"

She waves her hand in the air flippantly. "Oh, don't give it a second thought. Sounds like it was all in good fun. This—ahem—BITCH can take a good joke now and again." Suddenly, her eyes are steely and burning through me.

Before I can feel an ounce of regret or fear, Amber grabs my chin and studies me like a show dog.

"Wait—are you Jack?" Amber asks, a secret-knowing gleam flashing through her eyes. She's not fettered when I pull my face from her grip. She purses her lips and adds, "I've heard about you." By the way she winks at me, I can tell she doesn't mean from the gossip news.

Cherie talks about me? To her celebrity friends?

Cherie shoots her friend a warning glare and shoos both her and Danika away. She turns and looks me over, switching back to her more playful persona.

"You sure do clean up nice, Hansen," she comments, twisting the collar of my shirt between her fingers. "Here, this will make it better." She undoes the top button of my shirt so that it reveals part of my chest.

"That makes me look like a tool," I complain, but I

don't dare change it. If she thinks that looks better, then I'm okay with it.

Unexpectedly, her hand is in my hair, and she's messing it. "Too much gel," she says with a scrunch of her nose. Usually, this is a cardinal sin to me, but I'm too distracted by the feel of her fingernails against my scalp to pull away. I stand still and let her do whatever she wants to it.

"So, how did you get in here? Who are you with?" she asks again.

My mind snaps back to attention. I look around, realizing I've lost my group completely. Finally, I see Carly and Mica coming back for me.

"I'm here with some friends," I say, gesturing to the duo as they approach.

Cherie looks over at Carly and noticeably stiffens. "Who is she?" she asks in her signature snotty tone.

I stare down at Cherie, who suddenly looks like she's taken one shot too many of a mean potion. Carly approaches her with a friendly, unsuspecting smile while I'm inwardly cowering, sensing the worst.

"Hi, I'm Carly, Jack's friend," the poor, innocent girl announces, extending a hand. "I'm a big fan!"

"That's nice," Cherie snips, ignoring her. She turns two darkened, emerald eyes on me and forces a smile. "I'll let you get back to your friends."

Carly raises an eyebrow and looks disgusted as Cherie pushes away from me and parades through the crowd with her two "friends" at her heels. I turn and am sputtering an apology when Carly's mouth twists with humor.

"I thought you looked familiar," she says. I can feel myself turning all shades of red.

"Yeah, but—"

"Hansen!" Mica interrupts, firmly shaking my

shoulder. "Is that the girl from TV? What's her name—"

I nod. "Yeah. *That's* my stepfather's niece," I tell him, watching Cherie rush out of view with her friends.

When I look back at him, his eyes are bugging out of his head like a cartoon character. "That's the *cousin*?" he cries.

"*That* is *Trouble*," I say, and his mouth forms an 'o' as he howls laughter.

"Oh, my man—you serious?" he nearly screams. "Are. You. Serious!"

"It's not what you think," I grunt. I glance over at Carly, hoping she hears me, too. "She's just a brat I have to live with, and she drives me nuts." Now that Carly knows who I am, or at least whoever the media has made me out to be, I expect her to dismiss me completely. There won't be any convincing her that we are nothing more than family, especially after how Cherie just acted toward her.

But it's not only Carly that I have to worry about putting false pieces together; Mica has already finished the puzzle and is standing in humored sympathy. My face grows hotter. I know this is going to be a big conversation we will have tomorrow, when Carly is out of the picture and it's just us in the gym.

"My brotha," he sighs, resigning to wait until tomorrow for the full story. "Let's get this man a drink!" He puts his hands on my shoulders and pushes me toward the bar.

"Oh, my favorite bartender's on tonight!" Carly cries out, her eyes like two bright lights on her face. Her body dances toward the bar, as though she is possessed by the music, where she is attended to immediately. Some things are so easy for girls that they are just wrong.

"Here you go," the bartender says with a flash of his kindest smile, presenting three giant cocktails. His leering look in her direction annoys me.

I pull out money to pay for the drinks, but the bartender waves me off, yelling, "It's on the house!" I'm puzzled and put the money on the bar anyway.

When Carly cocks an eyebrow at me, I say, "Gotta tip, right?" I want to impress her, and tipping is impressive, I think.

Or maybe not. She shrugs and sips her drink delicately.

I realize she may still be peeved about our run in with Cherie, so I extend a weak apology. "I'm sorry about Cherie; she's always like that. It's not you."

"Actually, it's you," she replies with a playful wink. When I don't catch on to her innuendo, she adds, "She's clearly jealous; I would be, too, if my ex-boyfriend was hanging out with another girl."

I feel my eyebrows rise in disbelief. "I'm not her ex-boyfriend. I was never her anything."

"Could have fooled me," she says.

I shake my head. "I'm not, I promise."

"Okay. I believe you." Carly giggles and takes my hand, blessedly forgiving. She nudges Mica for his attention. "Where do you want to go first? Balcony? Dance floor?"

"We'll look around after this," Mica says.

I'm not listening to either of them, instead staring at the drinks that Mica begins removing from the bar. He offers me a glass, but I hold up my hand and refuse it.

"No, thanks," I say.

They gawk at me. "What? You don't drink?" Mica teases.

I smile and pat my stomach. "Gotta watch my figure."

"Yeah, right, take this," Mica replies, shoving the drink back at me.

"No," I protest. "I can't, really. I have to drive, remember?" I won't say the real reasons though. I glance back out at the dance floor, watching for Cherie and for people taking her picture. She's drunk enough for both us. I don't know why, but I feel the need to be alert in case something happens. I also don't need anyone snapping a picture of me drinking, too.

"Whatever, more for us," Mica chuckles. He takes one of the drinks and practically throws it down his throat in seconds.

Carly gawks at him, laughing, "Oh my!"

"What? I'm thirsty. A hot club can do that to you," he comments.

As they drink languidly, I keep an eye out for Cherie, who I finally find back in her VIP section, center stage, making a complete spectacle of herself. She sways and swoops her hips to the music. I like watching her dance, but so do many other guys in the club. She relishes the attention.

Danika comes up behind her to dance against her body. She grabs Cherie's hips and lets her hands travel down to her knees as she sinks lower to the floor. She twists slowly back up, and Cherie mimics the move. They giggle to each other, completely aware of the pairs of male eyes stalking them as they move together.

I hear Carly say, "Hey, we're gonna go check out the second floor. You coming?"

But my eyes are locked, and I'm not listening. I watch a stocky young guy, dressed in jeans and a striped collared shirt, dance his way toward the girls. He looks familiar, but it's hard to tell with the flashing lights and the distance between us. Cherie shakes her head and wags a finger at him playfully. She seems to know him. With a flick of her wrist, Danika sends Striped-Shirt back to his friends with his tail between his legs. He is aggravated but tries to play it cool by laughing and shrugging dramatically. I'm relieved.

When I look toward Carly and Mica to finally give an answer, they're gone. I know I should go look for them, but I decide to stay put instead and keep an eye on Cherie and Striped-Shirt.

"Jack!" My head swivels, and a camera flashes, blinding me.

"What the hell, man?" I demand, shielding my eyes.

"Sorry, Jack," the cameraman says. "Derek from Dirterazzi.com. It's good to see you! What are you doing in here? You're Cherie's age, aren't you?"

I think fast. "No, I'm older."

"Huh. Not by much though, right? Are you here with Cherie and the girls tonight?"

I shake my head and turn around to face the bar, ordering a bottle of water. He continues to fire questions and takes another picture while I pay.

"So what's going on with you two?" he presses. I ignore him. "How do you feel about her being seen out with Caz Farrell this week?"

I grunt, "Get lost, man," and take a big swig of water. I feel fire building in my throat, as if I could spit flames at him.

He leans against the bar beside me. "Hey, man, I'm just trying to do my job, you know? They pay me to get pictures of you guys. You give me what I need, and I can help you out, you know? Use me, man, I can write your story for you, get the truth out there."

"Oh, is that how it works?" I grumble sarcastically, hoping he'll get the hint that I'm really not interested in talking to him.

"Yeah, man, that's what we do for each other out here." He thumbs the air behind us. "Just the other night, Danika called me to come out for her 25th birthday party.

I got a lot of great shots of the Kidz Channel girls and, in turn, she got a story written about her on the blog. Builds her brand, you know? It works out for everyone."

I turn and squint down at him. "25th birthday? Danika's 25?"

He grins. "Yeah, man, she's an assistant. What, you thought she was a kid? How would she be Cherie's assistant if she had to go to school and stuff?"

I'm dumbfounded and stare at him, trying to make sense of it all. Danika, nearly ten years older than Cherie, is the one enabling Cherie to drink and party? She even drives her underage employer to and from the parties and clubs and probably buys the bottles of booze for their late night Jacuzzi ventures, too. Now, more than ever, I want Cherie to fire Danika. If she won't, then my mom and Jim will.

Reminded of her, I search the dance floor for Cherie and her friends. When I find them, the song changes, and the girls decide they don't like the new song so much. They make their way toward the bar and right into me in a fit of laughter. Derek snaps away.

"Derek, can you give us some space, please?" Cherie says sweetly. "I'll give you a few stills later, okay?"

"Of course. Thanks, Cher," he replies. He snaps one more picture of her, and he walks away.

I gawk. "Seriously? That's all it takes?" Cherie meets my marveling gaze and gives me a smug smile. She peers over my shoulder, noting that I'm alone.

"Lose your lame friends?" she asks. I shake my head and roll my eyes. I don't like this version of Cherie. She reminds me of the Cherie I met on Christmas Eve, and I feel her getting under my skin.

"Shots?" Amber shouts out, although it was really more of a command than a request. Cherie nods eagerly, and Danika orders three lemon drop shots. Suddenly, she turns, and her eyes flash menacingly at Cherie.

Too many guys and cameras lurk nearby, watching them, watching me, waiting for something to happen. I try not glare at the strangers, but I can't help it. Danika whispers something in her ear, and Cherie grins, nodding vigorously and giggling. Positioning my body possessively beside them to ward off their predators, I'm distracted from asking what they're up to.

When I look down at the girls again, the scene is staggering, and I almost choke on my water.

Danika is primed and ready for the cameras to flash once more, a shot glass sitting snuggly inside of her cleavage. Cherie winks at her. Gracefully, she arches her neck and puts her lips to the rim of the shot glass. Once she has her mouth firmly planted around the rim, she yanks her head back and swallows the shot. She proceeds to lick any spilled drops off of Danika's skin. The small crowd roars, and my brain turns to mush while other parts of me jolt with alarm. I can't process what is happening fast enough to react.

"My turn!" Danika cries enthusiastically. Cherie carefully places a shot glass inside of her own cleavage and presents it to her assistant. I watch, befuddled, as Danika takes her shot with vigor. Whooping and clapping erupts from a group of men at the bar who have gathered to watch, and even a few bachelorettes prepare to pay homage to the scene by ordering up their own shots.

Cherie looks up at me and gives me a coy smile. "Want one?"

I promptly shake my head no, but I do. I can't hide the panic that I feel rising into my chest. Cherie is making a lot of bad choices and attracting all the wrong kinds of attention. She's making me mad and nervous at the same time. Worse, she's choking the sense out of me and turning me into one of her panting admirers.

"Cherie, what is wrong with you?" I try to scold, regaining some of my dignity. But her friends are whisking her back to the dance floor. Danika and Amber laugh giddily to each other, and Danika reaches for her hand to pull her away. Cherie looks up at me, and I give her a warning glare. Does she know she is beginning to crack through my senses and make me nuts? Is that what she wants?

She smiles up at me. "Dance with us?" she says, and I catch the hopeful pitch to her tone. She reaches out for my hand. I want to say yes. I want to follow her and protect her from the men lusting after her right now. I want to touch her. I see headlines again, and I shake my head.

Watching the groups of predatory males who move in toward the girls like lunchtime in a zoo, I reply through clenched teeth, "I'm going for a walk."

I slip away into the crowd while she follows Danika and Amber begrudgingly in the opposite direction. Behind me, I hear the girls shout about me to one another.

Amber: "Where's he going?"

Cherie: "A walk. If he comes back with that girl—"

Danika: "Relax! He probably has to go jerk off."

Classy.

Chapter 30

My mouth tightens, and I'm ignorant of passersby as I enter the men's bathroom, slamming into them if they don't move out of my way. Someone curses at me, but I maintain tunnel vision and move swiftly to the sinks, thrusting my hands beneath the automatic faucets. The cold water does little to calm me as I sweep it over my face with my fingertips. I drench my eyes with it, desperate to clean away the image of Cherie putting on such a crude show in front of so many people.

What is she thinking? How could she do something so trashy? I try to convince myself that this behavior just isn't like her. When other people are around, Cherie is a monster, doing whatever it takes to pacify the crowd, following and indulging her friends' whims. I can feel my blood boiling at the thought of how she changes her entire persona depending on who is in the room.

An old, familiar possession threatens to overtake me. A fire is blazing in my chest and spreading through my arms. I look down. My veins are bulging. My knuckles are white from how hard I'm gripping the sides of the sink.

I should leave. I should go home before something bad happens. I feel like I could turn into King Kong and burst out of this club with Cherie inside one of my fists. I'd carry her to the top of a building, too, just to take her away from all of these eyes that are watching her implode.

But this is real life, and I can't control her; she's not my little sister, she's not my real cousin, and she's certainly not my girlfriend. She made it clear to me today that what I think, what I need, doesn't matter. She can and will do whatever she wants. All the nights in the world spent sleeping next to each other won't suddenly make her care how I feel about her drinking or her slutty performances.

Still, I can't watch her do those things and let it go because I'm into her, big time. Every night, I've fallen a little harder, trusted her a little more, and risked losing my control with her. She's the one who crawls into my bed and breaks down all the walls I've tried to put up, but I'm the one paying for it.

No one else knows this, of course. No one knows because I am Cherie's biggest secret that I'm keeping, and that secret is instantly raging inside of me in this setting, where I have to watch other guys stalk her and lust after her; my feelings for her have permeated my senses and make me want to claim what's not really mine with force.

No way, I tell myself. *I'll only end up looking like an ass or getting into some kind of fight.*

I wait a few moments by the sink, taking deep breaths and reassuring myself that I can handle Cherie's antics and not lose my cool. I close my eyes and count to ten. When I open them, I vow to ignore her for the rest of the night. I'll find Carly and Mica and enjoy their company, hopefully forget Cherie is even there.

I stride out to the club's center confidently, and I notice Cherie and her friends are planted in the middle of the dance floor again, grinding on each other and moving provocatively for all of their lolling-tongued spectators. I order a beer from the bar and climb the stairs, determined to stay true to my own promise.

"Jack!" Carly calls when she sees me approaching. They are coming back down to the main floor and meet me in the middle of the stairwell. "The upstairs room is playing lame house music. We were just coming back to find you!"

"Same here," I laugh. "Great minds think alike."

She beams and bats her long, flirting lashes.

Mica points to my drink and raises his own beer bottle. "Yes!" he laughs, and we clink bottles. "Now it's a party! Drink your troubles away, playa!"

I nod and turn to follow them. Carly takes my hand in hers and parades through the crowded bar area, pulling my hand up to rest on her hip as we walk. It's a bold, possessive move, and now she has my full attention. When we get back down to the lower floor, Carly guides me toward the dance floor.

"Dance with me!" she pleads. I nod and take a big swig of my beer. I haven't danced with a girl in a long time, but I'm more than game at this point. I pull her close, letting the sweet scent of her hair sweep over my face. She moves with the beat, and I shadow her motions blindly. She rolls her hips in circles and presses her back to me. A deep hunger churns inside my groin. I close my eyes, lost in the moment.

I open them only to find Cherie dancing nearby. Her eyes catch mine, and she forces an arrogant grin. Then, she looks over at Amber and scowls. Amber gives Carly a death glare. If I didn't know any better, I'd think Cherie was actually getting jealous.

Carly yanks my vision back into focus by turning around to face me and pouts, as if she knows I was distracted. I grab her small waist and pull her closer, and then I'm ripped back into Cherie's world by a whooping crowd. Cherie is running her hands up and down Danika's body. I'm pulled in and out of monitoring Cherie's situation by Carly's teasing hips as they trace figure eights against mine and send shudders through me. My hunger whips into a frenzied starvation, causing my fingers to dig into her waist. She bites her lower lip and pins me with one of those "I want you now" stares.

Another dull roar of cheering buffoons snaps me out of the trance. I scan the crowd that's formed around Cherie. Striped-Shirt lurks close by with eyes narrowed into slits like a snake. He's ready to strike, and I feel my muscles stiffen. This time, Danika and Amber do not send him the message to back off.

Cherie glances over at me, probably expecting me to foam at the mouth like the rest of her fans. Instead, I turn my full attention back to Carly, keeping in time with her. When I glance up again at Cherie, her eyes are burning a hole into the back of Carly's head.

And that's when Striped-Shirt moves in for the kill.

He begins grinding hard against Cherie's body as though they were *thisclose* to being naked. She steps away to put space between them and pretends to laugh it off, but he draws an arm around her waist and pulls her tight against him. My hunger flares into anger as I watch his hand fan out along her lower abdomen. The tips of his fingers graze a part of her I know he shouldn't touch. I pause, and my limbs quake with fury.

Carly follows my gaze. "What is it?"

But I'm barely conscious of Carly now. The position of Striped-Shirt's hand has triggered panic in Cherie, and her face contorts with discomfort. She squirms, but he is strong and holds her tight against him, smiling and saying something into her ear as if they're old friends. She pulls and pushes, and his hand drifts lower, until finally she throws an elbow into his ribs with a shriek.

"Get off of me!"

He doubles over, clutching his side. "Hey!" he yells. "Why are you being such a bitch?"

Like dynamite, my rage explodes. Without thinking, I'm in motion, bulldozing through the crowd and immediately jumping between them. I draw back and swing my fist into his face. Striped-Shirt is off of his feet and splays backward like a crash-test dummy. Someone screams. My knuckles blaze with pain, but I pursue him anyway, until someone drags me back a step. Two guys, possibly his friends, come right for me. The bigger one aims a punch at my face that I dodge while the other tries to keep the peace by getting in the middle. Striped-Shirt returns with a vengeance, his mouth bleeding, his eyes blazing, and froth spitting from his mouth as he threatens me. Immediately, brave onlookers move forward to break up the fight, putting distance between all of us.

"If you ever touch her like that again, I'll kill you," I threaten him.

"Come on, kid, I'm right here!" Striped-Shirt taunts.

Cherie cries, "Jack! Jack, stop! What are you doing?"

My teeth grind together, and I'm driving through the peace-making friend who tries to hold me back from killing Striped-Shirt. My eyes burn with fury.

"Try hitting me now, punk!" Striped-Shirt shouts. "I'm ready for you this time! C'mon!"

"Let's go, then!" I reply over his short friend's head.

Cherie grabs me. "Stop it, now!" She pulls me away, but I won't back down. Striped-Shirt and his friend are ready to fight, and they continue to taunt me. Mica and D'shawn shove through the crowd to come to my aid.

"Stop him, please!" I hear Cherie beg my friends, and Mica swoops in to pull me further away from Striped-Shirt.

The bouncers, led by D'shawn's cousin, are closing in, just as I calmly shake off the hands grabbing at me, including Cherie's. I hold up my arms, showing surrender. Striped-Shirt and his friend still try to plunge through Peacemaker and the bouncers, who are forcing them back. The crowd joins the bouncers' efforts, turning the dance floor into a pit of struggling bodies. The two shout curses at me, and I ignore them, but Mica shouts some choice words back in my defense.

Danika takes Cherie's hand roughly and drags her away from the crowd as it grows more violent and chaotic, and now the cameras are really snapping away at both of us.

"Cherie, is he your boyfriend?" a man calls, taking a video of her. I viciously swipe the camera from out of his hand and glare at him.

"Jack!" she nearly scolds. She looks furious. I obediently go to her side. "Let's go. Now." She grabs my arm once again. She hastily leads me through the crowded club to a hallway that opens to a set of bouncers guarding hidden back doors. They step aside and let us through, eying me as if they know I'm the cause of the fight. Mica follows, too, using his manners and charm to distract them. We emerge from the club into an alley.

"Wait—where are we?" I ask, looking around.

"Getting out of here, and fast!" she mutters. "What were you thinking—you could get arrested!"

Only then does it hit me: Cherie is desperately trying to sneak me out of the club because I could be in serious trouble.

But I'm only in this mess because she had to act like a complete slut tonight.

I stalk forward and away from Cherie as fast as my legs will take me; my jaw is as tight with anger as my chest is with anxiety. I ball my hands into fists, even the one that feels broken. Mica is at my side, trying to calm me down.

"Dawg, what happened?" he asks, glancing back at Cherie and her friends.

"Wait, Jack!" Cherie shouts feebly, trying to keep up with me in her stupid high heels. Danika growls something incoherent under her breath, and Amber is lagging behind all of us, typing on her cell phone.

"I'm sorry," Cherie slurs under her breath. I won't look at her.

"You shouldn't ask for trouble in the first place," I grumble.

Cherie is offended at the implication. "What are you talking about?" she demands defensively.

"You knew what you were doing," I groan. "Winking at guys, dancing like that with Danika, *doing body shots!*"

I make the mistake of meeting her gaze. Cherie quickly tries to hide her satisfaction. Even Danika forgets her resentment for a moment to look back at her with a sly grin. My comment confirms that I've given her exactly what she wanted in the first place: attention. That little victory gives her nerve, and it infuriates me even more.

She taunts, "I don't know what you are trying to say, but it's not my fault some guys can't control themselves—"

I turn on Cherie then, my body looming over hers, enraged. I feel a primitive urge to physically shake sense into her, and I have to lock my hands at my sides to avoid grabbing her. She instinctively shies backward, shocked and frightened.

"Do I look like an idiot to you?" I bellow. Mica steps in and puts a hand against my chest to hold me back. I must look like I'm about to pummel her next, but I'm fuming and don't care. "I saw everything! You're just as much to blame! What, do you want guys to drool over you until some fool like me has to jump in and fight them off—is that it?"

"I didn't expect you to fight with anyone!" she tries to say, but I won't hear it. I'm a pot that's finally boiled over.

"What do you expect from me, huh? Do you expect me to look the other way when you're practically inviting guys to mess with you? You sleep in my bed, for Christ's sake!"

The alley is silent; even her friends gawk at me. Apparently, only we knew this secret. I know I shouldn't unveil everything, but I have lost my filter completely, along with my patience.

She's mortified, her voice trembling. "I'm not your girlfriend, Jack. I can do whatever I want."

My voice is guttural. "If you're going to pretend there's nothing going on between us, at least have the decency to do it behind my back, not right in front of my face."

Her stare is frigid. I feel an explosion is imminent, but I'm not sure which one of ours will have the most impact.

"I didn't think you would get like this over one of our dumb guy friends—"

"*Friend*? That guy is your *friend*? Friends shouldn't touch you like that. I don't touch you like that!" I yell.

"I never asked you to, and I certainly never asked him! I was just having fun, Jack," she insists, humiliation filling her cheeks with pink. "He went too far—"

"He went too far because you asked for it!" I lower my voice and growl, "If you don't want guys to disrespect you, you should try to have some respect for yourself!"

"Don't talk to me like that—you're not my father!" she shouts.

"Well he's not here, so someone's got to step in!" I growl back. I press my mouth shut and instantly regret the comment. Her face crumbles, but she quickly recovers herself, as if she remembers she's surrounded by an audience.

Mica whistles low; he knows I've crossed a big line. It adds more fuel to her smoldering fire.

"Oh, yeah?" Her face turns beet red, and tears well in her eyes that she tries hard to blink back. "Where's *your* dad, Jack? Oh, that's right—he ran away because he didn't love you!"

I'm quiet for a moment, trying to understand why it feels like the ground is being pulled out from under my feet. Her words fill my ears, and my mouth hangs slack.

She knows she's got me, and she goes in for the kill. "At least my dad is dead. *Yours* hates you so much he *chose* to leave and never looked back!" Cherie spits. She races off, her heels tapping on the concrete, her friends chasing after her.

Mica curses low and quiet, like he feels the growing tsunami inside of me and knows his hand is not going to be enough to hold me back. Her words slice into my very being and release the dark, rabid animal that bursts out. I roar loudly and start to chase after her. I don't get too far before Mica is on me, grabbing my arms and pulling me into a tight, frantic embrace, preventing me from going forward. I get one arm loose and swing at him, but he is able to dodge it and secures my arms to my sides again. I twist but can't escape his hold.

I can't escape period. I can't run fast enough to get away from the four years' worth of emotion that rises up into my throat from my gut and burns the air in my lungs. Mica is desperate to help, but he can't communicate with me now. I drop down to the concrete and bury my head in my hands, fighting an uphill battle against the words that echo in my ears.

Unloved. Abandoned. The words are screamed at me by unseen banshees that suddenly swirl around my head. I want to close the door on them, but now that Cherie's opened it, I don't have the strength. I'd been dodging those words for four years, but Cherie Belle hurled them at me in half of a second. She went and shined the biggest light she could find on the skeletons in my closet, illuminating my worst fears and dragging them out from the darkness.

How does she do that? How does she know what to say to completely debase someone without a single ounce of regret?

Mica's down by my side, and he puts a hand on my shoulder. I sigh heavily and fight the tears hard. This can't happen here; not in front of Mica, not here in the street. I can't let her win like that.

Cherie warned me. I should have listened. I should have known that she meant it when she said I'd better watch out. Stupid pranks aside, the girl had a penchant for really using my worst insecurities against me. The Cherie Belle Mean Machine knows no bounds, and she finally found what she needed to truly break me.

It takes me a long time to recover enough that I can get to my feet.

"Sorry," I croak, grateful I didn't cry but feeling anything but victorious.

"Nah man, I'm sorry. I wish I knew what to say."

"There's nothing to say." I take a woozy step forward.

Mica holds my arm to steady me and murmurs, "C'mon, let's get you home, dawg." And, for the first time since we've met, Mica is speechless.

Chapter 31

When I pull in to the driveway, it's nearly one in the morning. I do my best to sneak in to the casita undetected.

Cherie's waiting for me, sitting on my bed, looking tear-stained and washed with relief as I enter.

"Oh, thank God—"

"Get out," I interrupt immediately, pointing to the house.

"Jack—"

"No, I'm not kidding. Get out."

"Jack, I'm really sorry—"

"I don't care," I state firmly. "Leave me alone."

She looks stricken with grief. I see tears welling in her eyes, but it doesn't have the same effect on me this time.

"Look, either you get out, or I'm calling Mom and Jim in here right now and telling them everything," I threaten.

She's unfazed, her lips pouting in that way that makes me forget stuff, like what I'm mad at. I can't let her do that to me this time. I'm done with her, and I have to stand my ground.

"Jack, can I just say one thing?"

"No—nothing!" I crow, slicing the air with my bruised hand. "I am done talking to you. I am done being your stupid security blanket. Go call Caz and cry on his shoulder."

"You don't mean that," she whispers, and I hate her for knowing that little bit of truth. She adds, "And I didn't mean what I said before." I can't keep listening to her because she's going to make me believe her. I have to lock myself in the bathroom and tune her out until she shuts up or leaves, preferably both. I reach for its door, and she jumps from the bed to stop me, grabbing my forearm.

"Oh, no! Your hand!" she murmurs. I look down at it, realizing that it looks more swollen and purple than it feels.

I hide it behind my back. "Whatever; don't act like you give a shit."

"Please just listen to me," she pleads. For the first time in a long time, she is stone-sober. I notice the absence of alcohol-scented breath and see her eyes are not clouded over. They're wide and green and pleading for forgiveness.

But I'm just too raw this time. "No, you listen. I've never let anyone in the way I let you in, Cherie. I told you everything out there today, and you threw it back in my face the first chance you got. You would think someone who claims to feel so alone in this world would have a little empathy for a guy like me, but no, that's not the case."

I feel my eyes burning with tears now, and there's not much I can do to hold them back. "Because you don't really know what it's like. Your parents didn't just leave. They didn't walk out and forget you existed. That's something I have to wake up and face every day. That's what I get to think about at night, in between worrying whether you'll come home in one piece and why you are keeping me a big secret."

Her eyes water, too. "Jack, I—" She's speechless and looks down.

"You know what's really scary? What's really scary is that you have the power to make me feel as low and worthless as my dad did. You, who doesn't want anyone to know that you sneak in here at night, you who treats me like garbage in front of everyone else but then climbs in my bed later. And I'm the asshole who takes it, who lets you walk in and out of my room, who knows you go out with other guys; I say nothing just so you can keep living a lie."

I take a step back from her. "You don't know what it's like to be really abandoned by someone, but you're about to find out, Cherie. Because I'm the only person who really gives a damn about you for you and not what you can do for them, and I'm done taking your bullshit."

Her meek voice squeaks, "You're right."

"What?" I demand gruffly.

"You—you're right, okay?" she stammers, pulling me toward her. I resist and shake my arm from her grip. She looks down.

"About what?"

"You deserve so much better than me, Jack," she murmurs. "I am so, so very sorry. For your hand, for being such a bitch, for what I said—that was—it was a terrible thing to say."

It was worse than any smack you could have given me, I think bitterly. I almost wish she had smacked me instead. Now I don't even want her to touch me.

She shrugs. "And I shouldn't have done all of that in front of you tonight. I—I had no idea you had those kinds of feelings for me. I mean, I wanted you to notice me, but I didn't think you really cared what I did."

So she *was* trying to turn me into a panting mess. "It's sad that you need so much attention all the time." I'm shocked by my own cutting words, but I don't take it back. I don't even feel badly being cruel to her.

She swallows hard, injured. "I know," she admits, hanging her head. "But I don't just need attention. I—I need you." She looks at me then, all somber and heartbroken, and I have to wonder if it's more for dramatic effect.

I decide she's just acting again. "Give it a rest," I groan.

"Please just hear me out?"

I shake my head. "You don't need me, Cherie. I don't matter one bit in your big Hollywood world."

She's on the verge of tears now. Crocodile tears in my book. "But you do! I've been pretending that you don't matter to me because you're not supposed to. But the truth is I'm never happy until I come here. I feel safe in here, with you. I feel like I can be scared and sad. I can be me."

I shift uncomfortably, hating how her words are melting my resolve. I'm supposed to be furious right now, steadfast in hating her and refusing to let her get close to me ever again.

"I really care about you, Jack," she whispers.

"I don't believe you."

She looks at the floor, her eyes still glistening. "I guess it's hard to believe someone who's treated you like I have."

"Interesting how you have these mature revelations in the middle of acting like a stupid little girl every five minutes," I snipe. "Why do you mess with my head if you like me so much?"

She shrugs. "I don't know. Because you let me, I suppose?" She looks forlorn. "Because I love you, and I always treat the people I love like crap?"

I don't think I've heard her correctly. I retreat backward a step and catch myself against the wall. "What?"

She smiles, but it's a bittersweet smile. "Yep. I've been in love with you since that day in the parking lot. Hard to believe, huh?"

I nod dumbly. I don't believe her. Love is huge. It's

the biggest step someone can take, the strongest word you can use when you tell someone how you feel. I don't know if I love her. Do I? How would I even know? How does she know?

I can't believe she loves me already. But I want to.

Cherie shakes her head back and forth and looks up wistfully. "You were so calm, so strong; the way you took care of Britney, and me, all of it. I'd never felt so safe in my life. I was like, 'God, this guy is incredible.' Chloe and Claudia—they made it sound like you were cold and messed up because of your dad, but I told myself, 'No, no way. That guy is the sweetest, most caring guy in the world. He'd take care of me.' And I really, really needed that more than anything else in the world. I needed someone I could trust, someone who would be there for me and keep me safe.

"But then you said all that stuff to Eva and Jim, and it hurt me so much. It crushed me."

"I know," I whisper, and it's all I can say because I'm still stunned by these secrets she is suddenly divulging.

"I tried so hard to hate you. I did everything I could to make you hate me back so that you wouldn't catch on to how I really felt. But no matter what, I couldn't stay away from you. I couldn't just pretend that there wasn't another Jack I had seen that whole first week we spent together, and I wanted him back. I wanted you to protect me again. With my whole world so upside down, I just wanted to feel safe with someone. I still do, but not with just anyone. With you."

I can't tear my eyes from hers, struggling just to breathe. She turns and walks back toward my bed. "I don't know why I'm telling you all of this. It doesn't matter how we feel about each other anyway. We're supposed to be family, and we can't be more than that."

She sits down on the edge of the bed and stares at

the floor. I feel like I'm being broken up with, but without the fun of ever actually dating.

I muster the voice to say, "It doesn't have to be that way."

Her eyes perk up. "What way?"

"I—" I can't bring myself to say what I really want to say. "I could never pretend you're just another person in this family."

She meets my gaze, and there are a thousand things said by her eyes in that one fleeting moment. It all comes down to the words only she can manage to say: "We're already more than that, huh?"

"Yes."

She stands up and paces. "I tried to pretend these feelings weren't there. I convinced myself that this was all platonic—that you were just Jack and that sleeping in a bed together didn't mean anything. But the truth is I don't just come out here every night because I hate sleeping in that house."

My heart beats triple time. I think I know what she means, but I need to hear her say it. "Why then?"

Her lips tuck together like she's trying to hold the reason in. Like once it's out there, she'll never be able to take it back. She looks me dead in the eye, and I gulp under the intensity of her stare.

She says, "I come out here because I want to sleep next to you. Because I love you, and I want to be with you, and it's the only time we can be together without anyone else knowing."

A huge weight suddenly drops onto my shoulders and grounds me from the high she'd given me earlier. *Without anyone else knowing.* I will never be more than a dirty secret to her.

"So why can't we just tell them?" I ask softly, glancing toward the window then the floor, doing anything to avoid her gaze as the silence hangs heavy in the air.

"Well, we can't date each other, Jack. That would be weird—we live together, and we're family by marriage, at least—"

"So?"

She tilts her head. "Jack, be reasonable. Think about what they'll say. We're teenagers; we live together, and you're supposed to be my cousin in a way..."

"Yeah, I guess," I say quickly, doing my best to mask my disappointment. She's right; who am I kidding? I couldn't make her my girlfriend under any of these circumstances.

"I just—I saw how much I hurt you tonight, and I needed you to know how I really felt about you. I needed you to know that I never wanted to hurt you. I didn't know you even cared.

"But now that I do, I can't keep coming in here. It's not fair to drag your feelings through this, too."

My heart drops into my stomach. That will take some getting used to, especially when it means I won't know what she's up to or if she's safe at night.

But it's not supposed to matter to me, I remind myself. *She can't be my girlfriend, so I can't keep tabs on her.*

"Okay. So, I guess that's it," she whispers. I avoid her stare, which I feel resting on my face. "I'll stay in my corner, and you stay in yours. Just like we said a few weeks ago."

I nod stiffly. To think only a mere week ago we were trying to keep ourselves from strangling each other. Now, we must do everything in our power to keep our hands to ourselves for different reasons.

"Well this sucks," I grunt. It's the only thought I can come up with at this moment. That's all I'm thinking, and

I'm pretty sure she's thinking it, too, when she comes toward me with her mouth turned down sadly.

"It's better this way, before we do something we regret," she says, her voice lacking conviction. She rests a hand on my arm, and my skin prickles. "Before we do something we can't take back."

I raise my gaze to hers for the first time in what feels like forever, and I see a wistful set of green eyes staring back at me. "Like what?"

"You know…" Words escape her. She can't finish her sentence and pouts. "I'm happy to know you like me, too."

I swallow hard. "What would make you think I didn't?"

Her mouth twists to the side and she hides suddenly shy eyes. "We never… did anything. Like, we never kissed. I thought it would happen a dozen times, but you didn't try—not once. I've been sleeping next to you since Sunday, but you didn't even touch me. I assumed I was just another annoying little sister to you."

My jaw falls slightly slack. My mind draws up all of those intense, fleeting moments, where her eyes went dark and our mouths came too close. *She wanted me to kiss her?*

"What?" she asks, noticing my disbelief.

I shake my head at her. "You have no idea how much restraint that took."

"Really?" she murmurs with a smile.

I nod.

"Even now?" she says, and now all I can think about is kissing her.

My stomach muscles tighten, "Yes."

"Well, why didn't you ever kiss me?"

I shrug helplessly. "Why would I? You're… well, you're Cherie Belle. And gorgeous." She beams and looks away shyly. "You are. You know you are. You can have any guy you want. I'm just me—the kid you've hated for the last five weeks. I thought if I even looked at you funny, you'd slug me. I never in a million years thought I had a chance with you."

I look down at my feet, shuffling them against the carpet. "And it doesn't matter. I still don't. Tomorrow, you'll go right back to being you, and I'll be the guy you're pretending to hate so that no one catches on to the truth."

She nods her head once and then cocks it to the side. "There's still tonight." Her fingers slide further up on my arm, leaving a blaze in their wake, and her other hand creeps up to my cheek.

"Tonight?" I repeat dumbly, staring at her, my voice strained and hushed. It's hard to breathe again. Is she giving me permission to do what I've been trying not to do for two months? I think Cherie actually wants me to kiss her, right here, right now.

She closes the space between us another step, stroking my jawline. "Maybe… just this once… before we go back to forgetting each other exists—"

My lips are on hers before she can finish, and my arm swings behind her back to pull her close. She moans against my mouth and kisses me back, digging her nails into my hair. We're locked in a rough embrace that shakes my core, and I'm vaguely aware I just started something that I might not be able to stop.

She senses my urgency, too. "Jack, wait!" she gasps suddenly, pulling back. I release her and stumble away until my spine meets the wall. My nerve endings are bellowing and my body demands for a need to finally be met, but I withdraw and try to think of anything but her lips, her hands, or her body.

"I'm sorry," I grunt, breathing hard. I make the

mistake of looking up at her and find she is watching me with a new intensity in her eyes.

"Don't be," she says. I know she's asking for more. I can see it in her narrowed eyes and her parted lips. For once, I do exactly what my body tells me to do and tell my brain to shut up.

My primal side takes over; it's been dormant for too long and has no more patience for reason or hesitation. I rush forward and kiss her again, lifting her. She curls her legs around my waist as I carry her to the bed and lay her down. My mouth finds its way back to hers with ease, then the curve between her neck and her shoulder, and she writhes beneath me, which only encourages the frenzy. All logic engulfed, my hands explore her body, pulling off her dress and then my shirt with pure visceral strength.

She suddenly looks frightened. My chest tightens and I pause, brought to my senses briefly.

"Wait—have you ever done this before?" I pant.

Her wide, innocent eyes dart between my face and my zipper. "No. Have you?"

I hesitate to tell her the truth, but I think I've already given myself away. I nod. "Are you sure you want to?"

She swallows hard and nods rapidly. "Yes." But she doesn't look ready at all. She looks terrified.

"I don't know if this is a good idea," I murmur, sitting back on my heels. She's been making one bad decision after the next; the last thing I want to do is be another bad decision, especially with something as big as her virginity.

"I trust you," she whispers, sitting up. She swallows hard. "You're the only person I trust; I want you to be my first. I'll only get that once, and this is the last time I can ever be with you. It's just for tonight."

I've heard her say that before. Before I can argue,

she kisses me hard and slides her hands down my chest, tapping my primal side back into the ring.

DIRTERAZZI.COM

FIGHT CLUB! JACK HANSEN AND DOMINICK FURST THROW DOWN OVER CHERIE BELLE!

The rumors of Cherie Belle and Caz Farrell just may be pushing Jack Hansen over the edge. Cherie and Jack, her rumored on-again, off-again boyfriend, were involved in a major brawl at Fly last night, and it all started with a little dance off.

This is the first time Hansen has been seen publicly with Belle since late December. As we've previously reported, Cherie's been spotted several nights this week at Fly, often with Caz Farrell. Clearly, Belle is having her cake and eating it, too. Onlookers believe Hansen and Belle were engaged in a heated dance-off with different partners minutes before the brawl broke out. Our photographer at the scene claims Hansen was already incited when he watched Cherie, 16, take body shots off of her companions, fellow stars Danika Shields, 25, and Amber Stiles, 20, before an audience of cheering fans. They had an argument, and Hansen disappeared, only to return with a sexy brunette at his side.

Hansen started dancing with the mystery girl to make Cherie jealous, until Cherie retaliated by flirting with Dominick Furst, another Kidz Channel alum. Hansen was so enraged that he charged and laid Furst out with a knockout punch. As chaos escalated in the club, Hansen and Belle vanished with their entourage. If charges are pressed, Hansen could be arrested for assault, a misdemeanor that carries a fine and potential jail time. Calls to Furst's or Cherie's publicists have not yet been returned. Dirterazzi just wants to know: Where are Cherie's new guardians, aka Jack's parents, in all of this?

Chapter 32

I smell her hair, and I know she's still here. That, and the weight of her head on my chest. Yellow light peeks in through the blinds above my bed and bathes over me, but her skin on mine is the only warmth I can feel. The emptiness and anxiety I woke up with every other morning is replaced by relief and contentment.

It's the knocking on my door that jerks me out of the happy haze and back to reality.

"Jack, honey?"

Mom!

Cherie leaps to attention and looks at me, horrified. Panicked and still groggy, I rush to find my clothes and pull myself together. I can feel the blood leaving my face.

The door's handle jiggles. "Jack, are you awake?"

"One second!" I hop on one foot, pulling on a pair of gym shorts. My bruised hand is throbbing and stiff and practically useless. Memories of last night pour through my mind and distract me from the naked girl in my room who flits past me.

I look up and see Cherie pulling her dress over her head as she makes a mad dash to the bathroom.

"Where are you going?" I hiss.

"To hide in the shower!" she mouths then rushes inside. I hear the shower curtain scrunch and swish, and pretty soon, it's as if I'm the only person in the room.

I take a deep breath to calm myself, slowly reaching for the doorknob. I can't think straight; my heart is racing and adrenaline has all of my limbs trembling. Hiding my swollen hand in the pocket of my shorts, I glance over my shoulder to look at the bathroom and pray she won't be discovered.

When I swing the door open, I try to look sleepy and annoyed. "What is it?"

Her face is all frowns and furrowed brows. "Hi, honey. I'm sorry to bother you so early, but Cherie never came home last night, and I'm worried sick. Have you heard from her?"

Just the sound of my mom saying her name within the confines of these walls, mere feet from where Cherie hides, makes my heart pound. "Cherie? No idea."

"She didn't text you or talk to you or anything?"

I try to give her the *Seriously?* stare, complete with a head tilt and a frown. "Does it look like we talk, Mom?" Inside, my guilty conscience wants to shine a bright spotlight on me and scream, *We did way more than talk!* "She hates my guts, remember?"

My mom nods and sighs, hugging herself with her arms. "Yeah, I know, I guess I was just hoping…"

She pushes past me and walks into my room.

"Mom?" I call urgently. "Mom, I kind of want to go back to sleep."

But she's oblivious and broken. She plants herself on the bed and leans over, her hands clasped and her elbows propped on her knees. My mom is sitting where I just had sex. I want to puke. Why does she have to sit right there? I glance into the bathroom nervously, and my heart bursts back into panic mode.

Suddenly, my mom sniffles, and I snap to attention. Are those tears in her eyes?

"Mom?"

"I just don't know what to do anymore. I feel like I have no control," she whimpers. A tear streams down her cheek, and she sobs delicately. "I—I try to give her space, you know? I know I'm not her mom, and it's been so hard for her to adjust. . .but she's out every night, and now she doesn't even come home! I don't want to punish her because it will only push her away, but . . ."

I feel my insides cave. "Mom, you can't worry about what she's doing. She's almost old enough to do whatever she wants anyway."

"But she's mine now, Jack!" my mom exclaims. "I'm responsible!"

"Correction: Jim is. She's his, not yours." I know these words can get me in serious trouble with the girl behind my shower curtain, but right now I don't care. I've seen my mom cry enough in her life over selfish people, and it's not fair.

My mom waves me off. "Come, now, Jack, you know what I mean. Besides, Jim is never really around to help Cherie or be a dad to her."

I close my eyes and sigh. "Story of our lives, Mom." I look her dead in the eye. "How do you solve the problem with the twins when they don't listen?"

She shrugs, wiping a tear away. "I don't think that much about it. I mean, I'm more careful with them than with you and Brenton and Britney, but I still feel like their mother in a way. Cherie hardly knows me; it's only been a month!"

I'm about to level with her and remind her to be firm and take a stand, but I hesitate. Cherie can hear everything I'm saying. For once, I try not to be the guy with the answers.

"I don't know, Mom. Maybe you should try talking to Jim or something? I doubt Cherie is doing anything terrible."

Suddenly, one of the twins is screaming across the pool at my mother. "Eva! Eva, you're not going to believe what your son did now!"

My heart skips a beat. I jerk around and look across the pool. Chloe meets my gaze and waves, her grin wide and evil.

"You are so dead!" she laughs proudly.

My mom stands up and groans. "What did you do, Jack? Can you just tell me so I don't have to go over there?"

"I, um—I have no idea," I stammer, looking over my shoulder at the bathroom.

Suddenly, Jim is yelling out to us, too, and he emerges from the kitchen onto the patio. "Jack, get in here!"

Now I'm panicking. I feel my hands shaking all over again. Did one of the twins spy on me and Cherie last night? Did they see her come into my room? Did they sit outside my door and listen in?

I suddenly hear the sounds of last night echoing in the back of my mind, especially Cherie's voice gasping my name. I swallow hard. The twins could've easily heard us.

I follow my mom toward the kitchen. Jim glares at me and pushes a newspaper into my mother's arms.

"What the hell is this about?" he shouts.

I peer over my mother's shoulder and feel myself shatter inside. The newspaper is emblazoned with the headline: *Cherie Belle on the Road to Destruction: Boys, Benders, and Club Brawls!*" The headline screams from beneath a picture of her looking drunk, her dress riding up on her body.

Inside my arms.

The caption below it reads, *"Bonnie and Clyde 2.0: Jack Hansen, 17, gets intimate with Belle, 16, moments before he assaults her other suitor."*

"Jack...?" I can hear the desperation in my mother's voice to believe anything other than what she sees.

"It's not how it looks, Mom—" I try to say. My face is hot and my knees are quaking. I feel like I'm going to vomit. Assault? Bonnie and Clyde—what does that mean? Am I an outlaw for getting into a fight?

Claudia narrows her eyes and double takes between me and outside. I grow pale and look back, wondering if she sees Cherie, but there's no one out there. She still looks confused. "What—"

Chloe cuts her off, grinning haughtily. "It's exactly what it looks like. He started the fight; it's all over the gossip sites." She holds up her phone as a noisy, dark video plays. You can see blurry bodies colliding while Cherie screams my name.

"How…?" my voice trails off, and I'm speechless.

"Apparently Jack and Cherie are quite the item," Chloe snickers. I glower at her.

Jim senses my brewing temper and shields both of his daughters behind him. "Jack, what were you thinking? How could you take Cherie to these places and encourage her to drink when the whole world is watching her right now?"

I try to be patient. "I didn't encourage her to drink. I didn't even know she'd be there. This is all one big—"

My mom turns on me before I can even explain anything. "Forget Cherie—what are YOU doing in these places? You're not allowed to drink—Jack, are you drinking and—and fighting?! Why are you fighting again? Oh my God—I knew it was a mistake to bring you out here!" And she's lost to me, muttering to herself and staring at the newspaper in her hand as if somehow the story will magically change.

"Stop reading it, it isn't the truth!" I try to take it from her.

"Oh my God, your hand—look at your hand!" she nearly shrieks, dropping the newspaper and grabbing my wrist. I scrunch my eyes against the pain.

"Oh, Jesus, Mary, and Joseph! What did you do?" she whimpers, releasing me and covering her face.

"I got in a fight, Mom, that's all." I hide it gingerly in

my pocket.

"That's *all*? You assaulted someone—what were you thinking? Jack, you promised me no more of this!"

I am all thumbs when it comes to defending myself in the presence of her irrational side. "Mom, you don't understand—I had to do something! This guy was all over Cherie—she needed help!"

Jim folds his arms over his chest. "Jack, this is very serious. You should never have brought Cherie into that kind of environment. She is fragile right now."

"Stop saying that!" I finally explode. "It wasn't me—I didn't bring her there, she was there with her friends when I showed up with my own friends. This is not my fault; if anything, I protected her out there!"

"Why were you going there at all?" my mom cries. "You're not old enough to be in those clubs!"

"Everyone does it out here, Mom," I groan.

Jim holds up his hand to quiet my mother. "Hold on, Eva. Jack, who are these friends Cherie was with?"

I'm relieved someone is listening to me at last. "Danika and some other celebrity girl. Danika's been taking her to this club all week—she's the one you should be questioning. I just happened to see Cherie there, and she got attacked by some guy, so I stepped in."

"Yeah, right!" Chloe squawks. "That's not what it says on Dirterazzi.com!"

The photographer, Derek, flashes through my mind, and I see red. "Shut up, Chloe!" I don't know what it says on the blogs, but I know they are probably telling more of the full story than I am.

She pulls up a report on her phone and reads, "The rumors of Cherie Belle and Caz Farrell just may be pushing Jack Hansen over the edge. Cherie and her rumored on-again, off-again boyfriend, Jack Hansen, were involved in a major brawl at Fly nightclub, and it all started with a little dance off—"

"Chloe!" I shout, trying to swipe the phone from her hand.

She dodges my grasp and races to the other side of the kitchen's island. I chase her, but she stays just out of my reach on the opposite end. She continues to read, "This is the first time Hansen has been seen publicly with Belle since late December. As we've previously reported, Cherie's been spotted several nights this week at Fly, often with Caz Farrell. Clearly, Belle is having her cake and eating it, too."

Claudia watches my face fall and says softly, "Chloe..."

She ignores her sister and continues reading. "Onlookers believe Hansen and Belle were engaged in a heated dance-off with different partners minutes before the brawl broke out. Our photographer at the scene claims Hansen was already incited when underage Cherie took body shots off of her companions, assistant Danika Shields, 25, and fellow Kidz star, Amber Stiles, 20, before an audience of cheering fans. The couple had an argument, and Hansen disappeared, only to return with a sexy brunette at his side."

"This is ridiculous!" I cry out. "Mom, you can't really buy this stuff—"

Chloe raises her voice and reads over me. "Hansen started dancing with the mystery girl to make Cherie jealous, until Cherie retaliated by flirting with Dominick Furst, another Kidz Channel alum. Hansen was so enraged that he charged and laid Furst out with a knockout punch. As chaos escalated in the club, Hansen and Belle vanished with their entourage. If charges are pressed, Hansen could be arrested for assault, a misdemeanor that carries a fine and potential jail time. Calls to Furst's or Cherie's publicists have not yet been returned. Dirterazzi just wants to know: Where are Cherie's new guardians, aka Jack's parents, in all of this?"

My first thought is, *Striped-Shirt is an actor, too?* I quickly snap to attention when I notice all eyes are on me.

"What? You can't really believe that; it's just some stupid gossip site!" I shout at their gaping faces. I look at my mom. "Mom, you even said not to listen to those sites!" My voice whines, but I don't care. I will not allow some stupid reporter to make my whole family think I'm just some jealous nut.

But my mom is staring over my shoulder, watching the front door as Cherie walks in, all smiles. She looks well-rested and clean, and she's wearing clothes that make her look like she just came from the gym. I gawk at her and glance back at the casita.

How...?

"Hi guys," she says cheerily. Suddenly, her eyes narrow like she senses a problem. I've got to give it to her, she's a great actress. "Is everything okay?"

Jim is the first to address her. "Where were you last night, Cherie? You never came home—your aunt was worried sick!"

"I stayed with Danika," she lies with a shrug. "We had a late night, and I didn't want her to have to drive me home."

"Cherie, they know about the fight," I say softly, knowing I need an ally to vouch for me now more than ever. She shoots me a look that says, *"Shut up; I'll handle this."*

"Cherie, have you really been drinking every night?" my mom asks, and her voice is so gentle but so hurt, as if Cherie has stabbed her in the back. "Is that true?"

Cherie laughs and waves it off, noticing the newspaper on the table. "Oh, goodness, Eva, you don't really believe those tabloids, do you?"

Chloe is still smirking from the other end of the island. She holds up her phone and announces, "Says here Jack was drinking last night, too."

"I'm gonna kill you," I growl toward her.

"Do you really want to keep adding to your criminal record?" she snaps back, her mouth smug.

Jim cries out, "Hey! That's enough, from either of you." He turns and looks at Cherie. "Cherie, tell us what is going on. Right now."

Cherie turns her attention to him and forces a laugh. "I'm not drinking. I promise."

"So what does this look like to you?" Jim demands. He holds up the front page of the newspaper so she can see how drunk she looks and how tightly we are entwined.

"Um, that we were hugging? It's just a bad angle— those photographers are really good at making nothing look like something."

"Well, why were you and Jack at this club together?" my mom asks. "Is there something going on between you two like they say?"

"Not at all! We just ran into each other. Trust me, we don't hang out," she says arrogantly, stinging me. Now she won't even look at me. She's got her eyes locked on my mom and Jim.

Mom passes the newspaper to her and says, "This doesn't look like running into each other, young lady. It looks like he's holding you up." My mom looks at me. "If there's nothing going on between you two, then why did Jack get into a fight with some other boy?"

I look down. Mom's smart. She senses dishonesty and won't let it go.

Cherie takes a deep breath and puts on a great smile. "Eva, Jack was really helpful last night when a friend of mine got a little carried away. He stepped in to protect me, and the tabloids are probably just blowing it out of proportion."

I nod my head stoically and stare at the floor.

"We realized the club was not a safe place for us, so we left. I went to Danika's, and he came home."

Mom can't argue with that story, can she?

But Chloe will. "They're lying. Tell them what you just saw, Claudia."

Cherie and I glance up, and I find that Claudia has gravitated to her sister's side. She looks hesitant and avoids my stare. Deep in my gut, I know she saw Cherie outside earlier. She must have. I beg her silently not to say anything.

Chloe nudges her. "Go on, tell them."

Claudia's voice is a mere murmur. "Cherie just came from Jack's bedroom. I saw her sneak out."

Cherie's jaw almost hits the floor. "What?"

"That's not true." My own voice shocks me. It's a deep, angry threat, because now I have two people to protect—my mother and Cherie. "Claudia, cut it out. Right now."

Chloe shoots me a death glare and purses her lips. "But that is the truth, Jack." The last syllable comes out like a smack. "She just saw her."

Cherie recovers from her astonishment and scoffs. "Like that would ever happen." It burns a little more than her other comment, but I know why she says it that way, so I have to just take it and stand here quietly.

Chloe looks over at her father. "There are security cameras everywhere, right? Go ahead and check them."

The security cameras! I had forgotten all about the cameras around the property. I feel my stomach flip, and my expression must reveal how horrified I am right now because Jim raises his eyebrows at me. Cherie pales. I don't know what to do. Every shred of me but one is screaming to just tell the truth before my mom finds it out for herself.

"Well?" Jim says finally, exchanging glances between the both of us. "Would one of you care to tell us the truth?"

I ask myself, *What will happen if I don't say anything? Mom can check to see what happened last night. She can check every night if she wants, and she'll see it all. She would be devastated if I continue to stand here and lie to her.*

"Jack? What is it, honey?" my mom calls, jolting me from my thoughts. I look up at her, and see her face is flushed with panic. She fears the worst; her fear is the reality, but she doesn't have to know it. I can tell her just enough to keep her world intact and finally bring the inevitable end to my secret relationship with Cherie. I can tell her something—a half-truth at least.

But I can't get the words out.

After a long silent pause, Mom stands and says, "Chloe, Claudia, I think you both need to go upstairs right now. We have to talk to Jack and Cherie." When the girls depart, Chloe smirks at me but Claudia hides her eyes and puts a lot of distance between us. Cherie watches them with her arms crossed over her chest and her foot tapping. She looks like an irritated cartoon character, but it's all an act. In her tight frown, I can see she is anxious.

Mom's eyes are screaming, *"Please say no. Please say this isn't the truth,"* as they dart between the image on the newspaper's front page and me.

"One of you needs to tell us what's going on," Jim says finally.

I know I can't keep this a secret anymore. There's actual, recorded proof. Why should I lie about something they can check?

I turn and look at Jim. "The truth is she's been coming in my room every night to go to sleep."

Mom looks from me to Cherie and barely whispers, "Cherie, is this true?" She holds onto the edge of the breakfast table like her legs aren't strong enough to hold her up.

Cherie shakes her head indignantly. "No!"

I narrow my eyes at her. "Cherie—"

She turns a venomous stare toward me. "Jack, just be quiet!"

"Enough!" my mom scolds. Cherie clams up, and I just shake my head in defeat.

I obey immediately when my mom tells us to sit down at the table. I feel Jim's eyes on me, and I can tell he's not completely convinced that I'm innocent in all this. Maybe I'm not.

I think about how I had sex with his virgin niece last night, and I know I'm not innocent at all. I hold my head in my hands and avoid looking at him.

Cherie says stiffly, "I'm going to stand right here, thank you."

"No, you'll sit down," my mom replies. Her voice is firm and angry, and if I were Cherie, I would sit. Cherie realizes my mother means business and pulls a chair out. She still makes a show of dropping heavily into the seat and crossing her legs sharply.

Less than ten hours ago, she was wrapping those legs around me.

I shake the thought from my head and try to focus on the table.

"Both of you are going to tell me what's going on," my mom commands, leaning forward on the table. I feel like I'm nine again and just had a fight on the playground with one of my friends. "And I want the truth.

"Jack, would you like to go first?"

It's harder for the words to come this time, especially in this proximity to Cherie. "She goes out with her friends every night and when she comes home, she doesn't go upstairs. She comes to my room, and she stays with me."

"And she sleeps there?"

I nod stiffly. "She can't sleep in her room because her parents' room is right down the hall. It upsets her."

Mom's chest rises and falls before she asks, "Where in your room does she sleep?"

I hesitate and look over at Cherie. What does she want me to say? Should I tell the truth?

My mom snaps at me, "Don't look at her, Jack. Look at me. Where does she sleep?"

It's hard to look at my mother and lie to her. I feel my cheeks turning violet. I can barely get the words out. "In my bed."

"And where do you sleep?" Jim presses. My whole body is rocked with chills and I have to look down. I don't understand why they care so much.

When I don't answer right away, my mom calls, "Jack?"

I can't lie to my mom, but I can maybe fudge the truth a little, for Cherie. "On the couch." There is a long pause of relieved silence, as if Jim and Mom were expecting the real answer.

"What is this, a trial? Why are you interrogating him?" Cherie says defensively, painting an invisible guilty sign over both of our heads. I look up at her bitterly, wishing she'd just let me do the talking.

My mom turns to stone and reminds her of the rules. "It's Jack's turn to speak, Cherie. Jack?" my mom says again, her hands curling together, her voice urgent. "Has anything… occurred between you two?" I can hear my mom forcing the question out, as though the thought is so painful that the words won't come easily.

The implication sets my nerves on high alert. I shake my head and so does Cherie. I don't know why, but lying about my relationship with Cherie is even more painful than lying to my mom.

"So you both just sleep in the same room, right?" Jim clarifies.

As I look up at him, I can see that this thought relieves him. I'm willing to tell him whatever makes him rest easy and my mom happy.

"Yeah."

Mom presses, "Why do you let her stay with you, Jack? Did you ever tell her to go back to her own room?"

"Of course I did," I say indignantly. "She told me it hurts too much to be in here, so I didn't want to force her."

Then Mom asks the question I can't answer. "Why didn't you tell one of us this was happening?"

I shrug and try to think of any reason but the real reason. I knew this day would come, and I knew I wouldn't have something intelligent to say. My throat is dry.

"He was respecting my privacy," Cherie hisses.

My mom shoots her a threatening glare. "Jack?"

I clear my throat to buy time and think. "I dunno. Didn't think it was a big deal, I guess," I lie softly. I won't tell my mom that she has been drunk every night; I hope they can't see that on the video. I definitely won't admit out loud, here or anywhere, that I hid it because I liked sleeping with her.

"And what happened last night?" my mom insists. "What went on at this club?"

"The fight is true," I admit. "But I only hit him because he was groping her."

My mom nods pensively. She turns to Cherie. "Is that

what happened, Cherie?"

Cherie nods. Her eyes hold onto the floor. "Yes. Jack was just protecting me."

Jim, still confused, jumps in to ask, "Why do you go to his room at night?"

My mom chastises him with a look and says, *"We already asked them that."* She's turned into Supermom, and she will not let anyone interrupt her mission to uncover the truth. She looks at me and asks, "Are you sure nothing more has happened between you two?"

The question combusts between my ears, making my brain buzz with electricity. My mom knows me too well. She can sense the indiscretion between us.

But I look over at Cherie and remind myself that we should never speak of what happened last night. It can't ever happen again and, for this very reason, it should never have happened in the first place.

I shake my head and say flatly, "Nothing."

And Cherie won't refute my answer. She keeps her reddening, glistening eyes on the floor, kicking one foot back and forth absently.

"Can I go now?" I ask my mom. She watches Cherie, sees a tear roll down her cheek, and nods. I can tell this conversation is not over, though, because as I leave, Mom avoids my gaze. She knows there is more than either of us is letting on, and she will be at my door later looking for the truth, as well as an explanation for lying to her.

Or Cherie will cave and tell them the truth, and then I'll just be in more trouble. As I step out onto the patio, I look back over my shoulder. Cherie is in tears at the table while my mom and Jim comfort her and give her tissues. It hurts my stomach a little to see her so upset because I know I helped cause this. What I allowed to go on behind their backs, all those secrets I kept since that last night back in New York, the truth has finally exploded. She is exposed to my family, and now they know she is heading down a bad path fast.

But, I remind myself, *she'll get the help she needs now, right?* It needs to be this way, for now at least.

I see a missed call from Mica on my cellphone when I'm back in my room. I don't call him back; I don't want to have to explain everything to anyone right now, and he'll be nosy as hell. Instead, I crash onto my bed, which still smells like her. Frustrated, I tear the sheets off of my bed and strip the mattress until it's bare. But it's the room that smells like her, not just the bed. My skin smells like her, too. I'm suddenly worried my mom or Jim noticed that.

Now I'm restless and angry. I know I need to get out and go somewhere else, but I can't think of any place to go, and I refuse to call Mica. I take a shower, hoping that will clear my head and make her scent disappear. But Cherie's scent is following me. Maybe it's my imagination, but I can't get rid of it no matter what I do.

I decide to go for a run, convinced that staying trapped in that room, surrounded by Cherie and awaiting my mother's second interrogation, is going to drive me insane. Throwing my bedroom door open, I pull on my sneakers and gather my keys. My mom and Jim are talking alone at the table now, and that only means they've finished with Cherie. I wonder nervously if Cherie told them the truth about last night and, more importantly, where she is now.

The only thing I can do is let my feet carry me far away from my house and the trouble I'll face with Cherie or them later.

Chapter 33

I return from my run ready to face the worst. I know my mom will want to talk more, and I just have to be prepared for her to know the truth. I take a deep breath as I stand on the doorstep and suddenly hear faint yet angry banter on the other side. Jim and my mom are fighting for the first time, I think. I push the door open gently and step inside of the house just as Jim's voice rises a little. He and my mom are arguing in the kitchen, and they don't notice I've come in.

"He encouraged it, Eva!"

"Jim, I told you, it's in his nature to take care of others."

"Eva, look, I was his age once. If a girl like Cherie asked to sleep in my room, I'd have rolled out the red carpet!" he declares. Hearing the way he says it makes me sound real bad. "I'm saying it for the last time: Jack took advantage of a lonely, confused girl."

I'm furious that he would think something like that of me, but I'm even more horrified when my mom doesn't quickly slam the book closed on the thought. I sneak closer to listen in, hiding behind the foyer wall.

She finally says, "And why would a girl like Cherie ask to sleep in his room if she didn't like him? Why Jack and not the twins if it was all about seeking comfort?"

Jim is grasping for a reason. "I don't know! She's always fighting with the girls, and she thought she could trust him since he's supposed to be family!"

"Jim, don't be silly. If anything, *Cherie* took advantage of *Jack*. She knows he's a nice kid, and she probably knew he had a little crush on her. She's the celebrity, and one with a party reputation, obviously—

who knows what she does when she goes gallivanting drunk all over Hollywood?" My mom is defending me for the first time in ages.

Then her tone changes. "Look, it doesn't matter who seduced who. They clearly did more than just sleep together. You saw how hurt she was when he said he didn't have feelings for her. And I know Jack—he would never have had a problem being honest with me if there wasn't something big to hide. Say what you will, but he's never openly lied to me like that before."

My stomach flips. I'm caught. We're caught. But how? Did Cherie tell them? Humiliation floods through me. I can never look at my mother or Jim again. I wish I'd never laid a hand on Cherie.

"Fine," Jim says gruffly. "Now what do we do about it?"

My mom sighs. "I don't know. It's a sensitive thing to talk about. Cherie's been through so much, and this is clearly hurting her. I guess I should talk to Jack and tell him it's not okay and he can't have that kind of relationship with her."

Jim scoffs. "Eva, you were a kid once. You know that as soon as someone tells you that you can't be with someone that only makes it more appealing. We could have serious trouble on our hands; Cherie's been sneaking in and out of this house all week; she's even had boys over and I had no idea. How are we going to stop *them both* from doing anything when they live together?"

I realize then that he's looked at the video for sure and has seen her go into my room every night, even on Sunday after her friends left. Well, at least they knew I was being honest about that.

She replies, "Well, we have to trust Jack to do the right thing, I guess, until Cherie is more stable."

Jim sighs heavily. "That's not going to work, Eva."

"Well, what do you suggest?" Jim is quiet at first. I nearly hug the wall in anticipation, waiting for him to answer.

He concludes, "We have to separate them. What about Darla? She and Leroy love Jack; they'd love to have him live with them, and Jack would get to move back to New York."

I slump down to the ground and hug my knees to my chest. *He wants to get rid of me?*

My mom's voice nearly shrieks, "I am not sending my son away!"

"Eva, calm down, it's only a suggestion. Just think: he hated the idea of moving out here, and all his friends live in New York. He doesn't get along with the twins. Now he and Cherie are one bad decision away from getting her pregnant, and then he will really run for the hills. He's already missing; this is just a plan for if he even comes back."

"He will come back, Jim. I know my son," mom replies angrily.

"I'm just saying, apple tree..."

"Don't," she bites. I have never heard her speak so viciously. Then her voice wavers with a little uncertainty. "He will come home; he probably just went for a run."

"Well, even if he does, I'm sure he's dying to get out. Does it really pay to force him to live here?" he asks.

I can't believe what I'm hearing. I want to cover my ears to block out his words, but I'm frozen in place.

Jim makes it sound like I would choose to leave if I could; like I've already abandoned all of them just to get away from Cherie. As though escape is the only thing I want, and that I don't care how it hurts anyone else, especially my mom.

That's not me; that's someone else. That's someone I promised I would never be. Wrath builds like a roaring train shooting through my body. His assumption sparks a fire inside that is so fierce that I don't have the strength to rein it in.

I will never be my father.

I get to my feet, quietly sneak back outside, and go to the casita. I'm tired of people deciding what will happen to me, tired of falling into step with the plans of others. I'm taking my life back into my control and doing what I know is right, not what they think is right for me. I'm going to call Cherie and tell her exactly how I feel. It's up to her if I stay or go, not them, not me. I'm going to tell her that, if she wants, I'll be everything to her. I'll be her security blanket, her boyfriend, whatever. Jim and Mom are not going to keep us apart just because they think they have to; no one can and no one will.

I throw open my bedroom door and see my bed is perfectly made with new sheets and pillowcases, not bare like I had left it before. My bed's condition must have been how Mom knew more happened; she's not a dumb lady.

I swallow my shame, shoving it deep down so I can muster the determination I had a second ago. I pick up my phone and dial Cherie's number. It rings three times before she answers on the other end.

But she doesn't say hello. There are a lot of voices in the background, and hers is not one of them.

"Cherie?" I say. No response. "Cherie, you there?"

She finally clears her throat. "Yeah, I'm here."

"Are you okay?" I ask immediately, hearing the heaviness in her voice.

"Yes, I'm fine."

"Can we talk? In person, I mean. Are you home?" I hear how pathetically hopeful my last question sounds.

"No, I'm out."

Mom and Jim actually let her leave the house? I'm

beyond puzzled. What are they thinking? "Where are you?"

She sighs again. "I'm with Carl and Betsy. They wanted to take me to dinner."

"Oh." My guts swirl as I think back to that last night in New York, picturing Carl's swollen and stubby fingers trying to hold Cherie steady. Mom and Jim have no idea that Carl and Betsy are just as bad as influences as her Kidz Channel friends.

I try to shake the sudden worry from my head. "Cherie, please come home. I'm worried about you being with them."

"I'm fine, Jack. Thank you for your concern."

"No, you're not. We need to talk, about everything."

She's quiet for a moment before, with interview-worthy professionalism, she says, "No, Jack, we can't talk anymore. I think it's best we just stay apart."

"Huh?" My jaw almost hits the floor. My heart beats double. "Why?"

"I just don't think it's a good idea for us to be around each other right now," she interrupts, her tone saccharine. "I hope you can understand."

"Well, I don't." I'm getting mad. My neck starts to heat up, and my shoulders are tight. "Why are you talking like that?"

"Jack, we said that we couldn't be together anymore," she replies. "And now, after last night and how violent you were with Dominick, it just makes me nervous that you're too unstable for me. I'm recovering from a terrible tragedy, and I need to be surrounded by positive people."

The answer sounds manufactured by none other than Betsy. But this isn't the paparazzi she's talking to— it's me! I live with her; she's slept with me! Don't I deserve more than a programmed robot response?

"Me? I'm the negative force in your life? Are you serious?"

"I just need to be surrounded by positive people and people who want to see me get through this," she replies evenly.

I can't believe she thinks I'd buy this bullshit for one second. "Cherie, don't give me that damned prepared statement crap," I bark. "I'm not just some random jerk off the street—this is me you're talking to!" I know my anger is getting the better of me, and I try to soften my tone. "Cherie, please. Just give me a chance to talk to you—"

"I'm sorry, Jack," she says haltingly. I hear her sniffle a little before she recovers herself. "This is how it has to be, and I hope you can appreciate my boundaries."

"No, you owe me more than that," I growl. "Look if you really wanted space from me, that would be fine, but I don't think you do—I think they're telling you to say all of this. Where are you—I'll come and get you right now."

"I'm sorry, Jack." She hiccups a small sob, and it's the only thing that convinces me that she doesn't mean what she's saying. If it hurts her enough to make her cry, she doesn't want to say any of these things.

Right?

"I know you don't mean this, Cherie," I say firmly, never doubting myself more than I do in this moment.

I hear a voice in the background tell her to hang up. She whimpers, "I have to hang up now."

"Fine!" I laugh, seething, hoping Carl and Betsy can hear me. "Let them run your life for the next few hours! I'm not going to give up, Cherie. You know why? Because I love you. They don't—they love the money you make for them. They just want you to look perfect all the time, but I want you to be happy.

"Go ahead and do what they say, Cherie, because

I'm just going to wait until you come home. They might control you out there, but they don't control what happens in this house. When you get home, we are going to talk about this without your goddamn puppet masters controlling everything you say!"

I hear her sob, "I know. I'm so sorry." The voice telling her to hang up grows more stern.

I hear a whimper and more muffled noises. "Cherie? Cherie!" The line goes dead, and my screen blinks that the call has ended. I curse, slam the phone down on my dresser, and charge out to the driveway.

Why is she talking to me like this? How could she let them get between us? Whatever it is she's being made to say, she won't be able to hide behind her cellphone when we come face to face. I'm going to find out how she really feels as soon as she pulls into this driveway. And she will have to cross my path eventually. At least, I hope she does.

I open my car door and slide into the front seat. I'll just wait in my car so she doesn't have the chance to sneak in. I'll wait all night if I have to.

DIRTERAZZI.COM

AND CHERIE'S TRUE KNIGHT IN SHINING ARMANI ARMOR IS...

Someone, quick, pinch us, because we think we're dreaming! It appears someone is finally, FINALLY, stepping in to put a stop to the Cherie Belle tornado of trouble before she completely spirals out of control.

Carl Schwartz, Cherie's manager, has reportedly had it with her antics and her wild partying nights, especially in light of the recent debacle at Club Fly. He is putting Cherie on lockdown and plans to seek her removal from the custody of James Goldman, Cherie's uncle and current absentee guardian. We here at Dirterazzi think this is the best move for Cherie's health and well-being; her new guardians just are not equipped to handle the life of a young celebrity, are too overwhelmed with their current brood of children, and have allowed a sixteen-year-old to run rampant through the streets of Hollywood without any supervision. Sources close to Cherie's camp tell us that Carl plans to meet with her guardians later today to convince them to allow him to adopt her since he has no children of his own and loves Belle like a daughter. If they won't cooperate, Schwartz will seek more drastic measures to get the job done. Stay tuned!

Chapter 34

"I found Jack! He's in his car! Jack? Jack. C'mon, wake up."

I feel someone nudging my shoulder. I open my eyes to my steering wheel and the sun glaring into my windshield, forcing me to scrunch them closed again. I must have fallen asleep in my car waiting for Cherie to come home. I turn and see Claudia watching me. She's the last person I want to wake up to right now.

"You okay?" Her brow is furrowed, her eyes wide and frightened.

"No. Where's Cherie?"

"I'm not supposed to say—"

"Jesus, never mind," I grumble groggily, climbing out of the driver's seat and pushing past her.

I hear my mother's voice screech from inside, "Jack!" That's the second to last person I want to wake up to right now, and Claudia practically tags her in as she disappears into the house.

Mom runs out of the front door, her eyes wider than Claudia's and her hair frazzled. I know just by looking at her that she spent the whole night frantically pacing and calling police and crying. Was she really that worried about me? She races forward and throws her arms around me, smothering me with kisses and anger and tears of joy all at once.

"Oh, thank you, God! Thank you! What were you doing out here? I've been calling and calling you! How could you not tell me where you were? Do you have any idea how worried I was?" she gasps into my neck.

"I'm sorry, I guess I left my phone in my room… where is Cherie?"

"Cherie's gone. Oh, thank God you're all right!" she cries, pulling at the hair on the sides of her head.

I grab my mother by the shoulders and focus her. "Stop! What do you mean she's gone?"

She stammers out a useless reply. "She didn't come home last night. Her manager thought it would be best she say with them since her movie premier is today."

My stomach drops. "Are you serious?!" Our phone conversation replays in my mind, and a million stab wounds reopen inside.

"Cherie—what the hell, Cherie..." I moan, clutching at my rapidly pulsing head. I turn to my mother frantically. "When did you last see her?"

Her head tips to the side. "Oh, Jack. Not since yesterday afternoon, baby."

"Well, why aren't you with her? She can't be alone with those people!" I try to pull out of Mom's hold, looking over her shoulder to the front door. Jim stands stoically in the entrance, eying me with a frown of disappointment.

Seeing him reminds me of his comments to my mom the night before, and I want to punch the frown off of his face. "Bet you thought I was long gone, huh?"

He cocks his head quizzically. "What?"

I usher my mom to the side gently and walk forward. "I heard you last night. I heard everything you said about sending me to live with Darla." I'm feet away from him before I stop and glare heavily at him.

"Jack, Jim didn't mean that—" my mom tries to say.

"Sure he did," I say coldly, smirking at my stepfather. "The apple doesn't fall far from the tree, right Jim?"

"That's enough, Jack." Mom scurries between us as if she senses a fight, and I look down at her with disgust. Does she think I'm going to actually punch her husband? I'm not some kind of monster who starts fights with everyone, not anymore at least.

I look back at him and think that's exactly what Jim wants. He wants me to be the angry, violent kid I used to be. "Well, I'm not my father, Jim, but thanks for having that kind of faith in me."

Jim looks down in shame and nods. "I'm sorry, Jack. You're right; it was a terrible thing to say. I was upset, and I was worried about Cherie."

"Well that makes two of us. Where is she? Do you even know? Or did you decide to send her away, too?"

He shakes his head and sighs. "No, her manager thought it would be best that she stay with them in a hotel for the night."

"And you let her?" I roar. "They're not good people, Jim! They've give her drugs—they gave her ecstasy the other night! She's not safe with them!"

He shakes his head at me. "Come now, Jack, don't be ridiculous. These are adults you're talking about. I know her friends are questionable, but I trust Carl. She has the premier of her movie tonight, and she needs to be well rested. Carl was worried she wouldn't get the kind of peace of mind she needs here and, frankly, I agree with him."

"She definitely won't get it there," I grumble. "Where is she? What hotel? I'll go find her myself."

Mom puts her hand on my shoulder, less frightened now that she knows I'm not going to beat up her husband. "Sweetheart, I know you care very much for her, but right now she needs a little space—"

"No!" I cry out, pulling away from her roughly. "Don't hand me that bullshit. Tell me where she is!"

They stare at the ground and each other, but they won't look at me. Their lips are sealed.

I grind my teeth in frustration and push past them into the house. "Chloe? Claudia?" The twins are at the

kitchen table, eating breakfast with Brenton and Britney.
Britney shrinks in her chair and looks almost frightened of
me, and I realize I must seem like a madman to her.

I try to soften my tone. "Hey guys. Do any of you
know where Cherie is staying?"

The little ones both shake their heads, but Chloe and
Claudia exchange a quick look before agreeing to say no.

I look down at Claudia, the easiest target, and pull up
a chair. "Claudia, if you know, you need to tell me."

She scoots her chair away and avoids my gaze. "I
don't, Jack."

"Leave her alone, Jack," Chloe snips.

"Claudia, please. She's not in good hands with those
people. She needs help, and they don't really care about
her. I need to know where she is."

"We told you we don't know, Jack!" Chloe shrills.

"Jack, leave the girls alone, please," Jim says, and he
and my mother are suddenly beside the table. "They're
not going to tell you. They promised Cherie they
wouldn't."

"*Promised* her?" I demand. "Yeah right! Why would
she talk to them ever again? They're the ones who
started all of this!"

Chloe retorts, "We called her to apologize, and she
accepted, so apparently she isn't that tore up about it."

Claudia adds softly, "We wanted to apologize to you,
too."

"Yeah, we would have apologized to you, too, if you
weren't such a jerk!" her sister interrupts.

"Girls! Enough!" Mom scolds. She touches my
shoulder and coos, "Honey, the bottom line is Cherie is
around the people who know her best and that's what
she needs—"

"They don't know her. None of you do! *I* know her. *I*
should be with her. Carl and Betsy and Danika—they're

all in on it! They allow her to get drunk and take her to clubs and give her drugs!

"They don't care about what happens to her, and they'll keep putting her in dangerous situations until it's too late. Just watch, she'll come home drunk tonight—if she comes home at all!"

Jim shakes his head and says, "No, Jack, we will be there tonight with her. She won't be coming home with us, but we will be there. We have all been invited to the premier as her family."

I pause and stare at him, slack jawed. "Oh."

But before I can feel a spark of relief, Jim adds as gently as possible, "Well, actually, the producers asked that, you know, you do not attend."

The words fall hard upon my shoulders, and I nearly crumble beneath their weight. "What?"

"They think it will draw unnecessary attention from the movie and the actors if you're there. There's just been so much media hubbub over that whole club fight," Jim says. "You can understand that, can't you?"

"You're not serious." I glance up at my mother. "Mom?" She turns away from me. Just one look at her glistening, down-turned eyes tell me that no matter how much this idea hurts her, she won't contest it.

"I'm sorry, baby," she whispers through a sob, making her way toward the stairs. "I think you should just go get ready for school, okay?"

I get up abruptly from the chair and pull at the hair on the sides of my head. "This is insanity!" I feel like I'm trapped in an alternate universe where my mother is becoming a puppet to some Hollywood tyrants. Cherie's handlers have singlehandedly ruined my life in the last twenty-four hours. Forget about Cherie, forget about this stupid premier—since when does my *mother* allow someone to treat me like this?

The stab wounds begin to work their way up my chest to my throat until I'm voiceless. I'm on some Hollywood black list because I protected Cherie from some douchebag. Cherie refuses to see or speak to me, even after I've poured my heart out to her, and she trusts the twins over me. Everyone thinks I'm about to snap, even Britney. On top of it all, my mother has left me to fend for myself yet again. I feel the blood draining from my face.

"Jack?" Claudia stands up and takes a step toward me. Her eyebrows knit together in concern as if I look as dizzy as I feel, and she reaches out like she is about to catch me.

"Don't," I choke, backing up. I look around the room at the worried, pitying faces that stare back.

It doesn't matter what I say to Jim or my mom or anyone. Cherie told me exactly how she felt last night, and I'm only making myself look like a fool by fighting anymore. I look as crazy as they're all making me out to be.

Finally, the worst thought enters my mind: *What am I really fighting for anyway?*

I throw up my hands. "I'm done." I turn to Jim, adding, "You were right; I don't want to be here. I'm going back to New York—I'll stay with Darla, Frank, anyone. But I won't stay here."

Tears fall from Claudia's eyes as I storm toward my room to get ready for school.

Chapter 35

Mica is waiting for me in the parking lot when I pull in. He stands by my space and shifts his backpack on his shoulder.

"Hey," I say, trying to avoid his gaze as I get out and grab my books from the back seat. "How are you?"

"I can't complain. How are *you*?"

I shake my head. "I don't wanna to get into it." He sighs and falls into step quietly beside me. I think it's probably a sign of a good friend when they agree to just let silence fill the air between you.

If only everyone could sense that I didn't want to be bothered, maybe my morning wouldn't have sucked as much. At first, I'm a little self-conscious. In the halls, girls look at me and whisper to one another. Some guys nod in my direction and say something aside to their friends. I try to keep my eyes forward and not pay them any attention. A few kids who have spoken to me before go as far as to say hello and smile. As far as I'm concerned, they know I got into a fight and knocked out a famous actor, and that fact must make me a pretty cool guy. A badass, even.

But I'm barely in my pre-calc seat for thirty seconds when Jen, the girl in front of me with the fancy bag that's always on the floor, squashes my growing ego.

"Hi," she says.

"What's up?" I reply, opening my notebook and pretending to not notice that she's staring at me. Finally, I look up from my blank page and find her examining me with a frown.

"Are you okay?" she says, biting her lip and practically wincing. "I heard what happened, and I'm so sorry."

I squint and cock my head. "Okay? Why would I not be okay?" I look around and then down at my bruised hand, kind of surprised she would even notice. The swelling is gone, and it's just a little marked up.

"It's no big deal, thanks though. Just a little bruised."

Now she looks confused and follows my gaze to my purpled knuckles. "Oh, yeah, I heard you were in a fight." There's a long awkward pause. "I meant about Cherie."

My heart stops. "What about her?"

Her mouth twists to the side. "You know, your breakup and everything. That must be really hard."

I feel my eyes grow wide. I stare at her for several seconds, trying to find the right words to say, wondering how she knows anything about any of what happened other than the fight in the nightclub.

I say slowly, "We didn't break up… we weren't dating."

"Oh." She forces a smile and nods, as if she is certain I'm either delusional or lying to her. But she still tries to be polite. "Okay, well, good luck with whatever is going on."

I watch her turn to the front, and curiosity eats away at me with every quiet second that passes. I notice a few other girls in class turning to look back at me, and even a few guys stare in my direction. Now that I look at their suspicious expressions, I can tell they're not thinking I'm a badass at all. What does everyone know that I don't?

"Um, Jen?" Her head turns slightly. "What did you hear exactly?"

She swivels, a sparkle in her eyes now that I'm willing to entertain the gossip. She does her best to not look too excited to share. "Well, there was this article about a phone call between you two on Dirterazzi, and I read the site sometimes, so I saw it. I don't believe everything they say, you know, but then it was on the news this morning, too. Like, the real news. So, I just wanted to say sorry."

"Wait a second—a phone call?" I can't be sure I heard her over my roaring pulse. All I can think is, *How does anyone know about the phone call?*

Jen nods.

"Dirterazzi.com?" I clarify, immediately drawing out my phone from my pocket. "How do you spell it?"

Her eyes narrow as I start to type the site into my search bar. She spells it and peers over the top of my desk to my phone. "Don't you ever look at that site? I mean, they're always talking about you—wouldn't you want to know what they say?"

I shake my head and meet her gaze. "No." My voice grows as cold as my stare. "Because they're all lies."

She gets the hint and backs off. "Right."

At the front of the room, the teacher begins roll call, and Jen seems grateful for the excuse to turn away from me. I'm equally grateful for the chance to look for this article without her breathing down my neck.

I don't have to scroll far; it's the first story at the top of the webpage, titled, "Breaking Up IS Hard to Do." I swallow hard. My eyes scan the article quickly as I tune in and out of class, listening for my name to be called.

Cherie Belle has finally put the kibosh on her on-again, off-again relationship with Jack Hansen after a nightclub melee brought out his ultra-violent streak. A very reliable source close to Cherie confirmed to Dirterazzi reporter Derek Santos that the couple is officially done.

"Cherie just wants to be in a good, safe place right now with people she trusts," says the source. "She needs to be surrounded by positive energy."

And in a phone conversation overheard by our source, Cherie told Jack just that. Our source tells us that, even though Hansen sounded very distraught, admitted to loving her, and even threatened to wait for her to get home, Cherie made it clear she needed space from him. Dirterazzi obtained a recording of the conversation, and while we're not at liberty to share it all, some excerpts from Cherie's end include:

"We can't talk anymore."

"I think it's best we just stay apart."

"I just want to be surrounded by positive people."

"This is how it has to be, and I hope you can appreciate my boundaries."

Her words are right there, in black and white, and they echo in my ears as if she is saying them to me all over again.

"Hansen? Jack Hansen?" my teacher calls. I look up and see everyone has turned to look back at me. I can barely breathe.

"Here," I choke out, casually sliding my phone under the desk's top until he moves on to the next name on the list. When I'm sure no one is looking, I pull it back out and finish the article.

Our source tells us that Cherie is happy with her decision to pull away from Hansen, feeling the relationship was nothing more than a temporary distraction from the deaths of her parents. Cherie's manager, Carl Schwartz, is determined to keep the two apart and feels she will be able to get the space she needs from Hansen once she goes on tour promoting her film, This Side of Sunny, *later this month. Of course, she will have to go home eventually, and there's no telling what will happen once she's living under the same roof with Hansen. Something tells us this is not over... stay tuned!*

I stare hard at the words below the article and swallow the lump that's building in my throat. *Related articles.* I don't want to know, do I? I don't really want to see all of the things they've said and, more likely, made up about me. My finger hovers over the underlined link as I try to convince myself I don't want to look. It's like opening Pandora's box.

But I should know, I tell myself. I should know what the world thinks they know, right? I don't waste another second and press the Related Articles link.

A list of headlines using Cherie's name pops up, and it's organized in chronological order, dating back to before my mom and Jim were even married. At first, it's just harmless articles about Cherie as a new face of the Kidz Channel, then a few articles speculating about her and Caz as they're photographed leaving a restaurant together. Suddenly, the headlines become bold and capitalized.

EXCLUSIVE: CHERIE BELLE'S PARENTS KILLED IN TRAGIC CRASH

ORPHAN CHERIE BROKEN-HEARTED OVER PARENTS' DEATHS

CHERIE BELLE BURIES PARENTS

WHAT WILL HAPPEN TO LITTLE ORPHAN CHERIE?

Then, I see the very first kernel of gossip that made the world believe I had any significance in Cherie's life. As I continue to read, it becomes clear that this single kernel popped into a whole batch of new articles and curiosity about her and, even stranger, me.

WHO IS CHERIE'S MYSTERY MAN?

CHERIE BELLE'S NEW LOVE AFFAIR: A ROMANTIC COMEDY

YOU DON'T KNOW JACK: JUST WHO IS JACK HANSEN?

AND CHERIE'S GUARDIANS ARE...

CHERIE BELLE: CAZ FARRELL COMMENTS ON HER RUMORED LOVE AFFAIR

CHERIE BELLE RETIRING FROM ACTING?

JACK HANSEN AND CHERIE BELLE REPORTEDLY NOT SPEAKING AFTER MAJOR FALLOUT

CHERIE BELLE COZIES UP TO CAZ FARRELL AT NEW YEAR'S PARTY, GETS WASTED! JACK HANSEN NO WHERE IN SIGHT

MISERY LOVES COMPANY: CHERIE BELLE MOVES BACK TO LA PAD WITH NEW GUARDIANS AND JACK...AWKWARD!

UNDERAGE CHERIE BELLE SPOTTED IN NIGHTCLUBS

BOOTY CALL: CHERIE'S LATE NIGHT TRYSTS WITH JACK HANSEN

DRUGS, BOOZE, AND SEX: IS CHERIE BELLE A TRAINWRECK IN MOTION?

CHERIE BELLE OUT FOR ASSISTANT'S 25th BIRTHDAY PARTY: NO BOYS ALLOWED!

CHERIE BELLE: WITNESS CLAIMS SHE TOOK ECSTASY

FIGHT CLUB! JACK HANSEN AND DOMINICK FURST THROW DOWN OVER CHERIE

AND CHERIE'S KNIGHT IN SHINING ARMANI ARMOR IS...

Each article I read is more and more accurate, depicting everything that's happened between us and everything she's done in the past two months. But how would the media know so much? Did they have spy cameras in my old house? Have they been listening in on our conversations in my room?

I shove my phone into my pocket and lean back in my chair. I try to follow along and take notes from the board, but I keep wandering in and out of a stupor, so numb that the pencil barely stays upright in my hand.

The reporters know everything. They even knew about our whole conversation last night—every last detail. But who would tell them? I don't want to believe that Cherie allowed them to find out, but I can't help picturing that sleaze ball Derek sitting next to her with a voice recorder in one hand, listening in on our phone conversation, as she spewed those cold lines at me.

I'm sick to my stomach, growing colder and colder as if someone lowered the thermostat to 30 degrees. I hug my arms around my chest and do everything I can to just make it through class, promising myself that I'll go home the second it's over.

It doesn't matter, though. I won't be able to escape this invasion of my privacy the way I escape the twins or my mom. I can't just go for a run or drive to get away from something that is all over the news, all over the internet. I can deny it, but who would believe me? When I don't go to the premier tonight, and when Cherie, or someone very close to her, is sharing physical evidence, there's no way I can deny any of this.

I see the cars of photographers following me in the rearview mirror as I drive through the streets of Hollywood Hills to get home. I drive a little faster, trying to lose them, but they are skilled and relentless, staying so close to my bumper that they will definitely hit me if I have to slam on my brakes. Every light I just barely make they glide right under just to stay on my tail. I merge in and out of traffic and stop only if I really have to.

There's a crowd of them, too, outside the gates of the house waiting for me when I get there. I move through the cluster at a snail's pace as they snap their pictures and shout questions at me. I keep my windows up and blare music to drown them out, thankful for the sunglasses that hide my eyes from them. The gate that closes behind me and keeps them at bay gives me a great deal of satisfaction. Of course, no one is home to see any of this or help me by stopping them.

The minute I get inside my room, I drop onto my bed and put my head in my hands. I don't know what to think or what to do. Instinct tells me to run; to pack my bags and get the hell out of this house and this state. I know I can't do that, though. Where would I go, especially now, without being recognized? I've been on the front page of newspapers and magazines. I wouldn't get too far before my mom found me because the photographers will find me first.

I pull out my phone and look one more time at the page of articles about Cherie. I find the headline that says "You Don't Know Jack: Just Who is Jack Hansen?" I know I shouldn't do it, but the curiosity eats away at me and I have to read it. I have to know just what they think they know about me.

I'm not sure what the word misogynist means, so I look it up, growing more and more horrified as the definition flows into synonyms.

Hates women, mistrusts women, mistreats women. I know it's not true, but I'm apparently the only person who believes that. If there's anything I have ever tried to be, it's not my father, and yet all I am in the eyes of others is his shadow.

I fall back against my pillow and stare at my ceiling. Betrayed by Josh. Betrayed by Cherie. Betrayed by Mom. I'm exhausted, but my adrenaline is pumping so hard through my veins that I can't possibly sleep. My mind spins with scenarios of disappearing and various escape routes, none of which seem plausible.

Maybe the media was right; maybe Cherie and I are just a match made in haste; two dumb, lonely kids clinging to each other because they thought they had no one else.

But Cherie doesn't need me; she has plenty of people. Cherie's loved and wanted and protected, and I'm the only one who doesn't have anyone in his corner.

Chapter 36

I stumble through the rest of the week with a routine built around dodging my family and my classmates, all who have the same tired, awful questions I heard a thousand times when my father left.

"Are you okay?"

"How are you feeling?"

"Is all of that stuff about you true?"

And Frank, my oldest friend in the books, even he doesn't know any better than to ask, "Have you spoken to Cherie at all?" in his texts.

Mica hovers here and there, telling people to give me space and privately checking in on me the way a good friend would, without mentioning *her*. Years ago, I would have told him to back off. If he pushed, I would have punched him. This time, I don't even have the strength to look at him.

Cherie. Even when she's not here, I can't get her out of my head or escape the constant, nagging need to know where she is and what she's doing. I've turned to watching the news, even checking that damn website, Dirterazzi, every night, just to find some kernel of information about where she is or if she's okay. I feel like nothing more than an obsessed fan because everyone around us has done a great job keeping us apart and pretending nothing ever happened between her and me.

Mom brings dinner to my room every night. She knows there is no convincing me to come out of my room. I don't let her in, but I hear her place the ceramic plate down on the concrete outside and knock softly. When I don't answer, she sighs and pads away softly, and I watch her from the window, waiting until she's gone to retrieve the plate. I keep waiting for her to bring Britney as some kind of incentive to open my door, but she comes solo each time, which means either Britney doesn't want to come or Mom's not that desperate to see me.

It's now Thursday, and four days ago, the night of the premier, was the last time I'd heard anything about Cherie. As I watched her parade up and down the red carpet, looking beautiful and innocent in her gown, flanked by my family and her handlers, I realized that maybe I was the problem all along in Cherie's life. Maybe I enabled her by keeping the drinking and the drugs a secret from my mother. It's possible everything Cherie said about me wanting her around, needing her company as much as she needed mine, was true. At the premier, she looked happy and healthy and sober, and she has managed to stay out of the news since. I can really only blame myself because Carl is maintaining his end of his promise and keeping Cherie out of the nightclubs and the tabloids.

I still can't rid myself of the gnawing feeling that she isn't safe, though. Someone very close to her had to be telling Dirterazzi all of that stuff about us. What if that person is keeping her from me? What if that Derek guy is stalking her, or someone else—didn't Jim say she has stalkers? At night, I lie awake, watching my door, praying she will come home to me, sick inside that anything could happen to her and I'm not there to protect her. I spend a lot of the time scolding myself for letting her get away, for running that day when I should have stood by her side and told my mom the truth. No matter what it cost me to tell my mom what was really going on with her, and between us, it would have been less painful than this.

Then I spend some time wondering if that would have made a difference. Cherie might not even care.

Maybe she doesn't even think of me half as much as I think of her. I should never have left myself so wide open to yet another person who could just walk out of my life without a single look back over their shoulder. When will I learn? No one in, no one out. That's how it has to be.

Then, sometimes, that darker part of my psyche that I can't close the door on anymore wonders if the world wouldn't be better off without me. My father didn't love me. Cherie's moved on just fine as if I never existed, just like Dad. Hell, Britney doesn't even seem to need me anymore. I doubt I matter much to anyone right now.

That's the part that I've spent a long time shutting out, the part that wonders if I have any real value left in this world. I used to be able to pretend I did because I had to take care of Britney and Brenton. But now... well, now I'm just Jack. I don't deserve my father's last name, and I don't belong to anyone else, so why am I here?

Sometimes I craft my own Dirterazzi articles in my head:

EXCLUSIVE: JACK HANSEN FOUND DEAD, DROWNED IN CHERIE BELLE'S POOL, APPARENT SUICIDE

JACK HANSEN OVERDOSES ON MOTHER'S ANTIDEPRESSION MEDICATION, LEAVES LOVE NOTE FOR CHERIE BELLE

JACK HANSEN DISAPPEARS, NO ONE CARES WHERE

Chapter 37

It's nearly three o'clock in the morning on Friday when my cell phone begins ringing beside my head. I jerk upright in bed and look over at the clock before fumbling to find my phone.

"Hello?"

"Jack? Jack, it's Claudia."

I hang up the phone and thrust it under my pillow. Seconds after I lie back down, it's ringing beneath my head.

"What?"

"Please, don't hang up, please... please just listen!"

I hear urgency and sniffling, and I sit up. Those two things are never good. "What is it?"

"We're at some guy's house. We need you to come get us."

"Are you kidding me? No way!"

"Jack, please?" she begs with the same urgency. "Cherie invited us to some party and, well, it's getting weird here."

"Cherie?" I tilt my head and listen closely. "What do you mean? Where is she?"

"She's drunk, and I don't know... the guys here... we just don't feel safe."

Now my nerves are heightened. I shouldn't be worried for the twins, but I can't help it, especially knowing Cherie is involved. "Where are you?"

"I'm not really sure," she replies.

"Put Chloe on!" I bark. I need to speak to the smarter of the two.

But she's clearly wasted. "*Jack*!" she sings into the phone. "Ommigod, are you coming to get us?"

"Where are you?"

"Um, I think we're at Caz's beach house in Santa Monica."

"WHAT?" I sit up in renewed alarm. "What are you doing there? It's three in the morning!"

"No, really?" She is genuinely surprised. I can hear her pull the phone from her ear to look at the time. Somehow, she hangs up on me.

"Chloe? Chloe!" I growl at the phone and redial.

She laughs into the phone when she answers. "Hey, sorry 'bout that! So are you coming? We have school tomorrow, and I'm tired."

"Yes, I know we have school tomorrow—what are you doing in Santa Monica?"

"It's a really, really, really loooong story, Jack," she slurs. "We went to dinner with Cherie, and then Cherie was meeting up with Caz and some friends for an after party, so she invited us, and we said ok, and Danika drove, but we got lost, and then we found them at this beach house..." I lose focus on what she says as thoughts of Cherie and Caz Farrell together begin spinning rapidly through my mind like a CD on repeat. I'm disjointed from Chloe's story until a high-pitched, hysterical whine yanks me from my thoughts.

"...butnowDanikawontbringushomeandshesaidyouwillhavetocomegetus!"

"Me? Why me?"

"I don't know!" Chloe wails heavily on the other end.

I sigh into the phone and hold my head. "Just calm down, Chloe. Breathe. It's going to be okay." I've seen girls get drunk at parties before, and there's always someone crying or someone screaming or someone acting slutty to get a guy's attentions. I don't have to wonder which drunk-girl cliché Cherie is filling, and it fans a deep flame in my gut.

I can hear Claudia sniffle quietly on the other end as she takes the phone and says, "Jack? Jack, are you going to come?"

Glaring at the clock, I shake my head. "Dammit Claudia—can't you guys take a cab?"

"No way! It would cost, like, a hundred bucks! We'd have to pay by credit card, and then Daddy would find out when he gets the bill—Jack, he can't know about this! He will kill us!" She sobs again.

Jim flashes through my mind. "How am I supposed to sneak out without your dad hearing me? He's going to find out either way!"

"No, he won't—not if you're quiet!" I don't doubt her; Jim has missed all of the late night events these past two weeks. Clearly, the guy could sleep through a shootout.

But not my mom. I could picture her up and watching those video cameras, just waiting for me to try to run off the way my father did.

"Jack, pleeeeaaase?! Please just try? These people are weird and the guys are staring at us and we just wanna come home!"

I want to tell her no, that she and her dumb sister deserve this for all of the evil things they've done in their lives. But all I can think is that this is Cherie's doing, not theirs, and Danika is carrying out some sort of demonic plan her little boss concocted. Maybe Cherie did this to them on purpose to get back at them for outing us. Why else would she suddenly start hanging out with the two girls she can't stand most in the world? They should have known better than to go to a party with a girl they double crossed and the woman who works for her.

And Cherie probably wants me to have to come get them because she wants me to see her with Caz.

But why Caz? Why did Cherie have to go that far and twist the knife deeper in me, too? How could she go chase Caz right after everything that's happened between us?

Because she doesn't care, stupid, I scold myself. *You do, but she doesn't. She doesn't care about you, or the twins, or anyone but herself. It's the Cherie Belle reality show, and we are just extras.*

I picture my stepsisters, stranded in some Hollywood party full of creeps who are drunk or high or both. Do the twins deserve it? I don't know. Will I kick myself if something bad happens to them and I could have stopped it? Definitely. As much as I would want Jim to have to deal with his stupid, irresponsible, and drunk daughters, I have an aggravating big brother instinct that needs to step up and take action.

I grit my teeth. "Ask someone the address and text it to me. I'm on my way."

*   *   *

An hour later, after a few wrong turns and some cursing, I pull up to a row of massive beach houses. The twins race out of the front door of one of the nicer ones like they've never been happier to see someone in their lives.

"Jack!" Claudia cries out, and she throws herself into the seat beside me. They reek of booze.

"You guys owe me big," I grumble, watching Chloe flop into the backseat. "Where's Cherie?"

Chloe squeals, "Forget her, Jack. Just go."

"Why? Where is she?" I demand.

"Really, Jack, it's not worth it. She's with Caz," Claudia says softly, as if it hurts her to tell me.

Chloe is looser lipped. "She's wasted! They were out on the balcony, and then all of a sudden he was carrying her upstairs!"

"What?" I thunder. "What the hell happened to Carl's strict lockdown rules?"

"Chloe, shut up!" Claudia waves toward the windshield. "Don't worry about Cherie. Just go. She'll be fine."

"No way; I'm not leaving her out here so he can take advantage of her!" I turn the car off and take the keys out of the ignition, just in case they get any ideas. "Stay in the car."

I leave behind a flurry of screeching and pleading. "No, Jack! Just leave her alone—she'll be fine!" "Jack, don't go in there!"

"Jack—wait! Get back in the car! Please! That guy is coming!"

I probably should listen, but I'm too fixated on putting a stop to Caz Farrell's little private party with Cherie. She may not want anything to do with me, she may even be trying to hurt me by hanging out with another guy, but I won't let Caz do anything with Cherie if she isn't thinking clearly. Mr. Heartthrob is way too old for her, plain and simple, and she is probably too drunk to stop him.

I walk in expecting a wild, glamorous party full of beautiful people and dance music. Instead, I get the image of every house party I've ever been to in Westchester, just fancier. The rooms are dimly lit and people sit around on expensive-looking leather couches. A massive TV is on in the middle of the farthest room, and the six or so people in front of it watch two people play a video game. I'm tempted to be disappointed in this so-called Hollywood after party, but I remind myself that it is 4 in the morning, and there may have been a much cooler scene hours earlier.

The smell of weed becomes overpowering as I walk closer to the living room, and I note the empty bottles of pricey liquor and champagne strewn about the kitchen. One guy looks my way and acknowledges me with a head nod. "Sup?"

I'm about to ask him where I can find Cherie when I feel hands clamp down on my wrists and shoulders. I'm under attack, and I struggle to free myself, but it's of no use.

"Get off of me!" I cry out, trying to wrench myself from the strong grips on my limbs. There are two massive brown-haired thugs holding me, and the kid who greeted me watches with disinterest.

A girl steps out of the shadows of the farthest hallway, and it's her signature smirk I recognize first.

"Danika, what the hell is going on?" I demand.

"Hey there, *Jack*. How good of you to come. We were worried the girls wouldn't be able to lure you out here," she murmurs.

"What?" I shake my head, unwilling to believe her, seething at the thought of the girls being in on this little prank. "What the hell are you talking about, Danika?"

"Oh, we have big plans, kiddo. A few of us want a little payback," she says haughtily. My heartbeat quickens and I can't breathe, sensing I'm in big trouble. *A few of us? Who the hell is she talking about? Could the twins really be in on this?*

"Where's Cherie?" I demand.

"Hooking up with Caz, I'm sure," she says slyly. "We gave her a little vodka, and he brought her upstairs. Once Derek shows up, we will get enough photos to buy her compliance for years to come."

Rage explodes inside of my chest. "No! Cherie!" I writhe against the hold the thugs have on me until they twist one of my arms higher up my back, causing me to cry out.

Danika shakes her head to them. "It's okay, let him go. He doesn't scare me."

The guys release me, and on instinct I whirl and push one back as hard as I can. His friend shoves me hard enough to make me fall. I scramble to get up just as Danika holds out her hand for them to stop.

"Tsk, tsk, Jack," Danika murmurs, looking me over. "Such a temper. You're a little out of your league here."

"Go to hell, bitch," I bark at her. "Cherie!" I shout again, turning toward the stairs. Danika's goons stand in my path. I pivot in her direction and ask, "How could you? She's just a kid—you're an adult! She trusted you! How could you use her like this?"

"Use her?" Danika practically snarls at me. "She's the one who uses others, Jack! You of all people should know this."

"But she's only sixteen years old! You're ruining her life—don't you care for her at all?"

Danika smirks at me. "Do you truly care, Jack? Or did you just care about getting close to a hot celebrity?"

I glare at her. "You *know* I tried to get her to get help!"

"Oh, yes, your little truth or dare game. Well, look how far that got you," she sings with a chortle. "I wasn't fired, and she didn't get help. Looks like the joke was on you."

"Fine, I get it, you're mad about what I said about firing you—fine! Let them beat me up—you can do whatever you want to me! Just please don't take it out on her!" I plead.

Danika just shakes her head. "Oh, sweetie, please.

This isn't about your petty little comments. Your bed buddy was planning on bailing on all of us soon because she wants a so-called normal life. But I've got bills to pay, and our little TV princess isn't going to quit anytime soon."

My jaw falls slack as I look from Danika to the stairs. "Wait... but..."

When she realizes I'm confused, she adds, "Cherie had already planned to fire me, Jack. She wants to quit the industry; she was going to let all of us go next month because she thinks she won't need us. That would have been very bad for the people who make a lot of money from her. So we created a situation that will require all of her decisions be made by the right people and not your dumb family. Now that Carl is acquiring custody, Cherie won't be pulling the plug on her career anytime soon."

"Money? You're dragging her through the mud and seeking custody for money?" My teeth grind together. "You call all of this off, now!"

She takes a step forward menacingly. "I don't take my orders from you, or your parents, or Cherie. I take my orders from the top, because that is how I get paid."

"The top?" I repeat, staring at her, trying to make sense of her words. "You mean her producers?"

"No, dummy, her manager. You know, Carl?" she sneers. "Nothing you see Cherie do or hear her say happens without him and Betsy carefully crafting it. Now that we've proven that your mother and stepfather were awful guardians, Carl will have custody of little orphan Cherie. Every decision will be up to him, including whether or not she continues acting."

I feel my blood reenergized with a fresh fury. Carl is the one trying to keep Cherie in the news, the one place where she least needs to be, and for what? To sabotage my parents, who trusted all of them? So he can gain custody and keep the Cherie Belle money train chugging along?

"You can't do this!" I step forward and warn, "I won't let you."

Danika shakes her head. "Jack, Jack, Jack... haven't you learned anything about how it works out here? With the right connections and the right pictures, you can make anything happen, especially a few bad decisions by a good girl."

Suddenly, the twins burst through the front door, searching the room wildly. "Jack!" Claudia cries, rushing to my side first.

"Jack, we have to go!"

"Let's go, Jack. She'll find her way home in the morning," Chloe commands, and she pulls hard on my shirt. I look down at her, and it's like looking at a stranger. Her eyes are wide and fearful. Her lower lip trembles. Is there something she knows that I'm not realizing?

It doesn't matter because I'm not moving. I'm a wall of fury, unwilling to move from this spot without Cherie.

I stare down at Danika and say, "So what did you drag me out here for, you sick bitch? Just to tell me all of this?"

"Jack..." Claudia's tone is a warning, and her eyes are frightened, too. My senses are heightened, and I look around the room.

A hand grips my shoulder and I jerk out from under it, shoving both of the girls behind me.

Dominick "Striped-Shirt" Furst stares back at me with that familiar sneer and angry, narrowed eyes. I'm overcome briefly with the shock of coming face to face with my "victim," as the gossip blogs have so aptly labeled him. The purple welt below one of his eyes glares at me. Gawking down at him, I marvel at the size of his bruise; the bruise I caused, delivered by my still-aching fist almost a week ago. My flight or fight gears go into motion as I look from him to Danika's goons to the stairs and weigh my options.

"Surprise, Jack!" Danika sings with a giggle. "I told you, a few of us still have a bone to pick with you."

I glance over at her, my jaw clenching. They have me cornered, and she knows it, and now it all makes sense. I've been lured out here so she can watch me get jumped by a guy who's itching to shed my blood.

The primal smell of danger is overpowering. There is no flight, only fight. I force myself to stand tall and snarl at Dominick, "Back off."

But we don't have to say anything more. I don't even have to enact the plan that's forming in my head, where I deliver a second knockout punch to the other side of the actor's face and beat it to the door before either of the goons can jump in.

None of that happens because Caz appears on the top of the steps on cue, clearing his throat. He comes down, cool as a cucumber, rubbing his eyes as if he just woke up, oblivious to my presence. He looks disheveled and worn, and I can only think the worst took place between him and Cherie. I hate him with every fiber of my being.

Dominick snorts at me like a bull ready to charge. I feel one of the girls pull me backward a step, but I shake them off and plant my feet.

"Hey," Caz mutters to his friend on the couch. "What's going on?"

The guy gives him a wink and a fist bump. "Good night, my man?"

Caz grins and shakes his head at his friend. "Don't be an ass," he chuckles.

I wait for Cherie to follow him, but she doesn't. Since my voice is trapped beneath layers of rage, Claudia thankfully asks, "Where's Cherie?"

He finally looks up and meets my gaze, his eyes widening as if I startled him. "Hey, man. Jack, right?" There's something mischievous in his grin.

I don't smile. I give him the deadliest look I've ever given a person before. I can feel the heat pouring out of my eyes. "Where is Cherie?" I repeat, and Chloe nudges me in my side to not be such a jerk. Caz narrows his eyes at my tone.

"She's passed out upstairs," he tells me, his mouth a smug smile. "I have no use for her; she's already lost her v-card apparently."

Dominick snickers. My blood boils hotter and hotter. If he touched her, I'll kill him.

"You're gross," Claudia hisses with disgust. My instinct is to kill him—all of them. In my mind, there's only one way he could know that kind of information.

My voice rises to a roar. "What did you do to her!?" I rush toward him, and Claudia and Chloe pull back on my arms to stop me. Danika's goons shield him and keep me from getting too close.

"What did you do to her?" I demand again, my voice shaking.

Caz scoffs, "Nothing, asshole; Cherie's crying and shit upstairs about losing her virginity to you—she's a hot mess. She can't handle her liquor."

"Maybe she shouldn't be drinking with twenty-five-year-olds, *asshole*," I fire back, standing my ground. He smirks and says, "What can I say? If she wanted to be playing on the jungle gym at home with you still, she would be."

I take a menacing step toward him. "She will come home because I'm taking her, now."

Dominick snickers, "Oh, you're not going anywhere, kid."

I glare at him and the thugs still waiting behind him, my breath coming in shorter, shallower huffs as reality sets in and dread fills me. I'm likely not going anywhere; I'll be lucky if I'm still alive in an hour.

I turn to the girls. "Get in the car," I whisper, thrusting the keys in their hands and urgently pushing them toward the front door.

"You come, too," Claudia whimpers, gripping my wrist.

"I will. I gotta go upstairs and get Cherie. I'll be right there." I sneak a glance at the others in the house and doubt my own words, and I'm a terrible liar.

Worst of all, Chloe knows it. "No, Jack—now!"

But I've already turned back to Caz and his friends, who have started to surround us. "I don't want any trouble. I just want to take Cherie home."

"Shoulda thought about that before you came at me last week," Dominick says, puffing his chest as he steps forward. He's a few inches shorter than me, stocky and broad-shouldered. He looks more like an Oompa Loompa than an actor. I almost want to laugh at him, but the collection of angry, scornful faces staring back at me makes my confidence tremble.

"We have some unfinished business to take care of," he adds.

"No! Leave him alone!" Chloe shouts, getting between us. "We'll call the cops!"

Caz glares down at Chloe and moves toward her. "Don't even think about it."

"Hey, stay away from her!" I yell, stepping between them. I swallow my fear for the girls and look back at them. "Go, Chloe. I'll be fine. Please just go." I push her behind me and look back at her twin, commanding with as much authority as I can muster, "Claudia, get her out of here." I know I'm about to get jumped, especially once I try to go back upstairs for Cherie. I don't need them seeing it or getting hurt, too.

Suddenly, I'm getting spun, and the ground disappears beneath my feet. I'm airborne, and I come crashing down hard on my face. Claudia screams. The tin taste of blood seeps into my mouth as the world spins. At first, I think I've only bitten my tongue, but it's worse. The blood is coming from outside of my mouth and leaking past my lips. I try to get up.

"Stop it!" Chloe shrieks as the first foot flies into my gut. They're everywhere, like flies, raining knuckles, heels, and knees into my body. I manage to grab one foot, pull and twist it. Someone cries out and a thud follows. That's one.

But there are too many. I'm assaulted feverishly, and all I can do is curl up and try to protect my head and face from further strikes. Something hard collides with my rib cage, and I hear a sickening crack. The pain is instantaneous, and I clamp my teeth together to stifle the howl of pain I'm moved to release. I won't give them the satisfaction of hearing me whimpering like a beaten dog. Eventually, some hands pick me up and throw me against a wall. I hear one of the girls scream again as I slide to the floor in a heap of aches and blood.

"Jack? Jack!" a familiar voice cries out. "No, get off of me!"

Cherie. She's there, somewhere, but her words spark a new fear in me. What are they doing to her? Where are the twins?

I peer up and see Caz, Dominick, and their thugs in a scuffle with her and the twins. Cherie is desperately trying to get to me, struggling against someone's hold. The twins are cursing and shouting as they fight to free her. The guys look like they aren't afraid to hurt the three of them, or do much worse, and I'm not going to let that happen.

I don't know where the strength to stand comes from. Parts of me are broken, I'm sure. But I won't let them touch Cherie or my sisters.

"Is that the best you can do?" I taunt, getting to my feet, my words practically slurred by whatever they already did to my jaw. Dominick and his minions turn and look. "I'm still standing, Furst."

Dominick looks to Caz, and they share a quick laugh. They abandon the girls to their goons and come for me. Cherie screams my name, convinced I'll be killed. She's probably right.

Regardless, I mock them. "It's real easy to attack a man when there's four on one."

"What man? I don't see a man," Dominick scoffs, and Caz chuckles to his right.

"Maybe I should squat down so we can be on eye level," I reply stiffly, wiping at the blood on my lips with the back of my hand. I look down at the red smear across my skin and grow a little woozy.

Dominick snorts and snarls, "How about my bodyguards here just break your legs?"

I look toward the goons, who release the girls and come forward, and I know he's not kidding. Just when I think I'm done for, I hear a familiar scream-roar, followed by a loud thud, and one of them goes down at my feet. Claudia stands behind him with one of the fancy liquor bottles in her hand, breathing hard.

"What the hell!" Caz cries out. Claudia swings the bottle at his head, as he dodges it and jumps aside. She hurls it at him, and it collides with his back, causing him to cry out and stumble. She raises her other hand, producing a second bottle, and she holds it like a bat over her shoulder and prepares to swing at anyone else who approaches as the other guys stare at her.

Chloe emerges from the background and charges toward the other thug with her mini-can of pepper spray that Jim never lets them leave home without. As she sprays it into his eyes, I feel dumb for making fun of it once upon a time. The bodyguard screams like a girl and covers his eyes, running from her. Her weapon is fierce and dirty and so New York, and it horrifies as much as it delights me at the same time.

The people who had been in other parts of the house all this time are suddenly clustered in the doorway of the living room, watching in awe. The guy on the couch is no longer disinterested but on his feet and pressed against the farthest wall in cowardice, not wanting any of the chaos in the room to turn to him.

Cherie approaches Dominick and Caz, who can't make any sense of the scene unfolding around us. "I've called the police and Derek from Dirterazzi," she says, waving her phone. "Your careers are so *over!*"

Caz gawks at her. "You bitch!" He lunges for her.

"Don't touch her!" I shout, reaching out to grab a fistful of his collar and jerking him backward. I use all of my strength to throw him, head first, against the wall to my right. There is a loud *crack!*, and he trips backward, holding the front of his head. Blood gushes from a fresh cut in his forehead and pours down the front of his face. He grips the wall, practically fainting from the sight of his own blood. I hear Danika curse from somewhere across the room.

"Cherie, what are you doing?" she cries out.

Cherie turns to her ex-assistant and commands, "Stay back, bitch! I never should have trusted you—any of you!" Claudia moves beside her cousin, wielding another empty liquor bottle, her weapon of choice. Chloe stands in the corner, holding her pepper spray up to the eyes of the bodyguard she's managed to corner, who still can't see after her first round attack.

Dominick realizes my guard is down, and he charges, flying through the air toward me.

"No!" Cherie screams, but she can't act fast enough.

I'm knocked to the ground, trapped beneath his heavy frame. Fresh pain ignites within my torso, and now my left arm is limp and burning. I gasp for air, but it's hard to breathe, especially with him on top of me. He sits up, draws back, and lands the punch that puts me out.

DIRTERAZZI.COM

EXCLUSIVE: JACK HANSEN IN CRITICAL CONDITION AFTER GETTING JUMPED BY FARRELL, FURST, AND BODYGUARDS

Caz Farrell's Santa Monica beach house was the scene of a major brawl early this morning, according to police. Our reporter was on the scene just as Jack Hansen, 17, was getting carried away in an ambulance to Cedars Sinai. It all started when Hansen's twin stepsisters, Claudia and Chloe Goldman, 16, found themselves stranded at Farrell's residence while Cherie Belle partied the night away. Too young and drunk to drive, the girls called Hansen to pick them up. Being the good big brother he is, Hansen jumped in the car and came to the rescue. Little did the Goldman/Hansen kids know, the entire party was a setup designed to lure Hansen into the house so Dominick Furst could exact revenge for the shiner Hansen gave him last weekend at Club Fly. Words were exchanged, and Furst and his bodyguard, along with Caz Farrell and his bodyguard, attacked Hansen.

We're told Cherie and the twins entered the scene at some point and broke up the beat down by attacking the men with… get this… liquor bottles and pepper spray. It's like a gang war straight out of West Side Story, y'all! The dirty battle raged on for several minutes as onlookers watched in horror. Finally, someone called the police, but not before Furst managed to land a few final punches that left Hansen completely unconscious. Sources present for the scene say Furst was pried off of Hansen's limp body by the girls, who formed a protective wall around their fallen hero until help arrived.

Farrell and Furst, along with their bodyguards, were arrested at the scene for assault and battery on a minor, as well as criminal negligence and endangerment of a minor. Both actors have already been released on bail, but something tells us that their time behind bars may not yet be over. These charges carry serious weight, especially due to the ages of the victims involved.

Again, Dirterazzi just wants to know: Where the hell are the guardians in all of this?

Update, 6:37 a.m.: The Goldmans have arrived at the hospital's emergency room and were quickly shuttled inside. We have not yet received word on Hansen's condition, but we will keep you updated.

Chapter 38

Lights are flashing. Dark shapes surround me. Someone is asking me questions. I can hear them, and occasionally I can see them, but it's not consistent. My mouth hurts so much that I can barely answer them. I fade in and out to red lights, white lights, blurry figures. I'm bound to something. I'm moving. I feel things bump and jerk and slide beneath me. Nothing seems clear, but I can't ask what's happening. I don't need to because the pain is overwhelming any questions I could have.

Sharp pains and dull aches numb my other senses and throb sporadically throughout my body. I don't think I could move if I wanted to, which I don't. I just want to lie here, as still as possible to avoid hurting any more than I already do.

I imagine Cherie. I wonder where she is and what she's doing. When I picture her face, I can smell her. I can hear her laugh. I can't feel her though. I can only feel pain. I slip back out of consciousness.

When I come to again, there are voices around me, hushed and murmured, accompanied by sniffles and rustling. A faint, steady beeping grows louder. Other sounds become clearer. The pain is not as prominent. Maybe I can open my eyes.

As I do, I'm met by a sea of familiar, concerned, and tear-stained faces. I see my mother rise from her seat beside me, awash in white light and looking haggard.

"Hi baby," she coos, wanting to touch me, but afraid to rest her hand anywhere other than on mine.

"Mom?" I croak. I look around. It looks like a hospital room. It feels like a hospital room. What the hell happened?

"Where am I?" I ask, my voice ragged.

But she's turned and calling to Jim. "He's awake. Get the nurse." She looks back at me. "Hey baby. You're okay. You're in the hospital, and you're going to be okay."

"Where's Cherie?" I say, trying to get up.

"She's fine, you just—"

As I start to move, pain shoots through my left side and shoulder. I cry out and fall back.

"Oh, God!" Mom tears up, but she tries to stay calm. "Don't move, baby, okay? The doctors are coming; they have to examine you."

I can't argue with her. I can't move; I'm actually afraid to move. My heartbeat spikes. I realize my arm is in a cast. Something is tightly wrapped around my torso. My face aches and feels hot when I reach up to touch it with my good hand. Memories of the fight come flooding back through my hazy mind, and I panic that I could be badly hurt. Mom strokes my hair. I close my eyes and try to just breathe.

***

My mom won't stop apologizing, even after I tell her it's okay and that I know why she didn't believe me. She babbles on and on, shaking her head at her own failures. "*Danika and Carl and Betsy, they had everyone fooled, even Derek, the reporter. How were we supposed to know these people, who had been in Cherie's life all this time, would go to such extremes just because she wanted to quit the industry?*"

"People will do anything to squeeze one last buck out of a celebrity like Cherie, even endanger them," says an officer who comes to question me. He asks a few questions about last night to corroborate Cherie and the twins' stories about the events at Caz's beach house. He doesn't interrogate me too much because I don't really make a lot of sense with the painkillers I'm on. My memories are sort of hazy and broken into puzzle pieces that I can't connect properly.

"It's okay, son," he says as he gives up and turns to leave. "We have all the evidence we need to move forward with an investigation for now. Maybe we'll catch up a little later, when you're feeling better."

They won't let Cherie see me yet, even after the doctors and the officer leave my room. I wonder if I look that bad, or if they just don't want us around each other. When my mother steps out to talk to the doctors about whether or not I need to stay in the hospital overnight, a young nurse comes in to introduce herself and tells me she's my night nurse. I have no idea what time it is, but I'm guessing I've been here almost a full day.

"Can I have a mirror, please?" I ask with as much charm as I can muster. Her lips form a tight, pitying smile, but she complies.

"Here you are," she says gently. I take it in my good hand and prepare myself to be horrified by my own reflection.

But it's not so bad. It actually feels a lot worse than it is. The right side of my lip is busted and blackened with dried blood and a few stitches. Purples and reds cover my right cheekbone, and a deep, red and black wound stretches from my forehead down across my left temple. My hair is kind of messed and even has some dried blood in it, too. It's kind of badass, even better than having a beard. I look a little like the guy at the end of an action movie who walks out of the burning building, wrecked but alive and victorious.

All I need now is the girl, I muse to myself. I put the mirror down and try to lay still. The doctors weren't concerned about my face. They were more worried about the internal bleeding, two broken ribs and cracked left collarbone. I guess I should be, too.

Someone knocks on the hospital room door, and I raise my head weakly to look over. Cherie steps inside hesitantly, peering toward the bed. As our gazes meet, she tries to smile through tears that immediately begin to fall.

"Hi," she sobs. She covers her mouth as if the sight of me is too much for her to handle.

"It's not as bad as it looks," I say quickly, wincing as I try to turn more in her direction.

"Don't move!" she scolds, quickly rushing to the chair at my side. She runs her eyes over my body and sighs, "Oh, Jack."

I follow her gaze down my bruised and bandaged torso and shrug my good shoulder. "Eh. I'll live."

She shakes her head. "I am so sorry. This is all my fault."

"No, it's not," I say. "Things just got out of hand. You actually saved me for once."

I smirk, but Cherie just locks eyes with me. "No. I caused this. Don't give me any more free passes. I've spent two months making messes that other people clean up. This time, all it did was get you hurt, and you deserve better than that. You deserve better than me. I am so sorry."

I shake my head. "You know I don't care about this," I say, gesturing to my bandages. "I'd fight for you any day. I'd take a bullet for you, Cherie, and you know that."

Her face falls and I continue, adding, "I know now that Danika was the one leaking everything to the media. At first I thought it was you, but now it makes so much more sense—"

She puckers her lips as if she's about to speak then pauses and thinks for a silent moment.

"What?" I press.

"I—It wasn't all Danika."

I swallow hard. "Huh? What do you mean?"

"I did a very bad thing, Jack."

My stomach twists. "What is it?" Her eyes dart away from mine. She stays quiet. "Tell me."

She leans back in her chair. "Danika... yes, Danika did tell the press a lot of stuff the last few weeks. She was responsible for most of the stories the media knew. I had no idea. But... the phone call between us the other day... You see, sometimes, when we need to do damage control, we stage things with reporters we trust. They call it a 'very close source,' but it's really just us telling them."

The sun rises on the awful memory of our phone call. "So when you said we couldn't see each other..."

She nods. "Carl and Betsy arranged a meeting with Derek Santos, and they made me wait for you to call. They knew you would. They wrote down my responses and everything."

I nod. "I thought so. I knew that wasn't real." I stare into space for a minute before searching her eyes for reassurance. "Why would you do that to me?"

She looks up as two tears stream down her cheeks. "I didn't want to say any of that, Jack. I wanted to come home the second you told me you wanted to see me! And you told me you loved me—I knew you meant it because I could hear it in your voice, in how you yelled at me. No one has ever talked to me like that. Please believe me; I didn't want to let Derek listen in and hear you—"

"Then why did you let them? You have the right to say no to people, Cherie. Do you have any idea how much it hurts to be stabbed in the back like that?"

She sniffles and wipes her tears. "I thought Carl and Betsy were just trying to clean up the image I was getting in the press, and they told me you'd be the best person to pin it on after what happened at the club. They told me I had to or I was going to bring bad press to everyone; Kidz Channel, the movie, them. I—I didn't know what to do. Carl said you wouldn't be there forever, that I was only hurting one person who might be out of my life in a year instead of hurting everyone who's been there for me all of this time."

"A year?" I guffaw. "What—where is he coming up with that?"

She shrugs. "You're going to go off to college soon. You said so yourself last week. Carl said—"

"I don't care what Carl said!" I snap, irritated. Getting angry is becoming painful as parts of me start to throb. I try to calm down and soften my tone. "Look, Cherie, I'm not going anywhere, no matter what anyone says—Carl, your uncle, Danika—they didn't know what was happening between us. They still don't, right?"

She nods quickly. "I haven't said anything about that night." She blushes a little and looks down.

I breathe deeply. "Well, maybe it's time we tell them."

"No, Jack! We can't!" she whispers, her green eyes wide and frightened.

I shake my head. "You need to decide what you want. If you want me around, I'll stay, and I'll never leave you. But I won't be a secret anymore. I want you to get the help you really need and go back to your normal life, and I want to be by your side every step of the way." "You *have* always been there for me, and look what's happened," she whimpers. "I didn't want this—I didn't want to drag you into my drama! Don't you get it, Jack? You're going to get tired of it eventually and leave, and then where will I be?"

I sigh and reply, "Cherie, don't you see the pattern here? Every time you push me away, I come back. I'm always going to be here for you. I'm not just giving up and leaving you alone. If you don't want me, I'll respect that and live with it. But if you'll have me, I'm going to be there for you no matter what you do to me.

"But it's your choice to make. Not Carl's, not my mom's, not the producers of your movie. I'm here, and I'm not going anywhere unless you say you don't want me around."

Cherie rests her eyes on mine and then looks down at my bandages, her lips pressed tightly together. A fresh tear rolls out of the corner of her eyes.

"Of course I want you around—you're the only person I've felt truly safe with. I just... I thought you'd walk away once all the publicity got too hard, and then I'd be all alone again."

Her words hit below the belt, and my chest tightens. "It's going to take a lot more than some stress to push me away, Cherie. I'm not my father; I'm stronger than him, and I know what it means to take care of the people I love," I say, hearing my own voice waver a little. I fight the emotion that I feel coming on. "I love you. Look at me. You can be sure I'll fight to the death for you before I will just walk away."

She replies, "This is crazy. We're kids. It's crazy for us to feel this way about each other—we barely know each other. I'm broken right now, Jack. And you, you've spent so much time hiding from how you really feel about your dad that you can't even talk about him with me. We're probably only attracted to each other because we're both so messed up—two unstable kids like us shouldn't be together!"

I watch her rant herself into exhaustion. When she falls back in her chair and quiets, I lean forward as much as I can. "I know I've got my own issues, Cherie. I won't pretend to be whole in any way, and it's going to take some time for me to really open up about that stuff. But I can tell you that you've already broken down more of my walls than anyone else. I'll let you in if you stop making me your dirty secret."

She stares at the floor for a long time before saying, "I have really young fans. I—I don't really feel comfortable telling people everything. Do we have to tell everyone we had sex?"

I shake my head. "Of course not. We never have to tell people what goes on behind closed doors, even when we're fifty. That's between us.

"But it's what you let them see on the outside that matters to me. I want to be able to hold your hand and kiss you and take you places, and I don't care who doesn't agree with it or who takes a picture of it."

"Being in the public eye doesn't matter to you?" she asks softly, as if she can't believe what she's hearing.

"Not if it means I get to be with you," I reply. "Besides, aren't you quitting acting? All of this attention is going to go away eventually."

"Yeah, but what about all the things they'll say about us before it goes away?" she whispers. "We're supposed to be family—"

"But we're not family, Cherie, and anyone with half of a brain knows that." I shake my head and sigh. "Maybe you care about all that stuff, but I don't. I won't feel bad about loving you."

Cherie nods slowly. The silence pools around us and threatens to drown me. It's the moment of truth: Either she will stand up and walk out of my life forever, or she will agree to tell the world about us. I feel like I'm about to start sweating from the tension. I never realized how much the threat of losing her would panic me, even last night when I thought she was with Caz. Up until now, I knew she was a helpless puppet to people older and savvier than her. But at this moment, it's just her and me and the words she chooses. The decision she makes is entirely hers.

Finally, she looks up and whispers, "I don't want to feel bad about loving you either."

My voice is hoarse. I just need to hear her say it. "Then don't."

She shakes her head. "I won't. I want everyone to know that we're together," she says, and I can finally breathe again. "I love you, Jack."

This time I can say it back. "I love you, too." I laugh because I can't find the words to express how happy she's just made me.

Her lips spread into a smile as she reaches for her cell phone. "I'll call Derek right now and set up an in—"

"No, hold on," I say, reaching out for her phone just as she begins to turn it on. Her big green eyes stare at me, wide and innocent. I take a deep breath and try to keep my tone gentle. "This isn't damage control, Cherie. We don't need a staged interview and phony prepared statements. This is real life. We need to be real with each other, always. Okay?"

Her smile fades and she lowers her phone. I can see by the confusion on her face that this is a foreign concept to her. She's spent so much time carefully crafting every part of her life, every relationship, and she doesn't understand what it means to be real anymore.

"Well, then, how will they know we're together?" she asks softly.

I take her hand in mine and smile as much as my bruised lip will allow. "We just have to be together. That's all. They'll get the picture."

"Oh." Her face scrunches. "Really? You want to stage a photo shoot?" She grins and adds slyly, "You do photograph well…"

I force myself to take another deep breath, suppressing my frustration. I can tell this is going to be a long road to travel with her.

But one glimpse of her smile tells me it's a journey worth taking.

DIRTERAZZI.COM

Cherie Belle Needs Class

It's rare that young, retired celebrities make good choices these days, so Dirterazzi was fairly surprised that Cherie Belle, the former Kidz Channel starlet and media darling, is actually considering starting school in September. It appears that Jack Hansen, Cherie's boyfriend and notoriously straight A student, is turning out to be a good influence on the celebutante, who recently started interviewing with independent school administrators in the Los Angeles area. Along with his parents and stepsisters (those hot twins we love so much, who are also considering a move from public to private education), Hansen accompanied Cherie to a tour of the Pinton Academy this week. It is unclear whether Hansen will join Cherie at her new school, but he certainly has the credentials to attend, according to one of his former teachers. Sources close to the family say that Cherie is thrilled to start in the fall, which is good news because she may need an extra year or two of it just to catch up with her peers, especially if she plans on going to college.

This is a far cry from the Cherie Belle we saw earlier this year, who spent the first few months of 2013 spiraling out of control and partying hard. It has been revealed that her wild ways were due in part to a major conspiracy by her handlers, Carl Schwartz and Betsy Calves, and her assistant, Danika Shields, who are currently under investigation for a myriad of charges, such as fraud, endangerment of a minor, and defamation, just to name a few. The treachery was unveiled when Hansen, 17, showed up at actor Caz Farrell's beach house in Santa Monica to pick up his twin sisters. There, he was brutally attacked by Farrell, fellow actor Dominick Furst, and their bodyguards. Both Farrell and Furst, as well as their bodyguards, have been charged with battery and assault following testimony from Cherie Belle and her cousins, Chloe and Claudia Goldman. Both actors face jail time and community service, and Farrell also faces charges of endangerment of a minor for serving alcohol to the underage Goldman twins and Belle. Their sentencing will be held later this month.

As for Cherie and Jack, a source tells us their lives couldn't be more normal together. Last week, Cherie went with Jack to his junior prom, and she danced the night away with his classmates. According to one student in attendance, Hansen hung back in the shadows while his lady love stole the spotlight, only stepping out to ask for one slow dance. Onlookers report a magical feeling as they watched the lovebirds embrace each other and sway back and forth, their eyes locked together as if they were the only two people in the room. Fans of this modern day Romeo and Juliet are rooting for the duo to stick together for the long haul.

Dirterazzi hopes the magic doesn't fade, but teenage love can be fickle. Only time will tell if Cherie's attendance at school will bring new drama to their currently happy relationship. Stay tuned!

Acknowledgments

Writing is a journey. I know what you're thinking behind that eye roll: *"That's what my kooky sixth-grade English teacher told me."* But it's completely accurate. It's a journey you take alone at first, and along the way you find companions in the form of dear friends and family who are unwittingly roped in as readers and editors. These companions are brave enough to take the journey with you. My journey would not have been complete without those few in my life who took the time to listen, read, respond, and care about the process. To my createspace.com team and those ladies with whom I entrusted my heart and soul, I thank you. Melissa, you've always been my biggest cheerleader and laughed at all my dumb jokes, even when we were just two dorky freshmen at the U. Julie, I can always count on you for honesty, love, and friendship. Andrea, thanks for showing me the "mom side" of things. Preety, you are officially my editor-in-chief forever. Congratulations...?

I would like to thank my students, too, who gave me endless laughs, fodder, and support this year. For five years they performed in my silly plays and asked to hear my stories and taught me what makes a great writer. I'm so glad that, if I was able to teach you anything, I taught you that you were my friends. (That one is just for you, Alex V.!)

Your sixth-grade English teacher probably also told you to write about what you know, something in which you are an expert. I should thank my family, now, because without them I would not have the insight into what families do best together: fight, laugh, and cry. Anyone who has ever sat around a table at a mandatory holiday dinner knows exactly what I mean. I should thank my mother, in particular, for always bringing the family around the table for meals, big and small. As I was growing up, she was the ultimate Holly Homemaker, despite what my sister and I like to joke about now, and no one can set a holiday table or decorate a room quite like her. I thank God every day for my family and the laughs we've shared together.

I especially have to thank the person who started this journey with me long ago: my father. He spent years gathering my silly, four-page, notebook-paper tales about horses and dogs and more horses. He filed stories and poems together and saved them in this little wicker trunk that to this day still holds my earliest scribblings. He never once doubted my dream, making it his own and spending every dollar he had to give me opportunities to grow as a writer. He gave me the confidence to believe I would one day publish my work to the world. Thank you, Daddy. I just wish you were still here to see our dream come true.

Most importantly, I have to thank my husband, who I don't deserve. At all. Not one bit. But he's still here for some reason, so maybe he actually likes me, even though I really couldn't tell you why. I can tell you one thing for certain, though: he's my everything.

To my readers: Thank you for reading. Please connect with me if you have questions at jlevine361@gmail.com, or check out our website, spiralseries.com, or 'Like' the Spiral Facebook page for updates on the sequel and to share your thoughts on the story. All any writer wants is to share these fictional people and places and situations that happen inside his or her head with someone who will listen. Remember to always be young. Have fun. Go after your dreams and find what makes you happy.

Also, stop being so hard on your English teachers. You might end up putting their advice to good use one day.